MW01139934

# Post Grid

## An Arizona EMP Adventure

Tony and Nancy Martineau

Foreword

An EMP, or electromagnetic pulse, is an energy wave that can destroy electronic systems and components by instantaneously bombarding the earth's surface with thousands of volts of electricity. This can be a natural occurrence, e.g., a coronal mass ejection (CME), or it can be caused by the detonation of a nuclear device. A nuclear bomb's size and the altitude at which it is detonated determine how widespread its electrical grid-killing effects are.

Please take this book for what it is: a work of fiction. Even the top scientists disagree about the actual magnitude of destruction by nuclear devices detonated in the atmosphere. The military has chosen to harden its planes, radios and other vehicles to EMP, so for the purpose of this book, we will assume there is a threat.

We, the authors, consider ourselves more knowledgeable than most about survival, but still don't believe we could survive the scenario put forward in this work. We live in a desert with four million other people, *totally dependent* on the infrastructure for anything more than short-term water.

Special thanks to our tireless beta readers, copy editor, blocker, graphic designer and family, without whom this work would have suffered.

Please feel free to contact us with corrections and comments at:
PostGrid@cox.net

Join our Facebook page:
www.Facebook.com/NovelPostGrid

Cover Art by Linda Kage Covers
www.lindakage.com/covers.html

Copyedit by Champagne Book Editing
www.champagne-editing.com

Chapter 1
Kelly - Day 0

The fluorescent lights flared and their ballasts popped, emitting the tiniest bit of acrid smoke at each end. Then the fixtures went dark. Static burst from equipment speakers. Explosions boomed from the parking lot. All of the electronics in the room wound down like a washing machine at the end of its spin cycle.

Nurse Kelly rushed to the window and parted the heavily-lined drapes enough to peer out. Liquid fire dripped from the transformers, igniting their poles and making small pools of flame around their bases. She pressed an open hand against her chest as if to suppress a deep gasp, held it there for a few seconds, and then lowered it casually to her side. She turned slowly back to the others in the room. They looked at her with questioning gazes. Because she remained outwardly calm, so did they.

"It must be some kind of power surge," Kelly announced to the laboring mother, whose wisps of sweaty hair framed her face, and to the anxious, portly father standing at his wife's bedside.

A red-haired obstetrician sat at the business end of a delivery bed, nestled between a pair of metal stirrups that were supporting her patient's legs in a most immodest position. Kelly could feel the blood pumping in the arteries on either side of her neck. *Remain calm*, she reminded herself. *It's just a power surge. There was no bomb, no gunfire. This isn't a war zone; you're a labor and delivery nurse in a civilian hospital now.* She stood straight, tucked a hairpin neatly back into her bun and ran her hands quickly down the front of her crisp, navy blue scrub uniform. In her best ex-Navy lieutenant's voice she said, "No problem here, we're just glad it's daylight." She peeled open the curtains a foot or so. The blinding Arizona sun made a shifting rhomboid across the linoleum floor, illuminating the hospital room and all four people in it. Everyone squinted reflexively.

Kelly walked swiftly to the head of her patient's bed, took the fetal monitor and IV pump cords from their regular power outlets and plugged them into the red emergency outlets. She stood, frozen, waiting for the hospital generators to fire up. No generators. *Odd*, she thought. *Where are the generators and why didn't these other machines go to battery backup?*

The laboring mother began to vocalize. It was a long, low, guttural groan, the kind emitted by women giving birth without medication. The pain consumed her, making her oblivious to the outside world. With no time to assess the power situation further, Kelly stepped to her patient's side. She rested one hand lightly on the mother's shoulder and one on the father's.

The OB was preoccupied. She directed in a quiet but persuasive tone, "Push," and then began to count. "One, two, three, four..." Kelly knew that nothing, not even a power outage, would quell Mother Nature's persistent urgings to expel a new life.

"I need some extra hands down here. This baby is coming out with a nuchal cord," said the obstetrician, speaking deliberately in medicalese and in a hushed tone. Kelly's brain instantly translated the words to *a cord wrapped around the neck*. She felt the beat of her heart in her ears.

"Cindy, look at me," said Kelly to her patient. "Breathe like this." She demonstrated, blowing small puffs of air through her pursed lips. "Don't push, keep your face relaxed. Just keep breathing. Jim, help her do that." Kelly directed the father by taking his shoulders and pushing him gently into his wife's face. "You're both doing a great job. Just keep breathing."

With one hand Kelly reached for the call light to summon more staff; the other reached for gloves from the holder mounted on the wall. The blue LED above the call light failed to glow. She donned her gloves and moved to the foot of the bed to help the doctor. The smell of amniotic fluid and blood assaulted her nostrils.

Dr. Williams demanded the patient's attention. "Cindy, give us a gentle push with your next contraction. Nothing crazy, just push your baby out gently." The doctor, falling back on a nervous habit, unconsciously bit her lower lip. She kept it trapped there as she concentrated.

Cindy moaned but it came out like a growl, air and sound forced between her clenched teeth. She was pushing the baby forward but then holding back, thwarted because of the pain.

"The baby's head is almost out." The doctor held pressure against it to keep the rest of the body from emerging precipitously and tightening the sinuous cord. Kelly quickly gloved. It would take both women, doctor and nurse, to free the child. Dr. Williams supported the fetus while Kelly tried to work her gloved finger between the mother's body and the pulsating cord. Another attempt yielded slightly better results, but it took another whole minute before Kelly could tug enough cord free to lever it over the baby's head.

"Push now, Cindy," demanded the doctor. The mother pushed, her face scarlet, breath held. Four hands finished guiding the new life into the world, narrowly avoiding the infant's strangulation. The baby, blue and bloody, lay limp in the doctor's arms. Both caregivers instinctively began to rub the child with the blanket to encourage it to breathe.

*Don't you die on me*, Kelly thought, *I've seen enough death in my first twenty-seven years to last me a lifetime.* After a long minute with no response, Kelly reached for an ambu bag, a device to inflate the baby's lungs. She fit the face mask over the baby's mouth and nose and then gave the device a few little squeezes, causing the child's chest to rise and fall.

Suddenly the baby began to breathe, filling its own lungs with cool air. It let out a hearty cry and the mother burst into tears of joy.

The whole room let out a collective sigh of relief.

Kelly's eyes glistened with tears, as they did every time a new life emerged into this world vigorous and beautiful. "It's a boy!" she sang out. "Congratulations! Wow, what lungs!"

"Take the baby," Dr. Williams directed as she wrapped the infant in a blanket and handed him off to Kelly. She secured two cord clamps about three inches apart and sliced between them with a pair of scissors, freeing the child from its mother.

"Here, Daddy, I believe this is yours," Kelly beamed, handing the infant to him.

The proud father walked from the foot of the bed to the head, delivering the child into its mother's outstretched arms.

*BOOM!* The building shook so violently Kelly was knocked from her feet. The earth rolled and a low grumble reverberated through the reinforced concrete floor and ceiling. The glass in the windows shattered, making a sound like a hundred Mason jars being spilled from the ceiling onto the concrete floor. The heavy curtains blew inward and then flapped unrestrained as hot air filled the room. Dust sifted down from the joints of the suspended ceiling.

Kelly jumped up and threw her body over the mother and tiny infant, clinging to the hospital bed's side rail. She quickly regained her composure and tried to assess the entirety of her skin for pain or injuries. She felt no piercings or coolness that might suggest blood. A quick appraisal of the room told her that, although visibly shaken, everyone appeared to be uninjured. The glass from the window had not been propelled violently inward. Kelly knew from experience that the explosion must have been from the opposite side of the building.

She had had enough of whatever was going on. For the first time since the war, she allowed herself to shift back into a soldier. She wasn't going to recoil from an attack. Her military training kicked in. Jaw set, she looked the doctor in the eyes, then bolted for the door.

"Where are you going?" shouted the doctor.

"There are other patients that need me now. You've got these two."

Kelly slipped through the room's door into the darkened hallway, where chaos reigned. Patients, visitors, doctors and nurses all ran for the exits. The exit sign failed to glow red over the door to the stairwell.

"What the...?" She boomed in a voice fit for a drill instructor, "Cathy, Bridget, search the floor!" Kelly directed the two nurses she could identify in the dark. "See if anyone's hurt."

Both nurses stood, looking stunned. They glanced at each other, then stared back at her.

"We were going to help these people out," Bridget said, motioning towards the people in view.

"No, they can fend for themselves. Get the immobile ones out."

"How?" Cathy shouted over the confusion. The elevators are broken."

"Bridget, get them into wheelchairs if you can and have visitors push them. Find more people to help you. You may have to cradle some in sheets and have people carry them down the stairs. Cathy, have the nursery nurse get all of the babies out to their mothers. Do it *now*!"

The nurses' eyes grew large, but they changed direction and headed back onto the ward.

Kelly ran toward the patient rooms on what she thought was the blast side—the west side. She came to the first door and placed her palm on it, checking for heat. Feeling that it was cold, she entered. A tremendous wind, coming from the broken window, blew in her face. Black smoke roiled in the sky ahead of her. The window's frame was intact, but shattered safety glass was spread across the floor. Acrid smoke burned her throat and lungs. Her eyes swept back and forth for victims, but the room was empty.

She took a deep breath and forced herself to cross the room. It wasn't only the height of her third-story perch that daunted her, but what she might see outside.

Kelly reached out a trembling hand and let it glide along the wall, walking tentatively until she got to the window's frame. She took a deep breath then strained her neck to look outside, seeking the source of the smoke. It was then she made out a crashed jet liner. The huge plane's tail jutted into the sky like a monument, engulfed in smoke and flame. The last third of the hospital's south wing was consumed as well. Black plumes of smoke dotted the distance between the hospital and Sky Harbor International Airport, indicating there were more downed aircraft.

"Holy crap, how many planes?" thought Kelly out loud, startling herself with the utterance. A single tear left her eye and traveled down her perfectly made-up face. Violence had followed her home.

Kelly turned to continue her search in the all-business, autopilot mode she had been trained to engage during harrowing situations. Everyone in her unit used to say she was the coolest head in the bunch, their rock under pressure. Only Kelly knew that she became a quaking bowl of jelly when the terror was over. She suspected others did too.

There were more nurses and families in the hallway when Kelly returned to it. "A plane's crashed into the hospital, we're on fire! Search all the rooms," Kelly shouted, motioning with her hands toward the rooms. "We have to get everyone out, fast!"

Just then, the fire doors on the south end of the hallway opened. Two male nurses each pulled a patient behind them in sheets, sled style, across the slick linoleum floor. Heavy smoke followed them through the door.

The first nurse, Jim, made eye contact with Kelly.

"Heavy fire on the end of our unit and the power's out," he said breathlessly. "Close those doors when you get through," he yelled at Mark, the other nurse.

"Elevators are out," shouted Kelly. "You'll have to take them down the stairs, one at a time."

"We've lost some patients already," said Mark. "The explosion took out the last four rooms or so on both sides of the hall and a few of our nurses are missing." His words were rapid and panicked.

Kelly took a deep breath and held it, then let it out slowly. "How many patients do you have left alive?"

"Ten, but realistically, four or five might survive. We'll never get 'em all out, it's ICU down there. Most won't live through the move," Jim answered, still pulling his patient down the hall toward the stairwell.

"How many do we have on OB?" Kelly asked Bridget holding her by the forearm. She and Cathy had returned from their assigned tasks.

"We only have three post-ops, and one of those can get down the stairs by herself, so three. Oh, and one laboring," Bridget added, "but she can still walk."

"Have the two ambulatories go, as best they can."

"They already have."

"Good. Are all of the other fathers here?" Kelly asked.

"All but one," Bridget reported.

"Cathy, you direct the fathers to evacuate their wives, give what support you can. Bridget, you and I'll take the freshest post-op. Put a big sheet under her in a wheelchair and bring her other sheet too. Meet back here. Go."

"Okay." Bridget and Cathy took off down the hallway.

Kelly pulled her purse from under the counter at the nurse's station and grabbed her car key on its lanyard. She put it around her neck, then slipped her wallet and cell phone into her pocket.

"I've got her," Bridget announced, as she emerged from a nearby room, pushing a young woman in a wheelchair.

Kelly grabbed the second sheet from the patient's lap and ripped a three foot section from one end.

"Lift your arm," Kelly directed the mother. "I'm going to tie your baby to you. We'll be as gentle as we can, but getting you out of here may be a little rough. Let us know if you're hurting." The patient just sobbed.

The fabric made a big loop around the patient's back and under one arm. The mother clutched her newborn to her chest as Kelly adjusted the makeshift sling, then snugged the knot.

"That should hold him. Let's go." Kelly looked Bridget in the eyes, then steered the wheelchair toward the main stairwell, ultimately headed for the ER on the first floor and outside.

As they rounded the corner, people were streaming from the stairwell fire doors. With the doors held open, Kelly could see into the seven-story stairwell. Blades of sunlight filtered through huge cracks in the masonry walls, illuminating the thick smoke that swirled in the air.

"What's going on?" Kelly shouted into the throng.

"Stairwell's full. I don't think they're getting out downstairs," an old man said.

Just then, an out-of-breath nurse came bounding through the door, sweat dripping from his face. "Don't come down," his voice boomed, directed at everyone. "The doors are jammed."

"What do you mean *jammed*?" Kelly cried, noticing his nametag said Ryan.

"Just what I said!" Ryan retorted irritably. "There's dozens of people down there, but the doors on One and Two aren't budging. Stairwell's warped. The door opens inward, and we can't get enough pull."

"The only other stair off this floor is destroyed, on the crash end," Kelly's tone was treble. "We'll have to get the doors open from below."

"Good luck with that, *sweetheart*," Ryan said in his best Humphrey Bogart impression.

Kelly glared at him. "Okay then, we'll have to find another way out. Get these patients as far from the fire as you can and wait for me to get that door opened," Kelly directed Bridget.

"I'll go with you," said Ryan.

"Okay," said Kelly. "Bridget, I need you to get whoever is still in that stairwell away from the door. We'll try to ram the door in. If we can't do that, we'll be back and find another way out."

Kelly placed her hands on the mother's shoulders, forcing her to make direct eye contact. "We will get you out of here. I promise." The mother squinted her eyes, pinched her lips together and barely lifted their corners; it was half sob, half smile. "I'll be back." She gave a quick glance toward Bridget, who looked just as scared.

Ryan, moving nervously back and forth, said, "Come on already! Which way do we go?"

"I have to think," Kelly said. "We can't go through ICU."

"What else is on this floor?"

"Day surgery. It's Saturday, it's closed."

Both took off in a dead run for the surgery doors. Grabbing the handles of the double doors and rattling them soundly showed them to be secure. All doors into surgery were electronically controlled by swiping a badge in the card reader, or from the secured nurse's station.

"So much for state-of-the-art security. Nothing works without electricity," said Ryan. "Isn't there a waiting room that looks over the cafeteria courtyard?"

"Yeah, but it's on the other side of surgery."

Smoke began filling the room, hanging stormily overhead. "The window," Kelly said spotting the reception window. "Help me get that table."

Kelly threw the magazine rack and lamp from the end table, breaking the pottery lamp into pieces. Together, they hefted the table.

"Man, it's heavy," Kelly said, her face scarlet from the effort. Arms straining, they heaved it at the glass window. The window shook with the impact and the pair jumped back as the table flew back at them, crashing to the floor. They had only managed to crack the safety glass.

Smoke now cascaded down from the ceiling vents. "It's probably being pushed through the air conditioning ducts," Ryan said. "They're probably open to the crash site."

Kelly started to cough, subconsciously bringing her hands up to cover her mouth without relief. Crouching, she tried to get away from the volatile gases.

"Help me!" Ryan yelled at her. "Grab the table again."

"Here." Kelly picked up the broken pottery from the lamp and proceeded to bash at the window with it. Ryan followed suit. They managed to bash a hole the size of a trash can lid in the glass.

"I'll go first," said Ryan. He wrapped his arm in his scrub shirt and wiped the glass pieces off of the counter, then hoisted himself up through the hole.

"Come on," Ryan motioned to Kelly. "Be careful."

She placed her hands on the counter and pushed until she could get her knees up there too. *If only I had made the hole a bit bigger*, she thought as she squeezed through the hole and glass ripped through the skin of her upper arm. Balanced on her haunches, half in and half out of the window, she reached up a hand to inspect the sudden jolt of pain. Blood coated her hand.

"You're bleeding," Ryan said.

"Leave it be, just go!" Kelly could feel a tightness in her chest, the tightness she always felt before it made its way up her throat and out onto her cheeks in the form of tears. She swallowed hard, then leaped from the counter, landing in a squat.

As she crawled after Ryan, blood ran down one arm, both hands making sanguine handprints on the linoleum tiles. Her lanyard allowed her car key to scrape along the floor as she went. Crawling battered her knees, but it got her to their next destination: another door. They went out into the surgery's clinical hallway. Darkness crowded around them as the door to the reception area inched closed.

Bruised and bloodied, Kelly groped along the baseboards until her eyes adjusted. She could see Ryan crawling ahead of her, and then a faint slit of light appeared low to the ground ahead of him.

"There are no windows in the surgery suites. Is that sunlight?" Kelly asked.

Suddenly her hand did not find baseboard to her left. Her fingers rammed into something; a rolling cart, she guessed. There were alcoves in the hallways for supply and linen carts, to keep them out of the way. She trailed her hand along the plastic cover, another six feet, then found the baseboard again.

It wasn't long until she and Ryan were at the thin strip of light along the floor. Smoke was being sucked out under the door.

Knees aching and her arm throbbing, Kelly reached up and pressed on the door's latching bar. It gave easily.

"All of these doors let you out, just not in. This must be out," Ryan said.

"If this is another dead end, we might need to get back in here. Don't let it close," Kelly directed. She emerged into a third-story hallway with floor-to-ceiling windows, now shattered. Pieces of glass littered the floor. The smoke was heavier outside the building than in, and curled in through the gaping holes in the glass. Day was rendered twilight.

Kelly crossed the hallway, dropped to her knees in front of a hole in the glass, and peered down into the cafeteria courtyard. Air streamed in around her sweaty body, cooling her and offering renewed hope.

She leaned out to inspect the structure below. Panic filled her again. More broken glass, *Ugh*!

Kelly crawled back to where Ryan sat, holding the door open. "We can get out, but it's a long way down."

"What do we do?" asked Ryan.

"I learned rappelling in the Navy."

"We don't have any rope. What about a fire hose?"

"Not long enough, and I don't think I could keep a grip on that. *Sheets!*"

Kelly pushed Ryan aside, scrambling back into the darkened hallway. "I'll be right back."

"Where you going?"

"Right back," Kelly repeated. "I'm getting sheets."

Ryan let out a sigh. "You have one minute!"

Standing was out of the question; the smoke was too thick. Kelly bent at the waist, eyes watering with each step. The coughing became constant as she made her way back to the alcove. She unzipped and threw up the plastic cover. It held supplies. The one next to it held sheets, pillowcases, blankets and towels.

*How many?* Not waiting to run a mathematical calculation in her head, she grabbed a tall stack of sheets that towered from her waist to her chin, and started in the direction of the outside hallway. Her air was running out. She bent forward as far as she could, still running. Some sheets from the top of her stack fell to the floor. She started to bend even further to pick them up. *You can come back for them if you need them*, a panicked voice said from inside her head. *Get out!*

She pushed past Ryan, coughing and gagging. "We can't go back that way," she said.

Ryan pulled a sheet from her hands and stuffed it into the doorway, keeping the door from latching shut.

"I like to keep my options open," he said.

Next thing she knew, they were both sitting in a pile of sheets in front of the broken glass, hands struggling to tie the large sheets end-to-end.

"Too bulky, we need strips."

Ryan grasped a sewn hem and tried to rip it. Kelly watched him struggle, then had an idea. She made a quick scan of the hall, what she could see of it through the smoke, then looked down. Her car key hung around her neck. She flipped the metal emergency key up and out of its fob and raked it against the sewn hem. It took two or three passes, but finally, a slit was made.

"How many strips do we need?" Kelly asked.

"Let's see... six feet in sheet length times three—no, make it four sections—should be one story's worth of rope."

"We'll need extra for the knots and the tie-off." Kelly notched the sheets and passed them to Ryan, who made short of work of tearing them.

"Smoke's pouring out from the surgery door now." Kelly told Ryan. "Faster, faster..." Her breath came in quick pants.

"That's five sheets, we have twenty lengths," Ryan announced, coughing.

Kelly sorted through the stack to find the ends and then started tying the lengths end-to-end, with Zeppelin knots.

Ryan watched. "How do you do that?"

*"B over Q, B over Q...* That was how I was taught the Zeppelin." The memory aid still produced a vivid picture in her head of how to tie the knot.

"Here, watch."

It took Ryan quite awhile and a little practice to get the knot right, but he was finally able to help.

"What did that take? Fifteen minutes? I hope this holds," Kelly said, more to herself than to anyone else.

The tall windows were about four feet across. They had a three-foot-tall pane at the bottom and an eight-foot-tall pane at the top. The two panes were divided by a midrail. Kelly picked a section where both the top and bottom panes had been shattered.

Ryan kicked the remaining glass pieces from the frame, then tied the end of the rope to the window's midrail as close to the brick building as he could.

"Try to keep at least one foot on the bricks. The windows below you probably aren't in any better shape than these," Ryan said. "If they're cracked, they'll give way when you touch them."

Kelly inspected the tie-off knot and gave it a few hearty tugs. *No give—good.* She positioned a sheet over the rail to try to protect her rope from the window's frame and glass shards. The ground was a *long* way down, but it looked like the rope fell to within a foot or two of the gravel. Kelly ripped two more four-inch strips from the remaining sheet and made a few loops around her hands to protect them from rope burn, then sidled up to the window.

"Wow, except for training, I never rappelled once in the Navy. Thank God I learned." Kelly said, glancing at Ryan and then looking down.

"You have one on me," said Ryan. I've never done it. Don't you need a fancy harness or something?"

She stood, put the rope between her legs, brought it around her right hip, up and over her left shoulder, then back down so that her right hand could hold it snugly.

"This this a Dulfersitz rappel; I learned it in my ROTC confidence course."

"You sure you've got this?" Ryan asked, as much fear in his eyes as she imagined she had in hers.

"I've got it," said Kelly. *I've got this, I've got this, I've got this*, she repeated over and over in her head. Tentatively, she put one leg out over the window rail. She snugged the rope against her body, then straddled the rail. For just a moment, she shut her eyes so tightly that her cheeks hurt.

"Just walk down the building, walk slowly down the building," she said to herself, out loud.

Putting her second leg out, the bottom frame separated under her weight.

Ryan grabbed her by her upper arm, the one that wasn't bleeding, and steadied her as she pivoted. He yanked her instinctively, digging his fingers into her flesh. "Whoa there," he muttered.

Thud, her chest and shoulder hit the rail. Momentarily stunned, she held onto the rope and waited for the swinging and pain to subside. At last her body was still, her nose nestled against the soft, white sheet. From this position it was difficult to maneuver, but after a minute or so she succeeded in getting her legs and torso into a ninety-degree angle. The descent was slow going. At any minute, she feared she could lose her footing again. If that happened, she would be torn to bits by jagged glass.

Ryan peered down from above and called, "Slow, girl, take it nice and steady." Kelly did not look up or down; she concentrated on her feet and kept walking. She controlled her rappelling sling by extending and retracting her right hand. This tightened and loosened the harness and allowed her to wriggle down the rope. The knots were stiff and occasionally caused pain when they scraped along her body.

Suddenly Kelly's right hand lost hold of the rope; she had come to the rope's end and it had slipped through her grasp. A searing scream escaped her lips as she fell. The end of the last sheet struck her in the face as it passed by.

A tremendous jolt went up through her legs and into her hips when she hit the ground, but she remained standing. She looked up. The fall had been about five feet.

"You alright down there?" came Ryan's voice.

"I think so. You next."

"Oh, no... I'm fifty pounds heavier than you and have never even touched a rope. I'll meet you at the stairs."

"You can't!" Kelly called up, but Ryan's face had already disappeared from the window.

Kelly took off in a dead run for the cafeteria doors. They were unlocked; her first stroke of luck all day. It was only a minute or two more to the emergency department, then the stairwell. From the cafeteria doorway she could still see a few people rushing out of the building. The screaming and confusion had stopped; all that was left was the sound of coughing and shuffling footsteps. What was it, twenty, thirty, forty minutes after the crash? Kelly had lost all sense of time.

"Come on! You alright?" One man put out his hands to help her into the hallway, but upon seeing the blood caked on her arm, just held the door for her.

Kelly seized the man by both shoulders. "Help us, the stairwell is blocked. The whole south wing is trapped!" He looked at her quizzically, trying to comprehend what she was saying.

A male nurse came toward them, pushing a gurney. Kelly grabbed the bed by the end, impeding its progress, and looked the nurse pushing it right in the eyes. "The south wing is trapped!" she said frantically, reading his name tag. *Nathan, RN.*

"What are you talking about?"

"The stairs on the far south end are destroyed and the inner stairwell door is jammed. That way," she said, pointing behind him.

Both men, the door-holder and Nathan, followed Kelly down the hallway. As they got closer, banging emanated from behind the doors, but no voices could be discerned.

"Couldn't anyone hear that?" Kelly asked in an irritated tone.

"We've been a little busy down here," Nathan answered.

"We've gotta get 'em out. We'll need a ram of some kind," Kelly announced. She pounded on the door with her fists and shouted, "We're coming, stand back, get back!" The impacts caused flashes of blinding pain to radiate through her tired arms and shoulders.

"We'll use this gurney, maybe we can force it open," said Nathan.

"The banging's quit, they must have heard us," Kelly said, looking at door-holder man.

He took Kelly's bleeding arm and said, "I'm Dr. Cho. Let me have a look at that arm."

Kelly yanked her arm away from him. "Not now, later." It was then she noticed his hospital name badge hanging from his belt. "I'm sorry, Doctor, but we need to get these people out first," she said with a weak attempt at a smile.

Nathan had positioned the cart about six feet from the door, then everyone gathered at the head end and gave a great shove.

The plastic bumpers on the gurney shattered and fell into pieces on the floor. The fire door had a big dent and paint was scraped off where the gurney had made impact. The door had moved a mere inch, but it *did* move. Smoke briefly puffed through the opening, but was immediately drawn back. Air whistled as it was sucked up what was now a chimney.

Kelly leaned toward the opening and shouted, "We're coming!"

"Get back," Nathan shouted at Kelly, motioning her away from the door frame.

The men took another run at the door and it was displaced another inch. It took about six or seven rams; Kelly had lost count by the time it was open wide enough for her to get through.

She squeezed in, then looked back and called, "We need a bigger opening, big enough for wheelchairs." Then she disappeared into the smoky darkness. She turned the corner and was besieged by people.

"We thought you'd been killed," said Bridgette, yelling from half a flight up.

"Long story."

"*Very* long by the look of it," said Jim. She hadn't recognized the ICU nurse from before. He glanced down at her bloodied, battered form, hair falling from her once-neat bun. "We have crews ready to carry the invalids and they're all staged, ready to go, on the first floor."

Just then the door below them came loose. It slammed into the block wall, completely open.

"Let's go!" said Kelly, tugging on Greg's shirt sleeve, but Greg turned and headed up the stairs, against the throng.

"I'll keep things moving up there," he said.

Staff and patients flooded down the stairs, pushing Kelly along with them, flowing out into the emergency department and toward the sunlight of the doors that led out into the ambulance parking area.

"Kelly! Kelly, over here." Kelly heard the nursing supervisor calling and beckoning from the nurses' station. She made her way in that direction.

"Are you alright? Your arm."

Kelly put her hands on her knees and bent forward, still breathing heavily. She coughed repeatedly and said, "It's okay, a flesh wound, I think. The bleeding has slowed, if not stopped."

"Can you run?"

"Yes, I think so, why?" Kelly asked.

"We need you to run to the fire department—I'm assuming you ran in the military. We need an army, and fast. We've gotta get as many of these patients outta here as we can. The fire is taking the south wing and moving toward the north one."

Kelly looked up from her bent position, squinting against the sun, and asked, "What do you mean?"

"All the phones are out, even cells. We can't find even one car or truck that will start. There hasn't been a single siren."

Terror struck at her heart. *What did all of this mean? Who had done this?*

"If you think you can make it downtown on foot, the front hospital entrance is still clear, you can go that way."

Kelly didn't answer, but dashed down the hall past the ER medication room. An IV pole lay on the floor in a pool of shattered glass from the room's broken security window. Mike, an ER nurse she recognized, dodged out of her way at the last second, his vision impeded by the huge box of medicines that partially covered his face.

"Bring what you can carry," Mike urged.

"I'm going to the fire department to get help," Kelly shouted down the hallway after the swiftly-moving figure.

Mike turned back and called, "Take stuff you think you might need. There are likely people who will need your help out there, and this place won't be here long." He continued down the corridor, not waiting for a response or looking back.

Mike's pry bar had left the medicine-dispensing machine unrecognizable. Its drawers hung open, displaying their contents. Kelly threw medications into a patient's belongings bag. She chose antibiotics, nausea medicines, painkillers and other emergency drugs. Bins of syringes and other supplies hung on the wall. Handfuls of each were collected. The stockroom was right next door, but not locked. Items deemed necessary were thrown into a plastic bag, including gauze, soap, and sutures. Finished, Kelly took off running toward the main entrance and her Jeep.

Her desperate, uncoordinated hands dug at her lanyard and her car key. She pushed the fob. No beep.

The Wrangler's door had to be opened with the metal key. The key turned in the ignition, but the engine refused to turn over. In fact, it was silent.

"What the…?" Kelly ratcheted the key in the ignition again, more forcefully this time. She got out and slammed the door. Going around to the passenger's side, she retrieved her four-wheeling, survival backpack and set it in the seat, then upended the belongings bag into it. The medical supplies were added, along with the phone charger which she yanked from the cigarette lighter.

A large man, sweating heavily, pushed a wheelbarrow past Kelly, conveying a young woman. Her bloodied, singed blouse was torn by bits of what might be fragments of an exploded airplane. She lay there with her mouth agape, head bobbing, her complexion that pale grayish cast worn by the dead. The man did not stop, but pressed on in the direction of the ER.

Kelly took off running east before turning south, past the crash, in a gait the military calls the airborne shuffle—more than a jog, but less than a true run. *How many hours had she run like this during officer's training?*

How surreal it all was. She couldn't ever remember feeling this insignificant or inadequate. Tears welled in her eyes. *I can cry now, I'm alone and don't have to be strong for anyone.* Her sight was blurry at best while navigating the parking lot to the street.

Vehicles rested at odd angles in the roadway and over curbs. Fires, ignited by the exploding transformers, grew where they had fuel available from brush and homes. People were gathered on the street corners in awe, looking toward the crash site. The early September temperatures, still in the high nineties, forced people into whatever shade they could find.

"Go help evacuate the hospital," Kelly pleaded with everyone she passed on her way downtown. Most people just looked at her blankly. It was then she realized her scrub uniform was smeared with blood from clutching the newborn and her lacerated arm. Her long hair had escaped her neat bun, and unruly tendrils now hung, framing her face. She pushed it aside in vain.

"Get hold of yourself," Kelly said out loud. "Remember your mission… fire department, downtown, run!" This set her resolve.

Several blocks into her journey, Kelly saw a bicycle lying in a front yard. Her moral compass struggled, only momentarily, with stealing it. She approached the bike, scanning for anyone who might have an objection to her borrowing it, lifted the bike by its handlebars, then threw her right leg up and over. Adjusting her backpack straps, she hoisted the pack higher onto her shoulders. The yard sloped toward the street, making her departure effortless.

Kelly zigged and zagged along the street, avoiding people and parked cars. Ignoring those who called out to her, she pressed on, and the four miles to downtown whirred past. She rode up onto the sidewalk, around the light pole and potted plants, right up to the front steps of the fire department. Kelly had her right leg in the air before completing her stop. The bicycle landed up against a chunky concrete pillar, meant to keep vehicles from driving into the lobby. Taking the stairs two at a time, she hurled herself at the entrance.

Inside stood a rotund uniformed police officer. He opened the heavy glass door just wide enough to speak. "Hold it right there, miss." He looked taken aback by her appearance.

"My name is Kelly Wise," she exclaimed, breathless, lifting the ID badge pinned to her uniform to reinforce her statement. "I'm coming from the hospital. We need help. The hospital's been hit by a plane and is on fire. We have severely injured patients and our power is out."

"Emergency Operations has been set up here in the lobby because of the lack of lighting in the basement. Wait here, miss," the officer said, visibly shaken.

*How can he just leave me here, standing quietly, bursting apart on the inside?*

The officer let the glass door close. He kept one eye on her, but hurried into the large lobby and spoke to another man.

*"Come on, come on!" Kelly thought.*

The two men conversed for a moment and then the officer hurried back across the lobby and held the door open for her.

*It's obvious no one here had witnessed the horrific scenes playing out near the hospital. How can they all be so calm?*

"I'll need to search your backpack, Miss Wise," the officer said, putting on vinyl gloves from a pouch on his duty belt.

"I understand why you are doing this, but really, I need to talk to the command staff," she panted. "We need help, this is life and death. There's a jetliner crashed into the hospital. It's simple!" Her words spilled out half whine, half scream.

"I'm sorry, but we don't know what the threat is."

Kelly, exasperated, let her backpack fall off her right shoulder, but caught it with her left arm. It was so heavy that her whole frame jerked to the left. The officer grabbed the pack at that point and finished lowering it to the floor.

"I'm sorry, miss, but I need to search your person as well before I can let you in. Spread your legs and put your arms straight up."

She did it just like she had seen in police dramas. The officer frisked her.

Not waiting for the backpack to be searched, she bolted forward, leaving it at the officer's feet, and practically ran toward a long table near the reception counter. There were tables set up all along the room's perimeter, but the dry erase board behind her target table said *Incident Commander*, whereas the others were labeled *Operations, Logistics*, or *Planning*. Several men sat at the table with yellow legal pads in front of them; one had a name tag that read *Fire Chief Lane*. The "white shirt brigade" stood as Kelly approached. She stood at mock attention out of habit. "I'm here from the hospital. It's burning down."

All of the men behind the table and all those within earshot listened intently, brows furrowed, as the nurse started to recount her tale.

"Stop, stop," Chief Lane said after just a few words from Kelly. "Everyone over here," he said, waving his arm in a sweeping motion, beckoning everyone in the lobby. "You've got to hear this." Thirty people stood mute, glued to her account, until she finished.

Chief Lane let his large frame fall backward into his chair. He put his elbows on the table and ran his hands through his silver hair, his face pale and blank. "We sent two bike officers to investigate the plane crash, but they haven't returned," he said hesitantly, as if carefully composing the words that were to come from his mouth. "I really don't know what we can do at this point. The city doesn't seem to have a single running vehicle. We've seen a few old clunkers running around, but they weren't stopping for us. A few police officers and firefighters have reported to our makeshift EOC (Emergency Operations Center), but others have left to check on their families. We don't have any real personnel count. Our radios and phones aren't working. We'll try to round up some resources, but at this point, we have very little to offer." Chief Lane stood, bent forward, hands still on the table so he was eye-to-eye with Kelly. "This is not a routine plane crash or power outage." A grave look came over the chief's face and he looked down as he spoke. "It's much more."

"That's it?" Kelly shouted, slamming her hands on the table.

"Yes, ma'am." He said, looking up slowly, meeting her gaze again. "What would you have me do?"

There was an audible gasp from all present, including Kelly.

She stared blankly. She wanted to yell, jump up and down, something. Her shoulders fell. She didn't know what she had expected to find when she got to the fire department, but this wasn't it.

"Oh, my..." The words escaped her thin lips in a mere whisper.

Chapter 2

CAP (Civil Air Patrol) - Day 0

It was a beautiful morning. Jess, a strapping lad of sixteen, looked up from the Arizona Gazetteer, the all-in-one topographic map book for the state of Arizona, to identify the large mountain he saw on the map and try to get his bearings.

"Hey, Dad, is that Mount Ord?" Jess asked, pointing out the car window to a rounded, towering peak to the southeast with a cluster of radio antennas and cell towers on it.

"Yes, Mijo," Jose called Jess by his Spanish nickname.

Jess was a Civil Air Patrol cadet. The United States Air Force Auxiliary, the Civil Air Patrol, was a step in Jess's plan to get an ROTC scholarship and then fly F-35s for the Air Force. He had flown with his dad for as long as he could remember. Soon, he would solo.

Jess had interrupted his father and Major Rabbinowitz chatting in the front seats about some article in *Scientific American* magazine. Captain Jose Herrero looked down from watching the road and glanced at the GPS suctioned to the windshield. "What's our next turn, Mijo?"

"You've got the GPS right there on the dash, Dad, and I saw you program the coordinates at Mission Base. Can I stop this now?"

"No, you are supposed to be navigating by the map all day today, for practice."

"I got checked off a year ago on map and compass when I got my Ground Team qualification, and I'm getting a little queasy back here," Jess said, puffing out his cheeks to emphasize his discomfort.

Jose cleared his throat in a manner only fathers can do.

"Yes, sir," Jess said in the sing-song voice of compliance. "Looks like about a half mile to our turn-off. We're going to turn left, west."

"Good job, you're right—I mean correct," said Jose.

Jess smiled to himself. He glanced over at Cadet Sergeant Rabbinowitz, who was sitting in the back seat with him. The guys in her Civil Air Patrol squadron called her Lynn. The younger Rabbinowitz' long, jet-black hair was rolled into a tight bun at the nape of her neck, military fashion. High school volleyball had toned and tanned her entire body. Jess hoped he hadn't had a stupid look on his face when he glanced over at her.

"Let me see that map," Lynn said. She reached for it, but Jess moved it just out of her reach.

"I'm the map reader. You can be the survival expert, first aid person or anything else you want today," Jess said.

"Oh, come on," said Lynn. "It's not like we're looking for a real crash site or anything."

"No, but on these SAREXs (Search and Rescue Exercises) you have to pretend—prepare for the real thing."

"We don't get that many here, do we, Dad?" Lynn looked to her father for reinforcement.

"Don't get me in on this, Lynn," said Major Dennis Rabbinowitz. "But they do say we have too much good weather here in Arizona for many plane searches—the land of the never-ending sun."

"I got to go on a *real* search," said Jess. "It was in the White Mountains. A helicopter crashed in a deep canyon. We drove almost all night to get there, then went into the canyon at dawn.

"You did not," chided Lynn. "You couldn't have been qualified yet. I didn't get my SAR qual 'til six months after that search."

"Did too, you can ask my Dad. He was there."

"Yep, Lynn," said Jose. "He'd passed his SAR practicals not two weeks before."

"It was cool, there were two dead bodies," Jess said, then wished he hadn't said it with so much enthusiasm. Lynn wrinkled up her nose and turned her head away. "I mean, they didn't let us see them up close or anything, because we weren't supposed to mess up the evidence. Just Major LaGuardia got to go in, he's a paramedic."

Captain Jose Herrero slowed and steered the lifted, fire-engine red Ford Expedition onto the dirt road from the Beeline Highway. The phone in Lynn's BDU (battle dress uniform) pants pocket fired off three loud beeps.

"Dad, it's time for Ops Normal," Lynn looked at Dennis and held out her hand.

"Mic please, Major Rabbi Daddy."

"There you are, Sergeant Daughter," Dennis said as he handed the radio microphone over the seat to Lynn.

Lynn cleared her throat and got ready to transmit. "Mission Base, Red Rock Three Seven, over."

"Red Rock Three Seven, Mission Base, over." A young teen voice replied from the VHF radio speaker. Jess thought it sounded like a cadet in his squadron.

"Ops Normal, Red Rock Three Seven, out." Handing the mic back to her dad she said," Now the Incident Commander knows that we are safe and secure, I feel much better."

"That must have been John on the radio," said Jess. "I mean, Cadet Curry. I thought he was supposed to be marshalling aircraft on the flight line today, not working the radios."

"They could have him doing both. They were short on cadets today for Mission Base; most were out in the field," said Dennis.

"This is a very big SAREX (search and rescue exercise) this weekend," Jose said, "And it's especially important that Mission Base keeps track of us. Since we are the *special surprise*.

We are not on the regular mission plan, but are supposed to be off doing *something else*. We don't have a tactical call sign for this mission either. As far as anyone listening knows, the good chaplain and his helpers are out ministering to the troops. Dennis, why don't you have a more distinctive call sign—say, Gawd One?" Jose asked, changing God into a two syllable word.

"That is a bit much for a *humble* Torah student like me," retorted Rabbi Rabbinowitz.

Jess and Lynn both suppressed a laugh on hearing their fathers' banter. The SUV turned off the pavement toward the mountains, dust obscuring brown brush and small desert trees in their wake.

"We are crossing over the old, single-lane, Beeline Highway now and will take this dirt road an hour or so into the mountains and then drop into that valley over there," Jose gestured toward the mountains in front of the truck.

"So what exactly are we doing, again?" asked Jess.

Lynn rolled her eyes. "Weren't you listening? Our assignment is to place a practice ELT (emergency locator transmitter) and have it transmitting by noon. One of the mission aircraft has orders to return to Deer Valley Airport and stop answering the CAP radio, simulating a missing search plane. Our ELT is supposed to *be* that plane. That should shake up the mundane weekend training."

"Mission Base radio will know that something is wrong when the aircraft doesn't report Ops Normal on schedule," said

Dennis, unable to hide the excitement in his voice. "The radio operators will let the command staff know right away."

"How long will it take to send the planes from the practice search to look for what they think could be a real missing CAP aircraft?"

"That is what the SAREX evaluators want to know," Jose answered. "The Incident Commander has to be flexible and adapt to problems, sometimes very serious problems, during a mission. The 'real' missing aircraft has priority, of course. We will hear on the radio when our practice ELT is heard by search teams. We are supposed to be sitting here waiting for the ground team to locate us."

The SUV lumbered along the dirt road, skirting the hills following a dry wash. The truck left the wash and worked its way up the side of a mountain on a road that wasn't much more than a bighorn sheep trail.

"What's that?" asked Jess, pointing to a collection of dilapidated buildings in the distance.

"Well, what does the map tell you, Jess?" asked Dennis.

"There's a mine symbol," said Jess.

"Yes, that's the old Sunflower Mercury Mine and processing buildings, or what's left of them after the brush fire a few years ago," Dennis answered.

The Expedition crested the hill and began descending into one of the countless valleys.

"This is the area where we're supposed to set up," said Jose. "Jess, check the GPS coordinates, but this valley looks like the one on our mission map."

"Yep, it's a match. Pull over under those trees, and we'll pitch the sun shade," said Jess.

They found a spot with patches of shade among some low, scruffy junipers and parked. It was September; temperatures were still in the nineties. Lynn reported to Mission Base that Red Rock Three Seven had arrived at their assigned coordinates. The group quickly erected a shade fly next to the SUV, and placed a folding table and chairs under the fly. They positioned the practice ELT in the middle of a small clearing nearby.

"Ahhh, this is the life," said Dennis, stretching out his arms as he sat in the low-slung folding chair. "Some of the other ground team leaders are leading their cadets over rough terrain for a hot, all-day hike and we're *sitting* here, in the *shade*. We start the ELT transmitting in about a half hour. Then, I think lunch is in order."

"Dad, can I start a campfire?" Jess asked.

"That would be awesome," Lynn exclaimed.

"Let's see, it's ninety-five degrees and we don't need to cook lunch," said Jose. "City kids and campfires—they just have to have them. Normally I would say yes, but I don't want to give any extra help to the searchers by sending up smoke signals." Jose paused, then asked, "Anyone up for a game of cards?"

As the group settled into the card game, Dennis said to Jose, "That is quite the SUV you've got."

"Thanks. Jess and I spent hours and hours working on it. We lifted it, beefed up the suspension, fabricated the brush guard, added undercarriage armor, installed the CAP radio, mounted the winch and even added a snorkel. It may be overkill for our needs, but I'm a project kind of a guy and it is good for Jess to learn to work with his hands."

"I think it's a very *pretty* truck, too," said Lynn, poking a little fun. "You do good work," she said, looking at Jess.

He looked at her incredulously.

"*Really,*" she said sincerely.

"I had a lot of fun welding, bending metal, and wrench turning," Jess said. "Dad had me draw the plans for the brush guard and armor on his drafting program. He thinks I should be an engineer like him. But I don't wanna sit at a computer. Aeronautical engineering would be okay while I'm in ROTC."

"Oh really? So in college you'll do ROTC and learn engineering in your spare time?" Dennis asked. "Most of the engineers I know worked very hard to graduate."

"It's all about flying fighters with that kid," Jose said. "Dennis, you seem to know your way around science and math. The cadets really love your model rocketry program. I also notice that you know a lot about the Air Force. Is that a big part of rabbinical training?"

Dennis chuckled. "That Air Force knowledge was gained first hand. I joined as soon as I could after high school to avoid going to rabbinical school. *Oy vey*, my father the rabbi," Dennis said in an exaggerated Yiddish accent.

"*Oy vey ist mir*, my father the religion prof," Lynn mocked.

"What did you do in the Air Force?" Jess asked.

"I was a metrological tech. I enjoyed doing science. So when I got out, I majored in physics. By the time I received my bachelor's, I wanted to know what made people tick. That led to a master's in psychology. The next thing I knew, I'd graduated from rabbinical seminary and held a PhD in religious studies as well. Now, I'm my father the rabbi. *Oy!*"

"Lynn, when are you going to rabbi school?" Jess teased.

Lynn shot him an exaggerated stare. "I don't really know what I want to do," she said. "Dad has me on the math and music wunderkind track. So I spend half my school day at community college doing differential equations and playing violin. The rest of the day I'm in high school with the rest of my junior class. I'm not sure that I want to be a professional musician or do math or science. Felicia Day has a dual math and violin performance bachelor's. Maybe I will be an actress and have my own web series like her. Shall I start packing for Hollywood, Dad?" Lynn lifted her eyebrows and flashed an exaggerated smile.

Dennis reached over and patted Lynn's hand. "All I want is for my little princess to be happy," he said in mock seriousness. "Don't worry; your path will open to you." He broke into song, "La, la, la, winding road."

Wanting to change the subject, Jess turned to Jose and said, "Dad, I promised Mom that I would send a picture of us from camp this weekend."

"So she can show it to your cousins in Iowa, Mijo," said Jose. "My wife is back east visiting with her family for a week," he explained to Dennis and Lynn. "Her sisters all wanted to get together for some *girl time*."

"Why don't we all stand next to the truck over here? That way, the mountains will be in the background." Jess said.

After some cajoling, jostling for position and Jess setting the delay timer so everyone could be in the picture, the smart phone beeped three times and everyone smiled.

Jess typed on the phone for a few moments and then said, "I sent it."

"I'll start the ELT transmitting now," Dennis said, walking over to the small metal box with an antenna attached. Looking at the switches, he confirmed that it was set to the right frequency. The red transmit LED illuminated as he pushed the toggle switch to the on position.

"Now we sit back and wait to be found." He bent over to place the ELT on the ground.

A loud, very short screech burst from inside the SUV. Dennis straightened up, still holding the ELT, as Jose stood up and moved toward the open driver's window.

"What was *that*?" Jose asked. Poking his head into the window, Jose heard a very quiet hissing from the CAP radio. He opened the door and examined the radio. He saw that all the indicator lights and the display were off. Pushing the off/on switch made no change. Jose inserted the ignition key and moved the ignition to the battery position: no change. The idiot lights on the dashboard remained off and the door open chime was silent. Glancing upward, he noticed that the overhead light was off.

"Odd; if the battery were dead, then the radio wouldn't hiss," Jose said half to himself and half to the others gathering around the truck. "Jess, go see if the headlights come on." Jose moved the switch to the on position.

"On," Jess called back.

The SUV sat quietly as Jose tried to start it.

"It looks like an electronics or computer problem. I don't know what is happening and I don't know what else to do," Jose said. "I think we better call the SAREX evaluation team and let them know we are stuck here."

"I'll call," Dennis said. Finding his hands full with the ELT, he glanced at it then looked for a place to set it down. Something was not right with the ELT. Looking at it again, he saw that the transmit light was off. Flipping the on/off switch back and forth changed nothing. "The ELT is broken too," he said.

Jose moved to Dennis's side and watched Dennis flip the switch on and off. "It was on just before the CAP radio squawked, said Dennis. He handed the ELT to Jose and retrieved his phone from his pocket. He swiped his finger across the display. It remained dark. He tried to get the phone to come on. "No phone either."

Simultaneously, everyone else reached into their pockets and retrieved their phones. This is just too weird, Jess thought. "What's going on?"

"Looks like something has knocked out our micro circuitry," Dennis said. "The headlights work, but anything with a computer chip between it and its power source seems to be dead."

"Any idea what is going on?" Dennis asked Jose. "Could it be some kind of transient discharge from the truck?"

"I don't think so," Jose said. "All of our cell phones and the ELT were affected too. I didn't feel any current through the ground. There was no sparking."

"There aren't any power lines in the area," Dennis said. "There is a mercury mine over that ridge as well as other large mineral deposits scattered around here, but I doubt it was a static discharge or a release of ionizing radiation from the ground."

"Not the truck, not the ground... that leaves the sky"...Jose's voice trailed off. "Could it be a solar event? You know, a solar flare or a coronal mass ejection?"

"That's possible," Dennis said. "There have been several big radio disturbances from solar storms that lasted for hours, and some for a few days. That could definitely affect all of our electronics."

"Yes it could, if it were big enough," Jose said. "There was a major solar event in the mid 1800s. It went on for days and affected the telegraph lines, which were really the only electronics they had at that time."

"We're due for our Ops Normal report in about ten minutes," Lynn said. "Mission Base will try to reach us on the radio, then cell phone. After they decide that we're not just temporarily in a bad radio area, they will start looking for us."

"Let's assume for right now," Dennis said, "that just *our* equipment has been affected. We should get our signal mirrors out of the twenty-four-hour daypacks in case a plane overflies us. Use the cord to keep them around your neck so you don't have to fumble with them at the last minute. Jess, Lynn—after you have your mirrors, get some of the road flares out of the back. Make three piles of them about six feet apart in a triangle on the road. Keep a flare nearby to ignite the piles, but be careful the fires won't ignite nearby brush."

The team moved to the rear of the truck and quickly obtained their mirrors. Without discussion, each person looked through the sunburst sight in the middle of their mirror and practiced aiming the sun's reflection at trees and bushes. This spot of light would be aimed at a pilot flying above them. The teens took road flares from an olive-drab ammo box in the back of the SUV and began setting up the flare signals as directed. Jess knew when directions were orders and when his father had gone into command mode. It was evident that Lynn did too.

Lynn and Jess joined the two men.

"Okay, we are in a survival situation," Dennis said, looking at the teens. "What is the procedure?"

"Survival situation? We just have a broken truck," Jess said.

"And broken radios and broken phones," Dennis pointed out. "I think we're fine, but when things start going wrong you must take control of the situation before it takes control of you. Survival procedures, please."

"STOP—Stop, Think, Observe and Plan," Lynn said, looking pleased with herself. This was the mantra CAP cadets were taught to use in an emergency.

"Good job," Dennis said. "Captain Herrero and I are not sure what has affected our electronics. It might be a solar flare. If it is, it may last for hours or days."

"Hours or days?" Lynn whined. "Will we have to wait for the search planes to find us?"

"If our electronics are down, theirs may be as well. There may not be any planes up to search for us."

"What, we walk home?" Lynn's voice was more shrill.

"Well, I don't think we know enough yet to make those kinds of decisions," Dennis said, "but we should be thinking about all of the possibilities. Our first priority should be to take inventory of all our belongings and determine what does, and does not, work."

"I'm not walking home," Lynn said throwing herself into a chair. "Do you know how long that would take?"

"As long as it takes," Dennis replied. "I don't need the attitude."

Lynn exaggerated the sullen look on her pretty face. Jess stood with his mouth hanging open slightly and gawked at Jose. Jose shot him a fatherly glare as if to say, *Don't go there with me, son.* Jess set his jaw and stood a little straighter.

"Now get up from there," Dennis directed. "I didn't do this just to inconvenience you. We'll just have to make the best of it."

Lynn stood and walked toward the SUV, putting her feet down heavily for emphasis. The others followed her.

Each member removed a small daypack and a larger backpack from the rear hatch of the SUV. The smaller packs, known as twenty-four-hour packs, were designed to be carried in the field while searching. They held items needed to conduct a search and equipment to survive for twenty-four hours. The contents of the twenty-four hour pack, together with the contents of the backpack, formed a seventy-two hour pack. As implied by the name, they were designed to sustain searchers for seventy-two hours in the field. Because of the packs, the team was well equipped with camping and survival gear plus socks, underwear, and a change of clothes.

A gear check showed that the GPS devices and walkie-talkies did not work. Packed in the truck were ten gallons of drinking water, a large ice chest containing "real food"—not the MREs kept in the search packs—a high lift jack, a tool kit, a pull strap and a rope.

The tents remained stored for the time being so they would not have to be packed if help came before nightfall.

The afternoon was passed discussing theories of what caused the radio and general electronic failures. After much discussion, they agreed that theoretically, it had the hallmarks of an electromagnetic pulse—an EMP—but who might have done it, they did not know. Through it all, the group watched the sky and strained to hear any engine noise from airplanes above or from the roads below in the valley. Not a single aircraft or contrail was sighted.

As evening approached, wood was gathered. Tents were unpacked and flat, rockless spots, as rockless as one could find on a mountain in Arizona, were located and cleared. Sleeping pads and bags were rolled out and the camp was prepared for night.

"Lynn and I will close the day with our afternoon and evening prayers," Dennis said. "Want to join us?"

"Sure," said Jose. Jess rolled his eyes so that only his father could see him, but joined the rest of the group near the campfire and sat quietly.

Dennis prayed in Hebrew and then repeated the prayers in English, just like he had after lunch.

Jess's family was not a church-going bunch. Jess had been to Mass a few times and to Protestant churches with friends a couple of times. It all seemed so foreign, so mysterious to him.

The team cooked over a fire as the sky burst into a beautiful sunset, then turned twilight. After dinner, the group sat in lawn chairs around the campfire, staring into the flames. The teens fed the small fire, poked at burning branches with sticks and then waved their burnt sticks in the air. The red embers on the sticks' ends traced paths of glowing red through the air. The sky was pitch-black. The customary glow from Phoenix, a town of four million people only sixty miles to the southwest, was absent.

"Looks like town is blacked out too, doesn't it, Dad?" Jess said softly.

"Yes, Mijo, it does."

"We should all get to bed," Dennis said. "Let's set a fire watch so the campfire stays lit and have someone watching and listening for planes. Watches will be two hours long. Keep the fire burning low to save wood. Anybody have a preference for their watch?"

"I'll take first watch," volunteered Jess.

"Second," Lynn said.

"I'll take the last watch," Jose said. "I'm an early riser anyway."

Dennis rose and went to his tent. Following the team leader's example, Jose rose and shuffled to his tent. Lynn and Jess remained.

About four hours later, Dennis checked the luminescent dial of his still-ticking wristwatch. It confirmed that it was his time to stand watch. He grabbed his coat and boots, then unzipped the tent flap and squeezed his five foot ten-inch frame through the opening. Jess sat stirring the campfire with a stick. Dennis noticed his daughter, still wrapped in her sleeping bag, sleeping in a chair across from Jess. Dennis sent them both off to bed and settled into his chair. After what seemed like an eternity, Jose woke and took over the last watch.

"This desert sure gets cold at night," Jose said.

"Yep, hot during the day and cold at night. You can't win."

"Speaking of can't win, I'm afraid for the kids and us too. Lynn was right you know—town is several days' walk. More than seventy-two hours."

"I know. Don't panic the kids, though. We can take stock again in the morning and make a plan. We've got our seventy-twos plus the cooler. We have water too."

"I don't like this, Dennis."

"I don't like it either. Don't let it make you crazy while you're on watch, though. We need all the rest, calm and wit we can muster."

Dennis nodded and went off to bed.

\*\*\*\*

Jose heard rustling from the tents as dawn broke over the eastern mountain tops. Slowly, rumpled figures emerged from their olive-drab cocoons.

"Get all of your electronics out," Dennis urged.

Everyone met back at the SUV. No car ignition, no radio, no phones, no GPS. Blank faces were seen all around. Lynn fought back tears, looking much older than she had yesterday morning.

"Let's get breakfast," Dennis said. "Maybe some food in our stomachs will help us think better."

It didn't take any time at all to retrieve oatmeal packets, granola bars and Pop Tarts from their twenty-four hour packs. Jose ate a can of Beenie Weenies, cold. The meal provided physical and emotional nourishment in a world that was becoming uncertain.

"It's clear that whatever is going on is affecting more than just us," said Jose as he sat with the others gathered around the table. "The sky was black all night. I didn't see or hear a single plane. We aren't that far from Phoenix and should be seeing planes at regular intervals. The CAP Cessnas can fly without electronics; the flight controls use cables. They would be able to land, but the pilots wouldn't take them back up without GPS and radios. The newer airliners and military aircraft are all computer-controlled; who knows how they fared. Not well, I'd guess."

"We need to get ourselves out of here. We shouldn't waste any daylight if we're going to walk clear to Phoenix," Dennis said. "We have food for a few days, but we can't waste it sitting here. We can make it to the road in a day. *If* things get back to normal, we can just hitchhike back to town."

"We can see the highway from that hill," Lynn said pointing south. "I could see it up 'til about a mile ago when we went over the ridge."

"Let's take a stroll and get a better look," Dennis said.

The ground team pulled on their twenty-four hour packs and started up the dirt road. Jess thought about how no one was talking much as they walked. Usually, ground team members laughed and joked as they walked. No one felt like joking this morning. They were all worried.

After a short hike, the group rounded the mountain.

In the distance, far below, small dots lay spread along the thin ribbon of blacktop. Like the others, Jess reached into a backpack pouch and retrieved a small pair of binoculars. Looking through the lenses, he saw stopped cars and trucks spread along the Beeline Highway.

"Everybody's vehicles quit just like ours," Jose said excitedly. "It's true."

Dennis shot a stern look as if to say, *Don't scare the kids*.

"I see people. They're walking down the road," Lynn said.

"I think we should head back to camp and get ready to hike home," Dennis said.

Lynn hung her head and started walking. She sidled up to her father and bumped into him, announcing her presence. She put her hand in his. Dennis looked down at Lynn, pursed his lips and then smiled ever so slightly. His princess still needed her daddy. He let the smile fade and continued walking.

Back at the campsite, everyone gathered around the Gazetteer.

Studying the map, Dennis said, "We know how far it is to the Beeline Highway, and then it's thirty more miles or so to Fountain Hills. What about these buildings?" Dennis pointed at the map. "The ones here to the southeast, on the old Beeline, the part that was bypassed during the last road improvement. Aren't these houses in Sunflower?"

"There are some ranch families there along Sycamore Creek," Jose said.

"They might have a working landline or at least know what is going on. I think we would be better off at a house than walking down the highway with so many others."

The discussion continued until all agreed to walk to the houses in Sunflower—they were closer.

The large seventy-two-hour packs were unloaded from the SUV. Everyone combined the gear from their two packs. The Camelbak water bags, canteens and all empty plastic water bottles were filled from the cooler. The remaining water was drunk or used to douse the campfire. They shouldered their backpacks and adjusted the straps. This was it. They were officially in full emergency mode.

The "unauthorized" combat knife Jess had on the left shoulder strap of his pack caught Lynn's eye.

"Quick-draw knife, that's not allowed on missions," Lynn said and then realized how silly she sounded.

Jess smirked back.

The team took one last look at the camp and started down the mountain. After a break-in period, the group stopped to adjust straps and check for hot spots where blisters might form on their feet.

"We started later than I would have liked," Dennis said.

"Yeah, I know," Jose replied.

"We can't hike much more than an hour or two because of this heat. We'll wait out the worst of it, then get a couple more hours of hiking in this evening. The terrain is too treacherous to hike at night. We're not going to make Sunflower tonight."

No one looked pleased with this revelation.

"Look at that," Dennis said suddenly, waving his arm in a grand sweep across the horizon. God in all his glory, don't you think?" No one replied.

****

The day's trek was rugged but uneventful, with no injuries. Hiking downhill was always hard in the Arizona desert, where pebbles and small rocks slid like marbles under your feet. The dust swirled up from the ground when feet made contact with it. The sun bore down.

"Let's make camp here," Dennis said. "It's getting too dark to see the map well. A few more hours should get us into the village; we can make it before lunch tomorrow."

"The moon is pretty bright, Dad. Don't you think we could make it in tonight?" Lynn asked.

"We don't dare take the chance. I can't even imagine carrying someone down this mountainside, can you?"

Lynn did not respond. She knew her father was right. They often did night searches during the summer to avoid the heat, but never on steep shale hillsides like this one.

"Do you think we can see lights or fires in Sunflower from here?" Jess asked.

"Not likely," Jose responded. "We are still several ridges over."

"Let's eat some dinner and call it a night," Dennis said.

Camp was *very* uncomfortable. There wasn't a single place a body could stretch out and every bivvy, or one-man tent, was positioned at some sort of angle with feet pointing downhill. They didn't keep a fire going, but prepped some tinder and kindling, just in case. There was very little hope of attracting attention now; it was almost thirty-six hours post-event without seeing a plane.

\*\*\*\*

Mid-morning. the group found themselves turning south at the base of the mountain. They were leaving the parched, rocky hillsides, covered in nothing but sand, gravel, cactus and scrubby trees, to enter a rare oasis in the desert along Sycamore Creek.

"Wow, flat ground again," Lynn said.

"Over there," Jess said, pointing. "It's water in the creek, I can hear it!"

The whole group moved quickly toward the stream bed. White-barked sycamore trees towered overhead, providing shade, and huge boulders lay strewn around like a giant's playthings. Everyone jettisoned their packs and took off their boots. Toes were dipped in the cool water. The stream was only nine or ten inches across here, but it was big enough even for Jess to get his feet in.

"Why didn't we ever camp here?" Lynn asked Dennis. "It's beautiful."

"We didn't camp here before the freeway was improved in 2005 because this little canyon was teeming with people from the city on weekends. We didn't camp here after the freeway bypassed this stretch of road because the Forest Service blocked the road with a berm and a fence just north of the houses in Sunflower. They don't want people back in here anymore."

After fifteen minutes or so Jose said, "I think we should get moving. We don't know what the rest of the day will bring."

"I'm afraid you're right, my friend. Get your shoes on, kids."

A collective *harrumph* could be heard. Jess began drying his feet with a camp towel from his backpack, but Lynn sat swishing her feet in the water as if she hadn't heard her father.

"Young lady," Dennis said forcefully. "I don't like repeating myself."

Lynn dared not feign ignorance, as she was sitting not five feet from her father. She put on her boots.

The team followed the dirt trail paralleling Sycamore Creek. After about a half hour, the team could see the huge Beeline Highway Bridge over the canyon in the distance. This section of highway was at least six or seven miles farther east than the section they were looking at yesterday from the mountain top. As they climbed out of the ravine, they emerged onto old, cracked blacktop.

Jess saw first a mailbox and then a house a short distance off the road. "Look, we've made it!"

"Yes," Dennis replied, "but made it to where?"

## Chapter 3

Kelly woke in her bed. She lived in a historic area in North Mesa called Lehi that bordered both the big city and the rural Indian reservation. It still retained its horsey past; horse fencing crisscrossed nearly every yard, and "horsekind" abounded.

She heard nickering from her living room. Her mind wandered in and out of wakefulness, limbs still heavy with fatigue. The earthy smell of the corral drifted into her nose. Kelly loved her horses, Hokey and Pokey. Wait—they were *in the living room* of her tiny house.

There it was again—the sound of a horse. Startled awake, her mind cleared and everything came back to her. The hospital had burned down with all those they couldn't get out still in it. The bedraggled nurse had picked her way home through the neighborhoods in a state of exhaustion, hunger and delirium. She avoided the looters she saw in strip malls and convenience stores. Ash fell from the sky. Neighborhoods had banded together into armed groups to protect their families and homes. They allowed her to pass through only after interrogation.

Kelly had stumbled into her barn in the wee hours of morning, gathered her horses and their tack, and proceeded into the house. Fears raged in her head that they might be stolen during the night or be spooked and run off because of the smoke. She filled a couple of bowls, pitchers, and some large plastic tubs with the water remaining in her water heater, remembering that her bathtub drain leaked.

*I can't believe it. Yesterday I needed to find love, settle down, have some kids, but today the world is turned upside down. My goal for today is to live 'til tomorrow. My head aches— probably dehydration,* the nurse in her thought.

She didn't have time to waste reliving events from last night. Survival was at hand. By now people must be realizing, as she had, that no help was coming from the government, and that everyone's lives were in danger. The stupid ones would still be out looting televisions and computers.

Kelly rose quickly and made her way to the kitchen. She unwrapped her arm wound and scrubbed it with dish soap and water. *Not too bad, fairly clean. It has to be redressed well if it's going to withstand the long trail ride today.*

She walked to her desk in the living room and started a list of items needed to get her to her mom's house in Sunflower. Hokey walked up to her and nuzzled her neck.

"I hope you are ready for the trip, girl," Kelly said.

"It's going to be forty-five miles of hot pavement and scruffy desert for us today." Kelly took Hokey's halter and pulled her nose around, staring into her horse's eyes. She often spoke to her horses as if they understood her every word.

Sunflower, where her mother lived, was an enclave of homes nestled in a canyon halfway between Phoenix, the metropolitan area that included Mesa, and Payson, ninety miles to the northeast. The horses could travel that distance in a day, but it would be a long, hard ride for them. If she had to travel off the main highway, it would be rough going and add to the distance. After reaching Fountain Hills, the rest of the trip to Sunflower would be rocky and mountainous. That would give her thirty-five miles of washes, brush and cactus to pick her way through. Water would be another issue. Kelly could think of only two sources of water between here and there. Her horses were lucky that it was September and not July, but a night's camp might still be in order.

Hay was hauled into the house. *My poor carpet.* After caring for the horses, she started assembling the must-haves from her list. *I wish I could take everything. There'll be nothing left to come back to. Either looters or fire will take it.*

It was time to go into Navy stealth mode and really pare down. After about two hours, everything was packed and she had dressed herself for the trip. The outfit consisted of a long-sleeved button-up shirt, a large bandana, blue jeans, a pair of leather batwing chaps, and well-worn cowboy boots. Next, Kelly donned a leather belt and holster holding her Ruger GP-100 .357 revolver. Her dad had given her the gun as a present just before she left for Navy nurse basic school. The reflection in the mirror was of a true cowgirl.

"I wonder how Dad's doing… you don't think he would try to come down here, do you?" Kelly asked Hokey.

Kelly's dad lived on a ranch in Utah. He and her mother had split amicably when she was ten. He went off and bought his ranch, but her mom had stayed in Arizona, where she had grown up. Kelly loved spending her summers with her dad. The weather was cooler in Utah, there were cattle to herd and you could grow more vegetables in the garden because they had ample rain and fertile soil. Maybe they weren't affected there. Even if they were, the ranches would be better off because it was more rural and they were pretty much self-sufficient. She hoped so, for her dad's sake.

Kelly threw on her cowboy hat, saddled Hokey, a paint mare, and Pokey, a stallion quarter horse. She owned two saddles, but only one set of really nice saddle bags. Using her head, she fashioned two more sets of saddlebags out of laundry bags tied together with wide fabric straps. A bedroll was packed with extra clothing and a coat. One horse would be ridden until it showed signs of fatigue, then the other horse would take over. "A lighter load will lessen your burdens, my friends."

The last thing to be thrown in was a manila envelope with Kelly's bank records, birth certificate, retirement documents, nursing license, and the like.

The three of them, Kelly and the two horses, walked down the street away from the fires, away from their old way of life in the rural Lehi neighborhood, toward the sparsely populated Indian reservation and ultimately, to open road. Kelly called out to Mrs.

Horne, her next-door neighbor, "Take what you want out of the house."

"Where you going?" Mrs. Horne called.

"My mom's," Kelly called back, without as much as a cursory backward glance.

The desert heat rose from the ground in waves; the pavement looked more like a river than a road. Kelly sighed and tipped her hat lower over her eyes. The horses must have been hot too, but they were a steady team. Relaxation came over her body for the first time this morning as she listened to the steady clip-clop of hooves on the road.

The horses were excited at first to be traveling, but soon settled into a consistent pace, gazes toward the ground. It didn't take long for sweat to bead around Kelly's sunglasses and hatband.

She took Gilbert Road north out of Lehi toward Fountain Hills. Suburbia gave way to the rolling hills of open desert, tall saguaro cactus and low, scruffy trees growing in miles and miles of finely ground stone. All of this existed within sight of mighty mountain ranges to the north and east.

They covered eight miles easily in the first two hours. It seemed that Kelly was the only one *leaving* Phoenix. City folks wouldn't voluntarily head off into the desert without transportation; to do so would be suicide.

There was the occasional person walking into town on the desolate highway, or someone resting at the side of the road. Kelly was an impressive sight, sitting tall on her horse with firearm visible, but she remained wary and approached everyone cautiously. Each begged water. They didn't seem to know what had happened. She assured them that they should keep walking in the direction of the big cities, and that help would be coming. She wasn't so sure about this last statement—after what she had seen last night, town looked dangerous—but she didn't have any other advice.

Water containers could be refilled at the Verde River, so she portioned out water to each one if they had a container, or let them drink from her "guest cup." The plan was to reserve the last gallon for herself. These folks were thankful. Kelly wondered how it would be as people became more desperate.

The horses and rider were making the right turn onto the Beeline Highway when they saw an old truck driving east, away from town. She had seen other old cars running in town last night as well. The truck was packed tightly and covered with an old blue tarp. Mom, Dad and kids rode in the cab. It swerved in and out of the parked cars on the highway. *Odd. How did they make it run when so many others vehicles didn't?*

Now, more than twenty-four hours after the disaster, non-working cars sat abandoned. They offered no shelter from the heat and couldn't supply any water. Kelly wondered where the very old and very young were. Surely there had been old folks and families coming into town from the mountain towns in the North. Maybe they had stopped in Fountain Hills to beg shelter instead of trying to make it another ten miles into Mesa. Maybe they just traveled more slowly and she would see them on the road later. She hoped not.

Not one airplane had crossed the sky since the disaster. Even after the nine-eleven attacks, fighter jets had crisscrossed the valley. Kelly sat perched atop Hokey, deep in thought. If this was an electromagnetic pulse, were the military jets not hardened against such attacks? Were their pilots unable to get to the base? Maybe the ground electronics were out. What would they do up there flying about anyway? Her body swayed gently back and forth as the horses' hooves clopped on the pavement. Since she couldn't answer any of her own questions, the trip ahead of her filled her thoughts.

Arizona desert was hot, rocky and unforgiving. In the summertime, monsoon rains cut deep furrows in the ruddy-brown landscape when torrents of water cascaded down the nonporous mountainsides. All of that water ran off quickly, leaving the riverbeds dry most of the year. Small trees, shrubs, and cacti clung to life, hoping their roots would find an indentation in the rocky soil that would collect the precious few inches of rain that fell on the Sonoran Desert each year. Kelly knew that she could not give out drinking water on the longest part of her trip, from the Verde River to Sunflower.

Kelly spotted someone ahead sitting off to the side of the road. Every encounter now was a cause for concern. As she got closer, she saw that it was a man in a sheriff's uniform sitting against a tree. As she drew closer still, she saw an AR-15 resting against his right shoulder. Crimson stained his left shoulder and chest. Kelly drew her pistol and scanned the surrounding desert in case whoever had done this was still in the area. When she came right up on him, she could see that the stain covered a corner of the name embroidered on his shirt: Malloy. The blood was dry. His chest rose and fell rhythmically. He was still alive.

Kelly knew by the sheriff's uniform that he was a deputy from Fountain Hills, a few miles to the north. The town contracted with the Sheriff's Office for police protection.

Kelly's brain immediately shifted to her moral upbringing and military training—no man left behind—but this officer wasn't in the military, was he? She worked side by side with law enforcement now and considered them part of the "brotherhood." He would do the same for her. She must help him, even to her own peril. The others had a chance, but someone wounded like this...

"Officer," Kelly said more loudly than she had intended. It sounded almost hostile.

The deputy opened his eyes, squinting against the bright sunlight behind her, and made an effort to get to his gun.

"Don't," said Kelly, nodding her head toward his weapon. "I'm here to help."

The officer let his body slump back onto the tree trunk.

"Yes, ma'am, doesn't look like I've got much of a choice," the officer said weakly. "I must have fallen asleep. I stayed awake as long as I could. The arm's not working too well. I took a round in the shoulder a few hours back and it's got me slowed down. Hell, nothing's working." He slumped further in resignation.

"What's your name?" She knew the name, but thought this might be a good test. She had woken him from a dead sleep; if he had stolen the uniform, he might make a mistake.

"The name is Jared, Jared Malloy."

Kelly knew Jared had little choice but to assume that she meant him no harm. He was in no shape to fight her off. She slung her leg over Hokey's back and lowered herself to the pavement. Another thorough scan of the desert, up and down the highway, yielded no evidence of bandits. From what she could see, the coast was clear, so she stepped onto the shoulder of the road. Holstering her gun, she bent down next to the injured man, gravel grinding under her cowboy boots.

"I'm a nurse. Let me take a look."

Again, Jared didn't object. Kelly lowered the AR-15 from his good shoulder to the ground and removed his pistol from its holster, placing it out of his reach. Jared visibly stiffened.

"Don't worry, I'll give 'em back. Does it hurt much?" she asked. The words seemed to calm him.

The bullet wound was higher and farther to the left than she expected, and older too. The wound was fully clotted. He had lost a fair amount of blood, but after giving him a quick once-over, his heart, major vessels, and lung seemed to be spared.

"How'd you get shot?"

"Some punk kid was trying to take a microwave from a convenience store. Guess he thought I was going to try to stop him, or something. As bad as things are right now, that was the last thought on my mind. I was only out protecting innocents, but now my protecting and serving is over. I'm heading toward the hospital in Mesa."

"I'd be looking for a plan B if I were you. The hospital you were heading to is just a pile of ash now. Everyone else in town is out of water, electricity and patience. It looked really bad, and I left only twenty hours after the blackout."

"How bad? What's going on?"

"All of the power is out, even cars, radios, phones, you name it."

"I thought the power would come back on."

"Well, it didn't. Just about every transformer in town was in flames when I left, so it won't be up anytime soon. Right now I have to take care of you," Kelly said, all business. She took off the officer's heavy bulletproof vest and removed his shirt, starting with his good arm first. Where the shirt touched his skin, it was soaked in sweat. The bullet had caused a clean entrance wound without an exit wound. Kelly took care not to touch open skin.

"We had fires all over Fountain Hills, too," Jared said weakly, squinting in pain.

"Looks like the bullet is still in there. It will have to come out eventually. The side of the road isn't a good place to do it, though. I'm just going to take a quick look." She intended more than a quick look, but didn't want Jared to know yet. "Too bad it missed your vest. High and to the outside."

Kelly went back to her horses and got her canteen, some pain pills, a bottle of skin cleanser, some exam gloves and a bandana from her first aid kit. As she returned to her patient, Jared looked warily at the supplies in her hands.

"What you planning?"

"First of all, I'm going to give you a couple of pain pills." Then Kelly fired off a series of questions. "Are you allergic to anything? Are you sensitive to pain medicines? You aren't going to fall off that horse over there if I give you these, are you?"

"No I'm not, just give me the damn pills," Jared said as he put his hand out, palm up. The warm water from Kelly's canteen followed the tablets down his throat. "Ahhhh, even *hot* water is *so* good when you're thirsty."

"Hm, a little fight left in ya—you might just make it. I'm not going to dig for it here. But it sure would be nice if that bullet was near the surface so I could get it out right away. Less chance of an infection that way," Kelly said in an authoritarian tone, not looking him in the eye.

Jared knew he wasn't going to dissuade her, and probably shouldn't, so he said, "Yes, *ma'am*," slowly and with a little drawl.

She put on her gloves, poured warm water onto the clean bandana and added a touch of soap. The soap was worked into a lather, then used to clean the wound and the skin around it.

"Take a deep breath."

Jared's breath caught in his throat as Kelly poked her gloved fingertip gingerly into the wound. The maneuver made her squint in that way nurses and doctors do when they have to hurt their patients during a procedure. Jared held his breath, but didn't yell.

"I don't feel anything solid."

"Damn! Get your finger out of there then," Jared said, finally releasing his breath.

Both sat without speaking for a few seconds. Jared was breathing heavily. Finally he said softly, "Sorry. I'm glad you didn't find it, I think. At least it puts off that bit of torture for awhile. We'll let the doctors do it under anesthesia."

"I only wish that could be true." Kelly continued to dry and dress the wound. Jared bunched up his eyebrows and tilted his head slightly, like a dog asking a question. "I wasn't kidding when I said there was no hospital to go back to," she continued. "Did you see any clinics operating in Fountain Hills? I know they don't have a hospital."

"I don't think there is anything left open in Fountain Hills, unless you include broken-into," said Jared.

"The next closest facility is the Mayo Clinic in Scottsdale, but that is miles and miles in the wrong direction. Anything toward town is the wrong direction. Here, let me help you get what is left of your shirt back on." She tried to move Jared's bad shoulder as little as possible. "It won't do for you have a third-degree sunburn on top of that hole in your shoulder.

Kelly made one more trip to the saddle bags and got out a bottle of Rocephin—a powerful, wide-spectrum antibiotic—along with a small bottle of sterile water, a syringe, and a wad of gauze. She mixed the powdered antibiotic with the water, then rolled the vial between her palms. When it was thoroughly dissolved, she plunged the needle through the rubber stopper and withdrew the yellow liquid. Jared stared with dread in his eyes, just as any five-year-old would do.

"That needle looks three inches long. I have a feeling that this is non-negotiable too?"

"It's only an inch and a half. This is an antibiotic," Kelly said. "That bullet won't kill you, but the infection will. Give me a hip."

Jared grimaced. "It's been years since I've had an injection. I can't remember ever having one in the *hip*. You don't mean *hip* at all, do you?"

Kelly ignored that rhetorical question. "This won't hurt much and I won't see anything," she assured him.

Jared rolled very slightly to his right side, allowing Kelly access to the waistband of his brown uniform pants. She exposed about two inches below his belt to give the injection.

"Hold your breath," Kelly said. Nurses only said that to give their patients something else to think about. She plunged the needle in up to the hub. The plunger, depressed slowly, dispensed the medication. Then, with one smooth motion, the needle was withdrawn. "All done."

"Man, you're all business, aren't you lady?" Jared said, hiking up his pants with his good arm.

"No reason not to be. You're hurt and I'm a nurse. I'll do everything I can to help you, but there is no reason to be all mushy about it."

"I thought nurses were sentimental, caring types."

"I've been a war nurse and an OB nurse. I've seen people die and be born all of my adult life. I can't always make them live, and if I took ownership of that I'd be a mess. Don't you agree? You think I laugh or cry every day based on the life and death of my patients? Do you cry for your victims and crooks? They're all pitiful, aren't they?"

"No, I guess I don't much any more, but I'd like to think I still could." Jared paused. "For the innocents."

"I'm sorry, you're right. I've just seen too much death in the last twenty-four hours. I'm probably on the defensive." Kelly looked up and her eyes met Jared's.

A smile started from the middle of his mouth, then lifted the corners of his lips almost to his cheek bones. For the first time she really saw him, not his bloody shoulder or his uniform, but his square chin and day-old stubble, his caring eyes. She tried to look away and suppress a full smile, but failed.

"That's more like it," said Jared. "You're beautiful when you smile." He lifted his hand to touch her face.

Kelly pulled back, out of his reach, and let her smile fade. She kept her eyes trained down on her supplies, and fumbled with her hands. "How hurt are you? Can you travel?"

Jared furrowed his eyebrows and pursed his lips. "What did I say?"

"Nothing," Kelly said coolly. "Can you ride?"

"I think so. They make it look easy in the movies," he said, matching her frosty tone.

Her voice softened, but only a bit. "Don't worry, Pokey is gentle and I'll lead. All I need you to do is hold onto the saddle horn and let me know *before* you fall off, if you can. We're headed to Sunflower. My mother lives up there. She was a Navy nurse too; retired now, of course. She has a little spread up in the canyon. You can stay 'til you get stronger and things in the city find an equilibrium." Kelly said it stiffly, like she had rehearsed it.

She removed the large bandana from around her neck and fashioned a sling for Jared's left arm. When she stood in front of her patient and leaned in, she could smell his sweat, that deep, tinny smell found on working men. She reached around to tie a knot to one side of his neck, then folded some gauze and placed it between Jared's neck and the knot.

"That won't be very comfortable, but it will have to do for now." Their eyes met again. Instantly Kelly felt shy. There was something about this guy that was different from anyone else she'd ever met. Or maybe it was just that he was so vulnerable; injured, a patient. It wasn't just the wound, but the impending infection that worried her. She had seen many soldiers live through a wound and die of the raging infection days later, especially if they hadn't gotten immediate treatment. A good reason not to get attached.

"That feels better already," Jared said, betraying himself with a pinch of pain showing at the corners of his mouth.

"Yeah, the sling helps to support the weight of your arm so the injured muscles don't have to go it alone. Your next test is to get on that horse." Kelly tipped her head toward her second horse.

"That's a fine horse, she yours?"

"Yes, he's a sorrel quarter horse, gentle too."

"What does it mean, sorrel?"

"It's the color of the horse. If a woman's hair were that color, it would be called auburn. His name's Pokey. Rest here a minute."

Kelly got out a spare bandana and tied it around her own neck, then repacked her saddlebag. She fashioned a scabbard for the AR-15 out of a pair of jeans and two shoe laces. This was attached to her own horse Hokey's saddle horn. She knew that Jared couldn't work that big gun with only one arm. Jared didn't protest; there was little fight left in him.

"We need to get going." She placed Jared's right arm up over her shoulder and around her neck, holding his hand against her collarbone. Then she straightened up, pulling him with her. The two ended standing nose to nose, so close that Kelly could see the tiny flecks of blue, brown and green in his eyes.

Kelly steadied Jared then bent down for his gun. She took his Kimber .45 pistol and put it back in its holster, looking him square in the eyes as she did it.

"Trust me, huh?" asked Jared.

"Yes, sir, I do," she said.

The maneuvers it took to get Jared up onto Pokey weren't graceful, but did end in success. Jared's shoulders slumped forward just slightly as he sat in the saddle.

Hokey resisted momentarily before letting Kelly bring her head around, with the reins, to the northeast. Pokey followed.

****

The sun was high and made the trip uncomfortably warm. Kelly stopped at intervals to give Jared water from her canteen and drink herself. The pair made their way down the shoulder of the highway with relative ease. "Are you sure we should be going north, away from town?" Jared asked.

Kelly could only imagine what must be going through his mind. It must be scary to be leaving civilization so badly injured and weak.

"I'll take good care of that shoulder of yours. I have antibiotics and…" she stopped short of saying that everything would be fine. "And they should do the trick."

Oh God, what was she saying? She had just made a decision that could mean this man's life. From what she had seen in town, though, her only clear choice was to press on. She and Mom had both assisted in many surgeries and they had antibiotics. They would give it their best.

As the afternoon went on, she and Jared came upon a Coca-Cola truck that had been broken into. They took a few cans of warm soda and drank one each. The warm, carbonated beverage rolled down their throats, giving little satisfaction. It was a far cry from the icy-cold Cokes they both knew from the convenience stores. They continued on.

Later, they stopped at the Verde River. The horses went immediately to the water and started drinking. The way they threw their heads down and kept them that way, made it hard for Jared to stay mounted. Kelly dismounted, then helped Jared do the same. It took a lot of work to get Jared up next to a large rock under a tree. He was weaker after his ride. The shade, provided by the wispy desert tree, was dappled with sunlight at best, and provided little relief from the heat.

Heat radiated from the sand that stretched to the water's edge. Kelly walked to the river and untied the bandana from around her neck, dipping it in unceremoniously. She returned to Jared and wiped his face gently while studying his fine features. She rolled up his long sleeves and bathed his forearms with the cool liquid. Jared watched her silently, thankfully. Kelly returned to the river's edge and wet her bandana again. She raised it to her face and wiped it down around her jaw, squeezing it to release the water down her front.

"I'd do the same for you if this weren't dirty river water and you didn't have a hole in your shoulder," Kelly said as she returned to Jared carrying her canteen of clean water. She put it to his lips and let him drink. He gulped greedily, a small trickle escaping the corner of his mouth.

"I'll get you a bed roll for your head," Kelly said softly. "I think you should rest."

"You'll get no complaint from me," Jared managed.

Kelly helped Jared to lie down and positioned his shoulder for as much comfort as he could achieve. He fell asleep immediately.

As Jared slept, Kelly gathered firewood and started a small fire. She strained river water through a paper coffee filter into her coffee pot. After it had boiled for a few minutes, she filled an empty canteen. Repeating the process, every container she had was filled. It would be a long push to her mother's from here without another water source. Water was life itself in the desert.

After about an hour, Kelly whispered, "Wake up, sleepy-head. We need to put some distance between us and the river before the sun goes down. People and animals will be drawn to the water's edge and we both need a good night's sleep. Neither of us are fit to take watch all night long. I'm so sorry, Jared. I can tell you really could use the rest but…"

Jared smiled softly. He forced himself to get up. "Why do we have to hurry? I understand getting away from the river but..."

"Three reasons. Unless you have some food stashed in your uniform somewhere, we can't afford to be hanging around out here in the desert. I only packed for one person, me, and only brought enough for three days. The way I count it, that gives us each a day and a half, two days if we both go hungry most of it. It doesn't allow for any delays either. Two, people will become more desperate by the minute and be willing to kill for what they *think* we have. And three, I hate to remind you but that bullet *has* to come out, and soon too."

Kelly guided the horses about a hundred feet off the highway to avoid the people walking west. This made it rough going for Jared because of the brush and uneven terrain. In many places, it slowed their pace to a crawl.

As they traveled, Kelly talked out loud so that Jared could hear her thoughts.

"I figure it's about sixty miles between Fountain Hills and Payson. If people had been stranded on the highway, they would wait for several hours for help and then start walking. They would go north to Payson or south toward the big cities. In either case, at three miles per hour—the average human walking speed—it would take them twenty hours to get to their destination. Families and the elderly will take longer. That means that the road will have people on it for several days. As time goes by, some will succumb to heat and dehydration. It's sad, but I can't come up with a single remedy for them that doesn't put our own lives in jeopardy."

Jared didn't talk much; Kelly had to guess it was the pain and exhaustion. She watched him closely for signs that he was no longer able to ride.

At about five o'clock, Kelly looked for a suitable campsite. The arroyo to their left, a dry creek bed, would do. She guided the horses further into the desert. When she found a good spot, Kelly helped Jared down from his horse and leaned him up against a small tree. Hastily, the nurse made her patient a place to lie on the sandy, dry river bottom. Rocks had to be moved from the area by hand, but the sand bar, overhung with branches, was relatively flat and smooth. A sleeping bag over a serape—a traditional Mexican wool blanket—would serve as a bed. The long day had taxed the injured deputy, but he never once complained.

"Here, let me help you," Kelly said, pointing to the makeshift accommodations. Jared took her arm and pulled himself to a standing position. The two moved together toward their destination. Jared stumbled but Kelly caught him. She got him to bed, then went back to her horse for something.

"Here, take these." Kelly held out two more pain pills. "You're an angel," Jared said taking the pills and popping them into his mouth. He reached out and took the canteen. Their hands touched briefly and Kelly felt a definite spark at the contact.

The pain pills hadn't had time to take effect, but that didn't stop the officer from falling asleep. Kelly set up a picket line between two small trees for the horses so they could graze on whatever green vegetation they could find without wandering away. The next task was preparing a meal.

After an hour or so, a nice pile of wood was stacked next to the campfire, where water was heating for their noodles. Kelly wanted the firewood in case they needed it during the night, but she did not intend to keep a fire going any longer than it took her to heat water. It wasn't yet dark, but when the sun was fully down, a fire would be easy to spot in the desert. It would attract anyone looking for food and water. Kelly patted her trusty Ruger.

Camp wasn't much, but the sun was setting and it made a brilliant display in the western sky. Arizona was known for its sunsets and for good reason. Many, like this one, filled the sky with brilliant colors that played among the clouds.

Jared slept through dinner. They each had had a granola bar and plenty of water during their afternoon ride. Kelly thought it was more important that he get some rest. Dinner was a lonely affair that ended when she found herself sitting in the dark, admiring the stars. There was no ambient light from Phoenix, a city of four million people, to make the customary bright-white glow to the southwest. The stars shone more brightly than Kelly could ever remember. It was getting colder by the minute. When the sun sets on the desert, temperatures drop quickly.

Kelly tried to stay warm by wrapping her coat around her legs, but even with the chaps, they were cold. The desert floor was cold. Sand didn't hold heat very long. The ground would pull any remaining warmth from her body if she lay on it without insulation. An alternative was to keep a fire going all night and stay near it. Exhaustion made that option unappealing; front hot, back icy, sitting up all night. A pack of coyotes howled and yipped in their eerie way, making the night seem colder and the location seem even more remote. Kelly turned her head and gazed at Jared.

He was sleeping so soundly that he probably wouldn't mind if she shared "her" sleeping bag with him. Kelly reasoned that he had lost a lot of blood and could use her body heat to fend off hypothermia as well. Strong hands removed boots, belts, chaps and coat, and then a tired body slipped slowly into the bag behind Jared. It took some maneuvering to position the coat, with the guns in it, next to the head of the bed.

Jared didn't move. Kelly's body fit his nicely, and the whole bag was warm and cozy. Slow, steady breathing joined the sounds of the nighttime desert and marked the rise and fall of his chest. Kelly felt warm all over. She snuggled closer to Jared than she probably needed to. Exhaustion enveloped her. She worried briefly about her wounded officer, then worried no more.

****

Kelly woke when it was not yet dawn. Somehow she had turned over in the night and now Jared was behind her, with his bad arm draped over her. She dared not move unless she hurt him or startled him, which could be dangerous given their close proximity. It was still cold. The physical closeness evoked memories of a happier time. She lay there fantasizing that they were lovers lost in each other's arms. It wasn't hard to imagine.

Jared's breathing changed from the slow, deep, steady breathing of someone asleep, to the shallow, quicker pace of someone who is awake, or at least on the verge of being awake, but he did not move or speak. Kelly lay there for a few more minutes before she felt Jared stir.

"How's your shoulder?" she asked him quietly.

"Stiff."

"That doesn't surprise me. Hurt much?"

"Yeah, some. I think I slept on it wrong, but I needed the sleep. I can manage."

Kelly eased her way out of the sleeping bag, pulling her coat over her shoulders.

"Ugh," Jared groaned softly.

"Sorry, I was trying to be gentle."

"It's not your fault."

Jared lay in the sleeping bag for another few minutes, but then nature called. Kelly knew that relieving himself was going to be a challenge—not to mention painful—but she also knew Jared wasn't about to ask for help. Kelly watched out of the corner of her eye as Jared struggled out of the sleeping bag and made his way to the edge of camp.

A few minutes passed. Jared called back, "I'm sorry to have to ask, but..." As Kelly got closer, she could see his difficulty. He had managed everything except re-buttoning his pants. She modestly lent a hand.

Jared said softly, "I really appreciate everything you're doing for me."

"I'm a nurse, remember? I've done this for many people."

"No, I mean it." Jared reached out with his good arm and touched her sleeve. "I couldn't make it without you. Your husband is a lucky man."

"I'm not married."

"I just assumed... you're wearing a ring."

"That's just for show, it's easier. I've never been married. Came close once. You?"

"Me? No. Haven't found the right girl yet," Jared said, averting his gaze.

"Come on, you're in bad shape and we can talk while we ride. I've got to get us to Sunflower."

The two walked back to camp. Breakfast was quick and cold, a couple more granola bars and some soda, which had cooled considerably since yesterday. Kelly and Jared both stole little glances at each other as they ate.

"Breakfast of champions," Kelly said as she packed up the bedding. The horses were offered a small drink before the picket line was dismantled. Everything was ready to go except for getting Jared on his horse.

Jared could do little to help himself. Kelly pulled Pokey near a fallen tree and tied him there. She helped Jared step up onto a tree trunk that was propped up on a large rock. The trunk gave a little under his weight, but did not break. Kelly held out her hand and Jared used his good arm to steady himself. He inched his way up the trunk until he was tall enough to reach the stirrup. He threw himself over Pokey and landed with a thud, but was safely perched. Pokey let out a whinny while taking a couple of steps backward, as if to protest the mount.

"We only have three hours left, if I've calculated it right. Sunflower is roughly at mile marker 220."

There was plenty of time to talk on their journey. Kelly noticed that speaking with Jared seemed to ease his pain, or at least distract him. Jared had to be coerced to tell her all about his day and night in Fountain Hills after the power had gone out. He told her about getting back to the sheriff's station and how he and three other deputies had decided to patrol on foot. The officers hid the weapons and ammunition from the substation that weren't being used, so they wouldn't fall into unfriendly hands. He told her about being out on patrol and how he got shot.

"I knew I couldn't carry much and needed to get to a hospital. I did the only thing I could think of, walk."

The country got more mountainous as they progressed. It wasn't long until they had to use the shoulder of the road. They rode more swiftly when passing people. Kelly scanned everyone as if they might try to overtake them for their food and water.

"Jared, you see that?"

"What?"

"That woman, I think she's got some kids with her," Kelly strained to see the figure far up the road.

"Wow, looks like two kids, maybe three and five years old. That sucks. Are we going to pass them up too?"

"I don't think I can. What should we do?"

"I'm glad to hear you say that. I'm still struggling with this self-preservation versus helping people stuff. My mind says one thing, but my heart says another."

"Mine too. My mom's house is within reach with the water we would have left, if nothing happens." Kelly said those last three words much more quietly than the rest of her sentence. "I'm gonna stop."

\*\*\*\*

"They looked *bad* already and it's only been two days," said Kelly as they rode on. "Can you believe that mom was just camping, waiting for help?" asked Kelly.

"Sure, someone always comes and helps. Haven't you seen the roadside assistance commercials or the National Guard ones? Someone has always come before; why shouldn't she expect that now?"

"You're right, but I'm afraid help's not coming this time. We haven't seen it yet."

"That was a nice thing you did back there," said Jared.

"Thanks, but I doubt they can make it back to town or survive out here unless they get more water than those three dirty water bottles we found along the side of the road. Those two granola bars I gave them won't last long either."

"It's all you had."

"I know it's all *we* had." Kelly used the plural as if somehow *they* had agreed to give away the last bit of food. "I feel like I have multiple personality disorder."

Kelly struggled with her thoughts. *We will find out very shortly if we can afford multiple personality disorder. Fate is going to dictate charity or survival.*

\*\*\*\*

They hadn't been back on the road more than an hour when Kelly pulled on the reins to stop Hokey. The horse stopped, but pulled her head forward as if to protest the pressure on the bit.

"Look up there. Do you see that dude in the middle of the road?" Pokey came to a stop behind Hokey without any direction from Jared.

"He's pretty bold for being on the road two days from the blackout. I think I should ride ahead," said Kelly. "Something doesn't feel right about this guy. No one else has been walking down the center line; it's just too hot on the asphalt."

"Could be nothing, but I think we should stay together."

"If he sees you're hurt, he could think he has the upper hand," argued Kelly. "I can protect myself better than I can protect both of us."

There was no arguing with that.

Kelly picked up the pace, leaving Jared to fall behind. He didn't close the gap. She reached down and felt the stock of the AR-15 concealed in the jeans scabbard. She wanted to make sure she could brandish it quickly if needed. She reached up and felt the grip of the Ruger too.

Hokey walked toward the man without any heightened sense of alertness. Kelly thought this was a good sign, although she couldn't tell herself why. She was, after all, just a horse.

"Good day," Kelly offered from atop her mount when she was about twenty feet from the figure.

The tall stranger smiled, but didn't say anything back. It was an odd smile. The kind of smile an actor used in the movies, just before he killed someone, thought Kelly.

"Where you headed?" Stupid question, Kelly thought to herself. The only place he could be going is town.

"Have any water?" the stranger finally asked.

"Just enough for me and my friend here to make it to Payson," she said, motioning back toward Jared. She didn't want to tip her hand by saying she was going to Sunflower. "There was water in the spring back just a few miles in Sunflower, if you need some."

"I'd rather have yours," the man said, pulling a pistol from his waistband at the small of his back.

Already on high alert, Kelly's training kicked in. Her magnum roared to life the same instant that it cleared the holster.

The bullet found its mark, center of mass, followed a split second later by another round. Hokey reared and twisted, forcing Kelly to hang onto the saddle horn. The man crumpled in the street, dropping his pistol. Kelly scanned the desert, terrified that the man might have an accomplice, maybe even more than one. She yanked the AR-15 from its scabbard and brandished it in case others were watching. Jared rode slowly to Kelly's side while trying to hold Hokey's reins in his left hand and his Kimber .45 in his right.

"I'll get his gun," said Kelly, trembling as she stowed the AR and slid down from her mount.

"Make sure he doesn't have any *more* guns on him," said Jared. "I'll cover you." His pistol wavered unsteadily.

Her .357 pointing toward the stranger, she picked up the Smith and Wesson MP lying a few feet from his sprawled form and stuck it in her back pocket. He was still breathing. His hands were empty.

"Do you have any more weapons?" Kelly demanded, voice quavering. There was no response, just a dull stare. Forcing herself to move, she advanced to the bandit's side. She recognized the emaciated frame and splotchy, weeping skin as that of a meth user. This was something Kelly had only seen in civilian nursing. Keeping her pistol drawn, she reached toward him, but couldn't bring herself to touch him or his bloody clothes. A boot made contact with his side and she gave a nudge, trying to see if any guns were secreted in his waistband. The gesture didn't move him much.

"You can do better than that," Jared said with all of the conviction he could muster. "Your life and mine depends on it, Kelly. Get him rolled over!"

Kelly finally put her boot under his flank and gave it a good shove this time. The body rolled face down onto the asphalt. Kelly tapped around his waistband with her foot. "He doesn't have anything else on him."

"He was a walking dead man before you shot him, Kelly," Jared said gently. "Meth addicts are zombies."

"I've never killed anyone before. I'm a nurse, remember? I have to watch people die when other people have hurt them, but I never thought I'd kill someone after I left the Service." Her voice was almost inaudible. She stared blankly at Jared.

"I'm sorry," he said empathetically. "It needed doing, though. The other night, I tried to give someone the benefit of the doubt and look where it got me. Come on, let's get out of here."

Chapter 4

"What are you doing with that radiation badge, Rich?" Emma Wise asked her neighbor incredulously. Rich waved the small plastic disc in the air by its metal clip as the two stood on the porch of Emma's adobe ranch house. Rich was just under six feet tall and of average build. His light red hair was now as much grey as red, after more than sixty years of living.

"I'm trying to see if there is any radioactive fallout," he said.

"Fallout? Don't you think we'd know if there had been a nuclear attack? You know, the mushroom cloud, roaring winds, stuff like that?" Emma asked casually.

Emma stood about five feet four inches. Her cowboy boots gave her a little extra height. Old West cowboys would have called her a handsome woman. Her good proportions came from physical labor, not a gym, and were well displayed by her Wrangler jeans and short-sleeved western shirt. Emma was just a little younger than Rich, but in the same ballpark.

"You'd see that only if it were a full-scale ground attack," said Rich. Before he could continue, a noise from the driveway caught his attention.

Emma heard it too. They both stared down the road.

About a quarter mile away, two middle-aged men wearing dark blue BDUs with bright, hunter-orange t-shirts and blue boonie hats came into view. They hiked up the driveway. Behind them were a teenage boy and girl. The teens wore bright-orange shirts and woodland camouflage BDU pants. They all carried backpacks.

"Who on earth are those people?" Emma asked, not really expecting Rich to have an answer. She walked to the porch rail.

"I don't see any guns," Rich said as he moved nearer Emma's shotgun, propped near the front door.

The first man waved, leading the others up the driveway.

"Hold on—just one of you come up," Rich called.

The first man continued to the porch. The others looked around, confused.

"Good afternoon, chaplain—or do you prefer rabbi?" Emma asked respectfully.

"Either, but I prefer Dennis, Dennis Rabbinowitz. I'm guessing you were in the military, ma'am." Dennis tapped the silver Star of David and ten commandment tablets pin above the bronze oak leaf on his hat.

"I'm Emma Wise. Yes, I nursed in the Navy. This fellow is my neighbor, Rich. You folks look like the proverbial lost patrol."

"How right you are. We were on a practice search-and-rescue mission for Civil Air Patrol," Dennis said.

"What is Civil Air Patrol?" Rich asked.

"It's the US Air Force Auxiliary," Dennis explained. "We search for downed aircraft. Our teenagers are cadets, like junior

ROTC. We're a ground team for this weekend's search-and-rescue exercise."

"Come on up, folks." Emma waved to the others.

"This is my daughter, Lynn," Dennis said. "That's Jose Herrero and his son, Jess. We were hoping you had a working phone. Our truck and all of our electronics seem to have stopped working. No one came looking for us."

"Dennis, our phones are working just as well as yours," Emma said. "All of our electrical stuff is out too."

"That's what we were afraid of," Jose said. "We think it might be some kind of solar storm."

"Or an EMP—you know, electromagnetic pulse," Rich said. "I think that a nuclear device was detonated high in the atmosphere, knocking out most electrical equipment *for good.*"

Everyone, including Emma, looked at him, brows furrowed as if trying to grasp what he had just said.

Rich continued, "Solar flares only affect objects that are plugged in. During an EMP attack, a high nuclear blast, the whole ionosphere is charged. Macro and micro circuitry, plugged in or not, *fry.*" Rich's eyes grew big and he threw both hands up in the air. "POOF!"

Lynn jumped back, then shot a worried look at her father. Jess let out a *humph* of disbelief and rolled his eyes the way teenagers do when they think their elders are wrong. "There were no mushroom clouds. Everything looks normal."

"The bomb was set off too high in the atmosphere for us to see all that," said Rich resolutely. For all we know, it covers most of the United States."

"I had hoped it wasn't an EMP," Dennis said. "To my mind, that is the most devastating possibility."

"Is that a dosimeter?" Jose pointed to the radiation badge in Rich's hand.

"Yes, but there's no color change, so no high radiation level," answered Rich.

"I wish we had a survey meter to see what the radiation levels are and to see if they are rising, declining or staying the same," said Jose.

"Shouldn't we have a Geiger counter for that?" asked Emma.

"Same thing, ol' woman," Rich said endearingly. "The solar flare, or whatever this is, might break the meter because it's electronic too. As long as the badge stays the same color, we're fine."

Lynn's eyes widened. She looked quickly between Rich and her father. "What is he saying? What are we going to do?"

"Don't worry, I'll take care of you," said Dennis, drawing his daughter close to him. "We'll have to take this one step at a time."

Lynn melted into her father's arms. "Does this mean the world is ending?"

"No, of course not," Dennis answered unconvincingly.

Jess addressed his father sharply. "No way!"

Jose looked at his boots, then back at Jess. "I'm afraid it could be an EMP or solar flare. That would explain what's going on around here, but I think Rich is right. We can't jump to conclusions."

"What about Mom?"

Jose shrugged his shoulders. "I don't know. She's in Iowa, out on the farm with your aunt and uncle. If they are without power, everyone there could manage for quite a while."

Rich, after seeing Lynn's reaction, said, "Maybe we shouldn't hang our hats on the EMP hypothesis one hundred percent. Our minds could be playing tricks on us, or it could be something we haven't even thought of."

"I'm sure we'll get more information over the next few days. Stay here and have lunch. Then you can work out what to do," said Emma. "Lynn, you remind me of my daughter, Kelly, when she was in junior ROTC in high school. She went on to Navy ROTC and nursing school at the University of Arizona. She lives in Mesa now. I hope everything is alright there."

"Emma is right," Dennis said. "We have camping gear. We'll be alright for awhile. Relief should be flooding into the cities shortly. We have time."

"May I use your restroom, ma'am?" Jess asked.

"Well, actually, no," Emma said. "Our water comes from a well with an electric pump that Rich and I share. No power means no water. We have some left in the tank, but that's for us to drink.

Conservation is the name of the game right now—no flushing. We will build a latrine away from the house. For now, take a shovel from the barn and dig a cat hole over there to the south somewhere. Please use as little toilet paper as you can. It's in the bathroom."

"Do you have another source of water?" asked Jose.

"Just the trickle of water in the creek," Rich said. "That leaves us trying to collect enough water for our use, plus watering the horses, chickens and rabbits. It's a bit of a haul up to the houses too. Our gardens won't last long."

"The creek has to be filtered and pasteurized for drinking," Emma said.

"Does that old windmill out back work?" Jose asked.

"That windmill was the original pump to the well," Rich said. "The old workings are still up there. The well supplied water for a stock tank in this canyon before our houses were built. It was converted to an electric pump years ago. The windmill hasn't been used since before I got here."

"Let's take a look," Jose said. "I tinker with mechanical stuff. Maybe I can give you a hand."

"Yep, Jose tinkers with stuff alright," Dennis said. "He's a systems engineer who can actually turn a wrench. You should see what he and Jess did to trick out their SUV for search and rescue."

"How about we put the seventy-two hour packs under that tree?" said Jose, trying to hide a slight blush.

Emma interjected, "Why don't you put them on the porch?"

"Care to follow me?" Rich asked, looking at Jose.

Jose and Rich started up the hill toward the windmill. Rich called back, "Mijo, you can join us after you have finished your hole diggin'."

"Why don't the rest of you come in?" Emma said, motioning with her arms like she was calling a flock of chickens. "Let's go to the kitchen."

Emma led Dennis and Lynn through her combination western and overflowing bookshelves themed living room, headed toward the kitchen.

"This clock's off by forty minutes," Dennis remarked as he noticed the old grandfather clock sitting in the corner. He paused, glancing at his watch, confirming that it was still running.

"I set it yesterday." said Emma. "It needed to be wound. I don't think anyone's let it run for more than a day or two since my dad died fifteen years ago. He disconnected the chimes when I was a kid, saying they kept him awake."

"Mind if I set it?"

"Nope, let me help you." Emma opened the face by lifting a latch on the side and swinging the glass open so that the hands could be manipulated. "I made a guess at the time when I set it yesterday. Looks like I got pretty close."

Dennis moved the minute hand forward forty-two minutes, then closed the glass. "This ol' thing will be nice to have while the power's out."

Emma led father and daughter into the kitchen. Her counters overflowed with food. Pots were boiling away on the propane stove. Empty Mason jars sat in boiling water or in boxes piled on the counters. Sunlight and a warm breeze flowed through the window over the sink.

"I'm trying to can everything from my refrigerator and freezer and Rich's refrigerator and freezer too. Don't know how long the power will be off and I won't see all this go to waste. We have plenty for dinner with all this food awasting. I only have so many burners and this meat, especially, has to be pressure canned for a long time to be done properly."

"Is there anything we can do to help you?" asked Dennis.

"I'll take this lovely girl as helper," Emma said in a motherly tone, looking directly at Lynn. "This kitchen is too small for more than that. Why don't you pull up a chair at the table?"

"I don't think Lynn has ever seen anyone can food," Dennis said.

"Yeah, this all looks complicated," Lynn said gazing wide-eyed at the whole operation.

"It's not, really," Emma said. "Canning is all about keeping things sterile."

Lynn stood close to Emma and peered over her shoulder, watching as she took Mason jars from a boiling pot with a special lifting device, dumped the water out, and set them upright onto a clean towel. The glass steamed.

"Hand me those metal lids, would you, Lynn?"

Emma added the metal lids, rings and a pair of tongs to a small pot of simmering water on the back burner. She put a large, wide-mouthed funnel into a sterilized jar and ladled boiling meat into it until the meat and its liquid reached the shoulder of the jar.

"Now take those tongs and place a lid from the boiling pan onto the full jar," Emma instructed. Lynn tried to get just one lid with the tongs, but the lids seemed to be stuck together. Emma took the tongs and pried the lids apart carefully, then held one out, offering the tongs back to Lynn. "I learned to can by helping my grandmother and my mother. My daughter, Kelly, canned with me when she was younger."

"I wish my Mom could have taught me stuff like this."

Glancing over her shoulder, Emma could see the sadness on Lynn's face. "Is your mom gone?"

"She passed away almost six years ago now. Cancer."

"I'm so sorry to hear that. Is it just you and your dad?"

"Yeah, he's a great dad, tries hard, but there are just some things you need a mom for."

Emma and Lynn worked and talked together until all of the meat was packed into quart jars and the lids were in place. Emma took the screw-top rings out of the boiling water and laid them on the towel. She used an oven mitt and picked up one ring after another, tightening it over a lid and onto the jar, just enough to apply pressure to the lids. One by one, she lifted seven jars into the pressure canner, filling each open slot. The water in it was already hot, but not quite boiling.

Emma set the cooker's lid in place and said, "Now we're just waiting for the pressure to build up and the pot to eject steam."

She showed Lynn how to ready more jars of tomatoes for the water bath canner. After ten minutes of steam pouring from the pressure canner's relief stem, Emma put the heavy metal rocker on. The rocker made a quick *swoosh-swoosh-swoosh* sound as excess internal pressure was allowed to escape.

"Okay, ninety minutes should do it." Emma sighed as she lifted her shirt sleeve to wipe her brow. "Canning is hot business, I tell you."

Jess burst into the kitchen. "My dad is making a well torpedo, and he needs all the paracord from our search packs," he gasped, out of breath.

"Calm down, what's your dad making?" Dennis asked, raising his eyebrows.

"Dad's calling it a torpedo or bailer. Rich has some three-inch diameter PVC. Dad's making a one-way valve out of an end cap with a hole in it and a piece of rubber, a nut, a bolt and a washer. You have to lower the thing into the well with the paracord."

"Really?" Dennis asked.

"Water rushes into the PVC pipe by pushing the rubber flap up," Jess said. "As you pull the pipe up, the rubber flap closes because of the weight of the water. Dad thinks the torpedo will hold about two gallons. The water can be dumped into the holding tank."

"That well is probably two hundred feet deep," Emma said. "It's going to be a lot of work. That won't give us enough water around here. We need to get a pump going." Her face had a blank expression and she looked a bit pale.

Everyone walked out to the packs on the porch and began digging through their contents.

Jess gathered the coils of paracord and started toward the well.

Emma shouted after him, "We'll call you in for lunch."

"It looks like you gals have the canning in hand," Dennis said. "I'll get started digging your latrine. Just let me know where you want it and where you keep your tools. It's the least I can do in exchange for a fine lunch." He headed outside.

Emma smiled and said, "You pick the spot, and the shovels are in the tack room in the barn up the hill. Oh, and thanks."

\*\*\*\*

At about noon, lunch was ready. Emma stepped out the back door and clanged a metal bar around and around in a triangle. How many times had she called Kelly in for lunch or supper this way? The high-pitched clanging could be heard for the better part of a mile. It echoed up the canyons and along the creek bed. It wasn't long until folks, like ants, emerged from every direction, heading for the house.

"We'll be eating on the porch to catch a little breeze," Emma explained. She had put out lawn chairs to supplement the porch swing and glider.

Lynn and Dennis brought plates filled with steak, fried zucchini and salad. They each took a plate and thanked Emma in appreciation for the meal.

"It's the least I could do,"

"I have good news," said Rich. "Jose here thinks he can fix the well if we can acquire or fabricate a few parts. Bill Johnson, about three miles down the road, has a pretty fair machine shop for keeping his ranch equipment repaired. We're going down there after lunch to see if he can help us with tools and hardware."

Jose chimed in, "Let me get a few more measurements and make a list of what we need. We can take the remains of the old pump cylinder with us too. Dennis, Jess, are you going?"

Both nodded yes.

"I want to go to town too," said Emma. "I want to make sure everybody down by the highway is okay health-wise. I'll put on my community nurse hat and make the rounds of the residents while we're down there." Emma paused in thought. "Lynn, can you ride a horse?"

"Sure, I rode horses in summer camp. Why?"

"What do you think about finishing up the canning and then riding to Sunflower in a couple of hours?" Lynn's face lit up. "Just remember, my horses are real cow ponies, not dude ranch stable queens. You'll have to cowgirl up." Emma let out a chuckle, seeing Lynn raise her eyebrows and open her eyes wide, questioningly. "Don't worry. They won't buck you off or anything, but you'll have to show them who's boss."

Lynn nodded, not sure she knew what Emma was talking about, but eager to ride a horse nonetheless.

"By the time we see everyone in town, the boys should be done shootin' the breeze at the shop."

\*\*\*\*

Lunch consisted of food *and* conversation. They talked about two things; the first was the immediate steps needed for their survival. Even though living in the Arizona desert wasn't new to these folks, no one had ever done it without electricity. Secondly, what the Sam Hill had caused all the electronics to fail? Personal introductions were more substantial, talk of an EMP as thorough as everyone in the group could recollect, and fear acknowledged but not dwelled upon.

Emma cleared her throat and said, "Seems that we need each other right now—you all for shelter, food and stuff, and us for mechanical help. I'm making an invitation for you to stay here for the time being, until we can figure all of this out."

"That's very nice of you, ma'am," said Dennis. "I can't see us walking back to town with the food we have left in our packs. We don't want to be a burden, and will do everything we can to set you up; you know, help out."

Emma smiled. "We have a deal, then."

Everyone looked at each other around the table.

There was silence for a minute or so until Emma broke it. "I want to talk to you all about one more thing before we finish eating: sanitation. We are in very fragile circumstances and on our own, at least for now. That means no getting sick. Washing your hands is the most important thing you can do. Make sure the trash is taken out promptly and burned. Let me know the minute anyone feels ill or gets injured. We could also use a source of hot water that doesn't use up our propane. Any ideas?"

"There is always a camp fire," said Dennis. "Do you have a barrel and maybe some glass, like an old window or door? I might be able to rig up some kind of solar water heater."

"Great idea. I'll show you around my work shed when we get a minute," said Rich. "*After* we get the windmill pumping."

Emma got up and started to clear the dishes from the table, and Lynn followed suit. "I think we should all get back to work before we burn any more daylight."

The mood was solemn but purposeful. Having tasks to perform helped take their minds off the "whatever had happened" that had turned their worlds upside down. Rich, along with the other men, started out the front door.

"Emma, come quick," Rich yelled.

"What is it?" cried Emma. She grabbed the shotgun on her way out the front door, unsure of the cause of the commotion.

"There are two horses coming up the driveway!"

Emma emerged onto the front porch, gun hanging from her right arm. Lynn trailed Emma to the door, stopped and peered down the driveway.

"Don't shoot, Mom! It's me, Kelly."

Emma propped the gun on the porch railing and then ran, in that old lady sort of way, toward her daughter.

"Kelly, are you alright?" Emma asked anxiously, her breath coming in gasps.

"Mom, we need help. I have an officer here who has been shot. He's lost quite a bit of blood and I'm afraid infection is setting in."

Jared raised his shoulders as much as he could, winced, and then glared at Kelly. "You didn't tell me you thought it looked infected."

Kelly ignored him. "Let's get him to the house." Kelly rode Hokey to the porch railing. Pokey followed. "Help me get him down."

Rich and Emma reached up and guided Jared down. He would have landed in a heap on the ground if they hadn't taken his full weight.

"Thanks, guys," Jared managed.

"Let's get him inside, Rich," Emma directed. "Take him into the kitchen, there's better light in there."

Supporting the staggering Jared under his good arm, Rich led him toward the front door. Emma followed.

Kelly grabbed her mother's shoulder, and Emma turned toward her daughter. "Who are all of these people?"

"They're a search and rescue group lost in the hills. I can explain more later. You came from town by horse. I guess we can assume no one has power or vehicles there either?"

"No, but we can talk about this later too," Kelly's voice was strident with panic. "That officer has had that bullet in his shoulder for more than twenty-four hours. His name is Jared." She exhaled forcefully. Emma pulled Kelly into her arms. Kelly's muscles relaxed some. She let out one small sob and melted into her mother's warm embrace.

Emma took Kelly by the shoulders, pushing her away slightly so she could look her in the eyes.

"None of that quite yet," Emma said in a soothing voice, her eyes smiling softly. "There's work to do." She gave her daughter a squeeze.

"Sorry Mom, I'm exhausted."

"I know, hon, but right now there is a young man in there that needs our help."

"Yes, ma'am," Kelly said, almost in her military voice.

Emma hugged Kelly again, then they both straightened and put on their "all business" faces.

Emma wiped a tear off Kelly's cheek and planted a kiss where it had been. Kelly's face was so dirty from riding in the desert that the tear left a muddy streak.

"I'll help you in there, but I don't trust my hands. They might shake so badly that I couldn't remove the bullet," said Kelly.

Emma smiled and gave her an encouraging wink. The two women moved hastily into the house.

Emma burst into the kitchen, Kelly right behind her, and started giving directions. Rich had lowered Jared into a kitchen chair. Kelly could see he was struggling to keep himself upright. Lynn stood agape by the kitchen door, looking at Jared. Kelly made eye contact with the teen as she passed by.

"I'm afraid the kitchen is hot and in such a mess," said Emma. "Rich, help me clear the table. Lynn, clear the counter around the sink. Kelly, you get a mattress cover from the linen closet and grab a couple of pillows and towels too."

Kelly returned from the hallway with her ordered items.

"Hold these," Kelly said, handing Lynn the towels. She looked directly at Lynn and smiled as she said it. Lynn nodded and took them, looking eager to help.

Kelly placed the pillows at one end of the table and then the plastic mattress pad over all.

"Put the towels approximately where Jared's shoulder would go, Lynn... please," Kelly added as an afterthought, realizing she wasn't in a war zone talking to her regular crew.

Rich grabbed Jared firmly under his arm to get him standing, lifting much of his weight and nearly dislocating the poor man's good shoulder. He stepped backward with Jared leaning on him until the two men got to the table. Jared pivoted on his foot, then inched one hip onto the table. Rich helped Jared lie down by providing counter-weight and using his uninjured arm as a lever.

Lynn watched as Emma moved close to her new patient. Emma removed Jared's sling and peeled back the remnants of his shirt. She tried to dislodge the bandage, but the blood was dry now. She tugged the bandage to release it from the entrance wound. When it finally let go, it took some of the scab and skin with it.

"Ouch!" Emma said sympathetically. Jared just set his jaw. "It doesn't look too bad yet." Emma eased the deputy's shirt off his shoulder.

"God, I'm just glad to lie down," Jared said softly.

"Kelly, take his pulse," said Emma. "The rest of you, besides Lynn, had better wait in the front room. We don't need any more germs in here than we have to."

"About 120 beats per minute," announced Kelly.

"Early shock. We need to address fluids and infection." Emma said it as much to herself as to Kelly. "Adjust those pillows, Lynn, under the plastic. Kelly, put a new pot of water on to boil." To make up for the commands, she shot them each a kind smile.

Lynn moved quickly, with a determined look on her face. She pursed her lips tightly, took in a deep breath and let it out slowly, doing as she was told.

"Yes, right away, Mom," said Kelly, smiling back.

Emma disappeared down the hallway, but returned shortly with a small olive-drab bundle and a box of supplies. She unrolled the bundle, exposing an army surgical kit. Stainless steel instruments were all neatly tucked into their own little pouches. Emma saw Kelly putting a big pot of water on the stove. They needed boiling water to sterilize the instruments.

"Did I send you to boil water and get sheets?" Emma laughed, making reference to an old midwives' joke. She was trying to break the tension and the silence. Kelly smiled broadly. This was her calling, her life's work; it felt familiar.

"Mom, I'm going out to get some things from my bags. As Kelly passed through the front room, she said, "Rich would you unsaddle the horses and get them something to drink? We were in a hurry and didn't water them at the creek. They haven't had much water since the Verde." Rich headed for the front door. Kelly followed him out of the house and retrieved her saddle bags.

Hokey and Pokey were munching on the green grass that grew under the large sycamore trees in her mom's front yard. Rich picked up the horses' reins and started leading them to the upper corral.

Returning to the kitchen, Kelly threw the saddlebags over the back of a kitchen chair.

"I have some pain meds and antibiotics in here. I gave Jared some Rocephin yesterday, and I'll give him another one now."

Kelly drew up a dose of long-acting pain medication and a dose of the antibiotic. The two medications couldn't be mixed together, so Jared would get two shots. "I also want to give some morphine intravenously right before the procedure so he gets quick relief. I don't have a saline lock; it will have to be a straight stick."

"I haven't heard 'straight stick' in a long time," said Emma. "It used to be routine for us to put medication right into a vein with just a syringe. I didn't know you young nurses even knew how to do it."

"We do what we have to in field medicine," Kelly said.

"Lynn, help me get his boots off," Emma said.

Lynn stepped back, covering her mouth, then appeared to think about her reaction. She lowered her hand quickly and edged forward. She took one boot in her hands and pulled. Jared grunted softly. She stopped. Emma smiled at the teen and nodded, encouraging her to continue. Continue she did; she got the boot off and then the sock, even though Jared showed some discomfort.

Emma took off the boot and sock on her side.

Kelly positioned a sheet next to Jared from his waist to his ankles and undid the button on his uniform pants. The sheet was laid over Jared's body to provide privacy. Kelly and Emma stood across from each other with their patient between them. They worked in unison to lift Jared's legs at the knees while removing the upper part of his uniform pants. Next they both held the sheet at the top and reached under, pulling his trousers toward his feet. This was a dance that both nurses had performed countless times. Kelly had never nursed with her mother and was reassured to find that pants came off the same way for both generations of nurses.

The water was boiling vigorously and Emma returned to the stove. She put the instruments and a pair of very long, metal tongs into it. The tongs' handles stuck out of the boiling water. "The tongs are sterile where they're submerged, but non-sterile at the handles," Emma said to Kelly.

"I know, Mom," Kelly said, exasperated. She pursed her lips but then relaxed her face into a grin, and her mom smiled back.

"I forget," said Emma. "To me, you're still an eighteen-year-old girl on her way to college. I wasn't around while you were becoming an accomplished nurse."

Emma opened a package of sterile 4 x 4 gauze and placed it on a clean cutting board. "Lynn, I'm using these pads to make a sterile place to put the instruments. If I can't explain it to Kelly, I may as well teach you."

"My mom loves to teach. By the way, Lynn, I'm Kelly, Emma's daughter."

"I thought she was your sister," Jared joked in a weak voice. "Is every female in your family a Navy nurse?" He let out a single puff of air that was meant to be a laugh but didn't quite make it, turning into a little cough.

"Yes, they are, sir," Kelly answered, putting her face near his and raising her eyebrows playfully. Amazing how much more confident she felt now, being with her mother.

"You can meet Lynn and the rest of the 'lost patrol' properly later," Emma said. "Right now, Kelly, we need a scalpel blade in the pot. It should be in that box."

Kelly found the small box of blades without difficulty. She dropped a number ten blade into the boiling water. Different blade shapes and sizes had different numbers.

Emma stepped to the sink and began to wash her hands. Kelly joined her. Lynn watched, glued to every detail. Both women washed their hands and arms up to the elbows, paying special attention to their fingernails. Emma pointed to a drawer next to the sink and said, "Get two of those towels damp, would you, Kelly?"

Emma took a bar of soap from the back of the sink, then returned to her patient on the table. Kelly and Emma washed Jared's grimy neck and shoulders, then all the way to his waist. Kelly rinsed off the soap with the other damp cloth.

"Lynn, could you please get two clean aprons and two towels out of the kitchen drawer?" Emma asked as she dug through the cardboard box to get a pair of sterile gloves, a pair of non-sterile gloves, and two facemasks. The nurses pulled their hair back with ties and put on the masks. They washed and dried their hands and forearms again, thoroughly. Emma put on the sterile gloves. Kelly would be her mother's helper and didn't need her gloves to be sterile, just clean.

"Jared, can you roll on your right side?" Emma asked.

Jared rolled gingerly onto his side. He wiggled a bit to make his weight-bearing hip and shoulder more comfortable. Kelly reached under the plastic pad and adjusted the pillows, and Jared gratefully sank into the pillows that now supported his head.

Emma stepped up to the table and placed her two hands on Jared's left shoulder, one on the front and one on the back. Methodically she felt around, fingers arched. They waltzed on the flesh around the entrance wound, then they tangoed on the skin of his back. Emma bit her lip and kept the pink flesh held captive there as her search continued. Heavy breathing accompanied the hunt. All of the sudden Emma squinted then closed her eyes tightly, lifting her chin. Her second and third fingers began to alternately tap the skin above Jared's shoulder blade.

Finally, "I think I've found it. Yes."

That was Kelly's cue to inject the morphine. She put a tourniquet around Jared's upper arm and chose a nice, thick, hand vein for the injection. "Lynn, when I tell you, pull this end of the tourniquet until it pops off Jared's arm."

Lynn moved to Kelly's side and set her face in a determined way, mimicking Emma. *Sturdy girl, nursing material,* Kelly noted. That was all she had time to think before her attention returned to Jared. "You aren't allergic to morphine, are you?"

Jared, eyes shut tight, shook his head no.

"I'll tell you before I stick you," Kelly warned. "It will feel like a rush of warm liquid going through your body, then it will make you feel groggy, but won't make you unconscious. If I give you enough morphine that you don't feel any pain, your breathing would become too shallow. Getting this bullet out is gonna hurt."

Jared did not change his expression. He didn't acknowledge Kelly in any way.

Kelly steadied the vein with her left hand and gave the skin a quick cleaning. "Okay, here we go." One fluid movement put the tip of the needle into the vein. "Lynn, remove the tourniquet." Lynn pulled on the dangling end until it popped, releasing its grip. The blue faded and the red returned to Jared's hand. Kelly pushed the plunger of the syringe slowly, injecting the narcotic.

Jared's eyes opened slightly, then became glazed.

Kelly pulled the needle from his vein.

"Hold right here, Lynn," Kelly directed, placing a folded gauze over the injection site. "Press it hard so he won't bleed and bruise."

Lynn reached out hesitantly. Kelly took her index finger and pressed it on the gauze pad. "That's right." Lynn looked up from her finger to Kelly's face and smiled broadly. Kelly nodded in appreciation and encouragement.

"Looks like the morphine's working," said Emma. Jared's eyes rolled upward into a strange stare before his eyelids closed softly. His facial muscles softened. "Get those instruments now, would you, Kelly?"

Kelly placed the instruments onto the sterile 4 x 4s. Emma picked up the scalpel blade and attached it to the scalpel handle.

Her steady hand made a quarter-inch incision on the back side of Jared's shoulder. He moaned.

"Let's hope this is our new *exit* wound," Emma mumbled. She picked up a pair of forceps—the medical name for tweezers—and inserted the tips into the incision. Jared visibly stiffened and held his breath. Kelly held her breath with him. It didn't take Emma long to find her target. Out came a bullet, a .22. Emma dropped the bloody slug onto a gauze pad. There was a collective sigh of relief.

"I've seen exploratories for bullets go on for a very long time," said Kelly.

"Me too," said Emma. "But this one practically jumped out at me.

"What luck—or should I say skill?"

"I would like to think a little of both." Emma walked around the table and poked around in the entrance wound. She found two tiny pieces of fabric lodged there and removed them. "Get me some sterile towels to clean this up." Emma looked at Lynn. "On second thought, maybe Kelly should do that."

Lynn took a few steps back, putting both of her hands behind her, out of the way but ready to help.

Kelly went to the stove and threw two hand towels into the boiling water. After a few minutes, she used the tongs to take one out and let it drip into the sink until most of the water was out and it had stopped steaming. Emma stepped to the sink, took the towel from the tongs and wrung it out with her gloved hands. She went to

Jared and washed the entrance and exit wounds. This made them bleed in earnest again. She placed gauze over the holes then held pressure.

"Get a bottle of wicking gauze out of my box, would you?" Emma asked Kelly.

Kelly opened the small bottle of gauze without touching the inside of the lid or its contents. She edged close to Emma and tipped the bottle up so that Emma could reach in and grab the thin gauze strip with forceps. Emma cut an eight-inch section with the other hand, using sterile scissors from the instrument tray. She neatly packed gauze into the front and then the back wounds. Jared breathed heavily again, clenching his teeth.

"Jared, this gauze wicks any fluids and infection out of deep wounds," Emma said, but she was looking at Lynn. Lynn nodded to indicate that she understood. "Get two tablespoons of sugar, as clean as you can, please, Kelly."

Kelly had only *heard* about packing wounds with sugar or honey to prevent and treat infection. She had seen some recent studies, though, where it was coming back into vogue. She went to the cupboard and got the table sugar. She poured some of it into her mother's hands. Emma packed the sugar into both wounds, entrance and exit, then dressed them with 4 x 4 gauze and tape.

Kelly helped Jared back onto his back. She squeezed his hand tightly. Jared squeezed her hand back.

"What does the sugar do?" Jared asked, slurring his words, not letting go of Kelly's hand. Kelly positioned the fingertips of her free hand in a small groove in Jared's wrist, where she could feel his pulse. She watched his chest rise and fall. "It acts as an antibiotic by drawing fluid out of the germs, in essence pickling them. You know how you can leave jam out on the table? The sugar content is so high that germs can't live in it. Plus, we are sweetening you up for later."

Jared gave a weak smile.

"Everything went well," Emma announced. "Kelly, take Jared's vital signs."

"His pulse is 116 and his respirations are 20." Kelly had already taken them.

"I need a temperature too." Kelly stood and turned. She tried to pull her hand from Jared's, but he resisted. Kelly looked back at him and then gave several playful tugs, breaking his grasp.

Emma reached into her cardboard box and handed Kelly an *antique* mercury thermometer in a plastic case.

Kelly had never used one. She looked at it quizzically.

Emma stepped forward and took the glass rod from Kelly, motioning Lynn to her side as well. She raised it in the air and gave it a good shake in a downward motion, four or five times. She rolled the glass rod between her fingertips until she could clearly see the thin silver line of mercury between the two tiny scales printed on the glass. Satisfied that the line was resting below the 98.6 mark, Emma told Jared to raise his tongue, and stuck the bulbous end of the device under it. "Now try to hold it there and please don't drop it," Emma urged. "I only have two. It will take three or four minutes to read."

Jared was groggy from the morphine, but held it as he was instructed. "I could do this all day," he mumbled to Kelly, "if you stayed and held my hand."

Kelly took his hand and moved close. While waiting for the thermometer to register, she noticed his face. It was relaxed for the first time since she had met him, his brow no longer furrowed. His beard had grown as well. It was the same color as his hair: a nice, sturdy brown, not coppery, but a luxurious, medium brown. The stubble covered his strong chin up to his high cheekbones. It was a kind face.

After what seemed a sufficient amount of time, she removed the device and held it up to read it. The thin, silver line now reached 100.8. "It's one hundred point eight," Kelly said proudly.

"That's about what I expected," said Emma. "The morphine has relaxed him a little and he has a low-grade fever. Now all we can do is keep the wounds clean, give him antibiotics and fluids, and pray." Emma wished she hadn't said the last two words out loud.

Kelly took care of the final bandaging and placing of a sling. Emma went to work making a bed in the living room, with Lynn in tow.

Emma found Dennis, Jose, Jess and Rich in the front room, looking like expectant fathers. "It's over," she said to them. "The patient did very well and just gave birth to a .22. Why don't you wait for us on the porch or in the kitchen?"

Kelly helped Jared to his feet, keeping his sheet tucked around him. She guided him into the living room, nearly running into the guys as they came from the other direction. She helped Jared onto the couch.

"I'm going to clean up the kitchen," Emma announced. She glanced over at Lynn as if to say, *And you are coming with me, dear.*

"I owe you and your mom big time," said Jared once they had gone.

"Don't be silly," said Kelly. "We would have done it for anyone."

"But you didn't do it for anyone, you did it for me."

"Well. You are truly welcome. Now, my sleepy friend, off to bed with you."

"No one has ever uttered such sweet, sweet words," Jared said as he sank into the couch and pillows. His eyes closed one last time.

Kelly sat on the floor by the sofa. She watched Jared breathe slowly in and out. She brushed a wisp of hair away from his face, letting her fingers linger a bit at his hairline. *Be well*, she thought. She remembered doing the same for a young soldier in Iraq. She hoped Jared's outcome would be better because she didn't think she could take another young man's death, at least not one she had started to care for. Kelly's face flushed slightly as she remembered her night with Jared in the sleeping bag. She stayed for a few minutes longer.

Chapter 5

Kelly went back into the kitchen to help with cleanup. Her mother had been canning food when they came in, and went right back to her work when the surgery table had been dismantled and disinfected. Kelly walked to the counter and started washing canning jars.

"Now, I wish I had brought a couple of liters of IV fluid from the hospital. He could use it," said Kelly.

"We can make do with oral rehydration solution and broth for the rest of the day," Emma said.

"We should let him sleep a few hours first, don't you think? Poor boy looks spent. He'll be back to eating and drinking normally in no time. How many doses of antibiotic do you have?"

"I brought a flat of twenty Rocephin vials from the hospital and a good selection of oral antibiotics too," replied Kelly. "So we have plenty."

Rich was the first of the men to speak. "I hope lover boy is asleep."

"Shhh!" Kelly shot him an exasperated glance. She had always thought that Rich, her mother's neighbor, spoke much too freely and with little reverence to her mother and her. She did as she always did and ignored him.

"What I want to know is, what happened?" asked Emma, looking at Kelly. "It's rare enough I see you with a boyfriend; did you have to shoot one to bring him home?"

"Mom, I need you to sit down."

"Well, of course, my darling," Emma said in an apologetic tone.

The men and Lynn sat at the kitchen table. There were six chairs total; that left them one short. Seeing Kelly needed a chair, Dennis popped up and held his chair for her, then held the empty chair for Emma. Emma sat facing Kelly and took her hands in her own. Everyone else sat quietly, Dennis finding a place on a step stool in the corner.

Sweat trickled down Kelly's temples. She reached up and wiped it away with her sleeve, then unbuttoned her shirt, revealing a T-shirt underneath. She slid one arm and then the other out of her shirt.

Emma gasped, "What happened to your arm? You have bruises everywhere!" She reached out and grasped Kelly's elbow. There were multiple small lacerations surrounding a large, three-inch gash in Kelly's right, upper arm. "Did somebody beat you up?"

"No, Mom. Let me explain." Tears welled in Kelly's eyes as she told about the terrible plane crash and fires, the EOC, and the hospital burning down. They were riveted by her every word.

She continued her story about her trip on the Beeline, finding Jared and shooting the man on the road. Emma stared, aghast. Kelly tucked her head into her mother's shoulder and sobbed.

"I'm so sorry, my darling. I didn't mean to make light of your situation. We have only been inconvenienced here. We had no idea that it could be so bad in town. I am sorry that you went through that."

"Mom." Kelly directed her words directly at Emma. "I'm afraid. I don't think there is going to be anything to go back to." Her lips quivered as tears rolled down her face.

"It's okay now, my baby. You're safe at home." Emma kissed Kelly on the forehead. Everyone was quiet.

Finally Rich spoke, hanging his head and wringing his hands. "I was afraid of that."

Lynn burst into tears. Kelly looked up quizzically. Yes, this did affect everyone profoundly. She didn't know if she could deal with everyone else's grief right now.

"Mom," she said, staring blankly, "I'm so tired I can hardly stand. I'm going to take a nap, then I'll come back and help you."

"I'm going to wash up that arm of yours."

"Aren't you going to suture that?" Rich asked Emma.

"You can't suture anything more than twenty-four hours after it happens. Most docs won't suture if it's older than eight hours. It will just have to heal," said Emma.

"I'll wash it in the bathroom," said Kelly. "There's soap in there, isn't there?"

"Yes, but I'd be glad to..."

"No, Mom," Kelly said, cutting her mother off. All grown up now, remember?" Kelly wasn't good at accepting help, even from her own mother. "Love you, Mom."

Emma gave a sigh. "Get some sleep, baby. Love you."

\*\*\*\*

"That was a good lunch," said Rich to Emma. "Kelly's been sleeping a while now. I bet she sleeps all afternoon—she looked beat."

"I can't remember ever seeing her that tired or distraught, poor girl. Living through a plane crash and then seeing your own hospital burn down, knowing patients were still in it, is worse than anything I've ever seen, and that's saying something."

"That was some fine doctoring you did, Emma, and Kelly too. Did you learn that in the Navy?" asked Jose.

Emma replied, "I spent more than my fair share of time as a surgery nurse aboard the USS Repose, a hospital ship, off the Vietnam coast. The docs there did all the cutting, of course. Doing medical missions, I had to take a more active role, if you know what I mean. We did a lot of work in South America and Africa. I trained local medical providers, but ended up doing anything and everything you can imagine. I'll tell you a few stories some other time. Kelly nursed our soldiers in Afghanistan."

"You should see the ol' woman's photo albums. But only if you have a strong stomach," added Rich. "She still looks after many of the folks around here."

"Jared is lucky you have both seen what you have seen. His survival will depend on it," said Jose. He glanced over at Emma, who was blushing.

"Lynn and I need to get ready to go to town," she announced, getting up from the table. "Kelly's sleeping. Get her up if you think Jared needs anything. They should both be okay, though. Coming, Lynn?"

"Sure, Mrs. Wise," Lynn said, jumping up from the table.

"Just call me Emma, dear girl. Let's go get some riding clothes on."

"I'm afraid this is all I have."

"You look fine; just sayin' we should get ready. Why don't you wait for me in the living room?"

After a few minutes, Emma emerged from her bedroom with her Ruger .357 strapped to her hip. Lynn noticed it, but didn't say anything. Emma also grabbed her .308 scoped hunting rifle from a corner in the living room on her way out the door.

Both women rode Emma's horses, Buckskin and Traveler, three miles into the small community of Sunflower.

"You know," said Lynn, "I've crossed that freeway bridge a hundred times and never thought anything about the houses down here."

She was enjoying her ride down the canyon. Some houses lay hidden beneath the sycamores lining the creek; others, surrounded by corrals, sat higher up; and a few overlooked the valley from the surrounding hills.

"We're a small community down here, mostly retired," said Emma. "I've been here eighteen years now. I'm one of the old-timers."

People walked out onto their porches as the two horsewomen approached. Emma waved and greeted them all by name. At each house, she stopped and spoke with the homeowners, inquiring as to how they were doing and if they had any medical needs. None did as of yet. That was good news. Everywhere they stopped, people mentioned a meeting set for 7 p.m. at Bill's place to "talk things over."

"All the people seem tense," said Lynn when she and Emma were alone again.

"Yeah, they live close to the freeway and you'd be tense too if you had people coming up to your door looking for food and water. They see the people walking down the road and have done what they can. We're lucky we live so far back. All these folks seem to know is that the electricity is off and cars aren't running. I haven't been talking about what might be going on because I don't want to cause a panic, don't know much about it, and can't answer questions very well either."

"Most of them are wearing guns." Lynn opened her eyes wide to emphasize her amazement.

"Yes, this *is* Arizona and we have a long tradition of defending our territory, and nowadays our homes and families. We're a pretty independent lot."

When the two riders arrived at the Johnson's barn, Rich, Jess, Dennis, Jose and Bill Johnson were gathered around a worktable. Jose talked animatedly while pointing at drawings on the table and occasionally tapping on the pump cylinder sitting next to them.

"Bill, nice to see you," said Emma, "but I wouldn't let that crazy old coot come onto your place with a gun." She pointed at Rich, who had a holstered Colt Government .45.

"I, too, am inclined to keep my firearms close, given the current circumstances," said Bill, nodding his head toward a scoped hunting rifle propped next to the workbench. "You don't seem particularly gun-shy yourself, Emma."

"Nope. How's the pump project goin'?"

"Jose, here, is a mechanical whiz," said Rich. "He has dreamed up a way to rebuild the pump and repair the windmill."

"We are still missing some parts," said Jose. "They are common enough. A hardware store in Fountain Hills would have them."

"You may not want to go into town," said Bill. "Judging by the state of the people walking down the highway, the town might be... chaotic. At first we were handing out food and water, but we've been chasing people away from our houses since yesterday. There have been a couple attempts at break-ins. We know these people are desperate, but we have to keep our supplies for ourselves. The residents closest to the highway put up a sign telling people on the road to go down to the spring to the south for water, but not to come near the houses. We've been taking turns guarding the road and the fences."

"Kelly paints a pretty grim picture of town. She says it is dangerous, but we just can't get this to work without the new parts," said Jose. "Emma and Rich can't stay at their houses without water. Even if the stores have been looted, most would not be grabbing plain old hardware yet. A trip to town would give us a chance to find out what has happened and get supplies."

"I think Jose is right," said Dennis. "From what I've read about blackouts and natural disasters, the looting is mostly at night and burns itself out quickly because everything of value is taken. The kids can stay at Emma's, just in case."

Emma and Lynn left the men at the workshop and continued making nursing rounds. Lynn watched as Emma visited with the local families. Beatrice and Emmet Banting lived in a small house near the creek. Emmet was an insulin-dependent diabetic. He had a few weeks worth of insulin left, but his case would be tragic if he couldn't get more. Another diabetic, Charlie Best, a widower, lived near the freeway in a small house. He would not discuss his insulin supply with Emma. Chris Barnard had congestive heart failure and was on medications to increase his heart's pumping action. He could most likely be helped with foxglove tea, but Emma would have to do some research on the dosing. Chris had a three-month supply of his medicines, so his case wasn't pressing. Emma kept her visits short and noticed that Lynn watched her assessments inquisitively.

After the circuit was complete, Emma and Lynn returned to Bill's house. Bill and several other men and women were setting bales of hay out as seats around an empty fire pit. The riders put their horses in a corral and joined the others.

People arrived in couples or small groups. Everyone knew each other and folks visited for a while. Finally, Bill looked around and said, "Looks like about everybody's here, except for the two on guard. For those of you who have not heard, if the guards blow their whistles, they need help. When you hear a whistle, ring your dinner bell, make some noise for others to hear, then head toward the whistle, well armed. Speaking of guarding, I have the signup sheet for the next five days on the table. The guards say that there are a lot fewer people going south today on the highway."

"Good," said Emmett.

Bill continued, "We have two windmills pumping water. One feeds the stock tank near the freeway and the other feeds a holding tank up the hill. We just need to get the water to everyone's houses. Any ideas?"

"I have a 55-gallon water drum," said one of the residents.

"Me too," said a second."

"We can put those on my buckboard."

"A hundred and ten gallons of water sounds like a lot," said Emma, "but when you add cooking, dishwashing, laundry, baths

124

and watering the gardens, it goes very fast. Rich and I are using a well bailer that Jose, here, built for us. Sounds like we will all be spending a bunch of time moving water until the power comes back on."

"Jose, you said that the bailer holds about two gallons?" asked Bill rhetorically. "If we make some bailers for the houses without windmills, those households could at least draw water for drinking, cooking and dishwashing. We wouldn't have to deliver water to them as often. Jose, tell everyone how you made yours."

Jose listed the parts he used and walked the residents through the process. "Do you have the parts?"

After some discussion, it was decided that almost all of the PVC pipe in the community was small-diameter.

"Jose and I are planning to go to Fountain Hills for pump parts tomorrow," said Dennis. "We can look for PVC pipe and the other things you need, too."

"The wells look like they can gravity feed some of the other houses," said Jose. "We may be able to plumb the windmills' tanks to some house tanks with irrigation hose. Do we need to add that to the shopping list?" Several people in the crowd nodded. "Okay, it's on the list."

"We don't know how long it'll be before we get back to normal," said Bill. "Some of us should go out to the highway and salvage food from the semis before it goes bad. I'm planning on heading out first thing in the morning with my buckboard. Who's going with me?"

Several men and women volunteered.

"If I can't go to Fountain Hills, can I go with them?" Jess asked Jose.

"What do you think, Bill?" Jose asked. "Jess is a good worker, but is it safe for a teenager?"

"There's not many people on the road now, should be pretty empty tomorrow," said Bill. "We will be a large group and well armed. I just don't see having any problems. We could use a strong, young guy like Jess."

Jess flashed a smile. Lynn didn't want to be left out. "I'd like to help too," she said.

"I'm not sure that's a good idea," said Dennis.

"Bill said it would be safe. At least I can help instead of sitting around just waiting."

"I'll look out for her," Jess said.

"She'll be fine," said Bill. "We old codgers could use the help."

"I'll be okay, Daddy."

"Alright." Dennis looked Bill in the eyes as he said it.

"The boys up at Emma's think they may know what's happened," Bill said, putting his hands on his hips. "I'll give them the floor."

Dennis stood and spoke briefly about solar storms and EMPs. At one point, Jose stood and added his two cents.

"How long will the outage last?" asked Mrs. Branham.

"We don't know if it's a solar storm, which can last for days, or an EMP, which lasts only a second, but the damage done by both is permanent," said Dennis. They can both cover huge areas, maybe the whole country. That means power grids and electronics will have to be replaced. I have no idea how extensive the destruction might be or how long repairs will take."

"Is that the only possibility?" asked Mrs. Branham.

"Those scenarios fit the circumstances," said Dennis. "I'm open to other possibilities."

Lynn listened to the conversation, which continued for twenty minutes. It was too *crazy* to believe. She was grateful when the topic finally changed.

Emma talked about sanitation and health issues. "Come get Kelly or me if anyone needs anything," Emma said.

It was also decided that the creek bed, upstream, should be regularly checked for dead animals or any other contamination, whether the creek was flowing or not. Emma recommended that any water from the creek be pasteurized before drinking, cooking, or bathing with it.

Lynn just wanted the meeting to end. She was exhausted and terrified and it wasn't just her, from what she could tell by looking around the room. Everyone's eyes darted from speaker to speaker. The mood was tense; many of the attendees were disbelieving or shocked.

It seemed to go on and on. The grownups talked like they had solutions to all of this. None of their yammering seemed to fix *anything.* She wanted her friends back. She missed going shopping for her favorite clothes and yes, even school.

After the meeting, Lynn had to wait while the others chatted with the people of Sunflower. She watched her dad seeking out anyone who might need emotional help or just a friendly ear. *He's in his councilor/rabbi mode*, she thought. *This could take a while.* She hated to admit it, but her dad really was the kindest man she ever knew.

Finally, Lynn and Emma mounted the horses. Emma made Traveler walk so that the others could keep up on foot, but Lynn galloped as fast as Buckskin could go.

"Stop, Lynn!" Dennis shouted to no avail.

Chapter 6

Dawn was breaking as the group of would-be foragers left Emma's homestead. Dennis rode Traveler, a beautiful grey dun quarter horse with a silvery, sleek coat. Jose and Rich rode Kelly's horses. Kelly drove her mom's other horse, Buckskin, who, true to his name, had a coat the lush color and feel of moccasins. He pulled a large donkey cart that wasn't much to look at with its flat bed of old wood planks mounted on an ancient pickup truck axle, complete with chunky tires. Kelly's mom kept the cart for use around the house and on the range with her twenty head of cattle. "It won't get stuck like a truck," she used to joke.

Lynn and Jess sat in the middle of the cart for fear of being bounced off the sides. They were being dropped off at Sunflower to help with the freeway foraging. The others would continue to Fountain Hills. They had packed a minimum of overnight supplies, in hopes of filling the cart with scavenged booty.

Dennis was riding alongside. "Hey kids, it's almost time to get down. I just wanted to tell you to be safe out there."

Kelly stopped the cart in front of the last house before they got to the main road. Dennis motioned for Lynn to come to the edge of the cart.

"Put your boot in my stirrup and I'll lower you to the ground."

Lynn grabbed her father's forearm, then tentatively slid her boot into the stirrup Dennis's foot had just vacated. Traveler stepped to the side when Lynn's weight pulled on the saddle. She stepped down, lowered by her father's firm grip.

"Bye, baby girl," Dennis said. "We should be back tomorrow." Dennis reached down and roughed up Lynn's hair like she was a five-year-old.

"Love you, Dad." Lynn turned away. She hid the tears that welled up in her eyes, refusing to look at her father as she whispered, "You be careful too."

Jose rode up to Jess, who was adjusting his CAP-unauthorized combat knife that he could now display proudly on his pack strap. "Watch out for Lynn," Jose said.

"Okay, Dad."

"Love you, Mijo."

Lynn and Jess stood quietly as the adults rode away.

\*\*\*\*

The cavalcade made good time descending the Beeline highway toward the small city of Fountain Hills. Only abandoned vehicles remained. The group noted which trucks might be worth a future visit from the Sunflower scavenging party. Food and water trucks particularly interested them, even if they had been broken into, because people on foot couldn't carry much. The unmarked trucks were more of a crap shoot. They didn't spend time investigating.

As they rode on, the group animatedly discussed what they hoped to find in town and what items should take priority to be brought back. Space was very limited and decisions would have to be made on the spot.

Rich noticed a car ahead and motioned to the others to slow up as he went to investigate. He quickly doubled back, giving a hand signal for the others to stop.

"We've got two folks sitting in a car up here. How do you want to proceed?" Rich asked no one in particular.

"Why don't you and Dennis walk up there?" Kelly said. "One on each side of the road. Sneaking up will be easier on foot and two dudes like you don't want to get into a firefight from the back of a horse. I don't know who would be more unpredictable, the 'dudes' or the horses." She grinned.

"Watch it, girlie," Jose said. "If you want us to go do the dirty work, you have to be nice to us." Dennis smiled too.

Rich took the right side of the road and Dennis took the left. They tried to stay hidden among brushy trees. As they got closer, Rich motioned to Dennis that he was going to approach the car and needed cover. No one moved in the vehicle; it was as if they were asleep. Rich stayed low and took cover behind a boulder.

"Hey you, in the car, do you need help?" Rich called. There was no reply. He ran crouching to the back right quarter panel. "At least one of em's dead," Rich called. "I can smell 'em."

He held his breath and moved forward until he could see both corpses. It was an elderly couple. Then he took off in a dead run to the roadside, trying to escape the odor before he had to take another breath. It did not save him. He retched and retched, as if his body wasn't just trying to empty his stomach of its contents, but was also trying to force the very smell from his mouth and nose.

Dennis walked up to the passenger's side holding his breath. He checked the back seat in case there was anyone else. He recited a blessing.

"Poor bastards," Rich said. "Wonder what happened to them?"

"Probably didn't even leave their car," Dennis said. "They look pretty old. Probably knew they couldn't walk all the way to town. I saw a cane in the back seat."

"You would have thought that one of them would have tried it," Rich said.

"Maybe they just chose to stay together, to die together," Dennis said.

Rich shook his head. "Let's get out of here."

Rich and Dennis went back to their horses. The mood had shifted to a more somber one. Rich and Dennis started out in front, together. They headed down the road, intending to skirt the stench as best they could. The horses grew skittish as they approached the car. Their ears moved forward and their nostrils flared at the smell of death. Traveler balked at moving forward, snorted and jerked from side to side. It took all Rich had to make him pass. Jose was very stern with Pokey and avoided problems. Kelly worried that Buckskin would balk with the cart, but he seemed less affected than the others. She made it around without incident.

"I think we should put Traveler in the lead the rest of the way," Rich said. "Let's keep moving."

\*\*\*\*

"We need to avoid the Verde River Bridge," Kelly said. "There might be a lot of people from the highway and from town at the bridge, trying to get water. We'll turn north onto the dirt track paralleling the Verde River on the Fort McDowell Indian Reservation."

A large Target store sat just north of the highway on Shea Road. As tempting as the discount store was, it was certain to have been looted by now. The group crossed the low-flowing Verde below the sand quarry, pausing to water the horses. They went through the deserted We Ko Pa Golf Course and dismounted at the base of a ridge. Rich was left to hold the horses. Kelly, Jose and Dennis ascended the ridge that overlooked a manmade lake to their west; Fountain Lake. A large, white monolith sat in the middle of its green water.

"Hard to believe that that big fountain once shot water over 500 feet in the air. It was quite some engineering. Doesn't seem to matter much now," said Jose.

Kelly lay prone, peering through the scope of her mother's .308 rifle.

"What do you see?" asked Jose.

"Townspeople standing at the lakeshore filling buckets, bottles and five-gallon plastic containers with lake water. A bunch have rifles slung across their backs," Kelly replied.

"What are those columns of smoke?" asked Jose.

I can't tell if they're cooking fires or the remains of larger fires."

The others took turns looking through the scope.

"Everyone must be desperate for water. The lake water is stagnant and nasty from all those ducks. There are a lot of backyard swimming pools here. I wonder if the homeowners are safe, or if people are fighting over that water too?" Dennis said.

"Yeah, the next big source of water is the river behind us and that is a pretty long haul," Jose said. "I bet the river near town will be contaminated soon. There are going to be a bunch of sick people, if there aren't already. Let's get going; we're burning daylight."

Moving a little more cautiously, the foragers rode north and entered the city limits on Grande Boulevard from the reservation side. The riders trotted through a mile of houses and condominiums. Front doors and garages of several of the condominiums stood wide open. "I guess the owners of these condos are retired—snowbirds who haven't come back for the winter yet," Kelly said. "I'm guessing those houses have been looted."

Occupants of other houses stared at them from behind half-open blinds and drapes. From time to time, a person scurried from one house to another.

Kelly said, "I feel like a character in some science fiction movie just before the aliens attack."

The little troop turned south onto Saguaro Boulevard, toward Fountain Lake and the main business area. The businesses were looted too. Broken glass lined mostly-empty streets. A few folks were hauling water in a kid's little red wagon, while others used their bikes. Those they passed wore looks of fear and scurried quickly away from the approaching group.

Their first stop was the hardware store on Palisades Boulevard. The glass from the front doors lay shattered on the floor. Jose stayed outside, away from the building, with the horses. Rich also stayed outside to cover the large store window with his AR-15. Kelly, armed with her rifle, and Dennis, with Jared's AR-15, went into the store with weapons at the ready. They carefully cleared the building, making sure no one was inside. The battered cash registers lay open. All of the snack and candy shelves stood bare. The soda machine was empty and the ice cream freezer was full of melted, stinking ice cream. Most of the kitchen and camping supplies in front were gone, but further to the back, plumbing and hardware items were still there.

Kelly signaled to Rich and Jose that they could come in and start "shopping." Dennis positioned himself at the front doors to guard the horses and warn the others of interlopers.

Rich and Jose went straight to the plumbing area and then the hardware section to pick out parts for the well and water heater. Kelly thought that nails and screws would be needed, and picked up several boxes. She also pulled an assortment of hardware, rolls of wire, duct tape and leather gloves. The lamp oil was all gone, but scattered on the floor were a few wicks. She got black spray paint, a couple of small oven thermometers, and strip insulation for the solar hot water project. She emptied the store of seeds, along with rolls of plastic sheeting for the garden, thinking long-term.

"Look at this!" she said, "peanut oil for deep fat-frying turkeys. It's worth its weight in gold."

Jose picked out a selection of tools. Everyone went along the shelves and pulled items that they thought would be needed.

The group searched the store for about thirty minutes. As Kelly emerged from the store, she saw Dennis crouched behind an abandoned car. Sweat beaded on his forehead. His eyes darted up and down the street as though he was sure someone was going to jump out from around the corner of the building.

"I thought you were never coming out of there," he said. "My imagination ran wild. All I could think of were those scenes from the Middle East where the masked men throw Molotov cocktails."

Finally, loose supplies were bundled into tarps procured in the store. The bundles, rolls of irrigation hose, and PVC pipes were strapped to the cart.

"Well, that's it for the hardware store," Jose said. "Good haul."

Next, they focused on finding the cache of weapons that Jared and the other deputies had stashed in the old town offices the night of the blackout. They quickly discovered it would have been impossible to find without the detailed instructions Jared had given Kelly that morning. The buildings stood empty, not used for years. Inside a back office closet, the scavengers found the tarp covering a green garden wagon. Under the tarp were four Remington 870 shotguns, three AR-15 patrol rifles, an M14 battle rifle and cases of ammunition.

Jose hefted one of the ammunition cases. "Thank goodness the Sheriff's office had this cart. These boxes weigh a ton. I feel sorry for the horses."

The cavalcade proceeded north on Fountain Hills Boulevard to the northern edge of town, to Dusty's Tack and Feed. After they cleared the large store, Kelly took the horses around back and tore open a bale of hay to let them feast while the party gathered supplies. Looking around the store, Kelly remembered wandering down the aisles of feed stores when she was young, hanging onto her daddy's hand. She had loved looking at all of the odd things on the shelves.

"Wow, this place is almost untouched," Jose said. "I wish we had a semi or two."

"Maybe we could stash some things outside of town," Rich said. "It would be safer than coming back here later."

"Let's start making piles of things to take, sorted by priority," Dennis suggested.

The group stacked bags full of oats, chicken feed and diatomaceous earth near the front door. They also gathered all sorts of equine medical supplies including antibiotics, vaccines, skin remedies, and syringes. The feed store even had a few non-digital thermometers. Boots, socks, gloves, clothes, coats, and chaps got thrown on the pile too.

"Hey, look at these," Kelly said as she threw three pairs of Ditsy-Dots rain boots on the pile. The boots had polka dots and horses on them.

"Lynn, Mom, and I will have dry feet in high style."

"Let's get all of these seeds and this hand pump too," Dennis said. "What about this woodburning stove?"

"It's too heavy," Kelly said.

"I know," Dennis said, "but if we had room, I'd take it."

"If we had room we would take the whole stinking store," Kelly shot back. "Grab all the horse tack you can. It looks like we will be horse-powered for a while."

The group added to their piles: galvanized buckets, axes, hurricane lamps, lamp oil, candles, horse shampoos, cleaners, come-alongs, ratchet straps, bolt cutters, fireplace matches, tarps, rolls of plastic, duct tape, and rope.

Dennis brought several cast iron pans and some Dutch ovens to the front of the store. "We've already got some of those at the ranch, Dennis," Kelly said.

"I know, but it isn't my plan to stay with you forever. There's a lot of people in those small houses and lots of mouths to feed. I don't think Jose is thinking about staying forever either. This stuff will be hard to come by and a necessity if we strike out on our own," Dennis said as he added hand grinders to the pile.

Kelly cocked her head to one side. "What, you guys don't like being in Sunflower with us?"

"That's just it, Kelly," Dennis said without stopping his work. "It's *your* place. I don't see us leaving anytime soon, though."

"Over here," Jose called. He held up a chainsaw. "This thing might still work if it had gas and oil, and we've got plenty of that in the stalled cars. I bet some of the other small engines work too. Anything without electronics should run, like this water pump; it's got a starter rope. These generators have starter ropes, but I bet their voltage regulation circuits are shot," said Jose. "Let's take a few of these engines. I'll find something for them to do."

Rich and Kelly helped each other carry two water pumps, two chainsaws and a generator to the front, each time checking on Dennis.

Kelly heard glass breaking in the middle of the store. "What's up!"

"It's okay," Jose yelled. "I just smashed a glass case to get knives and multi-tools."

"Get a few, but let's wrap this up," Kelly called back.

It took a few minutes, but everyone brought the last of their treasures up to the front.

"Jose, you got a new knife?" Dennis asked. "A bit large for gutting chickens, don't you think?" He didn't give Jose a chance to answer. "If you ask me, like father, like son."

Jose just smirked.

"I think we should be out of here," Kelly said. We aren't going to get all of this back to Sunflower on our cart. Maybe we could hide some of the bigger things and come back for them."

"But what should we leave?" asked Dennis.

"Leave a few of those huge bags of oats and some of that chicken feed, but take the dried corn, that may be our only grain crop. We can get by without this pile too," Kelly said, motioning to a stack of things that had been put in the "contingent upon room" pile.

"I saw an electrical substation a little north of here," Rich said. "Bet people won't be looking in there for food. We can put a couple of these padlocks on it after we stash the stuff."

Rich picked up some padlocks and a cargo net. "We'll use this to secure the load," he said, holding up the net.

"Let's pack this stuff up and get it to the electrical station. We'll come back for the essentials, Kelly said. "Who wants to stay and guard this stuff and who wants to go?"

"I'll stay," said Dennis. "It's gotta be safer here than out there on the streets."

"Okay, Dennis, if you're sure," said Jose.

Rich got Traveler and hooked him up to the cart while Jose, Dennis and Kelly loaded it.

Dennis took up a concealed position inside the store as the others left. The stash team disappeared around a small hill.

Rounding a corner, a substation came into sight. The fenced collection of formerly battleship-grey metal boxes and cylinders sat blackened and torn open by explosions of the huge power transformers that lay inside the fence. Overhead, broken power lines and metal scaffolding dangled in twisted shapes. The high barbed-wire-topped fence surrounding the substation seemed to be partially intact. No one was in sight as they came to the gate. A quick snip with the newly acquired bolt cutters dropped the padlock to the ground. Within the compound, a set of large storage units was located. Second and third snips of the cutters laid the lockers open.

"This will do nicely," Rich said. "Move the equipment out to make room for our stuff." Rich and Traveler brought the cart up to the locker doors, and the group went to work moving supplies.

"I can't believe the damage to this place," Kelly said, looking around.

"There was a massive power surge," Jose said. "Look, the transmission wires are melted together. The transformers' circuit breakers couldn't trip fast enough or were overwhelmed by the flow. It must be like this all over town. Hell, who knows, it could be like this all over the country."

"From what I could tell, most of the transformers in Mesa exploded," Kelly said." It's been days and no one has come to help. I still haven't seen a single airplane."

After a few minutes, all of the items were stowed in the electrical compound. The group had bundled them in tarps. Rich secured the outer fencing with his three shiny, new padlocks. "I wouldn't count on any of this stuff being here when we come back. All we can do now is hope that no one saw us stash it."

"Let's get back to Dennis and get the rest of our stuff," Jose said. "I'd like to get out of town. Do you think we will make it home tonight?" Jose directed his question to Kelly.

"It's going to be a long haul for the horses with that cart," Kelly said. "We have quite a bit of elevation on the way home. If we switch them out often, it's a possibility."

"I was hoping to get home. A night on the desert doesn't seem very appealing and I'm feelin' sorry for Lynn. You know her mom's dead and now she's worryin' about her dad. It would be nice to get him back to her tonight," said Jose.

"Yeah, and I'm anxious about Jared too. My mom's a hell of a nurse. She saw plenty of wounded in Vietnam, but infections are tricky. We'll know something tomorrow."

The three companions started back to the feed store. As they got closer, the roads seemed deathly quiet.

Gunfire erupted.

"What the hell?" Kelly shrieked.

"It's near the feed store," Rich exclaimed, kicking Buckskin in the flank, urging him to run. "Dennis!"

Hokey lunged after Buckskin without any urging from Jose.

Kelly struggled to maintain control of Traveler. If she let the horse have his rein downhill at high speed, she chanced losing control of the wagon and killing them both. The stallion, determined to be with the herd, reared up, whinnying and snorting, fighting Kelly's restraint.

Hooves thundered on the pavement and sparks flew from their shoes. The two men rounded the corner in time to see six gunmen charging the store, firing their weapons. One of the attackers fell to the ground just outside the front door. Blood stained the sidewalk where he lay.

Jose and Rich grabbed their long guns from their scabbards while dismounting. Both ran crouched toward the store. Taking advantage of surprise, they knelt behind a door frame. Each chose a human target and fired. Double-ought buckshot exploded from Jose's gun, throwing his foe to the floor. Two 5.56 mm rounds slammed into Rich's target. The gunman began to turn slowly toward Rich, but was unable to complete the turn. His knees gave way and he dropped to the ground. One bandit dove for cover. The other two turned toward the front of the store, firing wildly. Jose and Rich had the advantage of time and position. They each sighted their second targets and fired. The rounds flew straight and true. "Five of six down," Rich whispered. "One to go. Load your gun full. Did you see Dennis?"

"No," Jose murmured, "but our last guy dove to the left."

"I'm coming up," Kelly whispered.

Jose scampered behind a long, cash-register counter running along the front wall. He reached into his pocket and fumbled, loading shells into his Remington. Rich crouched behind a display of goat feed on the left and motioned Kelly toward Jose behind the counter.

"We think we've shot all but one," Jose whispered.

Rich held up his finger before his lips, signaling everyone to be quiet. He scanned the store before tapping his ear, indicating he heard something, and then pointed into the aisle on his left.

Footfalls from the left receded toward the rear. Rich crawled quickly to the aisle's entrance. He saw the attacker pass rapidly behind a display of bottles, headed toward the bulk feed section in the back. Kelly rose quietly to peer over the counter, AR-15 at the ready. Quiet descended over the store. She could hear Jose's panting near her. She got his attention and motioned that she would go right while he covered the middle of the store. Together they moved silently down the aisles.

A barrage of gunshots erupted from the back of the store. Jose and Kelly dove for cover, peering around the corner. They listened as Rich's heavy footsteps thundered to the rear of the store. Suddenly the shooting stopped, as quickly as it had begun.

Kelly saw Rich peek around his corner. She motioned to him to hold his position and cover her. With her rifle ready to fire, Kelly "cut the pie" of the opening to the feed area, moving slowly with her weapon in a semicircle around the corner. The gunman lay sprawled in the middle of the floor in a still-forming pool of blood.

"Dennis, are you okay? Dennis, answer me!" She frantically scanned the large, barn-like space. Sacks of all kinds of feed were stacked on pallets, and high piles of baled hay surrounded her. No response. The silence was deafening and she grew more panicked. She glanced hopelessly at Jose and Rich.

"We'll find him," Rich assured her.

"Dennis!" Kelly yelled again. Her eyes drifted to the man lying on the floor. Blood still flowed from his wound. His outstretched hand nearly touched the grip of his pistol. She scanned the area for threats, then ran to him, knelt down and picked up his gun. She moved closer and checked his pulse at the neck. *Are the other gunmen still alive?* Kelly wondered.

"Rich, Jose, go check the other shooters. Secure their weapons and make certain they aren't a threat. This one is out of action." They went back toward the front of the store.

Kelly thought, *The gunman had been facing the hay stack to her right*. She eyed the high pile of bales. There was a stairway of sorts, made by removing the bales from the square stack. Nothing looked out of place. She moved cautiously to the side of the stack. "Dennis!" Then she saw him. He was lying on his back, rifle at his side, eyes open and staring at the ceiling. "Dennis!" Kelly screamed, voice shrill, tears coming to her eyes. She scrambled to his side, then dropped to her knees. Dennis blinked and slowly looked at her.

"Oh, I hurt... everywhere," Dennis groaned.

She breathed a sigh of relief and dropped to her knees beside him. "You better," she chastised him. "You scared me to death. Don't move. Let me take a look at you." She began the same quick field assessment she had used during the war. "What happened?"

Dennis tried to sit up, but Kelly put one hand on his forehead, holding his head still. "Don't move your neck. Does it hurt?" She put her free hand gently behind his neck.

"Nope."

"Does it hurt when I move it side to side or up and down?" she asked, moving his neck very gently.

"Nope."

"Okay then, slowly, try moving it on your own and see what you think," Kelly said.

"Everything seems to move okay," Dennis said, slowly pushing himself up into a sitting position. "I was climbing that pile backwards as fast as I could go, shooting as I went. I must have topped it and kept on going. Did I get him?"

"Yeah, you got him alright. We saw you defending the fort. Good timing on our part, huh?" Kelly asked.

"I didn't know I could shoot a man," Dennis said.

"I'm sorry you had to do that, but you've got to get up, we have to get going before anyone else decides they want what we've got." Kelly helped Dennis to his feet and together they navigated around shattered glass and pellets of dog food to the front of the store.

Jose and Rich had two of the injured gunmen propped up against the wall. One had a flesh wound to his right arm and the other had been shot through-and-through the left leg. One was pleading for his life, the other just crying.

"We aren't going to kill you," Rich said.

"We didn't mean to hurt anyone," the least hurt said. "We were just defending ourselves."

"Didn't look like you were defending yourselves. We saw six guys charging the store. What a waste of human life," Rich said. He spat on the ground in disgust. "There's plenty in here for us and all of you too. Now your buddies are dead and for what? You kids have been playing too many damned video games."

"Please, just let us go," the youngest pled, tears streaming down his face.

"Oh, we aim to let you go, but you're done shooting at people," Rich said.

"You take our guns mister, and we're as good as dead," the other kid said.

"Should have thought about that before you rushed poor Dennis here," said Rich. "If we give 'em back, you're just as likely to shoot us as not." He motioned toward the west. "Now, get on out of here while I'm still inclined to let you leave."

The kid with the flesh wound helped his leg-shot buddy stand, and they hobbled off.

"I hate this," Rich said. "Scrapping like thugs for things we all need."

Everyone else was silent.

The trip home was a long one. The horses fared the worst, but Kelly made sure they were rotated off the cart every so often. That meant that time had to be taken to unharness and harness the animals, which considerably slowed their progress. The small band pushed steadily on to avoid the vulnerability of stopping for the night. The horses pulling the cart set a slow, monotonous pace that the others naturally fell into. The clomping of their hooves echoed through the canyons. As darkness fell, the temperature plummeted, giving everyone a second wind. They did not see any other travelers on the road home; if there were any, they were probably all camped for the night, if they had even made it this long.

Everyone rode quietly, peering into the night in case of an ambush and privately pondering the events that had turned their worlds upside down.

Chapter 7

The group got in about 9 p.m., as measured by the grandfather clock. It had been Emma's father's and his father's before him. Dennis stopped, opened the glass face and adjusted the hands to his watch's time. He wound the clock, then went on to the kitchen.

"How did the trip go?" Jared asked from the couch as Kelly came through the front door. Someone had stacked pillows so that he was sitting at a forty-five degree angle, and his shoulder was supported with more pillows and blankets.

Emma interrupted, placing the shirt she was mending on the end table beside her. "You can tell all of us while you eat. I made dinner, hoping you would make it in. I'll reheat it." She got up and headed for the kitchen.

"How are *you* feeling, Jared?" Kelly asked softly. She pulled the ottoman over near the couch and sat just out of his reach.

"Sore today," he answered, forcing his shoulders back slightly until he winced. "Hoping for a better day tomorrow, though. It's good to see you home safe."

Kelly smiled, "Good to see you too. I worried."

"No need to worry about me. I'll be as right as rain in a week."

She smiled. "Well, a week may see you off that couch, but I'm not sure a week is going to get you back to where you were."

"Oh, ye of little faith," he said with a playful frown.

Kelly leaned forward.

Jared wrinkled up his nose and gave a good sniff. "I wouldn't come any closer if you want me to live."

Kelly cocked her head to the side and raised one eyebrow.

"You smell of road dust and horse, but you're still a beautiful sight."

"Bet you say that to all your cowgirls," she said, sitting back up straight, suddenly feeling self-conscious.

"Only the pretty ones."

"Do you know any other cowgirls?"

"No, not really. I only moved here two years ago. I think one of the court clerks has horses. I haven't ridden since summer camp, when I was thirteen."

"Summer camp? Where?"

"Michigan. Crabapple Lake, over on the west side. The nights were heaven. The fireflies made the woods sparkle at night. We used to catch them and put them in baby food jars to make our own personal lanterns."

"Did you go every summer?"

"Most summers, when Mom and Dad could scrape up the money or I could raise it myself. They liked me gone because they both liked to drink. Sometimes the camp money got used for booze before I could go. If they drank the camp money, they'd just leave me at home alone; nobody watched me."

"I'm sorry." Kelly paused, thinking of what to say next. "I didn't mean to pry."

"You're not prying. A lot of kids have crappy parents. That's probably what pushed me toward police work. When the police came to our house, they were nice to me. Maybe I was wanting to make a difference, but I'm not quite the social worker type."

"Noble of you, Mr. Malloy."

"I don't know how noble, but at least my folks' lifestyle taught me not to drink or do drugs. When you see what it does to people, you either fall into it or run away from it."

"Did you have grandparents?"

"I remember my mom's parents when I was small, say up to five or six, but after that they seemed to fall away. We moved a lot, apartment to apartment, trailer to trailer. We would stay 'til we got evicted for my folks' loud fights or not paying rent. I never knew my dad's parents." He appeared thoughtful. "Shoot, I'm not sure my *dad* knew my dad's parents."

Kelly sat upright on the ottoman, stretching her shoulders." We all know that stuff goes on but I, for one, was sheltered from most of that. I had a girlfriend in fourth grade whose dad used to drink and yell—maybe even hit her, I don't know. I'd gone somewhere with her and her mom in the car. We got back to her house and her dad had been drinking. He came out of the house screaming and yelling. I used to see my friend at school after that, but was too scared to go over to her house anymore."

"Yep, that was *my* house too. I'm glad to be out of that now, on my own. I've been out for ten years, since I was fifteen. Took me a long time to fit in. I have a few friends now, you know, other deputies. They understand a cop's life."

She stared at him, unrelenting in her gaze. "Can you talk to them? I mean, really talk to them?"

"We watch sports. They drink beer." He readjusted his arm on the pillow. "We don't really talk. I guess I never really learned how to be a good friend."

"That can change."

"I don't know—can it? If you miss all that as a child, can you learn to be a good, friend, husband, father for that matter?"

"I think you've got what it takes," Kelly said. She leaned forward again and laid her fingertips on his forearm. "Let's get you well, then find out." She smiled briefly, then stood. "I'll be back, I'm going to go get washed up. My stomach is growling. The guys are up at Rich's place cleaning up and they'll be back soon hungry as bears; I don't want to hold up the works. Can we continue this later?"

"I'd love to." He closed his eyes and sank back deeply into his pillows. "I'd love to."

\*\*\*\*

A few minutes later, smelling of soap and perfume, Kelly returned to the living room to find Lynn talking to Jared.

"Time to get up," Kelly announced. She helped Jared swing his legs off the couch and get into a full sitting position. Next, she stood to his right facing forward, bent at her knees, and lodged her forearm snugly in his right armpit. Lifting, she said, "Up." The attempt was only partially successful. Jared came up a couple of inches, then flopped back down. "Ugh," he said upon landing. Lynn stepped to his other side just in case she was needed, but wondered where she could hold on. She didn't dare lift him by his bad arm.

"Guess I wasn't ready after all. Try it again," Jared said determinedly.

"Okay, here goes. UP," said Kelly. "Ahhh, that's it."

Jared stood, not quite straight up, but *up* nonetheless. Taking short, tentative steps, he said, "Kelly, this young lady"—he tipped his head toward Lynn—"stepped into your nursing shoes while you were gone. Seems now I have two of my three nurses hovering about. I appreciate all of this attention, but I'm not going to die on the way to the kitchen."

Jared suddenly listed toward Kelly and she leaned into him firmly, propping him up.

"We know, we know," she said, giving an exaggerated sigh and grunting, as if bearing his weight were arduous. She leaned her face in toward his so closely, she could feel the warmth radiating from his cheek.

Emma had placed Jared's new favorite chair, the one with the armrests, at the kitchen table for a late dinner. Kelly and Lynn helped Jared ease into it.

"Thank you, ladies."

Everyone sat crowded around the table as the meal was served.

"You mean we get to eat *again*?" Jess scooped a huge mound of mashed potatoes out of the bowl in the center of the table.

Emma cleared her throat. "Yes, but *please* save the lion's share for those who haven't eaten any dinner yet." She narrowed her eyes only half-teasingly and glared at Jess.

Jess seemed to take the hint. He knocked half of the scoop back into the bowl, showing just a hint of remorse.

"Thank you," Emma said approvingly.

"What happened in town?" asked Jess. "No one has told me anything. I wish I could have gone," he said, speaking quickly, not giving anyone time to respond.

"Okay, okay, be patient," said Jose. "I thought we should wait to tell the story 'til everyone could hear it at the same time, instead of having to repeat ourselves. We were lucky to get the parts and other supplies. I don't think we could have done it if we had waited one minute longer. Just about everything in town had been cleaned out and people were willing to fight and kill for stuff already."

As Jose relayed the tale of their adventures, Jess looked to his father with pride, but Lynn was visibly pale.

Dennis noticed her fear. "Come here, sweetheart," he said, pulling Lynn's chair closer to his. He held her hand. Lynn stifled a sob and leaned into Dennis's arm, looking down at her lap.

"How was the highway shopping, Jess?" Dennis asked, diverting the conversation. "We passed some trucks that you had unloaded on the way back."

"Great. Bill Johnson, the 'freeway boss', as we call him now, says that we're done," Jess said. "We put everything in his barn. The whole town is getting together to divide it up at about one o'clock tomorrow. We'll have to take the cart. We won't get it all home in one load either." His faced beamed.

"Sounds like you had a pretty good day," Kelly said.

"We sure did," said Jess. "There were two trucks along *our* stretch of road, about five miles. They had already been broken into, but had a lot of good stuff still left. We had to make three trips with the buckboard. Lots of it was food. Most of it is on pallets that had plastic wrap around them. We didn't take things like toasters or cameras, but there was everything you could imagine. We got about three or four hundred cans of tomatoes off one truck. We got so many cans that we thought we would break the wagon. Some of the bread and bananas and stuff were already stinking. One truck had a bunch of meat and it was rank," Jared scrunched up his nose, "but we still got the other food. My muscles are sore, but it really was kind of fun. It was like shopping without paying. Bill's going to post a guard, several of them, down at the barn tonight."

"Did you see anybody else on the road?" Kelly asked Lynn, trying to include her in the conversation.

Lynn looked up, pressing her lips together tightly as if trying to gather the strength to speak. "Yep, and we shared things off the trucks when people came up." She spoke softly at first, then built up steam. "There were only a few folks, like eight or ten of 'em, and they couldn't carry that much. A couple took food away in boxes. They were going to have a hard time getting the cans open, so we showed them how to rub the end of the can on the pavement until the metal wore away. We learned that in CAP. Some of the stuff was produce, like oranges and apples, so we gave that out first because we knew it would go bad quickly if it wasn't eaten. The potatoes were still good, too. Everybody was pretty friendly."

"Sure they were—you were handing out food and water," Rich said.

"We found water bottles, sports drinks and that mocha coffee stuff too. I know you really like that, Dad." Lynn looked up at her father and smiled at him for the first time since Jose had started the story about the trip.

"Should we all go to the divvy in Sunflower tomorrow?" Emma asked.

"Maybe," Jess said. "I'm sure everyone will have different ideas about what is important, if we get a choice."

"I think Jose and I should stay and fix the well so we don't have to haul water with that torpedo," Rich said emphatically.

"We'll have to sort the things we got in Fountain Hills first thing in the morning and get 'em off the cart," said Kelly. "We went clothes shopping, Lynn," she said, grinning. "I picked up some of your favorite footwear at the feed store."

Lynn rolled her eyes, knowing this would not turn out well. She smiled, tipping her head and batting her eyelashes dramatically. "Yes, I've always wanted a John Deere hat and some rubber boots."

"Funny you should mention rubber boots; I picked out the cutest pairs of Ditsy Dots boots with polka dots and horses on them, just for us," Kelly said, matching Lynn's expression and tone. "We might need them for mucking out the barn," she cooed. Lynn wrinkled up her nose in mock disgust.

"Look, Jared's asleep," Emma pointed toward Jared, who had put his head on the table and was now breathing heavily. "It's probably because of all those pain pills."

"I'll take him to bed," Kelly offered.

"No, leave him there. I'll help you later," said Emma.

"Well, it sounds like Bill's barn is full," Rich interrupted. "Thank the Lord. But I have to tell you guys something. Now I know you're staying, it's a good time to share my secret."

Rich spoke in a softer volume, put both of his arms on the table, and lowered his head, like in the old-time movies when the villain was going to give secret instructions to the other bandits.

The others mimicked his posture as they waited to hear what he had to say. The sight made Kelly giggle.

"I've been keeping stuff for an emergency for years," Rich began. "My old church taught me to keep a year's supply of food and other necessities. When I was younger, I didn't see the need. It seemed that it took all of my money just to keep food on the table for my family, but these days, I've got a pretty good store of provisions. I've also got a few extra ham radios and some other electronics in insulated metal trashcans in case of EMP or solar storm."

"No way! Do you think it's safe to bring the radios out?" Jose asked.

"I've been checking for radioactivity with the dosimeter. This thing changes color if radiation levels are high, and it hasn't changed. It's been a few days now. If this is from a solar storm, it should have passed by now. I'm sure other ham operators have radios stashed, too. There's a government command center buried at the Papago National Guard facility in Phoenix that should be transmitting. Shortwave broadcast stations ought to be transmitting too. I'd like to start listening to see if we can find out how widespread this is. Jose, maybe we can talk to your wife in Iowa, wasn't it?"

"My dad is in Utah and he's a ham radio operator too. Do you think we could try to reach him?" Kelly asked anxiously. I don't know if he put any radios in trashcans, but my dad has always been the prepared type."

"We'll give it a try," Rich said with a smile, "but the well's got to be our first priority. Once we get that finished, I'll set up the radio and antenna."

"Dennis can work with me on the well tomorrow, and you can get the antenna up and running," Jose said. "There may be Civil Air Patrol radios in operation as well. I think it's important that we make contact with others trying to get things fixed."

"Water has to be our first priority, then food," Rich said sternly. "We also need to go to that meeting in town. Tomorrow we should all be on either the fix-it crew or the moving crew."

There were dozens of tasks to be done and they made their plans with equal amounts of excitement and trepidation. They spent another half hour talking quietly about supplies and carrying on with life.

"Let's take stock of what we have," Emma said. "Rich, do you have a written list of your stores?"

"I do," Rich said. "I'll go get it."

"Not tonight—I was thinking that I have a pretty good idea of what's on my shelves, but not a good list," Emma said. "Jared can help me take inventory by writing stuff down when we get a chance. I have a lot of food canned from the garden and also cases of food from the store that I bought to save money. I never intended to live solely on the food in my pantry. I would have stored differently had I known this was coming. I'm not sure I have a good idea what can be put together to make meals either." She sighed, overwhelmed at the thought. "I guess we'll have to figure it out as we go."

"I'll help you, Mama," Kelly volunteered. "We'll see what we have, what we get, and what we can grow, then start making meal plans."

"You both have large gardens and chickens," Jess said. "Rich has rabbits, too."

"Mom has about twenty head of cattle on the range," Kelly said. "Most people these days wouldn't know where to look or how to herd them. They should be okay for a few more days."

"They would have to have a gun to shoot 'em too," offered Rich. "You're right though, we need to expand all of those food sources. Our food will be touch and go for some time. A year's supply for me will last the eight of us about...." Rich paused to calculate.

"A month and a half," Jose said glumly.

Rich shot Emma an "Oh My God" glance as he realized the gravity of their situation.

"Yes, thanks, Mr. Engineer," Dennis said, shocked.

Rich continued, "We can't just eat all the eggs or chickens either. We need to make sure that the hens are sitting on eggs so that we can grow the flock. The same is true of the cows and rabbits. For the next while, we need to hunt game for our protein.

We can get jackrabbits and quail nearby. We'll have to go further from home, but can probably get mountain sheep and deer in the hills."

"The food we picked up from the trucks and town will help," Lynn said. The others nodded.

"It may look like a lot now, but just think about how many grocery bags we bring home every week. It's already looking like a lot less," said Rich.

"Dad and I keep 'Torah kosher,'" said Lynn. "That means that we follow the dietary law as given in the Bible. We don't follow the expanded dietary law from the Talmud, like orthodox Jews—things like keeping two sets of dishes for dairy and nondairy, or anything like that."

"What does that mean exactly?" asked Kelly. "I've noticed you and your dad don't eat some things, especially meat, and they are usually the same ones."

"We don't eat rabbit because they don't have hooves. We don't eat any animals that are shot. Animals must be slaughtered according to dietary law."

"That makes it tough for hunting for protein then," Rich said, staring at them slack-jawed.

"We can snare game birds and eat them if they are killed properly," Dennis said. "Lynn and I will have to be very aggressive in our snaring. That will allow the rest of you to eat rabbits or other game."

"I put my male and female rabbits together two days ago and reinforced all of the hutches," Rich said. "It takes them a month to have their young 'uns and another eight weeks or so 'til those are big enough to get much meat. We can just eat the males for awhile if we want to build their numbers."

"We need to expand the gardens as much as we can and make them produce longer," Emma said. "We can make tunnels from the plastic sheeting to extend the winter growing season and use shade cloth to protect the crops during the summer. Of course, we will need to let some of the plants go to seed at the end of the season. That reminds me. We need to sprout some potatoes and onions from the cupboard before they all get eaten. Some have already started to sprout without refrigeration."

"We can forage for plants, too," Dennis offered. "Most greens are edible and I know we can get prickly pear and saguaro fruit."

"The fruits are hard to work with because of all the spines and need lots of sugar to make them edible," said Emma.

"Mexicans have roasted prickly pear paddles for hundreds of years," Jose added. "I love them."

Lynn wrinkled up her nose.

"We can look through my native plants and herbs books for more ideas," Emma said. "My bookshelves are full of that kind of thing, but I must admit I haven't tried much of it."

"I wish we could fish from the creek," Jess said.

"The fish in that creek are mostly the size of a stick of butter," said Rich. "Next place to fish is ten-plus *hard* miles overland."

"Oh, I don't know," said Emma. "I've seen some decent fish come out of that stream, especially further down where it pools more."

The conversation meandered on for a while longer, exploring more possibilities for living life without being able to go to the store. Kelly watched as Lynn became more and more sullen and withdrawn.

"Let's get to bed," Emma said, picking up on Lynn's distress. "It's getting late. Everyone's got to be exhausted."

Emma got a candle from the kitchen counter and handed it to Lynn. She took it, then gave her dad a tight hug and wished him a good night. Kelly got pain pills for Jared and a glass of water from the kitchen sink. The men, except Jared, took the lamp for their walk back to Rich's house. Dennis removed the glass from the hurricane lamp and Lynn lit her candle from its flame.

Emma gently woke Jared. "Wake up, sleepyhead."

"Sorry," Jared said, lifting his head and wiping his mouth with his good hand to see if he had drooled. He hadn't. "What did I miss?"

"Nothing," said Emma. "You need your sleep and we'll fill you in on everything in the morning."

Kelly and Emma helped Jared into the living room. Emma quickly straightened the bedding on the couch, then Kelly helped Jared lie down.

Sitting down next to the couch, Kelly handed Jared his pills. He smiled at her. Kelly thought about how Jared never smiled at Emma when she gave him his pills. She smiled back and then took the glass when he had finished with it.

Kelly stood and gave her mom a kiss on the cheek, "Night, Mama. I'll get up and do that dressing change tonight."

"You don't need to," said Emma. "I'll do it. You need your sleep."

"No really, I'd like to. It won't take me long. The next one is due about 3 a.m., right?" Kelly asked. She already knew she was correct about the time, but Emma was very particular about the technique and the timing.

"Yes," said Emma. "'Night, baby girl, sleep well." She motioned to Lynn. "Come on, little one. Off to bed with you." Lynn held the candle in the hallway long enough for Kelly to make it to her own room.

\*\*\*\*

Emma and Lynn made their way to the bedroom they now shared. Lynn's bed was a small camp mattress next to Emma's bed. She got the nightshirt Emma had given her and went into the bathroom to change and wash her face, taking her backpack with her cosmetics and toothbrush in it.

By the time she returned, Emma was already snuggled in. She patted the bed next to her. "Come on up here. I think we should talk."

Tears immediately welled in Lynn's eyes. She sat down, but kept her distance. She had a cell phone in her hands she was rubbing repetitively.

"What's the matter, sweetie?" Emma asked. "I think I know, but I want to hear it from you."

"The damn thing won't work," Lynn said, motioning toward the phone. Tears and words started to flow. "I can't believe all of this has happened. Dad was talking at dinner about almost getting killed!" Her voice was one step below shrill. "How can he do that?"

"It's just something that happened. He didn't plan it that way."

"I'm so scared. He's all I've got."

"I know," Emma said.

"I can't cry in front of Dad. We both developed this 'being strong for each other' thing after my mom died. He was silent, so I was too."

"You can let it all out with me now, honey. It's okay to feel scared, mad, and cry if you want to. I think I'd give your dad another try too. He seems reasonable."

"Reasonable about other people's problems, maybe, but not about my mom." Lynn moved toward Emma and leaned into her shoulder. She started to sob uncontrollably.

Emma rocked back and forth, slowly holding the teen. "I remember holding Kelly like this when she broke up with her first boyfriend and when she wrecked her first car," she murmured. Emma thought about how trivial that all seemed now compared to Lynn's losses—the changing of the world as everyone knew it.

"This is never going to get back to normal," Lynn sobbed. "I won't be able to go to prom or graduate with my friends. Who knows, I might not even go to college. We could all end up starving to death."

"Now, now, honey," Emma said comfortingly, "things will never get that bad." She hoped her reassuring words were true.

They talked late into the night. Nothing was "settled," but emotions were given words.

Finally, after all of the tears had been spent, Emma said, "Goodnight, sweet girl," and blew out the candle.

Chapter 8

Kelly's internal clock pulled her into consciousness. *Was it 3 a.m.?* She fumbled for a minute, searching for the book of matches on her bedside table, and lit the smallest stub of a candle. She put on the large bathrobe at the end of the bed and proceeded through the living room to the kitchen to get her supplies. The grandfather clock read 2:40 a.m.

Kelly passed Jared on the couch on her way to the kitchen. He was sleeping fitfully, his rest erratic now that he was sleeping through a good part of the day due to pain pills. She gathered her equipment in the kitchen and returned to Jared's side, setting the tray on the floor. Maybe she should light another candle. *The one I'm holding is so small he'll barely see me,* she thought. What if he woke up abruptly, startled, and couldn't tell who it was? Police officers were known to come up off the bed swinging—or was that soldiers? Maybe that was only in the movies.

Kneeling next to the couch, she laid her hand ever so gently on his shoulder, taking the chance. Jared didn't rouse. Again, she laid a hand on his shoulder and shook a little this time. Still no movement. For a split second, a thought erupted in Kelly's head. *He's not dead, is he?* She couldn't tell in this light. Looking down she saw, starting at the corners of his mouth, the slightest grin begin to creep across Jared's face. She leaned back and exhaled. "That wasn't funny, Mr. Wise Guy!"

"I'm sorry. I wanted to see what you would do."

"I know what I *should* do," Kelly said in a tone that could only be described as scolding.

"Please sit down. I'm sorry; it's not as funny as I had planned." He shifted a bit, giving Kelly room to sit next to him.

Immediately, Kelly shifted into nurse mode. Speaking softly so as not to wake the others, she said, "I'm going to change your dressing."

Jared reached up and took Kelly's hand. He raised it slowly to his lips and kissed it softly. She pulled her hand back, but did not take it out of Jared's grasp. She was used to attention from all of her injured Marines and had spent several years resisting their advances. During her training she was told how vulnerable these guys were, having been injured and away from wives and girlfriends. Other nurses Kelly had known had gotten into circumstances with patients that had cost them their reputation, respect, and in one case, the nurse's commission.

"What's the matter?" Jared asked. "Don't you like me?"

Kelly peeled the bandage from his shoulder, making him wince. "I think you know."

"Then what is it, a boyfriend, a lover? Ow! that hurts. Be gentle, would you?"

"I'm being as gentle as I can, and no, nothing like that. I told you I wasn't attached. It's just that you're my patient and... "

Jared held her gaze until she finally looked away, uncomfortable under his scrutiny. The silence was palpable until he finally broke it.

"So what we have is purely professional?" He shook his head when she refused to answer. "I respect professionalism as much as the next guy. Cops, like me, and nurses, like you, well, we don't have much beyond our honor, but Kelly, you and I are in a unique situation. Right now, we don't know what rules apply in this new world."

She stared at his leg as he spoke.

"I enjoyed our talks, and those didn't seem purely professional. Neither did our night in that cozy sleeping bag. Believe me, that night made this gunshot worth it." Kelly's eyes darted up to meet his gaze briefly, then looked away. "I've seen the way you look at me throughout the day. I thought—hoped—that maybe there was something more there."

"I would love for there to be more, but..."

"But what?" Jared said strongly. "Here we are living in the same house and it looks like we might be together for quite some time.," Jared spoke through his clenched teeth in a tone just more than a whisper. His voice softened a bit. "Besides," he murmured, taking Kelly's chin between his thumb and forefinger, he turned her head so that she was looking straight at him. "Besides, I think you are the most beautiful, smart and caring person in the world. I'm not going to be discharged in a few days and you are not being paid to take care of me. You didn't have to stop for me on the road."

Pulling her chin from between his fingers, she said, "I had no choice."

"I know. I think nurses and police officers are cut from the same cloth. I wouldn't have expected you to pass me by, and you wouldn't have expected me to pass you by, if you had been in my shoes. I have been watching you around the house. I love the way you help your mom and talk with Lynn, the way you teach her about nursing and cooking. I'm getting stronger each day. Today, I walked the hundred yards to the canyon road by myself. Granted, I had to sit a few times to rest, but I made it. I'd love if you went with me sometime, sometime soon, but not as my nurse. We can say your mom is my nurse if that makes you feel better."

Kelly smiled. She raised their joined hands to her lips and kissed his hand softly. "Yeah, okay, I'd like that." She looked calmly into Jared's eyes. "I just need you to know that I have issues I can't talk about yet."

"You mean about the fire?"

"No, about men, relationships."

"What, Kel?"

"Don't push me just yet, okay Jared? I'll have to tell you when I'm ready."

"I'll understand; just tell me now."

Kelly looked across the room at the lifeless wood stove, avoiding eye contact. She could feel tears start to well in her lower lids. "I can't, just know, I can't."

"I didn't mean to upset you, really. Come here," Jared said as he scooted further toward the back of the sofa, turning on his side to make room for her. "For old times' sake," he said as he lifted his blanket, inviting her in.

"I'll have to think about it. If I lie there I may never get up, and I'd *never* get your dressing done."

"I wouldn't mind," Jared said with a devilish grin. "You could do the dressing first, then lie down with me."

Kelly squinted slightly, thinking the proposal over. "What would Mom and Lynn say if they found us together?"

"We're grown adults. Surely your mom doesn't think that you've remained a chaste young thing throughout your military career?"

"It's just different for me. It's my mom's house and we're out here *on the couch*."

Jared didn't push any further. "I don't know what your issues are, but I will respect them. And Kel, I will respect you and your mom too."

Kelly smiled and finished changing the dressing, then sat holding his hand a little while longer. "You're tempting, Mr. Malloy, but tomorrow will be another busy day and it's late. She took her leave reluctantly. Jared watched her disappear into a soft pool of light down the hallway.

\*\*\*\*

Rich, Dennis, and Jose got up with the sun to start work on the windmill. They had a quick breakfast of oatmeal and coffee on Rich's little camp stove. They ate on the front porch and then started up the canyon. Jose carried a large tarp and a Sharpie marker. Rich had a large box of well parts. The dew made the quaking aspen leaves shine like gold coins in the light breeze of morning. The grass was damp and fragrant. The men walked side by side up the well-worn path through the little canyon to the West. Dennis thought how lucky they all were to have come together in this place. Rich pointed out Emma's healing herbs and a separate garden for seasoning herbs, as well as the rabbit hutch and chicken coop. Further up they passed a small barn and one of the corrals on their way to the windmill.

The windmill stood at the mouth of the box canyon where it received the wind as it was forced through the narrow channel. Fifty feet higher than Rich's house and seventy-five feet higher than Emma's, the well gravity fed both houses.

"With a day as nice as today, you would almost think the world wasn't falling apart," Jose said. The men stood for a few moments to drink in the serenity and beauty of the spot.

"You must be worried about your wife," Rich said. "I'm sure she's fine with her family."

"I can't worry too much about that right now," Jose said simply. When both men stared at him, he shook his head, the fear he tried to hide threatening to overtake him. He cleared his throat. "I really can't do anything about it. I need to be strong for Jess."

"I'm no preacher, like Dennis, but maybe you need to be less strong for Jess," Rich said.

Jose stood with a puzzled look on his face and thought about what was just said.

"I don't think so," he said. "It's the boy's mother we're talking about."

"Exactly. Your being strong makes Jess think you don't care about his mom or him."

Jose frowned in thought. Maybe Rich was right. Maybe he was hiding his feelings from himself and Jess. Somehow it was easier to bury himself in all of the work around the small ranches. He could deal with feelings later. Jose raised his gaze, set his jaw, and went about starting work.

The men's first task was to service and reattach the gearbox to the windmill. The gears changed the circular motion of the spinning wheel into the up-and-down motion of the pump pole. The pump pole, pump rod, and cylinder—the actual pump— needed to be serviced and reconnected too. Rich and Jose laid out the big tarp, then began ripping apart the gear box.

"Hey, Mijo," Jose said as he saw his son coming up the path toward him. "I'm glad you are here. Maybe we can teach you something about the workings of a well and a pump."

"Sure, whatever," Jess said, looking down at his feet, trying to amplify his disinterest.

Jose furrowed his brow, but then let it soften. Maybe he could couch it in a way that would capture Jess's attention. "You know, son, a well pump is similar to a pump on a car or on a plane, for that matter."

Jess looked up, expressionless, waiting to hear what his dad would say next.

"They all work on the principle of compression and expansion," Jose continued.

Jess bunched up his lip on one side of his mouth, put both hands in his jeans pockets, and walked slowly toward Jose and Dennis, still silent.

"Look here," said Jose, "we've got these parts laid out on the tarp, you know, the way we do with the SUV..." He didn't have to say anymore. Jess silently took the pieces from Jose and arranged them. He carefully drew an outline of each part and then made notes, on the tarp itself, about its placement and information they would need to get it back together. Jess put every nut, screw, and washer next to its corresponding part and drew arrows to show its placement. Soon, his frown had faded and he was joking and talking with the other men.

\*\*\*\*

The morning went smoothly and by the time the sun was getting high in the sky, Jose noticed Emma and Kelly out in the garden hoeing weeds, planting rows and harvesting vegetables. It wasn't long before Emma called, "Lunch in an hour."

Dennis stopped his task and stood upright, stretching his back. "Jess, help me fold the empty half of the tarp over the well pieces. We'll have to secure it all the way around with rocks to keep stuff from being blown away."

"As long as some stupid old cow doesn't come by and walk on it, it should be good when we get back," Jess said.

Dennis said, "Jess, your dad and Rich have agreed to stay here this afternoon and get this pump further along. I'll need your help if we're going to get all the food supplies hauled and stored."

"Stored where?" Jess asked. "The house seems pretty full."

Hey, Rich, does it freeze here in the winter?" asked Dennis.

"We get about ten to twenty nights a year in the thirties, but I know where you're going with that," Rich answered. "There's a cave up here a bit where we can put away the groceries. That should keep them from freezing and they will be harder to find if any thieves come calling. I'll show you."

Rich led the band further up the canyon. To their left was a small path that looked like it was made by deer or other wild animals. They made their way through some low bushes until they were at the canyon wall.

"It's right in here," Rich said, pointing to a hole at the base of the cliff. "It opens up pretty good once you get inside. We'll have to send two people in when we bring the supplies up here: one to pass the goods through that hole and the other to stack 'em. We can take turns. The work will be pretty slow going because whoever passes will have to lie on his back. I have some stuff in there already. I'll take a quick inventory before we put in anything new."

"Cool," Jess said. His eyes lit up and his voice became animated. "Can I go in?"

"Not now, son," Rich said. "You'll get your clothes all dirty. You'll have plenty of time in that ol' cave later. You'll be begging to get out of it," he said with a chuckle.

"Do you think we should keep some food at the house as a decoy stash?" Jose asked.

"Not a bad idea," said Rich. "It will be easier to use, too, if we store it closer to the kitchen. We don't want to be making regular trips up here to get stuff either. Our tracks would be too fresh and we would put wear on the trail."

"Let's get down to lunch," Dennis said. "The girls are probably wondering where we are."

\*\*\*\*

Emma and Lynn had a small lunch on the table when the men got back. The kitchen smelled heavenly. Emma scooped the last of the canned corned beef out of the frying pan when everyone sat down. A big salad and a bowl of green beans rounded out the meal.

"I'd have liked to have had a big batch of biscuits for lunch too," Emma said, "but I don't want to be using all of the propane for baking. It's too hot to fire up the wood stove in the house yet. The lettuce grows faster than I can pick it though, so have a big helping of greens."

"We live in Arizona, the land of sunshine," Dennis said. "I'll build you a rocket stove and a solar oven when I get a chance. I would have liked to have had some biscuits myself."

"I made a rocket stove at camp, remember, Dad?" asked Jess.

"That's a great idea, Mijo. It won't take us fifteen minutes to build if we can find some bricks."

"Oh, I've got some bricks at the side of the house, but it's not just the oven," Emma said. "We seem to have plenty of oil, but we're pretty short on shortening." Everyone chuckled. "It would be easier to make biscuits than bread, but without shortening the result would be pretty dissatisfying. Speaking of bread, Lynn told me that she usually bakes two loaves of bread and makes meals for the Sabbath on Friday mornings. We still have two loaves of bread, but we'll have to be thinking about when we should start making more. Our bread baking will have to be cut way back to save our flour stores. I hope we get more flour this afternoon from the trucks."

"Lynn is a great baker of challah," Dennis said, smiling.

"What's challah?" asked Jess.

Dennis looked over at Jess. "It's a braided egg bread that represents the manna that fell from heaven every day but the Sabbath. A double portion fell on the sixth day so that no work had to be done gathering manna on the Sabbath. We don't cook on the Sabbath, so we make meals in advance.

"Lynn and I did a little more preparation for tomorrow's meals," Emma said.

"Where's Kelly and Jared?" Rich asked.

"Oh, they'll be right along," Emma said. "Kelly is doing Jared's dressing change. Jared thinks he will be able to make it to town for the divvy this afternoon. I sure am pleased with how well his shoulder is coming along."

Kelly and Jared joined them directly. Everyone found somewhere to sit in the crowded little kitchen. The men told everyone how the well was going and that they expected to have it back together by evening if all went well. Everyone asked Jess and Lynn about what supplies they could expect to find in the barn down "in town" as they called it now. Dennis told everyone about building a solar oven.

Lunch was over in a flash. Jose and Rich went back up the trail to work on the windmill. Emma went with Dennis to hook Buckskin to the donkey cart. After the horse was harnessed, everyone else was ready to go to the divvy.

"Kelly, get my nurse bag there by the front door, would you?" called Emma as Kelly and Jared headed out the front door.

"Lynn, Jess, let's get a move on," Emma shouted and the two ran out the front door, letting the screen door slam behind them. The kids ran to the cart and scampered onto its bed as Kelly helped Jared along. When they reached the wagon, Rich helped Jared up by having him step onto his clasped hands. Kelly pushed him from under his good shoulder as Jess pulled him awkwardly onto the wagon. Dennis put both of his hands onto the deck of the cart and hoisted himself up. Emma drove the flatbed contraption. Kelly observed quietly, amazed at how easily they had fallen in together as a group.

The cart bumped down the road. Dennis watched with a smile on his face as Jess and Lynn laughed each time they were thrown into the air. Kelly happily sat glued to Jared, steadying him.

The wind rustled through the trees, water trickled down the stream bed in a fine ribbon, and the sun shone brightly, as it often did in Arizona. Emma pulled into the rutted driveway that led to the Johnson ranch. Dust swirled up from the path where every wheel and foot made contact with it. All of the Sunflower families were there, from what Emma could tell. Most came on foot, some by bicycle, and there were a few carts pulled by horses. There was even one doctor's buggy that the King family had spent countless hours restoring for use in Old West parades. That investment was certainly paying off now.

Emma's clan dismounted the cart from every side like ants exiting a hill. Jess ran toward Mr. Johnson and a few of the other men that were standing near the door to the red, good-sized pole barn.

"Hi, Mr. Johnson," Jess said.

"Hi there, boy," Bill said. "I was just telling old Cliff here how I hoped you were coming today. You sure were a great help out there on the road. A nice young man." Bill switched his attention to Emma. "Where did you come up with such a fine-looking group?"

Emma grinned in pride. "Bill, I'd like you to meet my daughter, Kelly. This is Jared, and you know Dennis. He's Lynn's father."

"Why, yes, I do and it's nice to see all of you. Dennis, you have a fine daughter. She's a hard worker and strong too."

"Thank you sir, I quite agree," Dennis said, putting his arm around Lynn's shoulders. Fatherly pride showed on his face, and Lynn beamed, keeping her gaze on her father.

Bill turned to face everyone gathered around the barn. "Our nice young men went to Fountain Hills and brought back piping," he said, pointing to the pile of PVC and coils of flexible tubing on the ground next to him. "Everyone in need, please meet here tomorrow morning at 0800, or as close as you can figure it, so we can make a plan and get it installed. We should all go in," Bill said, making a sweeping motion toward the barn.

The crowd proceeded toward the small door to the barn. There were no windows, and each person was momentarily blinded by the darkness. The floor was dirt and a dusty cloud rose from it as more and more people entered. Bill moved to the far side of the barn and pushed open a door, twice his height and ten feet long, suspended on rollers. Light flooded in, illuminating the entire barn. Pallets and stacks of goods were piled all around the perimeter. Gasps escaped from the neighbors who had not seen it before.

After a few minutes, when all had had a chance to take in the sight, Bill addressed the audience. "Now folks, a lot of good people have collected what we could find from the trucks on the roadway. We took what we thought might be useful with the intention of sharing it among those in our little community. Each family that was able sent someone to help. It is not our intention to split hairs about how much work was contributed. We want our hamlet to stay a tight-knit group. This means we will be divvying up our finds by the number of people in each family. Everyone gets an equal share despite what they may have contributed to finding this wonderful collection. Those who weren't strong enough to scavenge will be expected to contribute in other ways. We all have skills and it's time to put those skills to use."

He paused, glancing around the group to see if there were any objections. When no one appeared concerned with the allocation of goods, he continued. "One-of-a-kind items will be shared by the community. After all is said and done, we'll get working on a barter system so you will have a chance to trade items you don't think your family will use for items that others may want to trade. If anyone has a particular need, now is the time to speak up."

"We're going to need some blankets," Janet Nickels called out. "We usually use this place in the summer and weren't prepared to spend the winter here. If this power outage is permanent, heat will be a problem too."

"Okay," Bill said. "Anyone who can give the Nickels a hand, please meet them out by the corral fence after the meeting."

"Anyone else?" Bill asked. The room was quiet, so he proceeded. "Now, I think that most everyone is here. Anyone know if we're missing anybody?"

"Charlie Best isn't here," Bill's wife, Patty, said. Charlie was the diabetic that lived over the creek and kept to himself.

Ted Matherson spoke up. "I think the Branhams packed up and left yesterday for town."

"Anyone else?" Bill asked. The gathering fell silent. "Well, if that's all we have for missing persons, I'll turn the floor over to Dennis. He'd like to make an announcement." He stepped aside as Dennis moved forward.

"Thank you Bill, and thank you all for your generosity in accepting us into the community. My daughter, Lynn, and I will be holding a Bible study session tomorrow at ten in the morning. Normally, we would be at synagogue then, but one has to adapt to current conditions. You are all welcome. We'd like this to be a nondenominational service. We're just interested in meeting with others who choose to take time for the spiritual realm."

"What do you plan on studying tomorrow?" Patty called out.

"We put some thought into this today and after some discussion, we finally agreed that the place to start should be 'in the beginning,'" Dennis said. "Any takers?" Several folks spoke up and said that they would like to come.

"Let's have it here, where there is plenty of room," Patty said. "The boys could drag a few bales of straw in. We could turn it into a modified classroom."

"We'll see you here at ten tomorrow," Dennis said.

Bill retook the floor. "Okay, let's get busy. The Branhams leaving throws my count off. The way I have it figured, that leaves us with twenty-four souls. Let's leave their portion over there," Bill pointed to a corner. "We can trade from their items, which will mark the beginning of our first general store. The count of every item is on each stack of goods. We'll start here at the front and work our way around, dividing everything. If it doesn't divide evenly, put the remainders on the Branham's pile, or should I say the store pile. If everyone will help, we can get this stuff hauled out to the driveway in no time."

After sorting the goods, Emma's group had the cart loaded with an eclectic mix of foodstuffs in cans and boxes. There were only three five-pound bags of flour. There were a few hardware and cooking items as well. The loaded cart waited in the driveway. Emma realized that even though the pile was large, so was their group.

Emma said to Lynn, "I think we should go by Charlie's house and check on him. He's a diabetic. We'll let the others get

Jared back to the house. I think this has all been a little much for him."

Jared protested, saying he was fine, but Kelly could see he looked tired. With a little rearranging of the load, everyone found a place to ride and headed back to the house.

As they walked, Emma took the time to teach Lynn about diabetes and insulin. Lynn listened intently as the pair made their way down the road.

"So you mean he will die without the insulin and you can't make any for him?" Lynn stressed the word *die* in that whiny teen voice she could put on.

"That's right, but maybe we can get some insulin and other drugs before then. The government should have stockpiles somewhere, I suppose," Emma said wistfully, with little conviction.

"I hope you're right," Lynn said a little breathlessly. "I was worried about food, but I guess others have it worse. I thought insulin had to be refrigerated?"

"It should be, but it's not as fragile as some would make out. If it's kept at room temperature, the manufacturer states it will last for twenty-eight days. I have a feeling it's actually quite a bit longer. Insulin does have preservatives in it, but when the proteins start to break down, it will become less and less effective."

A few minutes later, Emma and Lynn walked up to the gate in front of the Best house. Charlie's old dog stood slowly, stretching, then wagged his tail and let out a few happy barks from the porch.

"Charlie?" Emma called.

Mr. Best appeared at the front door. "Howdy, Emma," he said in his methodical voice. Emma had never known him to talk any slower or any faster. He was dressed in a T-shirt and overalls. His greying blond hair was on the longish side.

"We didn't see you at the Johnson's and thought we should stop by."

He came fully out through the screen door and settled into a lawn chair on the porch, putting a hand on his dog's head and patting it. The dog panted with what could be described as a dog smile on his face.

"Well, I ain't dead, yet," Charlie replied with a forced chuckle.

"Bill was planning on using his wagon to get your share of the scavenged food to you," Emma said.

"That's very kind of him, but I'm pretty well set. Other folks need that food more than me. Just let Bill know he can divide up my share with the rest of you."

"That's mighty kind of you, but you don't know how long this might go on."

"Like I said, I'm well off. Let's leave it at that."

"I'll let Bill talk to you about it. Is there anything we can do to help since we're here?"

"No, I've got things under control. Thanks for offering." Without any further fanfare, Charlie rose and went into the house, leaving the dog where he sat.

"Pretty rude, don't you think?" Lynn asked.

"No, that's just Charlie's way," Emma replied. "Likes to be self-sufficient."

They started their walk back to the barn. "That's the Branham's place over there," Emma pointed to a red house across the creek. "We'll have to see if they're back up here in a couple of days, or if they have gone for good."

"Gone where?"

"I don't know—maybe they had a house back in the city? Maybe they had family they needed to take care of or something."

"Could be. I hope... " Lynn stopped and looked puzzled. "I don't know what I hope. I was going to say that I hoped they made it back to the city okay, but then I was going to say I hoped they made it back here okay. Which one do you think is best?"

"No way to tell, Lynn. I'm here and here seems okay right now. From what I've heard of the city, it *doesn't* sound okay."

The two walked on. After some time, Kelly and Jess came bumping along atop the cart, heading back toward the Johnson's.

"Dad and Dennis got the well fixed!" Jess called, obviously proud of their accomplishment. "No more latrines. We can flush in comfort right into the septic tank."

"Now that's some of the best news I've heard in ages," Emma rejoiced. "Did you get the stuff put away?"

"Nope, just unloaded out front. We left everybody else home to haul it in, except Jared of course. We high-tailed it back here to get you and the rest."

Emma glanced up at the rapidly setting sun. "We still have two more loads to fetch. *Dang,* I'm tired." Her face looked drawn.

Chapter 9

The morning light bouncing off the steep mountainsides woke Kelly. She groaned and rolled over, not quite ready to face the day, but rose and dressed in her best cowhand outfit. She brushed her long blond hair, putting it into a loose ponytail at the nape of her neck.

The house was quiet. She stole from her room and headed for the kitchen, but when she reached the living room, she was greeted by Jared's voice.

"Morning, beautiful."

"Morning yourself, han—huh, huh," she stopped before she could complete the word *handsome* and feigned a half-cough to cover the last syllable. "Did you sleep well?"

"I've slept on many couches in my time and this one is, by far, the most comfortable," he said. His response was too overly enthusiastic to be true.

"I know that couch, and you're full of it," she said as she watched him struggle stiffly into a sitting position.

"Yeah, it's your mom's house, I daresay you do."

"I'm sorry," Kelly said. "The sleeping quarters are a little tight around here at the moment. I'd say that you could go to the men's quarters shortly, but I don't think they have any better digs for you up at Rich's place." *Besides, I like having you here*, she thought to herself.

"The scenery is better here." Jared kept himself covered as he sat on the couch. He stretched gingerly and gave a big yawn. Kelly averted her gaze, worrying that the sheet might shift during such a maneuver. "Could you do a guy a favor and hand him his pants?"

Without speaking, Kelly got the jeans, plaid shirt and socks that lay on the end table and tossed them in a stack next to Jared. "I'll step out now." She smiled.

"You're welcome to stay," Jared said, raising an eyebrow.

Kelly ran her hand through her hair as she stepped into the kitchen.

Dressing as quickly as he could, struggling with every piece of clothing, Jared followed her. He walked up behind her and put his good arm around her waist. Sliding in closer, he nuzzled her neck. She stood still, holding a kettle of water over the sink.

"Take a walk with me, Kelly," he asked in a voice that was a little huskier than he had intended.

Kelly allowed herself to lean back into him, standing quietly for a few seconds, then wriggled from his embrace. She still felt a little uncomfortable about Jared's forwardness. On the other hand, it made her feel sexy and beautiful, the way she had with... she didn't let her mind continue. Jared's warmth drew her to him.

"I'd love to go on that walk with you," she said, "but let's have a little coffee and get that shoulder looked at first."

Kelly helped Jared off with his shirt. She lifted the dressings to find that his entrance wound was diminishing in size. It had a hearty ring of whitish scar tissue encroaching on a soft, healthy looking center. "Good, no drainage," she said.

"Now that's romantic."

"It is, if you're a nurse."

She cleaned both wounds with soap and water. The exit wound, on the back of the shoulder, had just the tiniest open area to one side of the quarter-sized scar. "These look really good. Your healing has been remarkable."

"Because I've had the three best nurses in the whole world, if you count Lynn, and I do," Jared said, smiling broadly. "If it looks so good, why does it still hurt so much? I can't move it worth sh—crap."

"You can swear, Mr. Malloy, if the situation moves you."

"No. No one else around here swears except maybe Rich, and he curtails it around the women. I'm not in a locker room; I can too."

"As you like. I'm not encouraging it, mind you." Kelly gave a quick grin, then went into patient teaching mode. "The sugar has been keeping the skin clean and allowing it to heal, but all of the underlying structures have to heal too. Your muscles, tendons, and whatever else that bullet ripped through will take longer to repair than skin. Having it in that sling has limited your motion. I'd say with a little time and some physical therapy, you should make a full recovery."

"Well, I should hope so," Jared said, his voice hearty. "There's a ton of work to be done around here and I have been a burden long enough."

"Don't be silly," Kelly said. "We all know why you haven't been able to help. I think everyone here is glad to know that we work as a team and that they won't be abandoned if *they* need help at some point."

Kelly took Jared's left arm and raised his elbow slowly until he winced. "Oh, sorry about that," she said. "I know it's sore. You can start stretching these muscles a couple of times a day. Once you have mobility back, we'll have to work on strength."

Kelly moved her left arm up and back as far as she could over her head, demonstrating full range of motion. She moved close to him and manipulated his arm into several different stretches, mimicking the physical therapists she had seen working with patients in the field hospital. Jared felt Kelly's breath on his shoulder, slipped his good arm around her waist and pulled her closer.

"I'll be running the physical therapy sessions around here, not you," Kelly said with the slightest hint of fake exasperation. She playfully pushed his arm away from her waist. "Now, put your bum arm up here so I can put your sling on."

"Y-e-s, n-u-r-s-e," he said, drawing the words out just to tease her.

Kelly folded a large, clean square of fabric into a triangle and then tied the two ends together at his neck, fashioning the sling. "Nice," she said, admiring her work. "I think you'll be out of that in a couple of weeks if you continue healing this fast and do your physical therapy."

The coffee boiled on the stove and was soon dispensed into two coffee mugs from the drain board.

"Now, let me tell you about your exercises..." Kelly said. She could tell that Jared was trying to pay attention to her therapy descriptions, but his gaze drifted from her mouth to her hair to her hands. It unnerved and thrilled her all at the same time.

"Yes, nurse," Jared said again as Kelly seemed to complete the lesson. "Now how about that walk you promised me?"

Without skipping a beat, Kelly stood and said, "Okay, I'm ready. Do you need anything besides your boots?" She had her hands on her hips, waiting for a reply.

The expression on Jared's face was one of surprise. "No, no, that should do it. Right now?"

"Sure, why not?"

Jared tipped his head to one side and raised his eyebrows. "Sure, why not?"

They both went into the living room, where Jared sat in the big wooden chair closest to the front door. Kelly got his newly acquired cowboy boots from the rug and slipped them on his feet, but she knew that it would take more effort to get them fully over his heels. She pulled and pushed without success.

Frustrated, she finally appraised the situation and mumbled, "Well, this won't be very lady..." She straddled Jared's leg facing his foot and taking the tabs on either side of the upper boot, pulled until she felt a pop as the boot slipped fully onto Jared's foot.

"Nice view," Jared said.

"Careful mister," Kelly shot back.

"Just the truth, ma'am, just the truth," Jared said in an exaggerated western drawl. Kelly laughed and then proceeded with the second boot.

After both boots were on, she excused herself. She slipped into the bathroom, brushed her teeth and conducted a final inspection in the mirror. She rustled her hair with her fingers until she thought it looked tousled enough to be sexy, then went to her room. Taking her gun from the nightstand, she wrapped the gunbelt around her waist, then fastened the buckle. The belt rested at the widest part of her hips, showing off her curves. The brown leather matched her cowboy boots perfectly. Kelly caught a glimpse of herself in the dresser mirror as she was leaving her bedroom and smiled confidently.

"I've always liked a filly with a nice revolver," Jared said, smiling as she reentered the living room.

By the time they left the small house, the sun was fully up and the day was warm, but not yet hot. Together they walked down the driveway, east toward the creek. Trees lined the drive and dappled the pair in filtered sunlight. Jared took Kelly's hand and gave it a squeeze.

"Do you think life will ever resemble anything like before?" Jared asked.

"It's hard to say. After seeing Mesa and Fountain Hills firsthand, it's hard to imagine *everything* going back to normal. I can't imagine living in town for even a few days in that condition."

"I'm a very lucky man," Jared said. He paused. "Just think about it, Kel. That gunshot should have become infected and killed me. Even if it hadn't, I would have been fending for myself in a city of four million people with a bad arm and no means of survival. Instead, I was whisked to this little paradise to be among people who have the skills and equipment to take care of themselves *and* me too. I won the evolutionary lottery—I get to live."

"Don't sell yourself short, mister. I know you're injured now, but your tactical knowledge may be very useful to our little group. We also need manual labor, and you can learn other ways to help. I'm not so sure that all of us put together have enough skills or supplies to make it through this, whatever this is. It's true we're better off than most, but our supplies won't last forever. We can't grow enough food in this"—Kelly searched for the words—, "semi-desert area to support eight people."

"Why not? We have water, gardens, rabbits and chickens, even cows. And look at these trees." Jared motioned to the towering sycamores.

"This canyon has a small trickle of water, about six inches across, almost year round, making it a desert oasis. I've loved this place since we camped here when I was a kid. I think that's why Mom bought up here; she liked it too."

"I can see why," Jared sighed contentedly.

"It's always been a struggle making things work here, though. We have two growing seasons, but they're short; we can only grow in the spring until it gets too hot for the plants to produce in June, and then again from late August until the first frost in December. The ground is very rocky and needs augmentation—you know, compost and fertilizer."

"I'm not sure we have much choice other than to make it work," Jared said. "Where there's a will, there's a way."

"I hope you're right."

They made their way down a steep bank into the nearly dry creek bed, lined with huge boulders fallen from the surrounding cliffs.

"Wow, look at the size of these things," Jared said, pointing at the boulders. "How did they all get in the creek?"

"Flash floods. When the monsoon comes, the rain rushes down the sides of these mountains, loosening boulders and pushing everything down into the canyon here. Our rocky soil repels water instead of soaking it up."

"Yeah, I've seen it and you do have some impressive storms," he agreed. "Growing up in Michigan, it all just soaked in. I thought it was like that everywhere."

"Summer, with its monstrous storms, is my favorite time of year," Kelly said, smiling. "I love the monsoons. The clouds explode in the afternoon into huge towers of white, and blue curtains of rain fall from their bottoms. You can see the thunderheads for miles and miles."

"You make it sound wonderful, but *I* equate the monsoons with calls for service. You know, alarm systems being set off, power being knocked out, water roiling in the roads." He grinned.

"True, but we need the moisture."

"Arizona is something else. I never could figure out why it only rains like that in the summer."

"The temperatures get so high here that it creates a basin of low pressure over the entire region. Humid air is literally *sucked* northward from the Pacific Ocean to the southwest, and the gulf of Mexico to the southeast."

"Yeah, I've noticed the humidity gets unbearable in July, then the rains start."

"In the afternoon, when we're about 105 to 115 degrees, hot columns of air rise off the desert floor, pushing the moisture into the higher atmosphere." Kelly made great sweeps with her hands skyward.

"That would account for the HUGE clouds with the flat bottoms."

"Yes, and it's colder the higher you go up. The vapor condenses into clouds, then pours rain."

"Wow, a meteorologist too—multitalented."

"All of us Arizona kids learned that stuff in grade school. Not being from here, you missed it."

Jared motioned for Kelly to climb onto a large boulder. It was as big as a VW Bug and had a flat surface where it had been sheared in half during its fall from the cliff above. Kelly climbed up first, then reached down to Jared and pulled him up.

The two stood there hand in hand, the light breeze blowing through their hair, leaves rustling above them. The morning was getting hotter and Kelly unbuttoned her long-sleeved shirt, revealing her tank top. She hunched her shoulders and eased the shirt down both arms.

"What's that?" Jared said, shocked to see the large bandage covering her right upper arm.

"War wounds."

His eyebrows furrowed into a concerned frown.

"I might have left out *some* of the details about the hospital fire." Kelly raised her eyebrows, gazed to the right and tried to look angelic. "It's nothing, just some scratches. Nothing as bad as yours, anyway."

"You wouldn't have that bandaged for this many days if it were just scratches."

"Okay, I'll tell you. No reason for secrets is there?"

"No, but you don't owe me an explanation, if you don't want to. I'm not prying."

"Of course not, we're friends." Kelly filled Jared in on all of the details of her "war wounds."

"You never told me you got hurt during all that."

"Didn't seem important at the time. Mom's looking after me, and they're healing. You had your own 'war wounds' to worry about."

"You're probably right. I wasn't in much shape to help, and I *would* have worried about you. I promise I'll start worrying about you now, though. Your trip to Fountain Hills the other day just about killed me, you know."

"It did?"

"Of course it did. I don't know why, Kel, but you mean more to me than you know. I can't explain it."

Kelly gave him a smile, then her face turned more serious. "There's something important I need to talk to you about, if we're ever going to be more to each other than just friends," she said. She closed her eyes and breathed deeply, summoning the courage to tell Jared about... Peter.

"Go ahead..."

"Jared," Kelly said pensively. "I *need* to talk to you about us—about me, I mean."

"Are you ready to share that? You don't have to." Jared turned his gaze away, but tightened his grip on her hand.

Without having to look him in the eyes, Kelly felt more free to speak. "I am," she said. She raised her face toward the sky, staunching tears, and stood silent for a few seconds. "His name was..." she began.

Jared cocked his head to one side; Kelly could see it out of the corner of her eye. He was asking the question, *was?* as clearly as if he had spoken it out loud.

"Was Peter," she started again. "He was a co-worker of mine—more than a co-worker—and he died."

Kelly looked up at Jared, who sat absolutely motionless and expressionless, waiting for her to continue.

"We were seeing each other, in Afghanistan, I mean—it was a 'deployment romance.' He was a corpsman, assigned to our clinic on a forward operating base, or FOB. It started innocently enough: close brushes while working in tight spaces, comments about my hair. I loved the attention, and then it just happened. One night, after a routine emergency and replenishment of a returning team's medical bags, he and I went to midnight chow at the DFAC. There were maybe ten people in the place and he started flirting with me, something I didn't expect. His confidence was a turn-on, and the fact that he was *way* junior to me made it more so. Our relationship continued; professional during the day and physical after hours. This lasted and we grew closer."

Kelly glanced up again to see if Jared looked distressed. Maybe she should stop?

"Go ahead," he urged softly.

"One day, one of the units we supported needed an extra medic to go 'outside the wire,' to meet with an Afghan tribal chief in a village about twenty kilometers away. Peter had always expressed his wish for more 'gun time' and as a Navy corpsman, felt he should be seeing more action than taking care of the whiny FOB-bound troops. His leadership gave the okay, and onto the trucks he went. I didn't give much thought to it until a voice cracked over the Command Net, which we monitored in the clinic: 'FOX BASE, this is FOX SIX, we're comin' in by ground hot with three wounded, one critical. We'll need a helicopter. Request dustoff ready, have a med team meet us at the front gate past the blast walls, time NOW."

"The patrol roared through the gate and stopped in the designated area. I saw him, his face drawn and pale, eyes open, expressionless. Waiting for the helicopter, I—I mean *we*—tried to stabilize him the best we could before flying him to Kandahar, but his brain injury was pretty severe. From Kandahar he went on to Germany, where he died."

"That was the last I ever saw of him," Kelly sobbed. "We weren't supposed to be having a relationship and I was still deployed. Nobody knew about us. I couldn't openly grieve, couldn't go to be with him, couldn't go to the funeral," she said, still sobbing. "We had talked about marriage."

Jared turned Kelly toward him but she put her hand up, motioning for him not to speak, then buried her face in her hands. Jared held her silently.

After some time, when she had calmed her crying enough to speak, she glanced up at him and then hurriedly looked away, hiding her face. She couldn't bear to see him looking at her— seeing her so exposed.

"I'm sorry," he said quietly, flatly, then ran his hand through her hair.

"I've always thought that if I had gone with him, I could have saved him. I could have nursed him so intensely, loved him so deeply that he would have had no choice but to live," she said angrily, swiping the tears from her face. "Never mind, it's stupid. Her voice cracked, her breath caught in her throat and tears streamed down her face.

Jared hesitated, then took a small step forward, not sure what to say or do before quickly making a decision and closing the gap between them.

"That's not stupid," he said emphatically, reaching out and cupping her face in his hands. "Shhh, you're okay."

"I don't know why I told you," Kelly said, wiping more tears from her face. "My mom doesn't even know."

"Thank you for telling me." Jared held Kelly by one shoulder and pushed her out to arms' length to look her in the face. "It's clear you loved him deeply."

"I did, but I didn't think I would ever love again...," Her voice trailed off and she broke eye contact, looking down at her feet.

Jared leaned in abruptly and kissed her.

Their lips came together in a rush of need and for once, they opened up to one another completely. Only the touch of their lips, the melding of flesh was important.

Jared's hand moved to the back of her neck and the kiss became more urgent, more primal. She met him eagerly, his need becoming hers.

He pulled her down to the rock with him, the surface warm from the morning sun.

"Oh, Kel," Jared breathed. "You feel so right. This feels so right."

Kelly quieted his lips with a kiss.

Jared moved his hand down her neck and toward her collarbone. Kelly lightly took his hand in hers, stopping it where it was, and said, "Let's not go there."

Jared was breathing heavily. "We're not children."

"No, we are not," said Kelly, "so let's not act like ones. We are expected home and we're just off the road. Anyone can see."

"Damn it, Kel," Jared said in a low tone.

Kelly understood his impatience all too well. "Okay, okay, there's more, I'm afraid," she said between kisses. "If we go too far too fast, there will be consequences—privacy issues, family-planning issues."

"Okay, I understand, but shut up," growled Jared. "Just kiss me."

Neither moved to end their amorous encounter. Jared traced every feature of Kelly's face, even the tracks of her tears, with his lips, erasing their evidence.

"Did you hear that?" Kelly asked, breathless.

"What?"

"I don't know, but—"

Jared put his finger to his lips signaling Kelly to be quiet. "I think it's voices," he whispered.

"Yes, there it is again."

They both lay still, straining to hear what the voices were saying, but couldn't quite make it out. It was definitely a man and a woman speaking though. It was coming from upstream. It might have been possible to make out their words if it weren't for the wind. Voices and wind mingled, echoing down the canyon.

Jared pointed off the rock and Kelly rolled to the edge, then scrambled down. He scooted over slowly, without the aid of his injured arm, and Kelly assisted him down as quietly as she could. Both crouched behind the rock.

"You stay here and I'll go up and see who it is," Jared whispered.

"I think I should go," Kelly said. "I know you're the officer, but your injury..." She didn't finish her sentence or wait for his objection. Unsnapping the thumb break on her holster, she rose quietly. Looking down at Jared, she could see the concern on his face. "I'll be right back," she whispered, more confidently than she felt.

Kelly crouched low as she made her way upstream. It was a skill she had learned well in pre-deployment training. The nurses were made to simulate what she was doing right now. How ironic, Kelly thought, that she would complete her military duty without having to crawl in the dirt, only to find herself doing it in civilian life.

She picked her way around smooth, dry wood, heaped up against tree trunks and debris piles because of its tumultuous journey downstream in a series of floods. It was slow going, but after a few minutes, she was close enough to hear what the couple was saying. They were talking about making their way to the Mogollon Rim, where they could find water, and wondered out loud if it would be too cold to survive there this winter. They were afraid if they stayed here they would not be able to get enough water and food to sustain themselves. *How sad*, Kelly thought. So many must be in the same predicament.

Kelly did not want to be seen. She momentarily entertained the idea of inviting them home, but knew the stress that two more mouths would bring to her small community. With a deep sigh, she stole back downriver toward Jared and home.

It was getting much later than Kelly had intended. The family had planned on meeting the folks in town for a religious gathering at ten.

Jared was still crouched behind the huge rock when Kelly returned. "How did it go?" he asked. "Do you know them?"

"No," Kelly said. "They're travelers trying to make their way north. They didn't see me and I'm glad for that. We should be getting back. We have more than a half hour's walk. It's getting late."

"Seems like we were together for mere seconds," Jared said, smiling.

She gave him a quick peck that immediately turned into something more.

**\*\*\*\***

By the time they had returned to the house, the rest of their group was finishing breakfast.

Emma looked at the pair with a slight furrowing of her brow. Kelly and Jared looked at each other, puzzled. How had Emma figured them out? Did their appearance give them away? Kelly reached up as if to wipe away some stray lipstick she wasn't wearing. Emma glanced away and started speaking like nothing had happened. *Mothers!*

"Hurry up and eat something," Emma said. "I saved you some scrambled eggs and cream of wheat."

Kelly took a very small portion, leaving the bulk of the food for Jared.

"We saw a man and a woman down by the creek. They seem to be camped out down there," said Jared.

Kelly and Jared took turns relating the story, sans kissing. Emma and Rich seemed very concerned.

"We'll have to keep an eye on that, I tell you," Rich said as they finished their story. "I don't like it. It's too close to home."

"They aren't that close. It's a half-hour walk to their camp," said Kelly.

"Even that's too close for my taste," said Rich. Emma nodded in agreement.

Chapter 10

"All hands on deck?" Emma asked before nudging Traveler to pull the cart out onto the driveway. Dennis and Lynn rode alongside on Buckskin and Hokey.

Dennis grinned, surprised to see Rich joining them. "Rich, I didn't think a heathen like you would be going to Torah study."

"I'm not a churchgoer," Rich admitted. "I'm for Bible study and anyway, this isn't *just* Bible study, it's a way for the community to come together."

"Yes," Emma agreed. "In my time in the Navy and doing medical missions, we discovered that people grew closer and got along better when they shared a religious ritual. There's real comfort in ritual."

"You're starting to sound like my graduate seminary students," Dennis said.

"Jess here surprised me when he told me he wanted to go to the meeting," Jose said. "I grew up in a very Catholic family, but my wife and I haven't gone to Mass much."

"It was nice to see you, Dennis and Lynn, welcoming the Sabbath last evening," Emma said. "Lynn, you were so pretty when you lit the candles, covered your eyes and recited that prayer.

I felt the bond between you and your dad when he laid his hands on your head and blessed you."

Lynn offered a shy smile before glancing at her father.

"Jess, why don't you drive Traveler now?" Emma said suddenly. "All of you *dudes* need to get some practice driving the cart and some more saddle time, too." She waited for Jess to awkwardly make his way to the front of the moving cart. He sat beside her, then she handed him the reins.

"Thanks, I've been wanting to learn to drive," Jess said, rolling his eyes as he took the reins. "I had imagined something with a little more *horsepower* though."

Everyone laughed.

"Lynn, you can drive the next time we take the cart out," Emma announced, "since you can't drive a cart on the Sabbath."

"That sounds fun. I hear girls are better drivers than boys," she said, glancing sideways at Jess.

He ignored her.

"Great, and tomorrow you can both learn to muck out the stalls," Emma said , ignoring their looks of disdain. "It's time to find out how your cart gets its giddy-up."

Kelly smiled at the camaraderie, then reached out and took Jared's hand. She said, "Mom, you and I will need help when it comes time to move the cattle off the range. Jess and Lynn will make good cow hands, but they will both need some roping practice."

"A little shooting practice is in order too," Rich said. "We're lucky we got out of Fountain Hills without getting shot. Well, most of us." He glanced over his shoulder at Jared with a playful grin. "I don't think we should press our luck."

"I've never shot much," Jose said. "I could stand some lessons."

"That's why you have my shotgun," Rich said. "I have a bunch of .22 ammo back at the house and I'll teach you to shoot with my rifle. It's a perfect little gun for learning and keeping your skills up. "

"I'll help with that," Jared volunteered.

"I could use some range time too," Dennis said.

"We all could," Kelly said.

"I'll make up both basic and more advanced training for each of you," said Jared. "I'll have to get a feel for everybody's skill level first, but I've qualified expert on pistols and rifles since the academy."

"Do I have to shoot?" Lynn asked, trying not to whine but not succeeding. "I mean, I'm not afraid of guns, but I've never really seen myself as"—she thought about what word to use—, "aggressive."

"Your cousins in the Israeli army carry M-16s with them everywhere, on and off duty, " Dennis said. "Because of our circumstances, you need to be able to defend yourself."

"They are in a war—we're not. Teen attitude echoed through Lynn's words.

"Well, at this point I don't know what to say we are *in*, but I think it's safe to say we are in a survival situation until proven otherwise."

"Do I have to shoot the big guns?"

Jared answered that one. "I'll teach you everything you need to know. When you're confident, you won't be afraid of any of them."

"Okay, what if I don't want to?"

Dennis jumped in. "You might need to defend one of us too. How would you feel if Emma needed you, or Kelly, even me?"

"I don't know," Lynn said softly, anger still coming through even without volume.

"Talking about shooting practice," Rich said, "what about the stuff we left in Fountain Hills? I think we should go into town tomorrow and see if there's anything left of our cache."

"It's got to be done," Jose said. "I suppose the sooner the better."

By the time they arrived at the Johnson home, most of the people of Sunflower were there, some with family Bibles in hand.

After the discussion with Rich and Emma this morning, Dennis was not surprised to see the turnout. The family groups broke up, and individuals greeted each other and began conversing. Dennis circulated among the crowd, making small talk.

As 10 a.m. drew near, Dennis cleaned off a worktable in the shop and placed his chaplain kit on it. Dennis always carried the kit he had put together for Civil Air Patrol. He drew out his prayer shawl and pronounced a blessing before donning it, then set up a small white stand. He laid out a Hebrew Bible, the Torah in book form, and a King James Bible. On the stand he placed a miniature Torah scroll. It had a blue protective cover with gold designs and Hebrew writing on it. People noticed him preparing and began to drift into the building. Lynn, seeing her father ready to start, unfolded her prayer shawl, recited a blessing and placed it over her shoulders.

"Welcome," Dennis said. "Let's get started." He waved toward the lawn chairs around the tables. "First, thank you for coming to study with Lynn, my daughter, and me. This is our Sabbath, and these studies will be our substitute for attending synagogue. I hope each one of you will find joy and peace in our contemplation of the Torah, the five books of Moses." He paused for a moment.

"I'm assuming you folks are of a Christian background, am I right?"

Everyone nodded.

"I truly hope that your faith in God and your determination to follow the moral values of your religion is strengthened. From my perspective, Christianity is Judaism for non-Jews. We all worship the God of Abraham and base our religions on the books of Moses, as well as the other writings of the Hebrew Bible. We have a lot to share.

"I am not the final authority here. We each bring unique perspectives to the discussion. I encourage debate. We do not all have to have the same opinion.

"Some of you may be wondering about my views on religion. Well, I call myself a Jew without portfolio. I was raised and educated in the Orthodox tradition. I was ordained a Reform rabbi and attend a Reform synagogue. I'm less interested in the form of Judaism, but more interested in seeing how the teachings of the Torah and Jewish practices are adapted by individuals and communities to fit new circumstances.

"Enough of my blathering, I think it's appropriate to begin our gathering with a prayer. Would someone like to offer one?"

So began the first meeting of the "Christian-Jewish Synagogue of Greater Sunflower" as the residents came to call their spiritual meetings. The participants soon became animated as the discussion ranged from opinion to opinion.

Rich surprised Kelly with his insightful and erudite discussion of the text. A little of the shroud of mystery covering Rich lifted when Dennis asked about his ability to parse the meaning of passages. For the first time, Rich divulged personal information, saying, "Oh, I was raised Mormon and even served as a missionary in Italy. Later, I taught high school and community college English."

The hour passed quickly. Dennis brought the meeting to a close with a prayer in Hebrew and then one in English.

Study hour broke up with the neighbors thanking Dennis and Lynn. Dennis sought out the Bantings and had a long talk, exploring their fears of Emmet's diabetes. People continued to visit after the meeting, reluctant to leave the little community they had created, until one by one the family groups began to go.

**\*\*\*\***

The clan lazed about the house after lunch. "I could get used to this not working on Saturday thing," Rich announced.

Jess blurted out, "So, can you play horseshoes with *real* horseshoes?"

"Yes, you can," Emma said. "It's harder to get a ringer because the real shoes are smaller."

"I saw some horseshoes in the tack shed," Jess said. "Does anyone want to play?"

"I'd like that," Kelly said.

"Me too," Jose said.

"I'll get a couple of stakes and a hammer," Rich said. "Jess, go get some shoes."

Emma used the powdered lemonade packets they got when provisions were divided in Sunflower and made a big, celebratory pitcher, all the while pining for ice.

Shortly the clan was gathered in Emma's front yard, sipping gleefully.

"Boys against girls," Lynn called out.

"That's three against five," Jess said.

"That's all we need," Kelly said, pitching the first shoe. Jared threw with his good arm and did about as well as everyone else.

"Rich, I didn't know you taught school," Dennis said between pitches. "What did your wife do?"

"She was a music teacher. We met in college and played in a band together."

"You played in a band?" Dennis asked incredulously. "What kind of band? What instrument do you play? Wait, wait, don't tell me... the trombone." A big smile spread across Dennis's face and then Rich's.

"I messed around with guitar, bass guitar and upright bass. Betty had a beautiful voice and could play almost any instrument she picked up," Rich said wistfully with the sheen of tears in his eyes. "In school—remember, this was the 'sixties—we were in a folk band. Later we tried our hand at rock, bluegrass, country and some jazz. We loved being together and working out different styles."

"Do you still play?" Lynn asked.

"I get my guitar out now and then and pick a little," Rich said.

"Don't let him fool you," Emma jumped in. "He has some amazing licks. I first heard him playing sitting out on his front porch."

"Emma knows a thing or two about guitars herself," Rich said. "She joins me playing on the porch most times."

"I just strum chords enough so people can sing along," Emma said. "I never got beyond that. Lynn, do you play an instrument?"

"Violin and piano. My dad plays clarinet."

"Wow, we have quite the musical group, don't we?" Emma said. "I think we should play a little this evening, maybe a love song." She nodded toward Kelly and Jared, who were sitting together on the glider.

Kelly glanced up, surprised that her mother would say anything like that in front of the group.

"Like everyone hadn't figured it out," Emma said. Dennis and Jose both smirked, trying to stifle laughs.

Jared pulled Kelly closer to him. "Nothing to look at here," he said, raising an eyebrow and tilting his head to one side.

Kelly did not resist, and folded herself into his arms.

"I, for one, am glad to see it," Dennis said. "I think I speak for everyone when I say Jared here seems to be a nice guy, clean cut and polite. He's just what every mother hopes for for her daughter."

Jared's face turned just the slightest hint of red as he turned to see what Kelly would say.

"Mom, stop it. We haven't announced our engagement or anything," Kelly said.

"No, I didn't mean you had. I just thought it would be easier on everybody if it were out in the open," Emma said. "More lemonade?" She stood and moved toward the half-full pitcher.

"Thank you, Mrs. Wise. You are so kind," Jared said with a hint of sarcasm.

"You are welcome, young man," she said, mimicking his tone.

Jared smiled.

The group finished up their many rounds of horseshoes. Dennis and Lynn recited Havdalah at sunset, then all played, sang and danced on the porch well into the night. The day of rest and celebration had been just that.

As the others prepared to go off to bed, Jose gathered his twenty-four-hour pack and shotgun from next to the front door. He slung the pack over his shoulder and said, "I'm off to do my guard shift in Sunflower." He headed down the porch steps and Jess followed him.

"Dad, what time do you get off?"

"Two a.m., you know that." Jose cocked his head to one side.

"I know," said Jess, looking at his feet and kicking a small stone in the moonlight. "But..."

"What's up, Mijo?"

"I want to go with you," Jess said, lifting his gaze to look directly at his father.

"You haven't napped or anything. It's going to be a long night."

"I know. I'll be your back-up," Jess said. It was more of a question than a statement.

"I don't think it's a good idea. Your mom would have my head if I let anything happen to you."

"Mom?" Jess said, manly anger in his voice. "That's your excuse, Mom?"

Jose readjusted the shotgun in his left hand.

"My mom is dead for all we know. If she's not dead, she'll never find us in this stinking canyon in the middle of nowhere."

Tears welled in Jose's eyes for the first time Jess could remember. "I don't know what else to do, Jess." He lowered his head to hide his emotion. "I don't know if we could survive anywhere else right now. Your mom would be foolish to try to make it back here, across the whole country and then this desert."

"But we know where Uncle Tino's farm is," Jess said angrily, tears welling and standing in his eyes.

"How do you propose we get there? You're not three, you know better."

"Do I?" he shouted. "Mom's out there somewhere and you don't care!" His voice broke as he said it.

Jose pushed out his chest and stepped forward, right into Jess's face. "Don't you ever say that, son," he snarled, teeth clenched. "I loved that woman long before you got here and I still do. If I thought setting out on a long walk would fix this, I'd do it.

But I don't. We could be minutes—literally minutes apart out there and never find each other."

Jess dropped his shoulders and leaned back a couple of inches to increase the distance between his and his father's noses. "I miss Mom," he said.

"I do too, damn it. Get your coat... and your gun. We'll talk about this in town."

Chapter 11

Jess and Lynn were tasked with building a solar hot water
heater while the "away team" went to Fountain Hills. Jose had
explained to Jess, in detail, how to build it during their night on
guard duty. It filled the long hours in the dark and cold as they
walked up and down the fence between town and the freeway.

The plan called for a double-walled, insulated box that
could hold a coiled, one-hundred foot hose. One hundred feet
because that was the length they had picked up on their first trip to
Fountain Hills. The box also needed a good-sized double-paned
window to let the solar energy in.

"Let's go across the creek to a couple of those abandoned
houses and see if there is any glass lying around," Jess suggested
to Lynn. "Everyone here in Sunflower seems to have a shed with
extra parts and old stuff in it."

"I think we should tell Emma and Jared first," Lynn said.
"Kelly and Jared saw those people down by the creek yesterday,
remember?"

"Yeah, they're no problem—just passing through I bet."

"All the same, it's a good idea that someone knows we're
going. Race ya!"

The teens hit the porch at a dead run and let the screen door slam behind them on their way into the kitchen. Jess practically threw himself at the kitchen table, his hands outstretched to catch himself, and announced, "We're going to look for old windows." He was panting so hard, the adults could hardly make out his words.

"Wait a minute there," Jared said, lowering his arm from one of his therapy exercises. "I don't want you guys out there alone, it's not safe."

"But Dad said we had to make the water heater," Jess said.

"I don't think he meant for you two to be out wandering around by yourselves," Jared said.

"Then come with us," Jess said.

Jared thought for a minute. "My arm isn't one hundred percent and I'd never forgive myself if anything happened to either of you. Your fathers would skin me alive."

"I'm a good shot—especially with a shotgun," Jess said. "We can help you."

Jared considered. The chances that anything might happen were slim, and it would feel good to get outside and actually be of some use. He relented with a sigh, saying, "If we stay downstream, away from the visitors, we should be okay."

Jared put on his gunbelt, then snapped his .45 pistol into the holster. He sent Jess up to Rich's place to get another shotgun because he didn't want to leave Emma without one. All three met back on the porch a few minutes later.

The day was perfect, as Arizona fall days tend to be. Jared had to call out and remind the kids several times not to get too far ahead. Jess and Lynn were running and laughing amongst the trees along the creek. They were headed to the Branham's place to scavenge. The family was the one that had left Sunflower to go back to town when all this first happened, and no one had seen them since.

"I think it's over here," Jess said. He spotted a red house through the trees on the far side of the creek. The trio navigated downstream until they found the old concrete slab that had been poured across the stream so that a car could drive over it during times of low water.

"Yep, this is it," Lynn said. "Let's look around back."

Behind the house stood a two-car garage with a shed attached. This was just the sort of place people kept windows, wood and other building supplies. Jess turned the handle on the garage door and it opened with ease.

"It's not even locked," Jess said, surprised.

"Be careful!" shouted Jared from fifteen feet behind the teens. "Remember, I can't move quite as fast as you yet," he hollered. "Wait for me. I'll go in first."

Jared went in cautiously with his pistol drawn. Two newer-model cars were in the garage. Farther to the back of the garage was a tool bench and hand tools. Gardening supplies, insecticides and paint cans covered the shelves. Cabinets lined the back wall, holding bolts of fabric and sewing supplies, among other things.

"It's clear, come on in," said Jared, "but I don't see any windows except the small one in the wall over there."

"That's not big enough," Jess said. "We could use a roll of this insulation, though." Jess carried it outside. "The back of the house has a mudroom on it."

There were three large, double-paned windows surrounding the little lean-to, which made an airlock for the back door.

"These are good-sized," Lynn said.

The windows looked about five by four feet.

"They look good to me," Jess said.

Jared went into the lean-to. "I don't want any surprises. You kids stay out here while I clear it."

Jess looked exasperated.

"What? Did you forget that there might be others in here? Others that might not be friendlies?"

Lynn dropped her gaze like a small child caught with her hand in the cookie jar.

"You both had better start thinking that way, if you want to live." Jared opened the back door and went in, weapon drawn.

Jess ran back to the garage to get a hammer and screwdriver to remove a window for the water heater. He returned with two hammers, and Lynn took one.

They waited until Jared emerged, saying, "All clear. I'm gonna sit on that stump over there and supervise."

Both teens ignored him.

"Just pry the frame away from the opening, but don't break the glass," Jess said.

Lynn rolled her eyes.

"UGH, this thing is in tight," Jess said after he had scraped the caulk away from the outside of the frame and dug his hammer claw into the wood casing.

"I think we should go find another one," said Lynn wiping the sweat from her forehead with her forearm.

"What do you mean? We just got started. The same guy probably put in the rest of these windows, too."

Jared sat quietly, just observing, a chuckle buried deep in his chest but not touching his lips.

More muscle was applied to the frame by both Jess and Lynn. It took them more than half an hour, but when the window was finally removed, Lynn glanced through the empty space. "Whew, who knew it would be that hard?"

"Yeah, but we didn't break it and that's the important part," said Jess.

"Good job, you guys," said Jared.

"Now that we have the window, we should check the house for food before the rats get it. We would have to share it with the neighbors, of course."

"Why?" asked Jess. "They could have come and gotten it themselves."

Jess took a hold of the back door handle and gave it a turn. Lynn and Jess found themselves standing in a small kitchen with red-checkered curtains and a linoleum floor.

"Looks like they did. It's been raided."

Kitchen cabinets hung open. Dishes were stacked, untouched, but the food was gone.

"Well, can you believe it?" asked Jess.

"Yes I can, seeing as you were thinking about taking it yourself," said Lynn.

"What makes you such a goody two-shoes?"

"Duh. I'm a practicing Jew, religious..."

Jared stepped in. "Come on you two, let's get the glass back to the house. I'll help you carry it."

"No, you won't," Lynn said. "Kelly gave me strict orders not to let you use that bad arm yet."

"She's not my boss and I'm feeling fine." Jared stepped up to the end of the window Lynn held. She and Jess already had it hoisted in the air.

Jared slid the sling gingerly from his left arm and tried to straighten it, but the sudden pain caused his breath to catch in his throat.

"Please Jared, let us carry it," Lynn pleaded. "If you hurt your arm again it will only take you longer until it's healed *and* I'll be in trouble with Kelly."

"Maybe you're right," conceded Jared, fumbling with the sling to get it back in place.

"Let me help you," Lynn said.

"You've got that window, plus, I can do it myself. Thanks, but... I mean, I need to do things for myself."

Lynn and Jess carried the large window flat. The insulation roll and the shotgun sat on top.

They had gone about a hundred feet when Lynn sighed, "Ugh. This thing's heavy and it's digging into my fingers."

"Okay, okay," Jess said in annoyance. "This is going to be a long trip if you can't carry any further than this without stopping."

Jared walked up beside her and unbuttoned his shirt. It took him a minute or two, but he got it off and folded it, one-handed.

"Here, put this between the window and your hands," Jared urged, holding the shirt up to her and taking some of the window's weight with his good hand.

Lynn accepted the offer readily. "Thanks, you're the best. I see why Kelly likes you."

Jared smiled.

\*\*\*\*

"Emma, Emma, we got the window!" Lynn called from the front yard.

Emma came out and admired their find. "Looks great. Why don't you all come eat some lunch? You can get back to work after that."

After a lunch of rabbit stew (not for Lynn—"I'll have salad, thanks"), Jess and Lynn built a wooden box, about eighteen inches deep, that fit the window glass's dimensions.

"This is looking good," Jess remarked. "Won't our dads be surprised?"

"Yeah, not only surprised that we made it, but surprised it works—if it works," Lynn replied.

"We need some dark, flat rocks, almost black if we can get 'em," said Jess.

"Why?" asked Lynn. "Won't that make it too heavy?"

"When the rocks get hot in there, they'll heat the water up and stay hot a long time. At least we'll get a hundred feet worth of hot water per shower, you know, from the hose."

The two got the wheelbarrow. They wheeled past the front porch, headed for the creek bed. "We're going to the stream to get rocks," Lynn called out to Jared. Before they could leave the front yard, Jared came out of the front door holding his AR-15 in his good arm, trying to catch up to them. "Hold up you two, gosh darnit!"

Once the flat, dark, creek rocks were gathered, they were moved to the house and heaped near the solar water heater.

Using Emma's ladder, the teens placed the box on the roof over the kitchen. Jess pointed the glass of the box's lid toward the sun.

"What about legs on the back to give it more tilt? The sun's not shining right into the box," said Lynn.

"Uh huh. Let's make them adjustable. You know, so the box could be tilted when the sun's lower in the sky, like in winter."

The rocks were lifted to the roof using a bucket and rope and placed in the box in one flat layer. Many different configurations were tried. Jess even took some rocks down to the ground and bashed them with other rocks, splitting them, to make them fit.

"Is there enough pressure to get water onto the roof?" asked Lynn.

"The windmill tank is higher on the hill than the house. As long as the end of the hose is lower than the holding tank, gravity will push it. So, if we hook this hose up to this faucet, and then take the hose up on the roof, water will still come out of the hose in the bathroom."

"What made you so smart, Archimedes?"

"My Dad, I guess." Jess said, shrugging his shoulders. "He's smart, sometimes."

They formed as many concentric loops of hose inside the box, over the rocks, as they could.

They ran the hose from the heater into the attic, where they placed a "Y" connector. One section of hose dropped through a hole in the ceiling into the kitchen, and the other through a hole into the bathroom. Emma pulled the length of hose down into the kitchen sink. She cut it, then attached a connector and a garden sprayer to it. She repeated the process in the bathroom. Voila! A handheld hot water sprayer in the kitchen and bath. Both of the hoses were left long so they could be used in more than one part of the room.

While Lynn was working, Jess had gathered pipe insulation, which he used to cover the hoses after it left the water heater.

"Time to test the system," said Jess. Emma stood ready inside.

"Jared, open the water faucet," Jess called.

Emma opened the sprayer in the kitchen. Air rushed out as water filled the hose. Soon, hot water flowed from the nozzle.

"Turn it off. Turn it off!" Jess yelled.

Jared twisted the faucet handle as fast as his good hand could go. A small leak sprayed from a connection inside the box, and the teens removed the glass. Jess reached for the connector, but Lynn slapped his hand away.

Jess stared at her. "What?"

"*Hot* water, silly! I'll get some gloves for both of us. We need to go back into the attic and see if there are any leaks there, too."

Soon, the connections were tightened and Lynn was positioned to watch for leaks in the attic. This time the water stayed in the piping.

Lynn and Jess dropped through the attic hatch and headed back outside to the roof. Emma stood on the kitchen counter and used expanding foam insulation, scavenged from the hardware store in town, to seal the holes in her ceiling. She sent Jared outside with the can to throw to the teens on the roof so they could seal the heater. Jess and Lynn secured the double-paned glass to the top of the water heater box.

"Wow, Dad really will be impressed!" Jess said.

"I want to be the first to take a hot shower," Lynn said, running for the house.

Lynn and Jess ran straight down the hall and into the bathroom.

"What if the water is too hot?" Lynn thought out loud. She opened the sprayer carefully and directed the flow into the tub. It was hot, but not scalding. She moved her hand back into the flow and held it there for a few seconds. It was *very* hot. Maybe it would cool down as more volume moved through the hose. *Yes*, she thought, *you can probably regulate the temperature by adjusting the water flow.*

"Get out, get out!" Lynn said impatiently to Jess, pointing at the bathroom door. She slammed it as Jess's foot cleared the threshold.

Lynn showered and proved her mixing theory correct. Ahhhhh, a nice, hot shower. She washed her hair three times, using as little soap as she could, and rinsed it thoroughly. This was a true luxury. She found that a nice, small flow made the temperature just right. She had to be careful to leave it running though, or the water was warm from where it had been sitting in the attic, then suddenly too hot when the water from the heating chamber made it to the sprayer head.

Jess, Emma and Jared took turns showering and bathing.

"Clean, what a glorious feeling," Emma said.

The whole crowd was newly energized by their innovation: the simple addition of hot water.

Vestiges of civilization were slowly creeping back into their lives.

"*Back to the Future*," Jess said. "Dennis talked about building a solar oven too, but I'm not sure I want to do that without him. He was talking about gaskets and double-walled construction and stuff. I think we should get as many of the supplies as we can so that we can do it tomorrow."

"What do you need?" Emma asked.

"Well, we'll need another window, but not so big this time," Jess said. "The oven will be smaller so I think the wood scraps you have in the barn will be big enough. We can use the rolled insulation we got today and some screws."

Emma grinned at the teen's enthusiasm. "Just make sure it's big enough for two loaves of bread at a time. Do you think you can do that?"

"Sure, we can build it any size, but we'll have to find a window for it. The window will go in the lid and reflectors go around that to direct the sun into the box. Some backyard solar ovens get as hot as three hundred and fifty degrees. We were learning about them in science. Mr. Steiner brought his into school and we cooked potatoes in it. Oh, I forgot—we need mirrors for the reflectors."

"Well, I think you two have done more than enough for one day," Emma said, smiling. "Why don't you guys help me with dinner and then you can go out in the morning looking for your window and mirrors? Go outside and start me a small fire, would you? I'll need the coals for the Dutch oven."

**** 

The moon was nearly full; it shone almost fluorescent against the mountain cliffs all around. The night was so still, it was if the world had stopped turning. Kelly rode up to the porch, where Jared sat waiting for her.

"The others are just behind me," she said. "It's after midnight; I didn't think you'd wait up." She took off her cowboy hat and swung her long hair free, dismounted her horse gracefully, then started slowly toward the barn.

Jared opened the front door and announced loudly, "Everyone's home," then ran after Kelly and took Pokey's reigns. "I thought you'd never get back," he said as they walked side by side. "You look tired. How was the trip?"

It was just polite conversation while walking up the hill, and Kelly knew it.

When they got to the corral, the two stood still for a moment, staring at each other. Jared wasn't in the mood for staring or polite conversation. He threw his good arm around Kelly's waist, drew her in and kissed her deeply.

"I'm glad to be home," Kelly said breathlessly.

"I can see that, my dear. I should send you away more often if absence makes the heart grow fonder. It did for me."

They melted into each other again. Tiredness racked Kelly's body. She leaned into him heavily. He stood there sturdily as she rested her head on his chest. She felt him breathing.

Jared ran his hand through her hair. "You smell good," he said. He put his nose to the nape of her neck and inhaled deeply.

"Don't be silly," Kelly said, "I've been riding all day."

"No, I'd know your scent anywhere, follow you anywhere."

Kelly stood motionless, taking it all in: the night, the warmth, the closeness.

The sounds of the other men's horses soon interrupted. Kelly stood upright and turned toward the barn. Jared opened the corral gate and led Pokey in, releasing him to feed and water.

Dennis and Rich brought the other three tired horses to the corral gate and unbridled them, setting them loose as well. All four walked back to the house together, Jared and Kelly hand in hand.

Lynn rushed out onto the porch and folded herself into her dad's arms. "I'm so glad to see you back home, safe and sound." Dennis wrapped his arms around her, grateful to have a daughter who still missed him.

"Dinner is on the table," Emma said, tossing a dish towel over her shoulder.

The delicious smell of chicken stew, made from canned soup with added greens and garden carrots, revived their tired bodies enough to be hungry. Everyone made their way to the kitchen, where they sat and related news of the trip while they ate their small rations. They had skirted town as much as possible and kept their weapons high profile. The padlocked enclosure where they had left supplies was undisturbed and the group loaded quickly and hurried out of town unchallenged. They had seen a dead body along the way, but the circumstances of the death were unclear. When beggars or thugs approached on the roadway, they had kept their weapons in sight and at the ready.

"Thanks for getting the supplies," Emma said. "We need everything we can get our hands on."

Jose glanced at the new plumbing and whistled. "Now that's something. Who did that?"

"We did," answered Jess and Lynn enthusiastically. "Took us all day."

"It works wonderfully," Emma enthused. "No fuel to heat for dishwashing, and my shower was heaven. Too bad for you; it's after bathing hours, sun's down."

"Looks like we'll have to wait until tomorrow and pray for sunny skies," Jose said. "I'm glad to hear you guys did such a good job." He smiled at Jess and Lynn. Both of the teens beamed.

"We did it just like you told us, Dad," Jess said. "The water gets really hot too. We didn't work on the solar oven today, though."

"We can build the cooker tomorrow. I think I've had all the fun I can stand for today. It's time for bed."

\*\*\*\*

In the morning, Dennis and Lynn went to the Branham house for another window and a mirror for the solar oven. They made a better search through the building for food, but found nothing worth scavenging. Lynn chose a few bolts of fabric from the garage to take home.

The others unloaded the cart and worked making row covers for the garden to keep the winter frost at bay.

When the scavenging party returned from their mission, everyone met back in the yard and started construction on the oven. The window that had been salvaged was two by three feet. Jess and Jose made a frame to fit around it. They built an insulated box with a forty-five degree angled glass lid to collect the sunshine. It took them all afternoon to finish the oven and build a frame to angle the mirrored reflectors correctly.

"Fine job," Emma said. "Makes me want to bake something."

"Not today, I'm afraid," Jose said. "We are getting short on daylight. Baking will have to start mid-morning and finish up by sundown. We'll have to experiment with timing and temperatures, I'm afraid. I don't know how hot it will get either. It will depend on if it's pre-heated and if there are clouds that day."

"Preheated!" Emma laughed.

"Yes," said Jose. "You heard me right. You'll have to turn the glass to the east the night before so that by mid-morning, the bricks on the interior will be hot enough to maintain temperature. Solar ovens take a while to bring their contents up to temperature and need mass to keep the temperature steady.

"Great," Emma said, "another skill set to learn. I'm ready."

Chapter 12

The morning chores completed, Rich led the clan to his house. *House* may have been a bit of an overstatement; it was more of a cabin. Built of stone walls and a wood-shingled roof, it sat behind and higher up the canyon than Emma's house. With the exception of Jared, the men had all slept in the shed near the barn up until this point. They had been on the porch for breakfast and in the crowded living room once, but had never really been invited in any further than that. Rich now led the group through the small living room lined with books. A table in the dining area—it couldn't be described as a whole room—was covered with electronic equipment.

Colored charts and maps covered a huge pushpin board on the wall. This was Rich's ham radio shack. The radios were scattered across the table, unusable since the power outage.

Rich led the others into his tiny bachelor's kitchen and opened what seemed to be a pantry. He turned his shoulders sideways to make his body as narrow as possible and squeezed through the small, hidden doorway. Kelly blinked, baffled at what she had just seen, before stepping closer to peer into the small space. Rich had descended dusty, wooden stairs into a rock-lined cellar and stood at the bottom, bathed in the soft glow of an oil lamp. The pitch black had been forced back and the yellow glow revealed a large room lined with metal shelves that were loaded with canned goods. Platforms hung from the ceiling beams, holding boxes and wrapped bundles. Boxes were stacked in the corners. Rich placed the lamp on a table in the center of the room as the others filed down the narrow stairway. Despite the stored items, the basement was spacious, having the same footprint as the house upstairs.

"Here it is," Rich proudly announced with his arms open wide. "This is my year's supply."

"It's like a secret passage in a movie," Lynn said. She brushed away a few cobwebs from the ceiling beams as she descended.

"Or a haunted house," Jess said as he ran his hand along the cool rock wall.

Kelly felt the cool, dry air as she entered. The room smelled of dust.

Where are all the five-gallon buckets of wheat?" Dennis asked. "I thought preppers ground their own wheat into flour."

"I never understood that," Rich said. "I used to look at the suggested year's supply list and see four to six hundred pounds of wheat and sixty pounds of sugar per person. Then I looked at what I ate. It wasn't even close. Nobody I know uses that much flour. I decided that I would store the kind of foods that I would normally eat. No need to use somebody else's list."

"Mostly canned goods," Emma said, looking around the room. "How come you didn't show me this before, ol' man?"

"Not everything is your business, ol' woman."

"I guess you don't bake much," said Emma.

"I do bake," Rich said. "There's enough flour to bake a couple of loaves of bread a week and plenty of extra for other cooking and baking. I don't plan on grinding any wheat. Wheat lasts forty years, flour only lasts ten. I used the food down here every day and replaced it when I went to the store. If I can't use up my initial stock of flour in ten years, I'm storing the wrong stuff." He walked down the line of shelves, motioning to various items. "I keep plenty of beans and brown rice, too. They're good for protein. These cans have a good selection of meat, fish, vegetables and fruits. With a little creativity plus my garden and animals, I can dine like a king."

"A *bachelor* king, or a prince maybe," Emma quipped.

"I've been dining at the queen's table," Rich said looking Emma right in the eyes. "And I have no complaints."

"Pretty clever," Dennis said looking around the room. "It's not just food either."

"Which brings us to these trash cans over here," Rich said. He looked at the paper labels taped on the can lids. "Ah, this one," he said, removing the metallic tape sealing the can and lifting the lid. Styrofoam lined the inside, which was in turn filled with cardboard boxes. Rich easily extracted two small FRS radios and batteries. "Here, put these batteries in and let's see if they work." He handed Lynn and Jess each a walkie-talkie.

With the batteries inserted, the teens pushed the power buttons. "Hello, hello," Lynn said holding the push-to-talk button.

"I can hear you. Can you hear me?" Jess said into his radio from across the room.

"Yes, I can," Lynn responded, not bothering to transmit.

"Looks like your Faraday cage worked, Rich," Jose said. "What kind of goodies did you stash in these cans? This is better than Christmas."

Rich selected another trash container and opened the lid. "This is a radio station in a trash can. We can set it up in the dining room."

He handed out parcels and bundles from the container and everyone started up the stairs. Lynn and Jess helped clear the ham shack table of all of the now-useless electronics as Rich unpacked an olive-drab radio that bristled with several knobs and switches.

"That looks like real military stuff," Jess said.

"It's British Army surplus," Rich said. "They call it a Clansman PRC-320. It's a high-frequency radio for long-distance communication. You can carry it on your back or hook it up to a vehicle. I have two."

"We had HF radios in Civil Air Patrol, but we didn't use them often," Lynn said.

Rich unpacked a microphone, speaker, Morse code key, and a green box with a hand crank and other parts. In a few minutes, the pieces were connected.

"This is the hand-cranked power supply to charge the batteries," Rich said, looking directly at Jess and then Lynn. "I'll need help outside repairing the antenna before we can fire her up."

He removed a coaxial cable from a burlap bag. The group moved outside to the green telescoping pole set vertically on the side of the house. Two wires hung from the top of the mast, which formed the true antenna. Rich removed a pin from the pole, causing an upper section to slide into the lower section. This process was repeated until the entire mast was collapsed and they could easily reach the top. Finally he removed the ruined coax and replaced it with the new one. He climbed up a ladder and passed the new coax connector into a conduit under the eaves of the house. Rich and Dennis worked together to lift the pole section by section until the antenna was back in its full upright position.

"That should do it, let's go in," Rich said, brushing the dust from his jeans.

Everyone followed him inside and watched as Rich made the final connection to the back of the Clansman. Running his finger down a frequency list on the pushpin board, he scribbled a note, then sat down at his radio, turning dials to set the frequency, and then adjusted the antenna tuner.

"Okay, let's see what happens. Jess, will you do the honors?" Rich pointed to the hand-cranked generator. "There should be some residual battery power." Jess cranked for a few minutes and then Rich threw the power switch. A quiet hiss emanated from the speaker. "The background noise is very low."

"What does that mean?" Dennis asked.

"Normally, it means you didn't put the antenna on the radio." Rich chuckled. "Today, it may mean the receiver isn't working or that background emissions are low. Things like power lines, street lights, car alternators and most anything electric put out a radio signal. Those signals mix with cosmic radiation, and the radio itself generates electrical static, making the background noise. When this happens, hissing, crackling and popping come from the speakers. With the power grid down and no electronics working, its pretty quiet." He adjusted the knobs again and listened closely. "I've tuned into the frequency of the Arizona Emergency Net."

"Is that a government net?" Jose asked.

"No, it's an amateur radio net for passing messages. It doesn't seem active. During a disaster, the frequency should be jam-packed with stations handling messages."

"So does that mean the receiver is broken?" Jared asked.

"I'm not sure. I'll tune around and see if I can hear anything else," Rich said. "The Arizona Emergency Net is in a band that's good for local communication during the day and long distances at night. Let's see if there are any shortwave broadcast stations on the bands for long-distance daytime communication."

"What if we don't hear anything?" Jess asked, visibly shaken.

"Just because a long-distance station is transmitting doesn't mean that we can hear it," Rich said calmly. "The radio waves go up and bounce or skip off of the ionosphere and come back down. For us to hear those signals, we have to be where the waves come down." He opened a book lying nearby and scanned its pages before making further adjustments to the radio dials. "Voice of America, nothing." He readjusted the radio. "BBC, still nothing." Rich continued tuning.

"So we don't know if the radio is broken, if the stations are not transmitting, or if they are transmitting and we just can't hear them," Jared said.

Suddenly a new sound came from the speaker. It sounded almost human. Rich turned a dial very slowly, making minute adjustments until they could make out a scratchy voice, broken and barely audible. The group could only understand a small part of the words being spoken by the broadcaster.

"It's Radio Australia, the Australians are beaming radio signals toward Asia and the Pacific like they always do," Rich said. The clan was glued to the speaker.

*"Prime Minister... Governor General... Australian Defense Force... Europe... United States... supplies... Iran... Israel... Japan... China..."*

So went the broadcast. It was just enough to hold all of the group's attention and provided no real answers.

"Hey, can someone else peddle this thing?" Jess asked, sweat glistening on his brow.

"Oh, sorry, forgot about you," Rich said. "That's a pretty good workout."

Lynn touched his hand and Jess recoiled from the sudden tension. Their eyes met for the briefest of seconds, but it was enough. "I'll take a turn," she said. No one seemed to notice their brief exchange.

"I think I would like to set up my other radio," Rich said. "It's a Yeasu and it will let us see if the Clansman is receiving correctly. We can also listen for VHF, very high frequencies, and UHF, ultra high frequencies, on that one.

"Why don't we try calling someone with the Clansman radio?" Lynn asked.

"Just because someone has a radio doesn't mean they are friendly," Rich said. "No need to attract unwanted attention. Now is the time for listening. First, we'll check for local activity on VHF."

Rich returned to the basement, this time returning with the Yeasu FT-817, a small, portable HF/VHF/UHF radio, a VHF/UHF antenna and two solar battery chargers. He set it up near its bigger green cousin and using a small antenna on the Yeasu, checked to see that both radios were sending and receiving correctly. When he tried listening to the Australian station with the smaller radio, the signal was no better. Next, two solar panels were placed outside the cabin and connected to trickle charge the two radios' batteries.

The mast outside was lowered and the eight-foot VHF/UHF antenna was attached on top.

Obviously committed to getting a signal, Rich began to scan VHF frequencies, listening to static until finally, the group heard a voice.

"Phoenix North, this is Ord Relay. Go ahead." Once again the radio went silent. Everyone looked around excitedly at each other. Jared, who was standing behind Kelly, wrapped his good arm around her waist and drew her in close to him. The group could not hear the other station's reply, but the first voice replied, "Lehi Staging, this is Ord Relay with traffic. Lehi Staging, Phoenix North reports they are two hours from your location and request a camp assignment. Phoenix North, you will be north of the old Beeline dragway and south of the Central Arizona Project canal. Mesa Kimball East will be east of you."

"Somebody's organized," Emma said. "They aren't military; no acronyms. They can't communicate without them." Dennis, Kelly and Emma chuckled simultaneously.

"It's not the Sheriff's office," Jared said.

"Nope, it's the Mormons," Rich chuckled. "This is the LDS Cannery frequency. Sounds like they are bugging out en masse."

"Why are they going to Lehi?" Jose said.

"They said Lehi Staging," Jared answered. "In the Police and Fire Department's Incident Command System, staging is a temporary holding area for staff, cars, equipment, anything that needs to go into a scene. Sounds like the Mormons are getting together and waiting, camping next to the canals and along the Salt River. Ord Relay is referring to a radio operator on top of Mount Ord." He glanced at the map on the wall, checking the elevation. "That's almost 11,000 feet. Someone stationed up there could communicate with most of Arizona."

"If they're headed north, they're taking the same way I did," Kelly said, pointing at the Arizona map on Rich's wall. "That means they'll be coming up the Beeline Highway through Sunflower." She traced the route with her finger, letting it rest on their little canyon.

"They'll head northeast to Snowflake, Taylor, Pinetop and the other little Mormon towns up north," Rich said, making a grand sweeping motion across the entire northeast corner of the map. "There are only a few places they could move so many people to in Arizona. They'll need a reliable water source and land to farm."

"How many people do you think are on the move?" Jose asked.

Rich shrugged. "This sounds big. Mesa Kimball East and Phoenix North are names of Mormon stakes. A stake is made up of several congregations. Who knows how many stakes are heading to Lehi? The number of people could be in the thousands—even the tens of thousands."

"Will they be here tonight?" Emma asked.

"Nah, it will take time to organize that many people. I don't think they would move them all at once either, but every day they wait puts them one day closer to freezing winter temperatures. They need to get where they're going and set up shelter before the first snow. They're liable to lose quite a few people, but they would lose more if they stayed in a chaotic city without water."

"Things must be getting bad if they're heading up north," Kelly said, leaning in closer to Jared.

"Well, the folks in Sunflower ought to know about this," Emma said. "There isn't anything we can do about it. The best we can hope for is that they only stop to use water from the stream."

Rich spoke up. "I think we should put together a Sunflower contingent to meet with the church leaders and set up some ground rules about sanitation, maybe discuss our expectations and basic courtesy."

"They need to know that we don't want them past our fence on the north side," said Jared. "They outnumber us. If they want to come in and take over our houses, piss in the creek and steal everything we have, they could do it. I'm not saying that is what they will do; I don't believe they will."

"I truly don't think they are looking to cause problems," Rich said, "but it helps to know what the expectations are—on both sides." He stretched and yawned. "But there's nothing we can do about it today. I'll try to find a shortwave broadcast after dark, when the conditions are better for a long-range signal to reach the states. Then we can share whatever news we hear, if we hear any, with Sunflower." Rich stayed glued to his radio like any good ham.

The others listened for a while, but drifted away when nothing new was heard.

****

The next day, Jared scheduled each member of the Wise troop for shooting practice. Making notes of each person's abilities, he worked on a schedule of firearms instruction. Kelly gave Lynn and Jess their first roping lesson when Jared was done with them. After learning some basic roping techniques, the teens were set loose to practice on every young cowpoke's first "roping cow," a sawhorse with a pair of horns lashed to one end.

Rich didn't come to dinner. After the last dinner plate was washed, the group left Emma's house to walk up to Rich's ham shack. He hungrily wolfed down the plate of food Emma had brought along, while announcing that he hadn't heard anything important.

"I was just about to tune back into that Australian broadcast station we heard earlier," Rich said. A turn of the dial and the speaker came to life.

"Radio Australia news, Karen Nguyen speaking. More than a week since the devastating attack against the northern hemisphere, the Australian government continues to assess the impact on Europe, North America, China, Japan, and the Middle East 'going dark' after a coordinated electromagnetic pulse attack." The group gasped. "Iran launched several missiles with small nuclear warheads and exploded them very high over major countries in Europe, Asia and North America. The EMPs, or electromagnetic pulses, have rendered most electronic equipment in those areas useless."

Kelly and the others sat dumbfounded as the news presenter continued speaking about the collapse of international trade and the need to cooperate with the other "powered" countries of the southern hemisphere. Iran claimed responsibility for the attack, stating they had "silenced the infidels and the Great Satan" to paralyze its more powerful enemies as a prelude to its nuclear attack on Israel. Australian commentators thought that the reasons for the Iranian attack were Iran's unbridled hatred of Israel and an attempt to cause massive chaos that would induce the return of the Twelfth Imam, the Islamic coming. No one would even know for sure because Israel managed to deliver, as a last gasp, a nuclear counter-punch.

"My God," Dennis finally uttered, breaking the silence that had settled over the whole group. "The announcer named just about everything north of the equator. I don't think we can comprehend total blackout to the Northern Hemisphere. Israel is gone too, if I understood her correctly."

"What does it mean, Dad?" Lynn asked.

"I don't know." Lynn helped her father sit down in the nearest chair. He felt like the air had been knocked from him. "I really don't know."

Lynn began to sob and her father put his arms around her.

"Living without electricity for a week is one thing," Kelly said. "But we could be like this for a very long time."

Staring into space, Jose said, "We may never find our loved ones again." He let the stream of words flow from his mouth unchecked. Jess moved to face his father. Their eyes met. Seeing his son's bewildered face, he said, "I'm sorry, Mijo." He grabbed his son forcefully and drew him to his chest. Jess laid his head on his father's shoulder and cried. Jose joined him.

The group sat quietly, each processing the information.

Finally, Emma stood up and wrung her hands in her apron. "We pick up from here," she uttered in a voice that was barely audible. "We pick up from here," she continued, her voice growing stronger. "Humans have always just had to 'pick up from here' and move on."

****

Breakfast was a somber affair the next morning. They focused on the business at hand. The clan had decided the night before that they and the people of Sunflower needed to thoroughly scavenge the Beeline Highway before the waves of migrating Mormons arrived. This would be their last chance to remove anything useful. Another area of great concern was Emma's cattle on the range south of Sunflower, near Bushnell Tanks. The cows needed to be gathered closer to the house so they did not end up as steaks for hungry travelers.

The cart and horses were readied for the day. Food, water and hand tools were loaded onto the cart, leaving as much room as possible for their finds.

Emma and Jared waved from the porch to the away team heading for Sunflower. It was decided that they would stay back; Jared because of his shoulder, and Emma to watch the place and continue farm chores.

By the time they arrived at Bill and Patty Johnson's house, the first rays of the sun were shining through the clouds.

The Johnsons could not believe the news of the attack. Patty leaned heavily on Bill, grasping his arm tightly as they listened to the details.

"It's true," Rich assured them. "We got pretty much the same stories from Australia, New Zealand and South Africa throughout the night. It seems the only state not affected by the EMP was Hawaii; looks like they were far enough to be out of range. Our biggest priority is that the Mormons may be migrating north, traveling along the Beeline."

Bill stared at Rich, nonplussed. "I don't think they will be hostile."

"Me either," said Rich. "But it takes a lot of resources to care for a group that size—resources we don't have a lot of, not to mention the sanitation and health problems. We'll need to meet with the church leadership and establish some ground rules."

"We're heading to the highway to make sure we get anything we need before someone else gets it," Jose said. "You need to tell the folks here what has happened and get them out gathering from the highway *today*."

"I'll get the word out to the residents," Bill said. "It's going to take a while to give them the news and get them ready. I'll try to have everyone out there by early afternoon."

"Hopefully we have more than just today," Kelly said.

"We have seen a couple of small groups of riders going up the highway and returning," Patty said. "I wonder if they were scouts?"

"Probably were," Rich said. "The church is very focused on planning, and they're incredibly well-organized. If any of us see any scouts, we need to find out what we can and ask to meet with a representative. When you talk to townsfolk today, see who wants to go to this meetin'."

The group headed out of Sunflower and turned south as the bell at Bill's house pealed.

Kelly suggested that they start the scavenge as far south toward the Lehi staging area as practical. The highway to the north could wait for a bit. Unlike the first sweep of the roadway, this time anything considered to be remotely useful in the future would be stripped from the vehicles.

A lifted Jeep was their first target. The battery, mirrors, toolbox, gas cans, tire jack, pull strap and Hi-Lift jack were placed on the cart. ATVs on trailers provided batteries and gas cans.

"I wish we had more wagons," Rich lamented.

"What about all the trailers we see?" Jess said. "Could we could rig a harness for the horses? I bet some of the lighter ones would work."

"I think you've got something there, Mijo." Jose smiled, patting him on the shoulder. "We will need wagons for all sorts of things in the future, and now is the time to get 'em."

"What kind do you think we should get?" Jess asked.

"Something medium-sized, I would think," said Kelly, "and with a good axle. It will need to sit high if horses are going to pull it."

"Most of the trailers out here are for ATVs and sit low to the ground," said Jose. "We can use those for parts. The real prize will be something that can be modified to ride about three, even four feet off the ground. We need to think about pulling these wagons too. We'll need harnessing material. I don't know... straps, belts, rope, maybe even seat belts."

"Yeah," Kelly replied, "Mom only has one set of harnesses for her team, and what we got in Fountain Hills was bits and pieces. If nothing else, we'll need materials to repair them over time."

"I'll need long, sturdy pieces of wood or metal to connect the harnesses to the wagons," said Jose. "We have quite a bit of wood, but it would be nice to find something more... ready-made, and probably longer. Oh, and tires too. Look for tires that have big diameters, but don't weigh a TON."

In the course of scouting the vehicles, a small, two-wheeled ATV hauler was selected as the first trailer to be brought home. Using scavenged chains and pull straps, it was attached to the rear of the cart. This arrangement proved to be workable, though a little unwieldy. The trailer bumped and scraped along the pavement whenever the roadway was the slightest bit uneven. The team dared not put any weight on the trailer.

The group continued harvesting mirrors off the vehicles for their solar reflectors. They collected anything of value, such as propane tanks, tarps and even a few sheets of diamond plate steel.

Some of their best finds were in motorhomes and camping trailers, where they found pots, pans, oven mitts, utensils, blankets, sleeping bags, salt, lanterns and stoves, candles, lighters, matches, skewers and all manner of camping gear.

"Make sure you get those coats," Dennis said emphatically, pointing into a closet in one of the motorhomes. "Winter's coming. In fact, take all of the adult clothes. If we can't wear them, there might be someone in town who could."

"These look like old people's clothes," said Lynn. "Shouldn't we leave some for the Mormons?"

"They'll have their own clothes because they're coming from their homes. All we have is the jumble we got from the feed store in Fountain Hills. As hard as we're using them, we'll need more pants; shoes too. There may come a time, young lady, you'll be glad to have these."

Tears welled up in Lynn's eyes.

"I didn't mean it like *that*," Dennis said, pulling down the corners of his mouth, frustrated. "I'm sorry."

Lynn sniffled, a tear spilling over her bottom lid.

"You know, if you find material today, maybe Emma could help you make some clothes?"

Lynn cheered just a touch and gave her dad the tiniest, short-lived grin.

A contractor's truck provided a wealth of tools and building materials, and two pairs of blue overalls that fit Jose.

By mid-afternoon their cart was overflowing and they headed back home. When they came upon some Sunflower residents, they had to pull off the road and wait for their wagon to pass.

"The pickin's are getting slim out there. Highway's empty though," said Rich. "Be careful."

"Thanks," said Bill, and everyone waved.

Chapter 13

Jared and Emma waved goodbye to the others as they climbed into the wagon.

"Be careful," Jared whispered, touching Kelly's hand.

"Always."

He watched as they left, dirt kicking up from hooves and wheels.

By the time Jared made his way into the house, Emma was pulling feathers from some quail. She handed him a potato peeler and he silently accepted the tool, awkwardly peeling the eight potatoes in the sink. Meal preparation started early, as food for a group this size required extra time in a solar oven.

"Dinner will be ready in the late afternoon or early evening," Emma explained as she loaded the large pot. "I'm excited to see how well she works with a big meal in her."

"Will it really get hot enough to cook a dinner this size?" Jared asked.

She wiped the sweat from her forehead and glanced up at the sky. "We'll have to position the oven toward the sun throughout the day, but I'll bet she'll be boiling our dinner before two."

"Did Rich shoot those birds?" asked Jared.

"No, he snared them and wrung their necks," said Emma.

"Well, Dennis and Lynn will have to relax their standards about eating anything killed with lead if they continue to struggle with their bird snares."

"We'll see about that. They are pretty determined. Anyway, these two birds will make a fine meal today. I'm happy to cook 'em."

The morning was spent pulling weeds together and harvesting okra, eggplants, melons, tomatoes, and greens from the garden. Emma made a big salad of mixed greens, carrots, cilantro, and boiled eggs for their lunch then whipped up a quick dressing of vinegar, sugar, and olive oil. Both were hungry. Everyone was expending more calories than usual because of their intense physical activity. The two talked and ate leisurely, enjoying the lull.

Right after lunch there was a knock at the front door and they both froze. No one had knocked at the door since the attack. Since then, people in Sunflower called a greeting from the road before going to a neighbor's door. Emma went to the living room, then glanced over her shoulder at the kitchen door. It was ajar. She could make out the barrel of a gun jutting from the opening. Emma instantly knew that Jared was covering her.

"Who is it?" Emma called, her voice flat with an unspoken warning.

"My name's Tim and the wife here is Mary. We are just passing through, but need some directions. We aren't from here and seem to have lost our way."

Emma considered their words, not believing for a moment they had taken a wrong turn. She wrung her clammy hands, thinking.

*They left the highway at some point and only this road would lead them back there. If she gave them directions they might just leave or they might become aggressive.* Emma glanced back at the kitchen door, hoping for inspiration.

"Follow the road north," she called through the door. "It's a loop. When you reach the highway, take it left going toward Payson."

"We could use a little food too," the man said feebly. "Just to get us on our way."

*Oh my gosh, think fast, Emma. What to say? How to say it?* She wished that Jared would come to her side, maybe they could discuss this. She knew he wouldn't leave his cover because, if the couple got in and thought it was only her in the house, he would be a lethal surprise.

Emma finally responded. *"We"*—she used the plural, trying to bolster her position—"need all of the food we have. I'm sorry, we can't give you anything. All I can suggest is that you stock up on water from the creek and head north."

Silence filled the air. Long minutes passed. *Had they gone? No, I would have heard their steps on the porch. Will they shoot their way in or bash the front door from its hinges?* Not having a gun, she retreated to the kitchen doorway.

"What should we do?" Emma whispered.

Jared was all business, shifting easily into police mode. He handed Emma his gun. "Take this. Cover the front room. If they try to come in, shoot first and ask questions later. I'll get my pistol and cover the back. Stay low."

"Okay," Emma said breathlessly. She glanced, from a distance, at the front window, but didn't see anyone. She crouched near the hallway, where she could hear any movement but still remain somewhat secluded. She held the shotgun at the ready. Emma's own breathing roared in her ears.

After a few minutes, Emma's thoughts turned to her own discomfort. Crouching was not good for old ladies, she thought. Her ankles threatened protest at the unusual position, and she wondered how long she could stay like this. Jared hadn't said anything about how long to wait. Certainly if the visitors were going to storm the place, they would have done so by now. Staying low, Emma made her way to the front window. What she saw surprised her. Tim and Mary were walking down the road, away from her house, hand in hand like two love birds out on an afternoon stroll. Relieved, Emma plopped to the floor and let the long gun rest next to her.

"They're leaving," Emma called to Jared. She felt like crying from fear, relief, and a sense of guilt. A month ago she never would have turned anyone away. She didn't see how crying would help things and it definitely wouldn't fix the world's problems. She slumped against the wall under the window, letting her adrenaline rush fade a little before trying to stand.

Jared took a place by the window, curtains held back. He shifted his gaze between Emma and the retreating couple.

"They might be the ones Kelly and I heard down by the creek." He let the drapes fall back, leaving a foot of sheers exposed so they could see out. "I guess it doesn't matter."

Jared held his good hand out to Emma, then helped her up. Together they stood looking out the window, staring down the driveway.

"We have been very lax about security," Jared said quietly. "I'm surprised we haven't had others up here like that. Maybe next time, they won't be so docile."

"What should we do?" Emma asked.

"Oh, there will be plenty to do," Jared said. "First, we need to secure these doors and windows and make an escape plan. We'll have to wait for the others to get home, but I will outline a comprehensive plan. Right now, I think we should take a walk around and see if anything has been disturbed or taken. We might be able to tell if they've been up to Rich's place or the barn. This is going to slow things down around here. We'll have to take turns playing security guard."

\*\*\*\*

By the time the donkey cart returned, loaded with everything one could imagine *and* pulling a small ATV trailer, minus the ATVs, Jared had already gotten a good start on security. Kelly led the procession as the tired animals lumbered up the driveway. Jared emerged from the bushes on the driveway at a point about fifty feet from the road. Kelly hopped off Pokey, took his reins and walked toward Jared.

"What are you doing out here, babe?" she asked. "You should be resting."

"We had a couple of visitors today." Jared relayed the story as the group made its way to the house. They commenced cataloguing the items from the cart, adding them to the master list while putting them away.

"So what is our security plan now that we've been infiltrated, deputy?" Kelly smiled, holding up a can of beans.

Jared ticked off the items on his list. "Detection, cover, concealment, and fields of fire are the first things that come to my mind," he answered.

"What's the difference between cover and concealment?" Jess asked.

"Concealment means just that, you can't be seen," Jared said. "Cover is something that stops bullets. Rich's house is made of stone. Emma's house is adobe. Both are good cover. Wood and stucco houses are just concealment. Remember, detection comes first."

"The Marines used tin cans on barbed wire in Vietnam for warning and to slow assaulters," Emma said. "I think we should put some cans on string or wire around our property. Not just one line, but two or three lines of wire different distances from the perimeter, so any attackers have a good chance of making noise. We can put up a perimeter line of string pretty quickly. There is plenty of barbed wire around here too. Repurposing it into tanglefoot may be a good long-term project."

"The tin can alarms won't help unless someone is there to hear it and decide if the cans are clanging because of attackers, wind, or wild animals," Dennis said.

"We should stand watches overnight," said Jared. I'll do the majority 'til this arm's healed. Remember, even if our watchmen sound the alarm quickly, there will still be a delay getting everyone ready to fight."

"I might have a few ideas for more advanced security," Rich said mysteriously. "I think I can rig up working headlights and car horns. The horns will alert people here at Emma's and up at my place. We can shine lights into the yard and down the road at night too."

"Won't that surprise 'em?" Jess said.

"I'll say," Jared answered. "Today we should at least get the basics done. Lynn and Jess, come with me and we'll get some fishing line. We'll start laying out some alarms; I'm well enough to do that. Kelly and Emma, can you start gathering some of our old cans and punching little holes near the rims so that we can put them on the fishing line? Dennis and Jose, how about finishing puttin' the rest of this stuff up?"

Everyone got to work. Lynn and Jess ran through the yard like school-aged kids, with Jared and Rich supervising the work. They were laughing and stringing different lines from tree to bush to bush to tree. They tried to get the line to lay in the crooks of the foliage at about two feet off the ground. Rich had told them that the number of animals setting off the alarms would be less at that height.

Jared and Jess started building a stone observation point, about three feet square, surrounded by short stone walls in the front yard for the watchers in case of a fire fight. This would allow a 320-degree view of the front yard instead of the partial view afforded by the front porch. He designed the stone escarpment to draw fire away from the house as well. It was slow going; with only limited use of his bad arm he couldn't lift the heavy rocks, but he could supervise and chink the rocks. Jared's strength had been growing day to day, and it was showing in his work.

Kelly and Emma had to make a trip up to the old burn pile to retrieve cans. After an hour, seventy-five cans with holes punched in them were ready. The cans were attached in groups of three to every length of line. Small branches were removed as needed to allow the cans to hang freely but still remain out of sight.

"If anyone walks into the strings, we'll hear 'em," Rich said finally.

Indoor security fell to Emma and Kelly, who moved furniture around in the front room. They moved the big hutch in front of the picture window and put the tallboy dresser next to the front door, where it could be slid over to block the door. In the kitchen they built large brackets that would hold two two-by-fours so that the door could be barred on the lower third and upper third.

The whole group met back at 5 p.m. for dinner. Emma sent Lynn out back with Jess to get the stew pot out of the solar oven.

Lynn and Jess bounded out the back door.

"Hey, Lynn," she called after them. "You might need these!" She held up a set of oven mitts. "I know it's a sun oven, but the pot will be hot."

Lynn returned to the back stoop and retrieved the mitts.

When the two got out to the oven, Lynn looked through the glass at the cooking vessel. "Look, Jess," Lynn said. "The broth is boiling right in the pot."

Both youths watched as bubbles broke the surface of the soup.

Jess opened the oven and held the lid while Lynn removed the heavy pot of quail and potatoes. A strand of black hair fell into her face, in front of her eye. She blew at the strand without result, unable to brush it aside because her hands were full. The weight of the pot caused Lynn to struggle with it as she made her way to the back stoop.

"Here, let me carry that," Jess said, putting his hands out toward the hot pot. He felt suddenly embarrassed that he hadn't gotten it in the first place. Why did he feel this way? He had probably watched Lynn do this or something just like it before.

"It's hot, silly, and I'm wearing the pot holders," Lynn said, looking back at him, saying it with a giggle in her voice.

Her voice attracted him. It was like she was singing the words, joking with him, *flirting* with him. Was she? Flirting?

Clumsily Jess said, "No, I mean it, it's too heavy for you." He could feel his ears turn warm.

"I've got it." Lynn pursed her lips and squinted her eyes. She lifted the pot two or three times, gesturing with her head toward the door, then waited for Jess to hold the screen door open for her.

He jumped up onto the stoop, swung the screen door open, then jumped down, giving Lynn room to pass.

The two entered the back door and supper was served. Jess paused to block the back door by putting the two-by-fours in their cradles, then took his place at the table across from Lynn. Emma set out a single loaf of beautiful bread. Kelly ladled broth, quail and potatoes into everyone's bowls.

The sights and smells were heavenly.

Chapter 14

"Mom was pretty shook up," Kelly said as she hugged her legs in front of her. Jared sat next to her. The swing moved slowly, creaking under the weight of the pair. A sliver of moon dimly lit the cool evening. A piece of thick diamond plate leaned up against the porch railing. Kelly listened for the tin cans to rattle. She reached up and fingered the lanyard that held the whistle she wore around her neck since their trip to Fountain Hills. Jared and Kelly had volunteered for the first watch.

Kelly said very softly, "I'm glad Dennis and Jose had an uneventful trip into Sunflower."

"Yeah, that was good, but I think this unexpected visit from the strangers shook everyone's sense of security," Jared said. "I'm glad I was home. Your mom's a tough lady, Kelly. Maybe that's where you get it from."

"I get it from my mom and my dad. Both are rugged individuals. Growing up, it was made clear that I was expected to be the same."

Jared reached over and pulled Kelly to him, making her release her legs and fall toward him. The bulletproof vest he had given her to wear felt bulky and stiff. She leaned her face on his warm chest. His arm felt strong around her shoulders. The two sat leaning against each other, quietly listening to the sounds of the desert.

"Kel, I've noticed that your food portions have been smaller than those you give the rest of us," Jared said. "I thought I was imagining it at first, but now I'm worried about you."

"I don't need as much as you men or the kids, for that matter."

"You wouldn't be saying that if it were your mother cheating herself."

"That's different."

"I don't think it is. I don't want you to lose any more weight. Just in these, what, nine days we've known each other, you're thinner."

"You are too, Jared, and you know it."

He pulled Kelly to him more tightly, giving her two quick hugs.

Jared changed the subject. "Rich was sure in a hurry to get to his radio after dinner. The rest of the guys were going to move their stuff from the shed into Rich's basement before turning in. They thought it would be more secure. No one has asked me to move yet."

"No, and they probably won't now that we are an *item*. There isn't a lot of room in the basement anyway. Plus, it will be too cold to stay in the shed in a few more weeks. They are probably glad not to have to share what little space there is with you, if the truth be told."

"I can only hope that they are all jealous." Jared grinned widely.

"You men are always so competitive, especially over women."

"Yeah, true, and if there's anything around here worth having, my dear, it's you. You're pretty, hard-working, and can take care of medical situations to boot. Any guy would be a fool not to want you for himself."

Kelly blushed. "That is very nice of you to say, Mr. Malloy. Flattery will get you everywhere." Kelly raised her face toward Jared's and was about to plant a soft kiss on his lips when they heard the jangling of cans.

"Damn it!" a voice hissed far forward and to the left.

"Holy...!" Jared said, spitting the word out in a whisper between his teeth. He lunged to his feet so quickly he nearly dumped Kelly onto the floor. He drew his pistol. Kelly dove for the AR-15 leaning against a piece of diamond plate steel that had been put there for cover. Jared took up a position on the left of the metal sheet; Kelly took the right. They scanned the front yard as far into the darkness as they could see.

"You don't think that was Rich, do you?" Kelly whispered.

"No, be quiet." Jared hissed authoritatively. "See if we can get a better fix."

*Oh,* thought Kelly, *I like this side of Jared.*

A full minute passed.

Jared reached down and took his whistle and placed it between his teeth. He blew as hard as he could. Kelly did the same. Her weapon was trained into the darkness toward the offending sound.

Suddenly, the yard was lit by four headlights.

"Wow, Rich has been busy," Jared whispered. "Let there be light!"

One person was lying on the ground and a second one was standing over the first. The man standing held a revolver. Both were frozen in the light.

"Don't move!" called Jared in his command voice.

In one fluid motion, the man grasped the woman's hand and pulled her to her feet. Both darted into the brush. Gunfire erupted from the darkness where the two had retreated.

Kelly and Jared shot at the muzzle flashes. The headlights went off, enveloping the yard in darkness.

Kelly slid quietly from the porch to the stone observation post Jared and Jess had built that afternoon.

Jose's voice came from the direction of Rich's house. "There are many of us and we are heavily armed."

"Stay put!" Jared yelled to Jose. "We've got two in the dark, in front to our north."

Emma and Lynn, shotguns in hand, exited the back door and came around to the front porch.

Kelly crouched behind the stonework, scanning and listening. She strained to make out the tiniest unusual noise, but the night was teeming with the sounds of a rural homestead: bugs, owls, snorting horses and the wind. The wind, which Kelly hadn't even noticed while on the porch, now sounded like a hurricane.

Finally a bush moved. Kelly's gaze darted in that direction and she leveled her rifle. She could just make out a figure lying in the brush line, then heard the *click, click* of a revolver's hammer snapping on empty chambers.

"You're out of bullets, or haven't you been counting? Don't move or you're a dead man!" Kelly shouted with a little more fear in her voice than she would have liked. She sighted her weapon.

"Put the gun down in front of you!" With no option left, the man complied. "All of you come out of the bushes with your hands up!" The first figure, a man, stepped forward, followed by a second figure, a woman.

"I've got two!" Kelly yelled over her shoulder without taking her eyes off the pair. She spoke to the couple. "Who else is with you?" No response. "Damn it, speak up!"

"Nobody's with us," quavered the woman's voice.

She heard Jared belting out commands one after the other. "Jose, go to Kelly. We'll cover you." Kelly heard Jose's footfalls approaching quickly from the direction of Rich's house. "The other men go cover our front flanks. Rich and Dennis moved quietly to positions on the right and left of the front yard. "Jess, stand by for lights when I call for them. Kelly, I'm sending someone else over to help you." Jared looked at Lynn and motioned with his head for her to go to Kelly. Lynn looked at the ground and didn't move.

Jared turned to her again and gave her a "psst." When she looked up, he shot her a cold stare. Lynn moved quickly toward Jose and Kelly.

"Lynn, shoot this guy if he does anything funny," Kelly commanded. "Lights, now!" she shouted.

Jess illuminated the front yard. Everyone but Kelly and Lynn scoured the yard for more unfriendlies.

"Man only," Kelly said, "walk slowly toward my voice and then lie face down, now!"

Lynn pointed her weapon at the man while Jose trained his weapon on the woman. Only then did Kelly leave the protection of the stone enclosure and make her way the three steps to her first prisoner. She searched the man for weapons. She removed a pair of handcuffs from Jared's armored vest and fumbled putting them on. Handcuffs weren't part of her skill set. The process was repeated with the woman. Jose retrieved the revolver and then checked the bushes for more accomplices and weapons.

Lynn escorted the detainees, shotgun at the ready, to the porch for safekeeping.

"Those are the ones that were here today," Emma said to Jared.

"Shhh, don't speak 'til I'm done," Jared hissed.

Emma furrowed her brow but complied.

Jared separated the two prisoners. He was very angry, so angry that he felt as if he were shaking visibly. As a street cop, he had learned the need to control his emotions. A good cop does not yell because he is angry, but as a tool to accomplish a goal. He drew a deep, slow breath and held it for a moment, concentrating on relaxing. It was what the birth coaches called a "cleansing breath." He chuckled to himself, realizing that Kelly's job and his had *one* similarity.

"Kelly, Rich, take the woman to the back stoop. Don't take her in the house, don't talk to her. I'll be around in a few minutes."

Rich and Kelly walked the shaken woman to the back.

Jared interrogated the man. "What's your name?"

"I'm Tim and my wife's name is Mary. We weren't doing anything."

"You were doing something," Jared said. "Just tell me the whole story."

"We were out looking for food—ah, rabbit hunting," Tim said uncertainly. "Um, I didn't know you, ah, that there were houses here. We didn't mean anyone any harm."

"It doesn't look like you got any rabbits. Did you see any?" Jared said.

"Well, no. We haven't seen any."

"It's not too likely, wandering around in the dark without a flashlight. Why don't you just stay right here. I'll be back." He left Emma with her shotgun trained on Tim.

Jared made his way to the back of the house, where he found Kelly and Rich guarding the second prisoner.

"Now, ma'am, would you tell me your name and why you are here?" Jared said as they stood in the dark on the back stoop.

"I'm Mary. We came up to the house earlier today. It looked like there was just an old lady here. We thought we could get some vegetables or chickens or something out of the yard. We weren't going to hurt her."

"Tim was pretty fast on the trigger tonight," Jared said.

"I suppose. He was pretty scared. We are getting pretty hungry. The weeds and jojoba beans down by the stream don't hold off hunger very long. Look at my clothes, they are already hanging off of me and it's only been nine days, a little over a week."

Jared left Rich and Kelly with the woman, and moved back to the front of the house to address his other prisoner. "Tim, we have had just about enough of you and your wife. I think it's time for the two of you to be moving along."

"Sure, sure we'll leave, just let my wife go," Tim pleaded.

"Not so fast. No one is going anywhere tonight. You've already shown yourselves to be untrustworthy and downright dangerous. We'll wait 'til the morning and then let you know what we have decided."

"Please, please don't hurt us," Tim said.

"No one here plans to hurt anyone. I'll have them bring Mary back around front. You two can stay together tonight."

Kelly brought Mary to the front porch. Both prisoners were re-handcuffed in the front and bound by ropes about their waists, ankles and wrists, and tied to the porch swing. Emma couldn't bear the thought of the two being cold or more uncomfortable than they had to be, so she brought out pillows and blankets. Both were given water, which they drank greedily. Nothing was said in the prisoner's presence.

Jared called to Jess to come down from Rich's house. The teens were instructed to watch the prisoners while the rest of the clan held a family meeting.

"Shouldn't we give them a good dinner?" Emma asked Jared.

"No, I'm afraid that would just prove that we have food to share, and they would be a threat in the future," said Jared.

"Not anything?" asked Kelly. "I don't think I could do that to a stray dog."

"Kel, you and I were just talking about how all of us are losing weight, how the food we have now has to last through the winter. Every bite we give them may mean a bite Lynn doesn't have, or Jess."

Kelly hung her head. Emma leaned closer to her and gave her a hug. "I know, it's just so hard to wrap your head around. I've struggled with it *every* time we have seen someone without."

"That's natural," said Emma, "but it's survival now. We all have to change our way of thinking; them or us. I hate it too. I won't sleep all night thinking of them out there, cold and hungry."

"Remember, they were willing to kill us tonight," reminded Jared.

Kelly shook her head in acknowledgment.

"We're not going to hurt them," Dennis said as a statement, not a question.

"No, of course not," said Jared. "I can't condone first-degree murder."

There was a collective sigh, even from Jared.

It took almost a half hour's discussion around the kitchen table to come up with the plan.

****

The next morning found the away team—Dennis, Lynn, Jose, Jess, Kelly and Rich—riding on the donkey cart and horses, heading north from the ranch along the old road. Tim and Mary, still bound, sat sullenly on the cart with their scant possessions, which had been gathered from their camp by the creek. Everything they had with them fit in a daypack, except a single light sleeping bag. They had a few matches, a few articles of clothing, a can opener, a small fry pan, two forks, a pocket knife and a cell phone.

The group came to the junction with the Beeline Highway, well north of Sunflower, and continued toward Payson. When it was deemed they had gone far enough, Tim and Mary were set down, their restraints removed, and their gear thrown at their feet.

"Payson is that way," Rich pointed. "If we see you in our neighborhood again, you will be shot."

The couple walked silently northward until they were out of sight, carrying their bags and the sandwiches Emma had made them for lunch.

"Oh, my God," Kelly sighed heavily. "How could our world come to this? Did you see what they brought with them? How did they think they were going to survive?"

"They didn't," said Jose. "We all have had survival training, some in the military and some from camping or search and rescue. Remember, there are many in our population that have never struck a match. We don't have pilot lights any more, their barbecue grills have a push button start, and there are butane lighters for their scented candles."

"Yeah," said Dennis. "I'm willing to bet that the majority of Americans have never stayed overnight in less than an RV."

"Very few are going to make it," said Rich.

"We will," Kelly said in a voice not much more than a whisper.

"Yes, we will," said Jose sternly.

The clan scrounged with renewed vigor. Today, they used the northern route to the house from the Beeline instead of using the southern route through Sunflower, saving them several miles. In addition to the trailers brought home, the great find of the day was an overlooked tanker truck carrying corn syrup. It was actually high-fructose corn syrup used for making soda pop. When Emma heard about it, while the group was dropping off a load at the ranch, she insisted that they fill several large, scavenged water containers and a fifty-gallon drum with the liquid sugar.

During the late morning, the team heard motors; vehicles coming toward them from the South. As they got closer, everyone could see it was a convoy made up of old trucks—pickups, surplus military trucks, stake beds and jeeps, many towing trailers. The sound was so foreign as to be unnerving.

Dennis wanted to talk with them, but the drivers' and their passengers' determined, wary expressions convinced him not to bother flagging them down.

"I bet they're moving supplies for the Mormons," opined Rich. "There has been a lot of activity on the LDS radio net in the last twenty-four hours. I think we should leave them alone. That is all we can ask of them in return."

**\*\*\*\***

After the cart made its final trip home late that afternoon, Dennis and Rich decided to make a trip into Sunflower to tell the residents about the encounter with Tim and Mary. Riding into the settlement, they saw folks unloading their wagons of salvaged goods. Rich and Dennis pitched in while telling their tale. As the unloading wrapped up, they heard teams of horse-drawn wagons approaching on the highway.

Bill, Rich and Dennis walked to the highway to watch the parade. Descending the access road into Sunflower came every manner of beast and wagon. Horses, mules, hennies, burros, and ponies pulled old buckboards, modern wagons on rubber tires, donkey carts, pony carts, replica covered wagons, and even a ranch chuck wagon. Dennis noticed rifles and shotguns within reach of the alert drivers and riders, some of whom also wore sidearms, but no one seemed threatening.

The first team pulled off to the side of the road to speak to the Sunflower contingent while the other wagons continued on the opposite side of the road, down toward the stream.

"Howdy," Rich called.

"Hi there!" exclaimed the driver. "I'm Warren Jones, the captain of this Mormon wagon company. Who might you be?"

"I'm Rich Freeman, and this is Jose Herrero and Dennis Rabbinowitz." Rich approached the wagon and Warren leaned way down from the driver's seat, offering Rich his hand.

"We are residents of Sunflower. You're welcome to camp down here by the stream, but we ask that you stay south of the bridge and keep your livestock out of the stream. We're afraid that too many hooves will foul the water," offered Rich.

"Very reasonable of you," Warren returned. "We are sorry that we have to inconvenience you like this, but we don't have any choice. We will be as clean as we can. We were planning on damming the stream to make a few small pools. Our families and livestock will be doled water from them and we'll tell everyone else not to go down there."

"We appreciate your sensitivity in this current predicament we all find ourselves in," said Rich. "How many of you are there and where are you headed?"

"In total, there are several thousand people that will be passing by here over the next week or so. We're heading north and will be spreading out to Snowflake, Springerville, Taylor, Show Low and the like. We can make arrangements for land and water there. My wagons will be here tonight and you should start seeing handcart companies around midday tomorrow."

"Handcart companies?" Rich repeated.

"Yes, sir. Without even knowing it, we have been practicing this great migration by encouraging our youth to reenact the Mormon pioneers crossing the Great Plains into the Salt Lake Valley in the 1800s. Each stake does a handcart trek once every four years for our youth ages fourteen to eighteen. Their trek, like this one, teaches them what our ancestors did for their religious freedom and what they felt was their survival. This migration is not dissimilar to the very journey our ancestors undertook more than one hundred years ago."

"I am very familiar with handcart treks," said Rich. "I went on one as an adult advisor."

"So are you Brother Freeman?" asked Warren with a chuckle.

"I haven't been active with the church in years," replied Rich. "I'm a ham radio operator though, and I've been listening to your ham net. Does each company have a radio?"

"No, I'm afraid not enough radios survived for each company to have one. This wagon company has one. I think one of the handcart companies, three or four companies back, will have one. The last company to come through will have one as well.

"I'd like to talk to your radio operator," said Rich.

"Sure thing, Brother Freeman," Warren said with a wink. "He's in that green, tall wagon there, the second one in line." The wagon master pointed toward the wagons south of the highway.

"Thank you much, Warren. Good luck to you and all your people. You'll need it," said Rich.

"As will you, as will you," replied Warren. The two men continued to talk for about 20 minutes. The Mormons were aware of the widespread blackout and relayed the sad news about the many deaths in the big cities. Both men shook hands with Warren again and they parted ways.

\*\*\*\*

Kelly made her way out to the living room and immediately noticed that the couch was empty. Jared's blankets were stacked neatly on the floor at the far end of the couch, with his pillow topping the pile. There was no light underneath the kitchen door. Kelly scanned the rest of the room and finally saw Jared sitting in the porch swing through the gauzy white sheers that hung between the recently repositioned hutch and the front window. She picked up one of the stacked blankets and made her way to the front door. She opened it ever so quietly and slipped out. Jared looked up and smiled sweetly at her. His eyes had that familiar glow of a young man in love. Jared motioned with his arms for Kelly to come and sit with him. She threw the blanket around her shoulders and climbed into the swing, snuggling up. Jared leaned over and kissed her softly on the top of the head.

"Good morning, my darling," he whispered.

Kelly responded to his words by pressing herself tighter to his side and nuzzling his neck. The sun wasn't up yet, but the sky had begun to glow pink behind the mountain peaks in the East. Both sat in the quiet of the morning, enjoying each other's company and their beautiful surroundings.

"What do you think of the Mormons coming?" Jared finally asked.

"Oh, not much. I just hope they can make a go of it in the North. Not too hopeful, though..."

"What? You don't think they should go?" Jared turned to face Kelly.

"I'm not saying *shouldn't,* but it all depends on what's up there already. Water and probably land, but can they work the soil, do they have any seeds, will they live through the winter long enough to plant? Those people aren't much different from most city folks. Probably a lot of IT guys and data-entry moms, not used to hard work."

"The difference may be the skills they have *collectively,* like us."

"Yes, that would be one of the determining factors: knowledge, supplies and hard work, but don't forget the weather. If the winter is hard, the other stuff might not matter. I just hope they have the calories they'll need for cold weather and hard work."

"Speaking of hard work, the others will be up soon and today is cattle round-up day, according to Mom. She thinks they should be moved closer to the house so that we can watch over them. She wants me and the kids to help out. I think Mom's right. We need to get them in before they become barbeque."

"How long will that take?" Jared asked. "I've never had to round up cattle."

"Most of the day I would imagine; maybe two. The cattle usually don't stray too far from the stream, but it depends on how far afield they have wandered."

"Will you have to camp out?"

"No, we would go out on multiple days if we need to, but for now Mom thinks it will be pretty straightforward."

"Good. I want you home at night. I worry about you enough as it is when you're out during the day, but the nights kill me," Jared said, turning his face to hers.

Kelly, seeing this out of the corner of her eye, turned her head toward him. "You're so sweet."

Their lips met in the middle. Their talk about cows had ended. They sat kissing and caressing, time forgotten, until they both heard people walking about inside.

Jared whispered, "I love these precious moments we get to spend alone together. You know how much I love you, don't you?"

Kelly's heart skipped a beat when she heard Jared's declaration of love. She sat silently for just a second and then said,

"I love you too... darling." Her heart skipped another beat at her own words, and another, and another.

Jared bent down and kissed Kelly passionately. He could not describe the joy he was experiencing. For the first time in his life, he couldn't think of spending his life with anyone but Kelly. "Don't ever leave me," Jared said, his voice low and breathless.

"I'm not going anywhere. Why would I ever want to?"

\*\*\*\*

Breakfast was simple: eggs and pancakes. Emma liked cooking over an open fire in the backyard, and so did Jose. Everyone gathered around the kitchen table to plan out the day. Emma, Kelly, and the teens would round up the cows. The men planned on readying the homesteads for winter. Harvest was in full swing. Garden beds needed to be turned; if fallow, new beds planned out and turned. More cover frames needed to be fashioned to extend the growing season, and then there was the ever-pressing need for firewood. This was also the day for Dennis to prepare food for the Sabbath—Friday night and Saturday.

The men stopped their gardening and watched as Emma and Kelly walked past toward the corral to meet Jess.

"I've always liked pretty cowgirls," Rich said to Dennis, loud enough for the women to hear.

"I heard that, you ol' coot," Emma shot back with mock sternness.

"Yep, Stetsons, colorful, fitted blouses, tight jeans, chaps and boots. That's a great outfit to show off any pretty girl's assets," said Jose, just for the guys' ears.

"Well, the six-guns and holsters might give one pause for reflection," Dennis said, drawing attention to the matching holstered Rugers worn by Emma and Kelly.

"What a wonderful image she is—I mean, they are," said Jared, smiling.

**\*\*\*\***

The morning found the wranglers working the canyons east of Bushnell Tanks. Emma normally kept a good eye on her herd and knew where to look for them. The task at hand was to find her cattle, separate them from any other cows, and move them to land near the Wise/Freeman homestead. A corral, one of the many spread across the Southwest for temporarily holding stock during round-ups, was located nearby. The plain, heavy beams had been placed by Diamond Ranch cowboys decades ago. The current ranches maintained and used the pens every year.

The teens rode around the corrals and closed all but one gate. Emma led the crew to a large, tree-covered area. Here they saw contented cattle chewing sweet green grass. The teens circled the trees, looking for any wandering cows. There were several cows up the incline of the canyon, but most were near the grass down by the stream. Kelly and Emma began driving the small knots of cattle together. Unlike in westerns, moving cows is a slow, deliberate process. Mother and daughter moved behind a small cluster of critters and, with a little shouting and nudging by the cow ponies, the cows started walking.

"Cattle are pushed from behind and guided by outriders along the flanks of the herd," explained Emma to the young 'uns. Kelly and Emma taught by example. They also shouted directions to Jess and Lynn: "Forward, hold steady, come back 'round, hold 'em," and the like. Both teens were fast learners and the herding seemed natural in no time. "I'll make true cowhands out of you both," praised Emma.

Little by little, the cattle coalesced into a herd. Down the canyon they sauntered, with Jess and Lynn steering from the sides. The steep canyon helped; the herd was pretty content just to follow the trails by the stream.

When they got to the holding pen south of the highway bridge, everyone worked in unison to steer them into the pen.

With the herd inside the fencing, Emma counted noses and looked for other ranches' animals.

"Kelly, you go with Lynn; I'll go with Jess. Let's make another sweep. The way I count it, I have five head missing. 'Course, I won't know for sure 'til I can inspect those younger one's brands."

The wranglers scoured the canyons, hills and meadows for another couple of hours until finally the last of the wanderers was joined up with the herd.

Now, the mini cattle drive home commenced. Lynn and Jess were a bit let down because they did not get to use their nascent roping skills.

In Sunflower, the herd was simply driven into a holding pen. The teens watched, enthralled, as Kelly and her horse cut the other ranches' cattle from Emma's herd. Kelly and Pokey put on a masterful display of cutting skills. Pokey danced beautifully, shifting from side to side. Facing a cow head on, the horse would bob and weave, blocking the cow's forward movement, and finally turn the ornery critter through the gate, into another holding pen. Most of the time, the target cow complied and moved through the open gate readily. Some were not as helpful.

"It looks like two basketball players," said Jess to Lynn.

"What are we going to do with the rest of these?" Lynn asked Emma.

"They're mostly Bill's and the Barnards'. We'll tell them where they can find their cows when we pass their places."

The herd, now slimmed down by several extra head, was pushed home.

Emma called ahead to Jose and Dennis out in the garden, "Open the gates to the corral, boys." The cows were driven into Emma's corral, where she looked them over for any medical problems. Emma took Lynn and Jess by her side while Kelly sat up on the top rail of the corral. She explained to the teens how they were looking for anything out of the ordinary such as skin, eye, hoof or mouth problems. They were also looking for ticks, sores, and wounds. Emma's little herd seemed well enough.

"A little salve on that calf over there for his leg wound and that should do it," exclaimed Emma. "When that calf weans, his mama will make a fine milk cow. I'm so hungry for butter and milk I can't stand it. We'll even be able to make cheese."

Everyone was tired and Dennis suspected they were hungry as well. "Hey cowpokes, lets get some grub," he called. "The sun has been hot and heavy today and I've made several meals in the solar oven. I packed it full. Dinner will be ready in about an hour. Tonight it's canned beef and roasted vegetables, and tomorrow's lunch is vegetable lasagna *sin queso*—without cheese." Dennis said this with a lilt in his voice. His meals looked good and smelled good, and he knew it.

The whole lot put up the horses, praised them for a job well done, and then headed toward Emma's house. Blissful, hot showers were taken one by one while Dennis finished dinner and got it on the table.

"Wow," exclaimed Jess. "Meat, potatoes and corn pudding, yum!" he said like a true teen with a big appetite. Lynn looked happy and dished food onto her plate as well.

Mealtime was truly a pleasure and the group was becoming more and more cohesive, more like family. Jess and Lynn went on and on about the roundup. Everyone could tell that the two were excited about their part in it.

"I think it was pretty rare in our society for children to be able to do a day's work that truly impacted their families and their own well-being," said Dennis. "The roundup today was useful and the kids can see that this will bring us meat and milk. I'm proud of everyone's hard work."

"I'm off to bed," said Jose. I'm going to try to get a couple hours sleep, since I'm guarding down by the highway tonight."

"Goodnight, Dad," Jess said. "Sleep tight."

"Thanks for covering for me on the Sabbath, Jose," Dennis said, "I've got your Tuesday."

## Chapter 15

Rich and Jess volunteered to stay behind to guard the place while the others went to Bible study.

After the meeting, on their way home, Dennis rode Buckskin alongside the donkey cart. "I was glad to see a couple of new faces in the crowd," he remarked.

"Yes, it was heartening," agreed Emma, "and I was surprised to see some of the handcarts coming in already."

Her words came to an abrupt halt as everyone on the cart flew into the air, landing with a thud on its bed.

"Sorry," Jose called. "I tried to miss that one, but it jumped out in front of the wheel."

No one responded.

"The families with the handcarts look better than I thought they would," remarked Dennis. "A bit thin perhaps, but otherwise in good shape. Leaving a decaying city and traveling five days with those handcarts, even in this heat, doesn't seem to have affected them much."

"Can you believe the travelers invited us to a dance tonight?" exclaimed Kelly, glancing at Jared expectantly.

Kelly glanced up at Lynn, who was riding Pokey next to the cart. Lynn saw the look on Kelly's face. Both broke out in a smile the way young women do when they are going to a "ball." Kelly then looked up at Jared, who sat in the front next to Jose, but there was no change in his expression.

When they reached the house, Jess seemed disappointed because there was no insurgent activity to report, but he perked up a bit when he heard the news about the evening's gathering with the Mormons.

After a light lunch, Kelly and Lynn started planning their outfits for the dance. Kelly flopped on the bed as Lynn came in to model her best pair of jeans and one of Kelly's white shirts.

"What do you think?" asked Lynn as she twirled slowly so Kelly could see the whole effect.

"Nice," she said with an approving smile. "But a little boyish for a dance, I think."

Lynn's expression went blank. Surely, Kelly knew that she didn't have any other "look" more appropriate for a dance.

Kelly said quickly, "I have an idea." She flew off the bed and bolted from the room down the hallway, Lynn trailing close behind. "Mom!" Kelly hollered.

Emma appeared in the hall from the living room and Kelly almost ran into her. "What is it, dear?"

"Do you still have all that fabric up in your closet? You know, the pieces I used to sort through for school projects and stuff?"

"Yes, but why?"

"Lynn and I need skirts."

Lynn's face lit up. Her expression turned to one of excitement and her eyes sparkled.

Emma led the two giddy young women into her bedroom. Way up on the top closet shelf was a stack of fabric folded into neat rectangles. Some of the pieces were very small and some were of very bright colors, but both Kelly and Lynn found a fabric they liked in lengths long enough to make skirts. Kelly's was a light blue with small white flowers; Lynn chose a deep purple tone-on-tone with swirls. Both young women were thrilled at the notion of having a new piece of clothing to add to their small wardrobes.

"I think these skirts should be a little longer than we would usually wear them," remarked Kelly. "The Mormons tend to wear modest clothing."

"I agree," said Lynn with only a hint of disappointment. "Some of my friends are Mormon and most of them wear their skirts well below the knee." Lynn draped the purple fabric around her waist, positioning the fabric so that it dropped about six inches below the knee. "Like this."

"Smashing," Kelly said sarcastically with an accent that was supposed to sound like an old Hollywood film star.

Emma took down an old wooden sewing hamper from the shelf. It was the kind that opened up and out from the middle, revealing two shelves on each side with a larger compartment down below. The lid was padded and topped with an embroidered fabric. She removed needles and thread of appropriate colors.

"I can't sew on the Sabbath," Lynn announced. "Not that I know how to sew anyway."

Kelly and Emma looked at each other, not knowing what to say. The silence was embarrassing until Emma stammered a little and said, "I'll make yours, Lynn, this time. We'll have some sewing practice later."

"That would be wonderful, Emma." Lynn's face beamed.

All afternoon, patterns were made, measurements taken and needles flew until the skirts were finished. The girls looked feminine, almost delicate, dressed in their light cotton skirts. Kelly and Lynn emerged from the back room into the living room. The Sabbath had ended; it was time to leave for the dance. The whole Wise clan was now assembled. No one wanted to miss the big social event. The house would have to watch itself during the dance.

"Well I'll be," declared Jared, seeing Kelly in a skirt for the first time. He grabbed her around the waist and twirled her in a circle. "I'll be with the prettiest girl at the dance tonight," he announced and then gave Kelly a big kiss on the lips that lingered.

"Get a room, you guys," said Rich, rolling his eyes at the two lovebirds disapprovingly.

Jared broke it off, realizing that he might have gotten a little carried away. He twirled Kelly again, holding her arm up over her head, and admired the way the skirt floated away from her legs as she spun.

"Miss Lynn, over here, looks beautiful as well," Jared said, grabbing her arm and giving her a twirl in the same manner. Lynn blushed, but it was obvious that she enjoyed the attention.

Emma picked up her picnic basket. Not having much to share, she had loaded two loaves of bread and a pint of her strawberry jam in a basket to take to the dance.

"I don't know if there will be food and drink because of the circumstances, but if there is, it won't be me that has nothing to share," said Emma.

"Mom, you are taking food for the party when we wouldn't share any with that starving couple last night?"

"There is a difference between sharing and being stolen from," said Emma. "Letting those two, who snuck up on us in the night and fired on us, think they could manipulate us into giving them food would have been an invitation for them to come right back here and steal us blind. I'm still not convinced that they won't. We had to make a strong show of force. I think we did that."

"Yes, you're right. That whole thing just makes my gut ache," said Kelly.

"I know, me too, but it had to be done." She paused and let the negative feelings drift from her body. "Let's get on to the party. Parties are for forgetting one's worries."

Jose opened the front door and held it for the women to exit. Rich had brought the donkey cart around and it was time for the second ride into town that day.

"Now don't get all over those fiddle and guitar cases," Rich cautioned the girls as he assisted them onto the cart's platform. Lynn got in first and took the smallest case into her arms. She held it tightly to her chest and closed her eyes in sheer joy. Lynn could play the fiddle and tonight she would.

As the group approached Sunflower, there was a pale orange glow in the valley, south of the highway bridge, as the cliffs reflected the light. Behind them, the stars shone brightly in the sky and dipped into the saddles and valleys between the surrounding mountains. The smell of smoke hung in the air. It wasn't only from the cooking fires, but also from the bonfire, whose glow they could make out as they got closer to the dance.

Music was wafting up the canyon. Instruments and voices joined together as hundreds of people gathered for the party. There were men and women, mostly in jeans and T-shirts, mingling with others dressed like cowhands and pioneers. There were so many people there that the little band from Sunflower wasn't even noticed. The men stayed behind to secure the horses and cart. Emma and Kelly picked out a little patch of ground on the embankment and laid out a blanket. Jess glanced over at Lynn and they were off like a flash toward the many young people dancing. Their forms were silhouetted by the fire until they became lost in the throng.

Emma and Kelly soon abandoned the blanket to visit with the other women who were gathered in groups. The young mothers gathered with babes in arms and toddlers close at hand. The older women had also gathered, a group that appealed to Emma.

"Hello ladies, I'm Emma Wise from Sunflower."

"Hello, Sister Wise, we're so glad to meet you. I'm Carol Clark."

Emma did not correct this church courtesy of calling each other sister or brother. She thought the whole evening might be lost explaining her connection, or lack thereof, to the church.

"How is your journey going?"

Many voices all spoke at once until the women again yielded to Sister Clark. "The Lord has been kind to us so far," she said. She proceeded to introduce the seven other women, then began to explain what had happened. "The church immediately gathered its members for protection. We chose one house with a pool in every neighborhood and moved in together, assigning cooks, moving crews and armed watches.

"Was it that bad right away?" asked Emma.

"No, not right off, but we weren't sure when it would turn bad. One of our neighbors was an engineer and it didn't take him long to figure out it was an EMP. We figured when people ran out of water to drink and the sewer situation got bad, say two or three days, we would start seeing acts of desperation, and we did. Making the decision to take action early helped us in so many ways. We weren't moving supplies when people were thirsty and hungry, and security measures had already been finalized. It wasn't hard to identify the stronghold of the neighborhood. You might say we were the big dogs."

"How did you talk to each other, organize?"

"Most of us went to the church or sent a neighborhood representative to the church building," said Sister Clark. "Right away the Bishop set up a nightly meeting at 4 p.m. to talk about anything members thought was important. Our young people relayed messages between neighborhoods, wards, and stakes on bikes. Groups of people would sit around kitchen tables and write copies of memos to go out, stuff like meetings, water purification, how to get a hold of nurses and doctors."

"Kelly and I are both nurses. Have you had any deaths?" asked Emma.

"A few, but they were pretty sick to start with. Sister Sessions is a nurse." She motioned to a kind-looking woman in the back, who gently raised her hand and waved. "The third night after the attack, we all went to a class at her house where she taught us a little about field medicine. She made a list of items that would be most useful in treating the sick or injured and had us collect over-the-counter medications and prescriptions." She took a breath and grinned at the woman. "She was very specific on things we should bring—like soap, bleach, sheeting for bandages, bedpans and wash basins, toothbrushes, lots of things." It was clear to Emma that Sister Sessions was somewhat of a local hero and an old-time nurse.

"Kelly here was working at the hospital in Mesa when it burned down. What did the other hospitals do?"

"I don't know about other hospitals because we lived too far away, but the nursing home a few blocks over shut down and let their people out on the street. It was a nightmare. Someone said that after awhile the staff went home to care for their own families. No water, no food, no toilets, no medicine. I wonder what they did at the jails?"

There was talk of those who were ill. They spoke about those who were too old or chose not to go for other reasons. Everyone in the group seemed amazed that they had been put into this situation and that those kinds of decisions had to be made.

"It took a few days, but after we decided that nothing was going to get any better, we knew we had to leave the metropolitan area, get to somewhere that had water, someplace more remote. Preparations were made for the journey. We made carts and wagons from anything we had access to," stated one woman.

"Everyone gathered their supplies and much thought was put into what would be most beneficial to take," explained another.

Emma looked around at the group in wonder, curious as to how they selected what they would take along and how everyday life was prioritized. She said as much, in awe at how organized and comfortable they seemed on the road.

An older woman, who introduced herself as Sister Wilke, continued the tale. "Of course, food was the top priority, and then we had to identify items that could help us grow more food. Some of us keep stockpiles in our homes, but most everyone has two or three months of food for their family. When it came to growing new food, everyone worked together to gather seeds and gardening equipment. Someone even said that Brother Ellis broke into a plant nursery or feed store or something," she said it more quietly than the other information she had imparted.

Another woman chimed in. "We decided against pipes for running water simply because they would take up too much room. We did bring some flexible piping for siphoning from irrigation ditches if we need."

"We all needed shelter, so tents, bedding, and tarps were a must," said a young woman in a blue dress. Her long hair spilled over her shoulders and Emma wondered what life had been like for her before she started on this journey.

"Every family made a cooking kit. We were told specifically to bring pressure cookers and solar ovens. Most everyone who camps had Dutch ovens," she shrugged. "The fact is, this whole trip has been like a huge camp out. Someone tried to bring propane bottles, but we decided they were too heavy and we could gather wood and debris along the way to burn for cooking and warmth. Let us show you our rocket stoves made out of stones, they work great and you don't have to haul them, you just use new stones."

"You're very organized," Emma replied. "Did you find yourselves missing things?"

"More clothespins," everyone said simultaneously, causing the group to erupt into laughter. "Everyone seemed to have rope or twine for the line, but few of us hang out clothes any more."

"Matches," said another woman. "Even our barbeques had instant starters. So few people had actual matches."

Emma and Kelly were lost in the conversations. Each topic was more engrossing than the one before it. The talk went on and on.

\*\*\*\*

Rich, Dennis, and Jose finally identified some of the men they believed to be leaders by the number of people gathered around them. As they drew near, they could hear plainly the men talking about how good it was for their people to have a party like this and enjoy their time together on the road. Dennis led his friends to the front, where he introduced himself and his companions.

"We are glad to meet you, gentlemen," said a middle-aged man dressed in a green flannel shirt and jeans. "I'm Mike Stroud, the captain of this handcart company. I'll let the others introduce themselves, otherwise I'll be introducing all night long."

After a few quick introductions, Dennis said, "What's happening in Phoenix? We've heard radio reports from overseas, but have no idea what is going on in the Valley."

The travelers from the city told of how the police, firefighters, hospitals, and National Guard tried to provide aid and protect the citizens, but that effort quickly ended. They simply had no resources for themselves, much less to hand out. Panic and collapse of the government was followed by a wave of lawlessness that was suppressed only by neighbors banding together for protection. Fresh water and food became precious commodities. Sanitation had all but been abandoned by many people. Disease and illness were already taking their toll on the weakened populace.

"We knew we needed to leave after a few days, get somewhere that had water and fertile ground for crops. Like the church has always done in the past, we are now going to places of refuge," said Brother Stroud. "Now, let's put all of this doom and gloom behind us, gentlemen. I believe we have a party to attend."

\*\*\*\*

Lynn ran back to the wagon to get the violin. She was out of breath when she reached the cart, grabbed the instrument, then twirled about in one fluid motion, her hair making a complete circle around her head, and she bolted back to the band near the fire. As she took out Rich's violin, the band leader, seeing the newcomer, took out his pitch pipe and gave her a "C." She tuned her instrument momentarily then began to play, letting the spirit of the music overtake her. Joy filled her heart. It was a relief to finally feel happiness surging through her veins.

Jess had been looking for Lynn when he noticed her playing with the others. He stood in the crowd, admiring her. Lynn was *so* hot. Jess felt that he could stand there and watch her all night. After three or four songs the band switched to a square dance tune that Lynn didn't know and she stepped back into the shadows, excusing herself from the group. Jess appeared at her side, handing her a cup of water.

"Wow, that was beautiful. I didn't know you could play like *that*."

"Yeah, I love it." She took the cup from him and drank it all in one gulp. "Thanks for the water, I'm thirsty."

A strand of hair was plastered to Lynn's face where the sweat had trickled from her temple to her jaw. Jess reached up and brushed it aside. She immediately leaned back and looked down, breaking the uncomfortable eye contact. Jess hooked her chin with his index finger and raised it.

"I think I'd like to be more than just friends," Jess announced to Lynn. "You know, boyfriend and girlfriend. How about you?"

She looked like a doe caught in headlights. "All of this is new," she stammered nervously. "You'll have to give me some time. I like you and all, but what would our fathers say?"

"I hadn't really thought about it. Do you think they would be angry? I mean we are sixteen and old enough to date."

"And what about that fact that I'm a practicing Jew, and you're not? That's been drilled into my head since I was little."

"That doesn't matter to me," said Jess.

"Well, it does to my Dad, and me too, I think."

"It's just with the attack and things, life is complicated already."

"It's not that I don't like you, because I do, I really do, but we need to think about this. Let's dance," Lynn changed the subject.

Jess couldn't think of anything to say to that. "Let's go dance then. Your dad won't care about that, will he?"

"Probably not."

Jess led Lynn back to the bonfire and put his hands around her waist, tentatively, and she put her hands around his neck, not too close. "This is nice," Jess said. "This is nice."

\*\*\*\*

Kelly and Jared fled the throng of dancers. They were breathless and sweaty from all of the frivolity. Jared led Kelly by the hand into the trees, just out of reach of the fire's glow. The night air was cool and refreshing.

"I had to get you alone, Miss Wise." Jared leaned in toward Kelly and she met him with a kiss. After a few moments, Kelly pulled away and wiped a tear from her cheek.

"What's wrong?"

"This might be the last dancing and socializing we'll do for some time. I guess I'm not used to being so secluded and I don't see us leaving Sunflower for... maybe years."

"I know it's hard. Every one of us has been holding up way too well in my opinion. We're all facing our own demons. Besides, I'll be here with you."

"I know you will, but it's not the same."

Jared took Kelly by both shoulders and peered directly into her eyes. "No, it's not the same and never will be. It's up to you and me to make a new life in this new world. I try to think of it as a 'grand adventure.' If you'll let me, I'll try to make you happy."

Kelly cut him off, her breath catching in her throat and tears welling in her eyes. "I know you will and I'll try to be stronger. Maybe it was all of the dancing." She collapsed onto his chest and he held her there as tightly as he could.

"Stronger? What do you mean stronger? I've never seen you be weak, Miss Wise."

"I don't know if I can do this, Jared."

"Do what? Live?" Jared felt Kelly shiver and repositioned himself to cover more of her bare arms. "I want to work with you to make whatever future we can together. Don't think I'm not scared, because I am. I think everyone is in a precarious situation right now, especially with food and medical care being in such short supply. Remember, I love you."

Kelly looked up into Jared's eyes and saw the love that he proclaimed, and crushed his lips with hers.

"Kelly," Jared said. Still holding her right hand, he bent down on one knee in front of her. "I know this is sudden, and if you want me to talk to your mom first I'll understand, but…"

Tears again welled again in Kelly's eyes, but this time they were tears of joy. "No, go ahead," Kelly said softly.

"Miss Kelly Wise, will you marry me?"

Kelly's head spun. She knew what she wanted. She had never been more sure. "Yes. Yes, I'll marry you, Mr. Jared Malloy," she replied fervently, and flew into his arms. "Yes, yes, yes!"

"You have made me the happiest man on earth, Kel."

"And you have made me the happiest girl in the world, Jared."

"Do you know when I first knew I loved you?"

"No, when?"

"When we first met and you stuck your finger in my bullet wound on the side of the road."

"You're kidding. That had to hurt like hell."

"No, I'm not. I said to myself, right then and there, if I live I'm gonna marry this girl."

Kelly smiled and glanced away for a second, thinking about that fateful day. Turning back, she said, "Kelly Malloy—it has a nice ring to it, don't you think? It will take some getting used to."

"It won't take long, I promise," Jared said, taking Kelly in his arms and kissing her deeply.

"Let's get back to the party," he said finally. "We'll have plenty of time to be alone together. Let's enjoy this while we can." He stepped back an arm's length from Kelly and tugged lightly. She resisted weakly at first, but then smiled and followed him back to the dance.

Different dances were announced and the music went on for several hours until, one by one, the families started to leave, heading back to their camps. The Wise clan finally said goodbye and loaded onto the cart for the trip home, exhausted in body but renewed in spirit.

Jared assisted Kelly up onto the donkey cart. Jess watched with newfound interest at how he attended to Kelly. "Here, let me help you," Jess said, extending his arm to Lynn.

Jared sat with Kelly in his lap and Jess sat next to Lynn as closely as he could manage. Dennis and Jose both took a second look at the seating arrangements, then looked directly at each other. Things had changed.

Kelly nudged Jared and nodded her head, first toward him, and then toward her mother. Jared nodded back, cleared his throat and began to speak. "Can I have everyone's attention?"

"That's kind of formal, Jared. What's up?" asked Dennis.

"Kelly and I have some news we would like to share."

Emma partially turned in her seat, looking at the couple until the horses began to veer to the left. She turned back around, brought the team to a complete stop and then gave the couple her full attention.

"Of course, this would have to be alright with you too, Mrs. Wise, but Kelly has said yes to my proposal of marriage."

Emma's face went blank momentarily, then a huge smile filled every crevice of her wrinkled face. "Alright? I'm thrilled!"

Kelly got up onto her knees and leaned into her mother's arms.

"I'm so happy for you, baby girl," Emma said. "I think Jared will make you a fine husband."

"I think so too."

On the ride home, songs and laughter reverberated off the canyon walls; celebration amidst chaos.

Chapter 16

Kelly and Jared were the last to join everyone at breakfast. "It smells wonderful in here," Kelly announced.

"Thanks, dear. Did you two have a nice walk this morning?" asked Emma.

"Yes, and as you can imagine, we had lots to talk about with the engagement and all," replied Kelly.

Lynn jumped in excitedly. "I just think it's so romantic! You two are just so right for each other."

"Well thanks; I would tend to agree with you, my dear. Would you be my bridesmaid?"

Lynn just about squealed her answer. "Of course! Can I help with the planning as well? I just love weddings. When is it going to be?"

"Jared and I were talking about it this morning. Now isn't a good time because there's too much going on. We all need to focus on the harvest and firewood. If we don't get the wood chopped and stacked, we'll be cold this winter. Even if we had it all chopped right now, it might be too wet to burn."

"I'm sure we can plan a wedding while we chop wood," said Lynn.

Kelly shot her an exasperated look. "There are many things that need to get done to prepare all of us for winter. I think we're going to shoot for sometime between Christmas and spring."

"I don't know if I can wait that long," exclaimed Lynn. "I may just burst with excitement."

"You might?" chuckled Kelly.

The table was spread with hot cereal and fried carrot fritters. The carrot fritters were Emma's answer to hash browns, since the carrots were in full harvest and potatoes would keep better in the cave.

"These fritters are good," said Lynn, "especially with catsup."

"It's a good thing we don't need a refrigerator for catsup," said Jess.

"Everybody eat lots of pecans," said Emma. "That's our protein for breakfast."

The nuts sat, unshelled, in a bowl in the center of the table, a few nut crackers thrown in. The pecan trees were dropping their nuts and Lynn and Jess laid tarps under the trees and gathered them every day.

All through breakfast, Emma noticed that Dennis seemed distant. He sat at the head of the table, looking down at his plate, unusually quiet. He seemed to be lost in thought.

"Hey, Dennis, what's up?" Emma asked.

"What? I wasn't listening."

"That's obvious. What's wrong?"

"I've been thinking." He took a long breath, then let it out slowly before continuing. "I know we've been talking about happy times, but I think it's time we talked about... everything. I'm afraid it's just as bad, or worse, than we had imagined in town." The pronouncement took Kelly aback, as it seemed to have come out of nowhere. Everyone stared at Dennis, not knowing how to reply.

It was Emma who was first to gather her thoughts. "I was hoping that things would start to get back to normal, but without leadership, electronics and supplies... well."

"The starvation rate will skyrocket in the coming weeks. You saw how skinny some of the folks looked already," Jose said quietly. It was a statement thrown out as fact rather than something open for discussion.

"How awful to even think about," said Lynn. "The people we are talking about starving were our friends and neighbors, and if the blackout goes all across the country, our family members may die, too."

"I know there's nothing we can do about it, but it has just felt like the elephant in the room to me, especially since last night at the dance and this morning's talk of weddings," said Dennis. "Many of the travelers were fearful that they would not make it through the winter because of the cold or lack of food."

"It is very chancy for them," concluded Rich, "but they have many factors in their favor. Mormon teenage boys are Boy Scouts, and the church has organized camping events for its members apart from Scouting. As a group, they have basic outdoor skills and equipment which most Americans in cities lack. They are more likely to be conservative, outdoor-oriented people who hunt and fish. Church members tend to garden and preserve food more that most, although Mormons, like other Americans, are becoming more urban."

"You guys have skills like that, but isn't it still chancy for us?" Lynn asked in her whiny, puppy voice.

"I think our little group will all make it, but it won't be easy," said Dennis. "We have to keep our noses to the grindstone and work hard. I just wanted to say thank you to everyone for all of the work they have been doing around here."

Kelly knew that their circumstances were precarious. She thought they had all known this for some time, but now there was no doubt. Their immediate survival was taking every minute of their time, and planning for the future was critical. The future had been put into an entirely new context. The past seemed so easy and distant.

"Let's get these dishes put up," said Emma, "and get to work."

****

Over the next few weeks, Lynn watched the group settle into a routine of canning food, gathering wood, tending to animals, and living day to day without modern conveniences.

"Hey, Lynn," Jess said, interrupting her thoughts. "How did we get stuck with the laundry again?"

"Just lucky, I guess. If we ever get electricity back, I'll never grumble again about having to put the clothes into the dryer and then fold them."

"Yeah, I know what you mean. Just tending the fire and heating the water has taken us more than an hour." He looked up and smiled at her. "It has been a very nice hour, though."

"Yes, it has been," Lynn said. She smiled coyly. Kelly and Jared's engagement had made Lynn look at Jess differently.

Jess's arms flexed as he lifted a heavy log and put it on the fire. Ash and smoke puffed into the air. Lynn put the dirty clothes into the big metal basin full of steaming hot water. She added a little powdered soap. Jess took a large wooden canoe paddle and stirred the laundry around in a circle. After about fifteen minutes, Jess lifted a heavy, soaked shirt out of the basin with the paddle and placed it in a clean bucket. The pair waited for it to cool enough to touch and then lifted it, letting it drain.

"Laundry is gonna take us all day," said Jess with a frown.

"Hey, guys, looks like you're making progress," Dennis called as he approached the pair.

"Yes, sir," Jess said.

"I've been thinking. I know we are pretty busy around here, but in the next few weeks I think you should both start classes."

"Classes?" Both teens spoke simultaneously.

"Yes, classes." He smiled at their reaction. "Harvest will be over in a couple of weeks and we should have a little more time for some study."

"But what do we need to study for now?" asked Jess.

Lynn echoed Jess's sentiments. "As soon as harvest is over, we will be right into planning the wedding and…"

Dennis cut them both off. "There will always be something to do besides study. The wedding is Kelly and Jared's, and you should have plenty of time off to help anyway. Everyone will help teach. Jose is good at math, Jared with law, Emma with medicine and I can teach some classes as well. Both of you were good students before all of this and I think you will enjoy your lessons now too. Now, back to work." Dennis took off across the yard toward the gardens.

Jess grumbled something under his breath.

"School isn't so bad, Jess," said Lynn, rolling her eyes at him.

"There has to be one kid in every class like you," Jess said, mimicking and exaggerating Lynn's famous eye roll.


**\*\*\*\***


The Wise clan passed the evenings reading one of Rich's English classics, playing and singing songs, and listening to news on the short wave broadcasts. During the night watches, the watchers did their best to find creative ways to pass the time and stay awake. Kelly relished her watch time with Jared.

Large handcart companies arrived daily in Sunflower and then moved on after camping overnight. Rich monitored their progress on the local Mormon VHF radio net. During the dance, he had talked to one of the ham radio operators at length, and he offered to relay emergency messages to and from handcart companies passing through Sunflower. He also learned of the Mormon radio nets held on HF frequencies, which were used to communicate over long distances. He began checking into the HF net covering Utah and the other states surrounding Arizona. Few radios had survived, but those that had were being put to good use.

A month or so after the first dance, Bill Johnson rode into the Wise farmstead mid-morning. He stopped his horse well away from the house and shouted up the driveway, "It's Bill and I've brought news." He waited to be acknowledged and told to come on in by Dennis. Dennis called to Emma in the house, and the whole clan came running.

Bill stayed seated on his horse. "I've got bad news." He removed his cowboy hat and set it on his knee. "Charlie Best has killed himself." There was an audible gasp let out by those gathered.

Charlie was the loner, who Kelly knew was a diabetic. A neighbor had found a note on Charlie's door that morning explaining that he was nearly out of insulin. He had decided to kill himself by injecting all of his remaining insulin so he wouldn't die a slow and painful death. Sure enough, Charlie was found out in back of the house lying in a self-dug grave with his old dog, dead, beside him. Lynn turned away from Bill as he spoke. Emma took her in her arms and placed her forehead on her shoulder. Everyone was stunned.

"*Baruch atah Hashem Elokeinu melech haolam, dayan ha'emet,*" Dennis recited softly. The words seemed to comfort Lynn and she whispered them with her father. "Blessed are You, Lord our God, Ruler of the universe, the true Judge."

"Dennis, would you lead a memorial service?" Bill asked.

"Of course," Dennis said. "Any death is a loss but a suicide is particularly tragic and wasteful. It is Jewish custom to bury the dead as soon as practicable."

"Yes," Emma said. "From a health standpoint, a quick burial may be best. When were you thinking of having it?"

"Tomorrow," Bill said hanging his head a little. "I've got some of the men working on a better grave now."

"We should see about making a simple coffin," Dennis said. A burial shroud can be made from his sheets. I would feel better if someone stayed with the body until the funeral. The watching, or guard, of the dead is a sign of respect."

"It's like when I was on the honor guard for a Civil Air Patrol funeral," Jess said.

"Yes, exactly, an honor guard," Jose said.

The next day, the people of Sunflower gathered at Charlie's house. Many wept openly. Dennis began the service by reading Psalms and then asked if anyone would like to speak about Charlie. A few people spoke, mostly about Charlie being a good neighbor, but the underlying theme was the harrowing times. Beatrice Banning, Emmet's wife, was barely able to control herself. Everyone knew Emmett was an insulin dependent diabetic. Just like Charlie Best, his days would soon be coming to an end. Emmett sat stoically patting Bea's hand. After placing the casket in the backyard grave, everyone with a shovel mounded dirt on the casket until the grave was full. Silence hung in the air. All that could be heard was the rustle of the leaves in the fall breeze. After the emotional service, the neighbors spoke among themselves but didn't linger.

Emma and Kelly stood with the Wise clan on the front lawn of Charlie's house. "I'm going to swing by Bea and Emmet's," said Dennis. "They are pretty tender now. I'll see if they want me to visit in a day or two."

"We're lucky to have you here, Dennis," Emma said. "Kelly and I are heading over to see Chris Barnard and check on his heart problem."

"Wait for me," called Lynn. "I want to go too."

"Sure, you can come. I was hoping you would take an interest," said Emma. "I've been interested in herbal medicine for a long time because of my medical missions. It looks like it will come in handy now." Emma addressed the men. "We'll take the three saddled horses. You can all ride the cart back. We shouldn't be long."

"What's wrong with Mr. Barnard?" Lynn asked, pressing her heels into her horse's sides to keep up with Emma's taller horse.

Emma wanted Lynn, as well as Kelly, to understand what the problem was. "His heart doesn't beat strongly enough. It's called congestive heart failure. The medicine he takes now helps him get rid of excess fluid, which makes his heart work less, and he'll be running out of it soon if he hasn't already."

"Will he die without it?" asked Lynn.

"Well," said Emma, "I'm going to try some juniper berry tea with him and see if works to get rid of the excess fluid, just like his diuretic pills—I mean water pills," Emma added for Lynn's benefit. She paused for a moment, considering the process she would need to follow. "First, we need to see how many pills he has left. If we start the tea now, maybe he can decrease his dose and make the pills last longer. Lynn, why don't you write down what I do to make the tea? That way, his wife will be able to make it for him again later."

"It's like playing with the chemistry set I got in third grade," said Lynn. "Brewing tea and saving people, imagine."

"Have you ever used juniper berry tea, Mom?"

"No, but one of my homeopathic books recommends it. I imagine it will take some experimentation on our part to get the dose right. There are other things we can try as well, but we'll start with this. I'm hoping we can use herbs to save him after his pills have run out."

As the women approached the white picket fence, they saw a sign attached to it warning against trespassing. It read: *Violators will be shot*. Kelly spotted Chris Barnard. He stood on the side lawn, speaking with Bill. "Hi, Chris," Emma called.

"What can we do for you ladies?" Chris asked.

"I was hoping to talk to you about your heart medicine," Emma said cautiously, hoping not to offend.

"Well, I'd appreciate that," Chris said with a big grin. Lynn recognized the grin as part of his "nature," the nature of patients Emma had been teaching her about.

"Do you mind if we all talk? Kelly is a nurse and Lynn here is an aspiring nurse."

"Well, I'll be. How did a man get so lucky as to have three beautiful nurses looking after him?" Chris said. His belly laugh made all the ladies join in.

\*\*\*\*

It was quite late the night of the funeral, but Kelly and Jared were still up, sitting in the living room, when they heard Rich yelling from outside.

"Come to the radio! Come to the radio!" His voice grew louder as he got closer to Emma's house. Kelly and Jared rushed out onto the porch.

As soon as Rich saw them he pivoted on one foot, turning back toward his place at a full run. Kelly looked at Jared, puzzled. They saw a light come on in Emma's room; she must have heard him too. The pair took off running after Rich, up the hill toward his house.

Rich was out of breath but already seated at his ham radio desk when they entered the house.

"I've got 'im," he said. Rich turned quickly to Kelly. "I've got your dad on the radio! I've been talking to Utah for a couple of evenings now and the pieces just seemed to fall together. I'll tell you more later, but just talk now while he's on."

"Dad, it's Kelly. Over," the younger Wise spoke excitedly into the microphone. The rest of the clan arrived in the ham shack, wearing puzzled looks.

"Hi, Cowgirl," Sam Wise's voice boomed into the room. "I sure didn't think I'd be talking with you tonight. I'm so glad you and Emma are alright. I was worried sick about you. I'm fine here. The ranch is pretty self-sufficient, you know. We have good water, big gardens and lots of milk and beef. How are you holding up? Over."

"I can't believe I'm talking to you, Dad. Mom's right here, too. We're doing okay. I left most everything behind in Lehi, but I brought Hokey and Pokey. You know how Mom is. She's in pretty good shape with her gardening, canning, and cattle. We do have a very full house, though. There's a total of eight of us here. I won't take the time to explain except to say one of them is pretty special to me. Over."

Jared stepped behind Kelly and put his arms around her shoulders as if Sam could see him through the radio.

"Well, I'll be. I'm glad to hear it. Tell your young man hello from me and tell him I expect him to take care of you as I would. I don't know what I can do to help from here. Everything is shut down hard. We don't dare travel yet. Over."

"We know. It's pretty dangerous to travel here too. We are well armed and our numbers help." The radio made a burst of static and then Sam's voice was broken. Rich took over the radio and tried to dial the frequency back in, but the signal was fading. Several more broken words were heard and then just static.

"I think we lost him," said Rich. "I'll try to get him back." He continued to work with the radio while all those gathered spoke amongst themselves.

"Wow," said Kelly, leaning against Jared. "Richard, you are a magician just to get him for that long."

"I'm glad your dad is alright," said Emma.

"Who would have guessed we could reach him?" asked Kelly. "He sounds good."

Everyone sat around Rich's living room for about half an hour, waiting to see if communication could be restored, but good radio propagation—the way the radio waves bounced off the atmosphere—had passed, at least for talking to southern Utah, and everyone was tired.

"Well, that was exciting, but I think we should all get off to bed," Jose said. "I've got chores planned for these kids all day tomorrow."

Jared stood and held out his hand to Kelly. She took it and he pulled her up from the couch where she had been sitting next to him. The evening air was chilly and Jared ran with Kelly toward Emma's house. Emma and Lynn walked leisurely, talking. It was good to know there were other people out there and some were even safe; at least for now.

Chapter 17

The night was cool and still. The moon was full; its light shone through the sheers of Emma's bedroom window. Maybe the moonlight was keeping her awake. Emma lay in bed thinking about the chores she needed to accomplish the next day: grazing the cows and horses, doing the wash, and canning carrots. Suddenly, she heard chickens screeching from the yard. Their pitiful squawks quickened and intensified.

"Coyotes!" Emma screamed, loud enough to be heard through walls. "Get a rifle!"

Lynn, startled, sat up in her bed as Emma reached the door to the hallway.

"Got a gun?" Emma asked, nearly knocking Kelly over as she exited her room.

Kelly turned on her heels and darted back into her room.

Emma collided with Jared in the doorway to the kitchen. Jared, still half awake, stepped back and let the determined lady pass, clad only in her night dress.

"I hope you've got a gun, it might not be coyotes," Jared shouted after her. He went directly to the couch and pulled his .45 from under the cushion.

"We can't afford to lose a single bird," Emma cried as she exited the kitchen door. "Shoo, get outta here," she screamed as she ran for the coop.

Panicked by the melee and concerned Emma would meet gunfire, Jared, wearing only his briefs, sprinted to catch up to the old woman and what he hoped were four-legged coyotes.

Rich was headed toward the fracas at top speed. "Emma, don't shoot uphill. I'm coming down!"

Everyone in the clan was headed for the coop.

Rich got there just in time to see three coyotes headed into the night, each with a large bird in its jaws. He got off a couple of rounds but failed to hit any of the three moving targets. The rest of the clan joined him, one by one, out in the back forty.

"I wished I could have shot one," Rich said in disgust. "We could have at least tried coyote stew or jerky in place of, or in addition to chicken."

"Damn!" Emma said. "I thought that coop could withstand those mongrels."

Rich walked up to the enclosure. "Looks like the fence was left open," he said, swinging the gate to and fro, hinges squeaking as usual. "No signs of damage to the chicken wire fence, but this coop door has been dug open," Rich pointed to deep claw marks in the plywood, "and there's hair caught all around the door too. Those damn mutts ripped those birds out of that hutch. They didn't have a chance."

The heavy, metallic smell of blood hung in the air. Feathers lay strewn around the chicken yard and a disembodied wing lay in the dirt. The remaining six chickens, clucking softly, stayed on their roost.

"Stupid birds!" Emma fell to one knee and wept. Kelly walked to Emma, leaned her rifle up against the fence and laid a hand on her mother's shoulder.

Emma sobbed, "I don't know why I'm crying. Is it for the birds or for us? Maybe both."

No one else said anything. Jose picked up the wing and exited the coop, rattling the lock to make sure it was tight. Everyone understood the loss; it put them farther behind on food production.

Emma stood up. Everyone stared at the moon silently, shoulder to shoulder. They were eight people fighting against nature, against mankind, against the world. Only the slightest hint of breeze rustled the leaves of the trees. How peaceful it was. Peaceful and daunting at the same time, just like every aspect of their existence.

Jess hung his head and started back uphill, alone.

Rich pulled Jose aside. "Your son gathered the eggs this afternoon."

"I was hoping it wasn't him. What should I do?"

"Oh, I think he'll take it hard enough to learn his lesson. I don't think I'd say anything, but somehow I'd let him know I knew. The boy can't think he got away with it completely."

The men, except Jared, went together toward Rich's place. Jared put one arm around Kelly's shoulders and the other around Emma's, and Kelly reached out and put her arm around Lynn. The four walked back to the house together.

\*\*\*\*

Jared ambled into the kitchen and sat at the table. The legs of the chair scraped across the wooden floor boards, making a *clack, clack* sound. Breakfast dishes had been long since cleaned and sat in the drainer. There weren't a lot of dishes this day, since the meal had consisted only of pecans and oatmeal made from the horse's oats, confiscated from the barn.

"What's up, Jared?" Emma asked. She was preparing a rabbit to go into a crock with other vegetables, and then the solar oven.

"I was sitting in the living room when Rich brought the kids in for their literature lesson."

"Rich seems like a pretty good teacher from what I could hear from in here."

"Oh, I'm sure he's great, and the kids like him."

"Where's Kelly?" Jared asked, looking around as if expecting to see her somewhere in the kitchen.

"She went up to tend the horses. She's been gone quite awhile," said Emma, finishing washing her hands and then flinging a dish towel over her shoulder.

"I'm goin' up there." Jared grabbed a plaid jacket from a hook next to the back door and exited, letting the screen slam as he leaped from the back stoop. As he passed Rich's house, he could see Kelly standing near the lean-to that made up the back wall of the corral. She had one foot up on the bottom rung of the split rail fence. He could imagine her chewing on a piece of straw like the cowboys in movies did.

"What's up, gorgeous?"

Kelly jolted around, face ashen. "You shouldn't sneak up on people like that."

"I wasn't sneakin'. You were a million miles away." Jared put his arm around her waist and pulled her tight. "Penny for your thoughts."

"What do you think of this old trailer?" She pointed at one of the ATV trailers they had acquired on the highway a few months back.

"I don't think much of it, why? You have plans?"

Kelly looked at Jared. She played nervously with the collar of his jacket and bit her lip. "I think we should leave. I don't mean tomorrow and I don't mean without telling everyone, of course, but I've come to the conclusion that this arid piece of desert cannot support all of us." Jared let her talk. "If we stay here we'll all die slowly. Anyone can see that we are using up our supplies faster than we can grow new ones. We lost those chickens last night, and we can't grow grain here."

"We're still in the early phase. The cows will multiply and the garden can be replanted in the spring. We can plant corn—it's a grain. We got some at the feed store."

Kelly pulled back, putting a little room between them. "That's just it. The cows will multiply, but slowly. Only the garden my mom has *now* can be replanted; there isn't enough ground for corn to make cornmeal. This is still the desert, even if there are trees down by the stream. The soil here is ground granite. It contains very little organic material and we can't drive to the nursery to get compost and fertilizer. It will take years and hundreds of man hours to collect and compost enough material to make it productive. We're all gonna die if we stay. We've gotta get to my Dad's." She sounded logical, practical, almost matter-of-fact, but her heart was pounding. Saying the words out loud about leaving her mother flushed a cold surge of guilt through her veins. She carried on anyway; it had to be said.

Noticing a quaver in her voice, Jared took Kelly in his arms and pulled her toward his shoulder for comfort. She lay her head against him. "Maybe you're right," he said. "We need to consider this carefully. I don't think it's going to be very friendly out there and it's like, what, three or four hundred miles of mostly desert to your dad's? Your mom and Rich are no spring chickens either."

"Mom and Rich will never leave. My mom would never go to my dad's anyway. She's got Rich and there's ample food for the two of them."

"You're talking about leaving her here?"

"If she won't come—and she won't—it's the only thing we *can* do."

"Okay, let's say we have to go. How do you propose we get there?"

"Horse-drawn wagons, like in the old days. We can modify this trailer for the horses to pull. We can sleep in it, cook from it. It will carry everything we need to get all of us to Utah."

"All of us? Who are you talking about?"

"Dennis, Jose, the kids, and us, of course. We will all have to go if Mom and Rich are to have a chance. It will be safer if all six of us go together, too."

"We're going to have to give this a whole bunch of thought before pulling out of here, Kel."

"I already have," Kelly said, pulling away and turning her back on him.

"I can see that, but I think the rest of us should be in on the discussion."

"I don't see any alternatives."

"There's always an alternative. I think we should all get together and run the math," Jared said, turning Kelly around to face him. "Figure out just how long the food will hold out."

"It's six months. May, by my calculations, and if we lose any more chickens, less."

"Come here," Jared gathered Kelly in his arms.

Impishly, Kelly said into his collar, "Can we change the subject now?"

"Sure. We're not going to solve that whopper this minute. Maybe we could talk about something here and now. The horses look good?" Jared said.

Kelly lifted her head and looked into the corral. "Yep, a little thinner, but I'm thinking of taking them down to the Branham's place today. They had grass on their front lawn and it's got a little height on it now. Should be a good lunch for our four friends here."

"I'll go with you. I'll look forward to it." Jared smiled and raised his eyebrows.

****

"Emma, that was the best corn pudding I've ever eaten," said Jared. "It's like sweet, buttery, gooey cake."

"That's probably the only corn pudding you've ever eaten unless you're from the South," said Emma.

"Well, that's true. I haven't had corn pudding before, but I've had cornbread. This is better."

"Lynn helped me make it. It's just some corn meal, canned creamed corn, corn syrup and some onion from the garden. I usually put a whole stick of butter in it, but I had to use a little peanut oil this time. Lynn and I gathered the greens out in the yard. And what do you think about the salad?" She glanced over at Jess, who had devoured his corn pudding but was pushing the greens around on his plate.

"It's good," he said sullenly, still not taking a bite. He pushed his chair back and stood up, taking his plate toward the sink.

"I'll take that, Mijo," said Jose, reaching for Jess's plate. Jess handed it over without speaking, then headed for the living room.

"You will turn Miss Lynn here into a fine cook," said Jared. "Now, if you will excuse us, Kelly and I are going to take the horses over to the Branham's for their lunch." Jared winked at Kelly.

"Jared," Kelly interrupted, clearing her throat. "I thought maybe my mom and I would take them down."

Jared looked at her, puzzled. "Sure." He paused, a little stunned.

"But I'll make it up to you," Kelly said, raising her eyebrows and nodding, asking for his approval.

"Okay then, another time." His voice and mood had changed from jubilant to disappointed.

"Will you go with me, Mom?" Kelly asked.

"Why sure, honey. Have something important to talk about?"

"Well, as a matter of fact, I do."

"Let me get some things. Lynn, can you wash up these dishes?" Emma didn't wait for a reply, but left the kitchen for the shoe rack by the front door.

"I'll go with you two," Jared offered to Kelly.

Kelly stepped within a foot of Jared and gave him a curt head shake. "Please. I'll explain later."

Jared waited for the door to close behind Emma before he asked Kelly to step out the back door with him. "I thought *we* were going to talk first?"

"No, I have thought about this and I think now is a good time to break it to my mom. Instead of us preparing to stay we *need* to be preparing to go and it will take us every second to get out of here in March. Really, we can't wait another day."

"I thought you said that the food would last through May?"

"Yes, if we take it down to the last mouthful. If we go earlier, we will leave more for Mom and Rich to use until they can get the late summer crops in."

"Why March then? Why not February?" impatience crept into Jared's voice.

"Weather," Kelly said, impatient herself.

"Okay, but I think I should go to the Branham's with you for security."

"No, thanks. Really, this is a talk my mom and I need to have alone. I have a history of leaving my mother. We still have issues. I left her every year to spend the summers with my Dad, I left to go to college and then the military. My mom was finally certain that I would be around, that I had come home to stay, and now this. Who knows if we'll ever see each other again. She'll be scared, sad, maybe even angry."

"Just be glad you have someone who is worried about your leaving," Jared said, his voice softening some. "Can we go out tonight, alone somewhere?"

"Sure, I promise." Kelly smiled, noticing Jared's downturned gaze. She gave him a peck on the cheek.

Emma stepped out onto the stoop wearing her cowboy boots and a nice holster to boot. "Ready?" Emma asked Kelly.

Kelly glanced at Jared and then to her mother. "Sure, Mom."

\*\*\*\*

Kelly and Emma saddled up two horses to go to the Branham's house. The other two horses, without saddles, were led by their reins. It had been quite awhile since Kelly and Emma had been alone together and could actually talk, *privately*. Every waking minute seemed to have been filled with contemplation, planning, and execution of survival.

At first the ladies rode in silence down the dirt road, turning to follow the meandering canyon. The water babbled in the stream and the sun beat down, warming their skin. Kelly was lost in thought as she sat atop Pokey, feeling his back sway under her saddle and her shoulders sway in response. She was trying to compose the right words to tell her mother how urgent and imperative she thought this move was.

"The horses seem keen to get away from the old homestead," said Emma placidly. "I think I needed a break too. We've all been working hard to keep ahead of everything."

"That's why I asked you to come with me today—instead of Jared, I mean."

"You were right. The grass is up to our knees," said Emma as they reached the Branham's.

Kelly and Emma dismounted and dropped the reins. The horses took immediately to munching the tall grass. It looked mostly brown on the tops but further down, toward the roots, the blades were still green.

"Fall doesn't give us much rain around here," said Emma.

"Mom, I don't want to talk about pleasantries, least of all the weather." She didn't mean it to sound quite so abrupt. "There's something big on my mind."

"Weather is important and—"

Kelly let out a frustrated "*harumph*," pursing her lips.

"Oh, I know that look. What's up, baby girl?"

"I'm afraid."

"I—"

Kelly held up her hand. "Let me finish. I'm afraid we might all starve. I think you and Rich can do well here, but the rest of us, we have to leave. We have to go to Dad's. That way, we all stand a better chance of survival 'til this whole thing is over."

Emma stood dumbfounded, her mouth hanging open. "We've all been working so hard."

"I know, but it's obvious we won't be able to keep up with food production. With eight of us here, our supplies are being used at an alarming rate. We have to go into Rich's basement or hike up to the cave almost every day to get food."

"You can't go. It's, it's... too dangerous. You'll never make it that far," Emma said hurriedly, trying to make a sound argument.

"We have to try. You can grow things there, *really* grow things."

"You're not going and that's final," Emma said in the same tone as if she had stamped one foot on the ground.

"I don't think you can talk to me like that anymore, Mom. I'm not a child and won't let fear keep me from doing what's right."

"Fear? You want to go charging off into the desert with those kids with the world the way it is? That's not right, honey, that's just plain crazy. Getting to Utah without a car is hard in the best of times. There are mountains to get over, tall ones, and then miles and miles of unforgiving desert, not to mention every human out there will be competing for your water, food, horses..."

"I know it's a gamble, but to stay is a certain, slow death and I refuse to take you down with us. I won't subject you to that." Kelly choked out her words, angry, sad and confused all at once. "I love you."

"I know you do. I'd gladly die for you and you know it."

"It wouldn't be you dying to save me, Mom. It would be all of us dying together. Is that what you want?"

"No! Damn it. But..."

"But what?!"

"But I never, ever want to lose you... again," Emma blurted out.

"You could come with us."

Emma fell silent, staring at the ground.

"Mom, did you hear me? You could come with us."

"No," Emma's voice slowed to a crawl. Her words were very deliberate. "No, I'm getting too old to make a trip like that. I've never imagined myself anyplace but here, living out my final days. This is my home. Besides, your Dad and I… you know, we... me and Rich wouldn't fit in."

It was Kelly's turn to be silent.

Emma continued, "What would Rich do?"

Kelly had no answer. Slowly the two women came together in a hug. Out of words and other possible solutions, it was all that was left. Both strong women were fixers, copers, used to looking after others. The tears ran silently down their faces until their collars were wet.

All of the unspoken words of the past flowed through them and out of them as they held each other. After a long time they let go and walked, hand in hand, toward the porch on the Branham's house. The horses continued to munch contentedly.

Mother and daughter talked until late afternoon started to fade into early evening. The sun sank below the cliffs to the west, putting their little canyon in yellow-grey shadow. Finally, they rode in silence together—really together—back toward the house.

Chapter 18

Kelly and Jared reclined on their favorite rock down by the creek. This had become *their* place to come and talk, a hideaway of sorts. Jared lay on his back with his jeans jacket rolled up under his head, and Kelly lay with her head on his stomach.

"Look up there, Kel," said Jared, pointing to yet another outcropping high on the cliff above them. "There's a nest up there, a big one."

"We have a lot of large birds around here, but I don't know of any that make a nest that size." Both shrugged. "Look at those clouds, though." Kelly pointed to some white, fluffy clouds with dark, blue-grey bottoms. "Looks like we have weather building from the west. We sure could use rain. I don't think we have had any since we've been up here."

"Nope, not a drop. It's hard to believe it's mid-November. Anywhere else in the country the snow would have started to fly, but here it's still in the seventies and only chilly at night. The first night I really needed a jacket was Halloween."

"I'm just glad we're here and not on our way to Utah. It won't be long before there's snow in the mountains of Northern Arizona," said Kelly. "I think Mom's relieved that we put off the move until March, but the delay will just make it harder on her.

You know, more time to think about me and to get to know you and the kids." She put that thought out of her mind and focused on the upcoming move instead. "When we go, we'll have to traverse desert for fifty miles to Payson until we start to climb the rim. Ninety-five miles in higher elevation to reach Flagstaff, two hundred miles of mostly high desert to Kanab, then fifty rough, mountainous miles to Alton, where dad lives."

"That's quite a trek," Jared said lifting his middle slightly to brush a small rock from under one hip. "Makes me tired just thinking about it."

"Makes me tired and hungry," Kelly said, rolling to one side and lifting herself up on one elbow. "Speaking of hungry, I was talking with my mom, who brought up the food issue for the horses. There won't be enough grass growing along the way, maybe not until April. We couldn't possibly carry enough feed for the whole trip even if we had it, so we will have to wait."

"Is that why we're waiting?" Jared asked.

Kelly nodded, but both of them knew that the logistics of the trip wasn't the only reason they were staying.

"How long do you think it will take, the whole trip?" Jared asked, picking up on her hesitation and sadness.

"Oh, three hundred and seventy miles, an average of ten miles a day, figure in rest stops—more than forty days, I guess. We need to plan it so we're out of here after the worst of winter and in Alton before the heat of summer."

"We should plan on delays for mechanical issues, injury, detours, stuff like that," said Jared.

"No way to account for any of that," replied Kelly. "We don't know what's out there."

"I think it will be fun," Jared announced. "A grand adventure."

"A grand adventure alright, but it scares the hell out of me."

Jared ran his fingers through her hair, just letting her know that he was there.

"But Jose and Jess have put a lot of thought into the wagons. Did you see the suspensions?" asked Jared.

She laughed. "They've been like mad scientists with this project. It's brought out Jose's ingenuity in the best way. The secret compartments built into the beds may just save our lives."

"Ingenious, huh?" asked Jared. "I never would have thought about an extra six inches in the floor or disguising a removable rail to access the space. Those custom water tanks are genius, too. The second half of the secret compartment fits tin cans and canning jars perfectly. We can hide anything we want in there."

"I just hope we can hide enough to get us by," Kelly rolled over onto her stomach and propped her head up with her hands.

"I think they look cool," Jared said. "The old-time covered wagon meets MacGyver."

"I knew you'd like them," Kelly said playfully. "The PVC hoops on top make them look like modern day prairie schooners. I wish we had something besides those huge blue tarps to cover them, though. Nothing that blue occurs naturally; they'll stick out like sore thumbs."

"The things I'm the most impressed with are the suspensions."

"You said that," Kelly pushed on his shoulder playfully, knocking him back.

Jared jerked back up to a full sitting position. "Now, what were we talking about? Oh yeah, suspensions... they sit high and ride like canoes, s-m-o-o-t-h."

"Yeah, Jose is proud of that," said Kelly.

"You know," Jared said, looking Kelly right in the eyes. "I didn't think Jose and Dennis were gonna come with us. How'd you change their minds?"

"Oh, I don't know," Kelly said with a drawl as she rolled her eyes to one side. "I might have laid down the law or begged for their help along the way, maybe both."

"Bill says travelers report that things are worse than ever in the cities. Nobody has seen anyone from the government except a couple Humvees with guns mounted on them driving through, and only a handful of those. No convoys of food, no water..."

"The longer this goes on with no direction from the government, the worse it's going to get."

"Do we still *have* a government?" asked Jared.

"Who knows?"

"What's our next big push? The canning and firewood chopping seem to be going well, if we can just keep wild-man Jess away from the axes. He darn near chopped into his own foot and mine the other day."

"Our next big job's got to be rounding up another couple of horses for the second wagon and getting them trained. That only gives us four months to find 'em *and* train 'em."

"What if we can't?"

"We don't go," Kelly said plainly. "Since I don't see that as an option, we'd better get busy."

"Wow, you mean I get to see Kelly the cowgirl again?" Jared asked, smiling playfully.

"I guess you do." Kelly rolled onto her back and took a deep breath. "It's so pretty here, I could stay all day."

"Too much to do—we should be getting back." Jared stood her up and gave her a long kiss before they departed.

\*\*\*\*

The clan was enjoying the evening, sitting on the porch, taking turns playing their instruments and singing. It was their usual nighttime activity because it didn't require any use of lamp oil or candles, and it was cooler on the porch. For the first time since early September, they were getting a little rain. This wasn't the violent, flash-in-the pan type rain they got with the summer storms, but a nice soaking rain that, after an hour, turned into a light drizzle.

Rich and Emma finished strumming and Kelly finished singing the last of verse of a song about a covered wagon.

*We are leaving Old Sugar Creek in our wagons stout and strong,*
*To make it to the valley before the winter nights are long.*
*Please pray for our safe arrival in a land to call our own.*
*In the spring will fall the rains where our summer wheat is sown.*
*... and the wheels rolled on, and the wheels rolled on.*

The pit-pat of rain resumed. The splish-splash sounds emanated from the puddles that had formed under the eaves.

Kelly said to Jared wistfully, "When I imagine our trip to Utah, I see it like that song: you driving the team, me sitting beside you, dinner around the campfire, a huge blanket of stars."

"Your idea of it seems a bit romantic, if you ask me. Sounds like a lot of hard work and cold nights. Didn't a lot of those pioneers walk alongside the wagons to save the teams and free up space?" asked Jared.

"I hope *we* don't have to do a lot of walking. We didn't when I was on the chuckwagon during roundups at my dad's."

"Yes, but on that roundup each of the cowboys had their own horse," said Emma.

"Your *remuda* looks like it needs more mounts," Rich chimed in.

"Really, I'd like four more horses: two each for the wagons and a team to trade out, "said Kelly wistfully.

"What does *remuda* mean?" Lynn asked.

"Well, young filly," said Rich, making the porch swing rock lightly, Emma by his side. "A remuda is the herd of horses for the cavalry, and remounts are the extra horses to be traded in when the ones you're riding on become tired."

"What makes you a horse expert, Rich?" Jose asked from where he was sitting on the floor with his back up against the wall.

"I've seen every John Wayne movie ever made ten times over," said Rich, putting his guitar down and picking up his banjo. He plucked the instrument and sang...

*If you want to have a good time, jine the cavalry!*
*Jine the cavalry! Jine the cavalry!*
*If you want to catch the Devil, if you want to have fun,*
*If you want to swell Hell, jine the cavalry!*

"Kelly's going to be the chief wrangler of this 'gathering remounts' detail?" Jared asked, laughing and poking Kelly in the side.

"I've spent more time in a saddle than anyone else here. Unless *you* want the responsibility, Mr. Malloy."

"How about I take over the security detail?" he bargained.

"Fine plan," said Kelly. "We'll need some cowhands too." She looked over at Lynn and Jess, who were sitting in lawn chairs near the railing. Jess was sticking his hand out past the roofline, where water splashed into his palm.

"I wanna go!" said Lynn enthusiastically. " My riding has gotten better and Pokey is my best friend *ever*."

"Fine," said Kelly. "We'll take you and Jess. It should be a fine outing."

Jess glanced away from his water play toward Kelly, looking pleased.

The wind picked up and the rain fell anew. Small drops of water landed on the back of the porch swing, where Emma and Rich sat.

Emma stood immediately to get away from the wet. "Well, get up, ol' man," she said to Rich. "You guys better get home before it really starts pouring."

"Oh, a little rain never hurt anyone, ol' woman." Rich said in his usual, slow drone, but he too stood.

"Just mind you don't catch your death." Emma raised both eyebrows and set her lips.

That was Dennis and Jose's cue to get up. They both brushed themselves off and Jose stretched, trying to get the knots out of his knees and shoulders.

"Come on, Mijo," Jose said. All four men stepped off the porch and then ran, in a mad dash, for Rich's place.

\*\*\*\*

By the end of the week, they'd had time to gather gear and make plans for capturing the wild horses that roamed the river near town. The predawn sun glowed red behind the mountain tops as the group trotted on horseback down the road, leaving small whirling clouds of dust where horseshoes hit dirt. Jared, Kelly, Jess and Lynn rode along the Beeline Highway. They had packed light and hoped to return home in two days.

"Will it be hard to find the wild horses?" Lynn asked.

"I've never known them to stray far from the river," Kelly said. "I just don't know what effect the collapse has had on them. We need to know what shape they're in. If we're lucky, we can bring one back with us."

"Can't we bring more than one?" Jess asked. "We have the ropes and tack for it."

Kelly chuckled. "It's going to be all we can handle to catch just one mustang and lead him back to the ranch. Okay, I know your horsemanship has improved, but I want you to be careful anyway. Jess, you and Lynn have really gotten good at roping in the corral, but that's not the same as convincing a full-sized, wild horse to leave his herd and come and live at our house. It will be downright dangerous."

They left the highway and went south on a dirt road that had been a playground for off-road enthusiasts. Kelly recognized the road, having roamed here in her pink "Barbie Jeep" with her "jeeper buddies" last spring.

Finally they left the brown scrub of the desert behind and wound down through the canyon and the dark green trees and brush lining the Salt River. The horses' pace quickened when the animals breathed in the inviting smell and humidity of water. When they made it to the river's edge, everyone dismounted and let the horses drink.

"I smell smoke," Jared said.

Kelly inhaled deeply through her nose. "Wood smoke."

The others were sniffing too. "You all look like a bunch of bunnies with your noses twitching in the air," said Jared, grinning.

Jess waded out into the river about ten feet from the brushy shore and scanned the banks. "Look, upstream. I see smoke from a bunch of little fires. There are some downstream, too."

The others took off their shoes and waded out into the flow. Kelly noticed that Lynn eagerly moved next to Jess and took his hand in hers. "They're spread out in the trees and bushes, away from the shoreline," she said. "Looks like individual camps."

"Who would be way out here?" Lynn asked, shielding her eyes from the sun with her hand.

"Anyone who could last this long," Jared replied. "It's going to be tough to look for horses by the river without having to deal with the locals."

"These are the people who were able to make it out here, away from town, and live out here for months on end," Kelly added. "These people have the equipment and skills to camp, hunt and fish. This is the only water on this side of Phoenix and it's the lowest I've ever seen it."

"Why, what happened to all of it?" asked Jared.

"There's never been a lot of water in the desert, but the Salt and Gila rivers used to flow year-round and overflow their banks each spring. That left good planting soil. The local Indians built irrigation canals near the confluence."

"Why don't the rivers flow anymore?" Jared asked.

"Geez, I guess you didn't have to take Arizona history in Michigan," Jess said. "We had to take the Dam Test in eighth grade and again as sophomores. You have to name all of the dams and reservoirs in the state."

"In 1903," Lynn said, "the Salt River Project started building dams and reservoirs along the rivers to supply Phoenix with water and power. The water here, near town, is held back by Stewart Mountain dam. The level is already down. The flow is blocked upstream by other dams."

"Thanks, Hermione," Jess said.

"Back to the problem at hand: looking for horses. We need to stay in the brush as much as we can and skirt around the camps," said Kelly. "We can come out to the river's edge between the camps and do our scouting. It's midday. I prefer to look for horses at dusk and dawn. Let's move away from the river and find a safe place to wait out the afternoon. Our horses need to rest anyway. Maybe we'll get lucky and a nice herd will wander into us," Kelly chuckled.

"I hope no one ate all the horses," Jess said.

Lynn's eyes widened. "You're so mean, Jess Herrero," she pouted.

****

Later that afternoon, Lynn returned to the group from the water's edge, holding the binoculars. "I didn't see any horses down there," she said. "I stayed on my belly, in the shadows, like you told me, Kelly. I saw one of the camps though. It's a family with a couple of small hiking tents and some lean-tos. Kids' clothes are on a rope between two trees. There are fishing poles set out into the river. It looks like a cow's skin is stretched out on stakes. It's like an Indian camp in the old movies. Whoever lives there must be gone or hiding."

The clan mounted and rode upstream as soundlessly as possible. They stayed a good distance uphill and away from the rocky, flatland of the valley, a dry floodplain with low scrub. As they climbed to a better vantage point, Kelly scanned the river with binoculars.

"What's that?" Jess murmured almost inaudibly. He pointed to a stand of green-barked palo verde trees about a quarter mile closer to the river than they were.

"Something's moving," Jared whispered.

Kelly played the field glasses over the area and saw long, brown hair through the branches. The group stared at the trees. Finally, Kelly saw straight, black hair hanging vertically as well.

"Horse's tails? Maybe they're headed for a drink?" Kelly said in a hushed tone.

"Let's go get them," Jess said enthusiastically, louder than he had intended. Everyone brought their fingers to their mouths simultaneously, reminding him to stay silent.

"Let's just watch them for a few minutes while we decide what to do," Kelly whispered. "It's always better to have a well-thought-out plan than to go in willy-nilly. We don't want to spook 'em."

Shortly after formulating a plan, Kelly rode Pokey a little closer to what she hoped would be a future mount. The other "cowboys" were spread in a semicircle downwind from the palo verde stand. Kelly watched the horses grazing on the sparse grass. There were about twelve animals of all ages. They looked in good shape. Kelly picked out what she thought might be the herd stallion and the boss mare. *What was that flash, a spark from a rock? I can't believe it*, Kelly thought. *At least one is shod!*

"Some of these horses may be domesticated," Kelly told Pokey, leaning forward and stroking him on the neck. "I hadn't even considered that. I bet we can just ride in, nice and easy so as not to scare them, offer them our sweet, molasses-laden oats, and go home with a couple horse buddies for you who are already saddle-broke. Shhhhhh, boy."

Kelly urged Pokey, in a slow, meandering walk, toward the horses grazing on tall grass under the palo verde trees. She slumped in the saddle to look less menacing, following them slowly, oats in the nose bag to try to get the attention of any domesticated animals. The horses, especially the black stallion, kept an eye on her, most of them wary, but a few interested. The stallion stood between Kelly and his herd, ears erect, head held high.

Kelly gave the nosebag a good shake, hoping the noise and smell of the oats would carry.

Suddenly the huge, black stallion pranced toward Kelly, raising his knees high, flaring his nostrils and shaking his shiny mane. He made a false charge at Kelly and Pokey, ending only five feet in front of them, then dropped his head and pawed at the ground three times. This was a direct challenge and Pokey met it by lunging into the air simultaneously with his aggressor. Hooves pounded again and again against both horses' chests. Unable to keep hold of the reins, Kelly was thrown to the ground, knocking the wind from her. Landing unceremoniously in the dirt at Pokey's feet, she drew herself into a fetal position, listening to hooves crash around her. *One hoof to the head and...*

The stallion was knocked off balance. He twisted his body so that he didn't fall flat on his back and landed close to his combatant. Pokey tore into the turned stallion's flank with his teeth. The black beast's legs buckled, and he dropped his hindquarters in an attempt to get away from his rival's teeth. Kelly

348

got to one knee, cried out, and clenched her arms about her head. Pokey released his jaws, but lunged again toward his adversary. The stallion kicked up both of his hind legs, but Pokey reared back, avoiding a kick to the head by two strong hind feet. Kelly let out another bloodcurdling scream, afraid she would be trampled.

Jess, hearing Kelly, took off at a fiery pace toward the fray on Traveler, and The others followed in hot pursuit.

"Jump right, Kelly!" Jess screamed as he rushed to intercept the powerful stallion.

She did so just quickly enough to avoid three of the four crashing hooves, her eyes shut so tight she could see stars. She couldn't tell if the offending hoof was Pokey's or the stallion's, but it hit her square in the shoulder blade, knocking her facedown in the dirt. "Don't," Kelly screamed at Jess. "They'll kill you!"

Traveler bolted into the fracas at Jess's ruthless urgings. Horseflesh collided with horseflesh as together, the team buffeted the black stallion. Jess managed to keep his reins even as Traveler reared high in the air. Pokey and Traveler stood together warding off the stallion, their bodies positioned between him and Kelly.

Pokey snorted, lowering his head. The stallion took off toward his herd, head held high, signaling his mares to retreat. The confrontation was over for now.

Kelly, still trembling, got to one knee, crying in pain and shock. Jared got to her seconds later, overcome with tears. He slipped from his horse and ran to her, landing on both knees at her side. "Are you hurt?"

"Mostly my pride." She threw herself into his arms.

"It's okay, it's okay," Jared said, his arms clenched about her.

"I should have known he was going to charge me. How could I have been so stupid?" She chastised herself for knowing better.

"You couldn't have known, Kel."

"That's just it," Kelly sobbed. "I did know, but I wanted those horses so badly I took a stupid chance and put Jess in danger too."

Lynn trotted up on Buckskin. Jess and Lynn sat atop their mounts, watching Jared and Kelly huddle together on the ground. "I think we need another plan," said Kelly.

Jared pulled her to her feet, ensuring that she could stand, and looked her over for open wounds. She made it up onto both feet but stood bent forward at the waist, holding her shoulder. Jared put his hand on hers and urged her into a full standing position, then held her as she took a few steps toward Pokey.

"I think I can walk." said Kelly.

"Let's get back to camp, it's getting late." Jared said. "It will take a little time to see how bad that arm is, and Lynn can make us some dinner."

\*\*\*\*

"Okay, this the last of the wire," Lynn said. It was now mid-morning and the group had been working for hours on Kelly's new plan. "Do you think this will hold the horses?"

Kelly inspected the ersatz corral constructed of scavenged Forest Service fencing and paracord strung between ironwood trees, palo verde trees, and boulders. Tents, sleeping bags, tarps, and brush were hung on the strands of cordage, which gave it a mostly false look of solidity. Two wings stretched out from the gate, forming a funnel to guide the herd into the corral.

"It doesn't need to be super-strong," Kelly said. "Most horses won't try to go through what they think is a solid fence. My granddad used to make horse traps like this in the White Mountains. It worked for him. I don't want a repeat of last night."

The corral had been placed between where the herd had been the day before and the river. Jess and Lynn arranged nibbles of oats, spread out in a line, leading from the grassy area where the horses seemed to graze, to the gate of the trap. A veritable feast of molasses-coated oats had been prepared for any horse willing to enter. Traveler and Buckskin chomped grass in the shade behind the trap. Kelly thought Emma's horses might help the strays to feel more at ease, or at least pique their interest. Jess took his position behind a bush on the left of the trap, and Lynn hid on the right. Each held a rope attached to a makeshift gate.

"Okay, everyone knows the plan?" Kelly asked. Without waiting for an answer, she spurred Pokey in a wide arc toward the last known location of the herd. It was important to come at them from the far side to drive them toward the trap. Jared rode Hokey beside her.

They rode slowly, silently, watching for the herd. The day was beautiful; it felt like one of the many joyrides Kelly had taken in this area before. She had to remind herself that this was serious business. Finally, they spied horses grazing. Jared stayed where he was as Kelly began slowly moving around the horses. She rode a distance behind them, then slowly encouraged the animals to move in the direction of the trap. She didn't want to push the herd too hard, just encourage them to amble in the right direction. After some time, one of the horses found the first deposit of oats. Shortly, another found more oats. Their pace increased as they searched for more treats. The horses grouped closer together, competing for the food. The black stallion, ahead of the others, sniffed the air, head held high and his body on alert.

Kelly decided to be the dominant "horse" at that point and let out an impressive "neigh" that reverberated off the surrounding hills. She motioned to Jared to rush the them with her. Dust rose into the air from Hokey's and Pokey's hooves as she and Jared focused on spooking the herd.

The stallion bobbed his head and neighed loudly, signaling to the other horses to follow his lead, then broke into a full run toward the makeshift corral.

"This is it!" Kelly cried. "It's working." She flashed a thumbs-up sign to Jared.

The stallion slowed as he approached the trap, dancing back and forth. He looked like he was trying to decide his next move, but his ladies and the junior males kept coming. Jared and Kelly drove forward until the entire troop was well into the wings of the trap. They circled a short distance back, along the rear and sides, driving the herd forward, pushing them through the gate.

Jess and Lynn closed the gate behind the herd as the horses ran around and around the perimeter of the enclosure.

"Looks like a circus act," yelled Lynn.

Kelly, who had joined her young friends, said, "Stay back in case one of them rushes the fence."

It took the horses a good fifteen minutes before settling down and standing quietly, taking in their predicament or simply grazing. All four horsemen leaned over the sturdiest part of the fence, observing the different horses and contemplating.

"Are we going to bring them all home?" Lynn asked, her voice jumping with excitement.

"No, most of these are wild." Kelly raised her voice to be heard over the breeze and the jostling horses. "I don't want to have to saddle break and wagon break broncs if it can be avoided. Besides, Mom's house can't support this many."

"Now what do we do?" Jess asked.

"Let them rest, calm down for a bit and eat the oats, then we can start cutting the wild ones out of the corral."

"I like the pretty pinto," Lynn said, pointing to a mostly-white horse with large, tawny brown bubbles of color splashed across her body.

"She is pretty," Kelly said. "We'll have to see if she will take a saddle. I'm so excited to have some domestic stock." Kelly moved about in her saddle, trying to contain her joy. "Let's see, I count five wearing shoes: four mares and one gelding."

It took the rest of the day, with plenty of rest breaks for both cowhands and horses, to get the herd cut.

"We're going to have to spend another night out," said Jared, flirting with Kelly by wrinkling up his nose and throwing his head back slightly.

"That's fine with me, Cookie," Kelly said. "I could use some chuck." She wrinkled up her nose, echoing the flirt.

Jess looked up at Kelly. "Huh?"

"Cookie means cook, and chuck is food," said Kelly. "It's a joke, a play on words. You know, Old West chuckwagons."

Jess still looked confused.

"I'm hungry, Jess, I'm hungry," said Kelly.

"Me too," he said, smiling. "I'm always hungry. As long as it means food, I don't care what you call it."


\*\*\*\*

Kelly woke early and quietly eased out of the sleeping bag she shared with Jared. She went to the corral, taking three bridles and some oats with her.

The stallion and what was left of his harem were still hanging around outside the fencing. His mares inside the fence whinnied to him softly from time to time. The stallion moved toward the rocky, brushy side of the corral, crowding the cliff as Kelly approached. He made noises in protest as she came closer.

Kelly ignored him and went to the corral. She began talking to the five horses inside. "Come here, girl," she said to the most inquisitive horse, the little pinto. "Lynn has her eye on you," she said soothingly, "and I can see why."

The pretty horse nudged Kelly's hand, which was now over the fence, with her nose.

"So you want a pet on the nose? How about some oats?"

The horse ate greedily what she was offered as Kelly rubbed her nose and ears.

Kelly made her way around to the gate and slipped in. She had to move a sleeping bag to work the loop of wire that held the corral closed. All of the horses rushed to the far side except the pinto, who stood patiently, probably hoping for more oats.

"Here, girl," Kelly said putting her hand out flat with the treat atop. While the pinto ate, she slipped a bridle over her head. "You've done this before, haven't you, girl?"

Interested now, the other horses approached Kelly and the pinto, looking for some of the same.

By the time the others reached the corral, Kelly had four of the five horses bridled. The fifth, the gelding, was still stand-offish.

"Lynn, what do you want to name your horse?" Kelly asked.

"What? I get the pinto?"

"Yeah, if you want her."

"Want her? You know I want her." Lynn grinned, then thought for a moment. "How about Beans? I'll call her Beans because she's a pinto. Get it?"

"Cute," said Jess. "Do I get one?"

"Which one do you want?" asked Kelly.

"I want that brown one, the one who looks like she stepped in white paint up to her hocks."

"Interesting face, don't you think?" said Kelly. "She has a thick blaze. If it had gone all the way around her eyes and nostrils, it would have given her a badger face."

"What do you mean by that?" Jess asked.

"It's a type of face mark that horses have, you know, like the star, the strip and the blaze," said Kelly. "It's like the horse is wearing a mask sculpted around the eyes, almost like the whole face was dunked in paint."

"Good choice, Jess," said Jared. "She looks sturdy, like she could handle just about anything."

"What are you going to name her?" asked Lynn.

Jess answered without a moment's pause, "Lightning, because her blaze is so distinct, like a flash of lightning against a dark sky."

"How poetic," said Lynn.

"What about the other two?" asked Jess. "They'll have to be for my dad and Dennis."

"Remember, all of these horses are meant to pull wagons to Utah," said Kelly.

"But we can just tell Dennis and Jose that these are their horses."

"Sure." Kelly pursed her lips. "It won't hurt anything." Smiling, she asked, "Do you want to name them or do you want to let them do it?"

"We wanna do it, don't we, Jess?" said Lynn.

"My dad's has to be Sapo—it means toad in Spanish. Grandpa had this friend who trained horses. He told crazy stories and would call every stupid, stubborn horse Sapo. When I was little I used to imagine a big, green, fat horse."

"Do you have a favorite?" Kelly asked Jess.

"Yep, that black one over there," Jess pointed to a dark horse with a long black mane and tail.

"She's a pretty one, but she's not all black; her coat has a nice brown undertone that makes her look velvety," said Lynn. "I had a dress like that once."

"Okay, Lynn, what about your dad's?" asked Kelly. "The only one left is that brown one with the little white dot on her forehead and white on her left front ankle."

"I like her, but I'll have to put some thought into it. Can I tell you later?"

"Sure. Hey, Jared, come get these girls." Kelly nodded to the four she had tied to a low-hanging tree limb near the gate.

Jared reached in and untied the lead ropes, then opened the gate just far enough to get the mares out, single file. The gelding made a lunge for the gate but Kelly jumped out at him, turning him around. He whinnied and threw his head back, making a show.

Kelly stood in the middle of the corral staring down the gelding, rope in hand. She'd made a big loop and now twirled it in the air to keep it aloft. The gelding pranced back and forth, daring the cowgirl to launch it in his direction.

Jess and Lynn climbed a small tree to watch the show.

Kelly threw the lasso but it fell short of its mark, landing in a cloud of dust on the desert floor. Hand over hand, she rewound the rope into nice loops hanging from her gloved left hand. Another loop was created and twirled overhead, then launched. The rope sailed over the gelding's head and around his neck. The beast's sharp tug on the rope pulled Kelly forward forcefully. She ran toward the gelding but then stopped and dug her heels in to no avail; he was just too strong. He pulled her in any direction he wished.

Jared, seeing her plight, made his way into the corral to help. He grabbed the rope with both his hands in front of Kelly's, and they both resisted. The result wasn't that much better.

"Jess, get me a switch," Kelly called. "Make it long, as long as you can!"

One solid leap put Jess on the desert floor under the tree he had been sitting in. His hand went to the knife tucked in his cowboy boot. He looked into the wispy, lime-green, desert tree and chose a branch about ten feet long and two inches in diameter where it joined the main trunk.

"It's going to take a couple of minutes," he said, hacking the branch at its base.

"This horse is mine," said Jared. "He's got some grit. He's handsome too. I'll call 'im Bullet."

Bullet paced back and forth, pulling on the lasso.

"We'll have to see if he'll calm down. This one might be staying here."

"I've got the switch," yelled Jess.

"Bring it in here, easy," said Kelly, motioning to the gate. "Jared, you had better go."

"What, and leave you in here alone? No way."

"I'll be fine now that I have my trusty friend here," Kelly said taking the long green switch and cracking it against the ground to see how it reacted in her hand. "Thanks, Jess. It's perfect."

Both men looked wary as they left the makeshift corral. Jared looked back at Kelly, who gave him a reassuring smile. Bullet had settled some, but was still a very large animal to contend with.

Kelly urged the gelding to go around the corral in a circle, clockwise, by pulling on the rope around his neck. He resisted at first by rearing, shaking his head and waving his thick mane. He started toward her. *Crack!* went the whip at his feet. His eyes went large and round, nostrils flared.

"This type of training is called round penning," said Kelly, "and you will see why."

He backed off; she had his attention and respect. Slowly, he started moving in the circle that his trainer wanted him to adopt. "There, there, boy. You remember now, don't you?"

The horse seemed to want to trot. "There you go, burn off some steam," Kelly cooed. She spun in a circle from the middle of the pen, just giving the gelding his head, letting him set his own pace. Suddenly, he turned to come toward her and she gave him a crack on the nose, directing him back to his circle. After ten times around, Bullet was slowed and his head directed to turn and start a counterclockwise trot. He did this willingly.

"See?" Kelly said, "he's not so bad, he'd just forgotten his manners."

Horse school continued for about an hour, until Kelly was satisfied that Bullet wouldn't give them any problems on the road.

"I think I've taken the fight out of him," Kelly announced. "Let's go home."

Chapter 19

Christmas, long awaited, had finally come to The Wise Ranch. Emma was excited. Just after dawn, she rose to stoke the wood stove and start breakfast. She almost tripped over the Christmas tree as she rounded the corner into the living room. The house was quiet and cold but the curtains had been drawn and it would warm up quickly once the fire was built up again. She tried not to make too much noise, as Jared was still sleeping on the couch. He just bunched his blankets up around his neck, turned toward the sofa back, and resumed his snoring.

Emma took some precious flour from the pantry and got out the ten eggs she had been saving for the occasion. Pancakes with high fructose corn syrup, salvaged from the tanker truck on the freeway, and scrambled eggs! She would need two eggs for her famous pancake recipe and one for each person, scrambled. Emma took her pail from the kitchen drainboard and headed to the barn. There would be milk and butter on the table too, an unaccustomed luxury. They had been getting milk from one of the cows for a week now. Today a second calf would be declared weaned, and his mama would be milked as well. They would even have enough milk to share with a few of the neighbors as a Christmas gift.

When Emma returned from the barn, Kelly was up, padding around the kitchen in her robe and some slippers she had fashioned out of the fabric up in the closet.

"Good morning dear," Emma said.

"Merry Christmas, Mom," said Kelly.

"Merry Christmas." Emma walked over and gave Kelly a long hug. She held Kelly out from her and looked her over as if trying to take in every detail.

"Can I help with breakfast?" Kelly asked.

"Why, of course. There's butter to be churned," Emma said without as much as a glance toward Kelly, who had wrinkled her nose in distaste. "The others can take turns as they meander in."

Just then Jared appeared. "Well, Merry Christmas to my two beautiful ladies," he said, kissing Emma on the cheek and then taking Kelly in his arms and planting a lingering kiss on her lips. The room was silent for a minute or so as the young couple kissed and Emma ignored them. "Hmm, that was a wonderful way to start the day." Jared beamed.

"Kelly here was just about to start churning some butter for me, maybe you would like to help?" asked Emma.

"Sure. Ever helpful, that's me."

Over the next half hour, everyone filed in. It took forty-five minutes to churn the butter, so everyone took a turn. Emma took the wooden paddle out of the tall wooden churn Jose had made, and scraped the congealed butter from its sides and paddle. She drained off the buttermilk into a small pitcher, then poured clean water into the churn.

"Churn that another minute or two," Emma directed Jess.

She repeated the process of draining off the diluted buttermilk and re-churning twice more, until she was satisfied the water ran clear. She scraped the remaining butter onto her marble candy-making slab and proceeded to beat it with two paddles to remove air bubbles and solidify the mass. "I learned this from one of my old Foxfire books. You have to use the marble and the paddles so the warmth of your hands doesn't melt the butter." The butter finally resembled what everyone had come to expect from store-bought butter, except it was softer and paler.

Kelly finished cooking the pancakes and eggs and they all sat down to a hearty breakfast.

"Can we open our gifts after breakfast?" enquired Lynn, eagerly.

"I don't see why not," said Dennis. "Like I said before, I like Christmas as an American tradition—a time of giving and sharing. You guys have celebrated Hanukkah and the other Jewish Holy Days with us, now we would like to share with you."

Lynn beamed. "There is a present for all of you."

As soon as breakfast was over, everyone gathered around the Christmas tree. It wasn't a typical pine tree but its desert cousin in shape if not in genus: the juniper. Junipers are sparse, light-green-bristled trees with silvery, green berries bearing little resemblance to the conical shape of the pine except in color. The fact that they were evergreen was convenient. It was decorated with scraps of material that the girls of the house had fashioned into bows, seed pods, and a small collection of special ornaments Emma had hung onto for sentimental reasons.

Kelly designated herself Santa and started passing out the gifts. "Remember," she said, "these are group gifts. The present is meant to come from all of us at the same time." There was an air of excitement as they began the familiar Christmas ritual of handing out presents to loved ones.

The first package went to Lynn. It was soft and about eighteen inches square. It was wrapped in light blue tissue paper. No tape was used; only a piece of brown twine held the bundle together. Lynn gently untied it and unfolded the paper. "Clothes!" she yelped. Inside the package was a white nightgown and three shirts. She clutched them to her chest, then reached out and took Emma's forearm. "Thank you so much, it's exactly what I needed." Lynn stood and held a shirt to herself, doing a complete circle for the crowd. "I love them."

The next package went to Dennis. It too was soft. Dennis removed the plain brown paper around his gift. It was a beautiful *tallis*, a Jewish prayer shawl, wool with many tassels.

"I helped Emma put the tassels on," said Lynn. "The number of threads are right." She smiled from ear to ear.

"It's beautiful," Dennis gasped, making a steeple with his hands and pressing the shawl to his lips. "I shall cherish it always."

He rose to his knees and leaned forward to give Lynn a hug, then held her head in his hands and kissed her on the forehead.

"Next is Jess," said Kelly. Jess got a small cardboard box without paper wrapping. He opened it and took out a leather belt with a large silver buckle displaying two horses standing on their hind legs. Jess looked up in amazement. His eyes went from one person in the room to the next. Kelly said, "It was my father's. It's a horseman's belt and that is what you have become."

"Thanks," Jess choked, turning to hide his emotion. He stood up and put the belt around his waist. It was large for him, and it looked like he might have to put a new hole in it. Jess turned the buckle up toward his face so he could see the silver horses. He beamed with pride.

"You'll grow into it, Mijo," said Jose. "Thank you, all," he said for his son, looking around the room at his friends.

Kelly handed Jose a large cardboard box about thirty inches square. It was heavy and Kelly's arms strained to lift it. Jose rose quickly and bent down to take the box from her. "Dang, that's heavy," he said. He struggled to stand upright with the box, then sat cross-legged on the floor with it on his lap. He opened it, revealing an old wooden tool tray filled with very old-looking tools, many with worn wooden handles. The metal parts of the tools were weathered and oxidized.

"Where on earth did you get these?" Jose whispered, blinking rapidly as he stared in amazement. He lifted the tray from the box.

Jess moved to sit next to his father. "Tools are important in a world without stores. We got them from the Branham's garage. These old tools were mounted on the wall above a workbench, and this old tray was there too." Jess reached into the tray and took out a chisel. "I'll help you clean them up."

The next present was small. It was in a little, pink velvet jewelry box. This gem went to Emma. "What on earth?" she said. Her fingers tugged at the hinged box. When it opened, it was an old high-school ring, a man's ring, on a gold chain. Emma looked up with a blank expression on her face.

"It's not much," said Rich, "but it means something to me."

"No, no, it's wonderful," replied Emma. "Help me put it on. This doesn't mean we're going steady, does it?"

"Well, if it did, ol' woman, I wouldn't admit it here in mixed company, now would I?"

Rich did not stand to help Emma put it on. Awkward as it was, Kelly stood and went to her mother. "Here, Mom, I'll help you." Kelly looked at Rich but he didn't change his expression.

The next gift was not lying under the tree, but was offered to Kelly by Jared. He pulled a small box from behind his back and handed it to Kelly. The tag was written in an unfamiliar hand. It was wrapped in white tissue paper and tied like Lynn's.

"This one is mine?" Kelly asked, grasping the small box with both hands and clutching it to her chest. She held it momentarily, as if waiting to calm a bit. She lowered the box to her lap and pulled at the string. The small bow gave quickly and the ties fell away. She removed the paper, revealing the tiny cardboard box. Her hands shook a little as she opened it. There, perched on a small, pink pillow, were her mother's wedding rings. Kelly looked up inquisitively, first at Jared and then at her mother. "But Mom, these are yours."

"Yes, my dear, but I know someone who could use them far more than I," said Emma.

Jared took the small box and lifted the band, which was set with a white diamond. He took Kelly's left hand and placed the engagement ring on her fourth finger. "I believe this makes it official, my love."

A tear of joy ran down Kelly's cheek. Emma had to blink rapidly to keep her own tears from spilling over her lids and down onto her cheeks. Kelly waved her hands back and forth in front of her face as if fanning herself. "I love them, thank you *both*." Kelly hugged Jared with one arm and her mother with the other as they sat, pulling both a little off balance. Kelly got up and sat in Jared's lap, admiring the ring on her finger. Jared pocketed the wedding band.

Lynn seeing her chance, plopped down onto the floor where Kelly had been sitting and announced, "Jared, the next one is for you."

The large box was as light as a feather, and Lynn threw it at Jared. He caught it easily and proceeded to carefully unwrap the brown paper covering. It was filled with packing peanuts, so he parted them with his hands and moved them around in circles, but could not find his gift. "Let me help you," Lynn said impatiently. She grabbed the box from Jared, stood it on one corner and then shook it lightly. She reached into the lowest corner and came out with a ring.

"It helps if you know what you're looking for," Lynn declared. She thrust it at Kelly as if she should take it.

Kelly took the ring from Lynn and laid it gently in Jared's outstretched palm. Both looked at it and then into each other's eyes. Jared closed his fist tightly around it, took Kelly's hand and turned it palm up, then opened his grasp, letting the ring fall into her cupped hand.

"Only 'til the wedding," Jared said.

"Rich, the last one is for you," Lynn announced. She handed him a very thin parcel of brown paper, about eight by ten inches, tied with a thin red ribbon.

Rich took it, giving a little nod of his head in appreciation. His large fingers fumbled with the knot and Lynn reached for the parcel to help him, but the tie let loose. The brown paper fell away, revealing a picture. It was a drawing of Rich's dog, done in pencil.

"Oh my God," said Rich and put his hand to his mouth. He looked up and scanned his audience. "Who did this?"

"It was me," said Lynn, her chin high in the air.

"How did you know? That ol' dog has been gone ten years!" He stared at it in amazement, studying every detail.

"I saw the tiny picture you had pinned to the wall near your radio. I didn't think too much about it 'til I saw the collar hanging by your chair in the living room. It's the same collar, isn't it?"

"Why, yes, I guess it is. That ol' mutt was the best dog ever lived," said Rich, brushing a tear from his eye. "All I had left of him was that tiny photo. I can't believe you drew him so true from that."

"I'd hoped you would like it, that it would be special. I didn't know what else to do."

"It's perfect, girl," Rich said, rising from his chair and leaning toward Lynn. She rose too and they met in the middle. Rich held the dog's picture way up in the air with his left hand and hugged Lynn for everything he was worth with his right. "You're a darn good artist. Thank you."

"You're welcome," Lynn said, looking down. Somehow it didn't seem right to watch Rich be overtaken with emotion; he was such a private man, and her elder.

"Now that the gift-giving is over, I have some more fun for us," Emma announced. "A special Christmas treat. Anyone who wants to make *fudge* can follow me to the kitchen."

Lynn and Jess looked at each other. Both said, "Yes!" at the same time.

Before Emma could get to her feet, Jess and Lynn were halfway through the kitchen door. Everyone else rose and stretched. Kelly gathered the brown paper and Jared stacked it neatly in a pile as Emma followed the kids.

Dennis and Jose got to the kitchen door and Dennis held it, waiting for Kelly. "You guys go ahead, we'll be in in a minute," Kelly said, grabbing Jared's hand and swinging it back and forth.

"Go ahead, look at your rings, you guys. Merry Christmas," Dennis said. He and Jose went into the kitchen. "What's up in here?" Dennis asked rhetorically. He ran up behind Lynn and tickled her around the waist. She jumped and giggled, trying to move away from the assault.

"Stop, stop! I mean it," she said, laughing breathlessly.

"No fooling around in the kitchen," Emma said. "I'm going to have hot things on the stove in a minute."

Dennis and Lynn jumped to attention, smiling devilishly and giggling.

Chapter 20

"Kelly," Emma said, walking up behind her daughter as she was drying dishes off the drainboard. "Why don't you put that down and come with me?"

"What is it, Mom?" Kelly casually draped the dish towel over her shoulder and turned, leaning back against the counter.

"We need to talk something over before the wedding. It's only two weeks away."

"Well, I know you can't be talking about the birds and the bees," Kelly joked.

"No, silly girl, it's about your dress."

"I thought I'd wear that skirt we made for the Mormon dance."

"That's one possibility." Emma smiled and held out her hand. "But I have another option for you to consider."

Kelly took her hand and followed Emma down the hall. On the hook next to her mother's dresser was a long plastic garment bag.

"Before you open it, I have to tell you that this was my dress; the dress I wore when I married your father. I don't know how you might feel about that, with him and I being divorced and all," Emma said quietly.

Kelly stepped forward, saying nothing. She took the thin metal zipper in her hand, tugging lightly until the bag opened and the dress spilled from its confines. She fingered the ivory silk, embroidered with hundreds of tiny, iridescent, seed beads.

"It's beautiful," Kelly whispered, running her fingers down the dress from the neckline to the waist, her fingernails popping over the beads. She turned to her mother. "I love it, but don't you think it's a little extravagant? I mean, Jared won't have anything fancy to wear, Lynn won't..."

"They aren't the bride. The bride should always steal the show. It's your day, honey. Unless you think it's bad luck or something..."

"I don't, I don't." Kelly fell into her mother's arms. "I'd be honored to wear your dress. You and Dad loved each other at the time; that's what matters." The fabric flowed from the garment bag like a magician's never-ending scarf. Kelly scooped up the train, so it wouldn't drag on the floor, and put it over her forearm. Holding the bodice up to herself, she turned toward the dresser's mirror, admiring how the dress sparkled; how the light from the window seemed to be reflected in every tiny sphere.

Kelly turned back to her mother. "Oh, I can't wear this. It will drag on the ground and get dirty. I'm not getting married in a hall. The chairs are going to be on either side of the dirt path out to the garden." She spoke quickly, thinking out loud.

"I know where the chairs go. I was there when we picked the spot, remember? And I don't have another daughter." Emma smiled from ear to ear, blotting her eyes with her shirt sleeve. "I'd love to see you walk down the aisle in that dress, with this beautiful train dragging in the dirt behind you."

"Can't you just see Jared's face?" Kelly asked, blinking back tears.

"Can't you just see Lynn's?" Emma said with a little snort. "I don't know who will be more surprised and thrilled."

Kelly placed the dress on the bed and stared at it for a moment before wrapping her arms around her mother. "Oh, thank you! No one will ever forget my wedding, least of all my husband." Kelly beamed and setting her lips in a determined smile, said, "You haven't told anyone, have you?"

"No, I thought I'd see your reaction first."

"I want it to be a surprise," Kelly said decisively. "The biggest surprise of *all*, on my wedding day."

\*\*\*\*

" Lynn, get your coat and sidearm and come on," Emma bellowed. "There's so much to do."

"Okay," Lynn called back, her voice tight with frustration, "it's not like we're on a time schedule or anything."

"You may not be on a time schedule, but I am. I wasn't going to tell you, Lynn, but I have a surprise. Well, not exactly for you, but..."

Lynn's face lit up. "What is it?" she asked impatiently as if she hadn't just been annoyed with Emma moments earlier.

"Wanna take a ride? We're going over to the Branham's to take a look at the place, and we need to get out of here before Kelly and Jared start back from the creek. Jared is supposed to be buying me some time and taking Kelly a little farther north today so she won't see us make the corner from the driveway onto the road."

"Take a look at the Branham's house? Why?" Lynn asked suspiciously. "And why is it a secret?"

"I thought you and I could fix it up for Kelly and Jared— you know, for after their wedding."

"You mean they're moving out?"

"Not exactly," Emma mumbled. Seeing that Lynn was still not catching on, she decided to be more direct. "For their wedding night. It won't be permanent because there's safety in numbers, but I have talked with some of the neighbors and they are willing to help us guard the place for a couple of days right after the wedding. You know, like a wedding present."

Lynn smiled knowingly, as though she had some great secret, and finished putting her boots on. Hurrying after the older woman, they climbed the small hill to the corral.

"I'll take this new girl, Sapo," Emma said, walking toward one of the mares Kelly had wrangled only a few days earlier. "I think she knows I mean business. You take Pokey. We'll leave Mr. Bullet here 'til he's had more"—Emma searched for the word—"schooling."

Lynn was very familiar now with saddling a horse. She led Pokey to the corral fence where she had placed the tack. She threw a colorful saddle blanket over Pokey's back, then hefted a large saddle over the blanket, being careful to ensure the blanket was smooth. Lifting the stirrup over the saddle horn, she reached under Pokey's belly for the cinch and threaded it through the rigging, pulling it tight around the horse's belly. Emma handed Lynn a bucket of cleaning supplies, letting the calmer horse bear the brunt of toting them. Opening the gate, she watched Lynn and Pokey trot out before mounting Sapo and following them down the main road.

"Watch for anyone on the road, or off of it for that matter," Emma instructed as she watched Lynn trot ahead of her, long black hair bouncing against her shoulders. "Slow up," she called.

Lynn headed back, making wide circles around Emma and Sapo as a game, a diversion, for the rest of the trip.

The ride to the Branham's place was cool and windy. Emma had Lynn wait at the road as she went up to the house, quietly, and looked in the windows. Some folks in the village had chased squatters from the house on and off, but it seemed to be empty now.

Lynn rode Pokey up beside Sapo and dismounted.

The two women stretched a rope between a pair of trees on the east side of the house, the side with the fewest windows, and attached the horses' reins to it. The horses could move freely between the trees, and took to munching the grass that grew there.

"Let's go in. Cover me like Jared has been teaching you," said Emma.

Lynn followed Emma up onto the porch, the old wooden steps creaking under their weight. She stood to one side of the front door while Emma stood on the other. Both had weapons drawn.

"Wait," Lynn whispered. "I think I'm going to be sick."

"It's just nerves, Lynn. Take a deep breath and let it out slowly. I'm going in."

Emma tested the screen door handle; the thumb press opened smoothly into the unlatched position. The hinges on the door were another story altogether. They squeaked as the door swung open. Lynn and Emma both winced at the noise.

Without delay, Emma pushed the door open. She hadn't expected to be blinded by darkness. She pulled back around the door frame from where she had just come. Lynn jumped back, thinking Emma had seen someone.

"What did you see?" Lynn demanded, eyes wide.

"Not a blooming thing," exclaimed Emma. "It's too dark. I expect if anyone was in there, they would have shot me by now. You stay here 'til I call for you."

Emma stood next to the front door for a minute with her eyes closed until they adjusted and she could make out the objects in the living room clearly. The wooden blinds were closed up tight, but the curtains had all been removed.

"Come on in, Lynn," Emma whispered, motioning with her index finger.

Lynn entered cautiously. Both women stood together silently, listening for any sounds that might indicate someone was in another part of the house. An eerie stillness enveloped the pair.

The sofa cushions were on the floor, lined up against the wall like someone had used them for a mattress, and there had been fires lit in the fireplace. The ashes remained, some spilling out of the hearth onto the wooden floor. Two old chairs completed the living room's decor.

"Looks like there's been people in here for sure," said Lynn.

Emma pulled on the blind cord and light shot through the slats. Dust particles swirled in the streaks of light, looking like miniature snowflakes in flight. Emma coughed more at the sight of the dust than from anything tickling her nose or throat.

"Looks like this room alone could take us all day," she said.

Together, they searched the rest of the house. The home was cold, and each room seemed to be more disheveled and dusty than the next. The downstairs bedroom had nothing in it but a naked, dirty mattress and a dusty nightstand. A broken lamp lay on the floor.

Rat droppings littered the floor and counters of the kitchen. Dishes had been left in the sink, as if someone had meant to wash them. The loft bedroom was dusty and the two mattresses filthy, but it was decided that that room wasn't needed and would be ignored, the door closed.

Emma drew in a deep breath, put her hands on her hips and announced, "Let's get to work."

Lynn took care of lighting a fire in the small wood-burning stove to take the chill from the crisp morning air. Then together they worked, sweeping, mopping and scrubbing. Finally, it was all they could do to haul the big mattress out on the porch, scrub it down, and tip it on its side to dry.

"Cold and windy today, but not humid," Emma said. "The mattress should dry quickly. We need to come and get it tomorrow and take it to the house, if we want it to stay usable. It's too heavy now, wet and all. I wish we had some special bedding for it. The beds at my house are all full-sized beds because the rooms are so small. That place was built back when a cabin was just that, not these mansions they build today. This is a queen-sized bed, I don't even think I have sheets to fit."

"I saw fabric out in the garage when we came to get the windows for the solar hot water heater, and when we got the tools for Jose's Christmas present too," said Lynn. "We could make some."

"They would have a seam down the middle, but that would be better than having something that didn't cover the bed. Let's take a look and see if it's still there."

Lynn led Emma to the garage. They entered it carefully as well. Slowly their eyes adjusted and Lynn strode to the back. There, in a tall cabinet, were stacks of fabric in many different sizes and patterns. Emma reached in and pulled several different colors from the nice collection. "Looks like Mrs. Branham may have been a quilter."

"Can we make a quilt?" asked Lynn.

"Well, it's been a long time since I've done any quilting, but I bet there are some women in town who could help us. It would be a wonderful wedding gift. I remember seeing a quilting loom at the Bantings' when we were down there for Emmet's funeral. Bea would probably welcome the company by now, and it's a fine reason for socializing."

Lynn and Emma pulled large pieces of fabric for the sheets and the backing of the quilt, then laid out smaller pieces, deciding which colors and patterns looked best together.

"These look fine," said Emma. "I hope we can get it done in two weeks. We should probably take all of this fabric tomorrow when we bring the cart for the mattress. I'm sure it will come in handy down the line."

"I can already see a few skirts and blouses for me," Lynn said. "Maybe if I learn to quilt, I can make myself something warm and cozy."

"Sure. You'll need blankets for your trip, too. That would be more practical than taking what Rich and I have," said Emma.

Lynn put two more pieces of fabric on the wedding quilt pile. "There's where we got the tools," she said, pointing at the workbench. We didn't take them all, they were too heavy. The guys should come down and sort through this garage for anything they might need for our journey."

Emma glanced up at the sun. "We need to get going. We've been gone a mighty long time and I'm surprised we don't have the men-folk down here looking for us. Close the garage and we'll go lock up the house. Let's pray that we don't have more squatters before the wedding."

\*\*\*\*

"Hi, Emma. Hi, Lynn," Bea Banting said, smiling as she answered her front door. "I'm glad you stood down on the road and yelled before you came up the driveway. I'm a woman alone now and I just can't tell you how unnerving it can be to have unannounced visitors."

Emma eyed the shotgun near the front door and nodded. "I can't even imagine, Bea," Emma said, laying her hand on the woman's shoulder. She entered the front door with a large basket over her forearm. "Do you feel safe down here, all by yourself?"

"No, not really, but I'm not willing to leave this house yet. Emmet and I lived here a long time and it's all I have left of *us*. You can understand, can't you?" Bea asked Emma.

"Of course."

Bea closed the front door and took the basket. "I can't believe you have been able to get all of this stuff out of the house without the kids noticing."

"I think Kelly has started to suspect something with Lynn and I disappearing every few days for a few hours at a time, but she'll just have to wonder," said Emma.

"Yeah, I think she knows something's up," said Lynn. "But she also knows the wedding is just around the corner, so she's not asking *too* many questions."

"I see you brought some more ingredients for the wedding cake," Bea said with a grin. She sorted through the basket. "Let's go to the kitchen, Emma. Lynn, take a look on the guest bed. We got some more piecing done last night and I think you'll be surprised."

Lynn headed for the front bedroom while Emma followed Bea into the kitchen. "It's really not necessary for you to take on so much of this project, Bea. But we sure do appreciate your help."

"It's a joy, really. Since Emmet died, I don't have that much to do. The garden is dead until spring, I've gotten all of my canning done, and the townsfolk have been so good about getting me firewood for the winter, that all I've been doing is rattling around this house alone and lonely."

"I know, girl, and we do appreciate your help," said Emma. "Your idea to hide the cake ingredients and then make it here was a stroke of brilliance. This should be the last installment except for the baking soda, so no one will suspect anything."

"Emma! Emma!" Lynn shouted from the front bedroom.

"What?" Emma asked as she reached the kitchen's door frame. Bea was right on Emma's heels.

Lynn draped herself in the quilt top that had lain across the bed. "Isn't it beautiful?" Lynn asked. "I've never seen anything so pretty. I didn't know it would look this nice when we cut all of those pieces."

Bea and the other women from town had taken hundreds of little fabric diamonds and joined them in a way that a swirl of color swished across the quilt top.

"The girls from town and I got that much put together yesterday. We still have to finish piecing the one lower corner and the border, then we'll be ready to stretch her out on the frame and secure the batting."

"Amazing," whispered Emma, fingering the fine stitches. "You are a true artist and the fact that you have taught the rest of us to piece a quilt is a miracle."

"Oh, I don't know about a miracle, but you all have really learned quickly and pulled together; otherwise, it never could have gotten done this quickly. I'd say two more days and we'll be done. A half day for piecing and a day and a half for the quilting."

"And none too soon," said Emma. "Can you believe the wedding is this Saturday? Only five days away. Lynn and I have the Branham's house done and the sheets finished—we even made pillowcases to match. The men have loaded the trailer up with some cooking utensils, food, firewood and such for the honeymoon. They aren't taking it over to the house 'til Saturday morning, the day of the wedding. We don't want it stolen."

"Tell Bea about Rich's plan to scare them." Lynn grinned mischievously.

Bea glanced questioningly at Emma.

"Oh, that ol' coot is planning a *shivaree*."

"What in the world is a *shivaree*?" asked Bea.

Lynn didn't let Emma answer. "It's like a party where you make the married couple get out of bed on their wedding night. Mean, huh?"

"Why would you do that?" Bea asked.

"For fun, I guess, if you're an ol' coot," said Emma. "It's an old, old custom. It originated back in France, or somewhere like that. It was something the young folks did out in the country, all in good fun. There wasn't a lot to do back then like there is now. That old man has his mind set on it and he's recruited Dennis and Jose. He's a prankster and I don't think I can stop him."

"I haven't even heard of it," said Bea, still with a puzzled look on her face.

"Oh, they quit doing it back in the 1950s or even earlier."

"I'm just excited about the wedding, and the cake... and the quilt," said Lynn.

"I know, isn't it thrilling?" said Bea, practically giddy, her voice a little squeak by the end of her sentence. "Your Kelly, such a beautiful young girl and that young man, so handsome."

Chapter 21

Kelly sat in a grey folding chair in front of her mother's dresser, which she could imagine as a gilded bench. Her knees knocked against the ornately carved, 1980s drawers. This was the closest thing in the small house to a dressing table. Makeup and hairpins littered the white linen table-topper, edged in lace, lying on the dresser. She stared at the reflection in the mirror of a young lady, her hair in rollers. It seemed foreign.

*My wedding day.*

The thought brought a smile to Kelly's lips that spread to her entire face. How long had she dreamed of this day? For as long as she could remember, she supposed, just like most other girls. Focusing on her hair, she removed the rollers one by one, and long tendrils fell over her smooth shoulders. It had been so long since she'd been able to pamper herself, to see herself as a woman, that she fingered the soft curls longer than she may have otherwise.

There was a knock at the door. "It's only me," Emma's voice came from the hallway.

"Come in, Mom."

Emma breezed into the room like a whirlwind, her voice rushed as she said, "Lynn and I have gotten most of the food done and finished the decorations for the arbor. Oh, wait until you see the lovely wildflowers we found at the top of the canyon! The men are..."

"Slow down, Mom. I don't think you've taken a breath." Kelly turned to face her mother. "I'm sure it will all be lovely."

Emma took a deep breath as she caught sight of Kelly's hair, and the tears came fast. "Oh, Kelly. You look... you look like a princess."

Kelly put a hand on one of her mother's and turned, looking back at herself. "Do you really think so?"

"I know so. Since the first moment I held you as a newborn, I've felt an overwhelming sense of pride watching you grow into a fine woman." Emma's eyes glistened with tears. She turned her back on Kelly quickly. "And now it's your moment, your time, to marry that young man and start your own branch of the family tree."

Kelly sniffled.

"Don't get me started..." said Emma, avoiding the word *crying* and wiping her face with her sleeve. "I have all day to be sentimental and there are too many things to get done right now."

The bride batted her eyelashes quickly, then waved her hand in front of her face to dry her own sparkling eyes.

"Can I help with your hair, just like I did on your first day of school?" Emma asked, taking a long lock of hair in her fingers and stroking it gently.

"Please," Kelly answered eagerly. "Remember when I used to beg you *not* to brush my hair?"

"I even let you go to school one day with a rat's nest, just to let the kids tease you," Emma said between sniffles. "Didn't work." Mom and daughter laughed and cried at the same time.

"Stop that," Kelly said, "let's make this a happy day, Mom—no tears."

"Oh, I can't guarantee that. If I didn't cry, the neighbors would talk," she said teasingly. Emma gathered one-inch locks of hair and wound it with her fingers, then secured each tidy roll at the back of Kelly's head with a hair pin. The long hair made a mound of joyous curls from crown to nape, then Emma took a can of hairspray from the dresser and drowned the updo.

"There, your veil should sit nicely just there," she said. Her hand, veiny and sun spotted, brushed back a few stray wisps of hair from Kelly's forehead up to the crown of her head.

"It's lovely, Mom, thanks."

Feeling her eyes going misty again, Emma turned and rushed toward the door. "I really should check on things, and people should be arriving soon." She turned back, hanging onto the door frame, and smiled softly at Kelly. "You have about half an hour. Call if you need anything. Sorry, Sunflower is a little short on caterers right now."

"Go on," Kelly said chuckling. "I have to get my makeup on. I shouldn't need any help 'til I have to get into the dress. Say, twenty-five minutes?"

\*\*\*\*

The men had worked for several days to ready the backyard for a wedding. They built an arbor for the ceremony that was constructed from curvy sycamore branches, its smooth, white bark making a perfect bridal statement. The grass had been hand cut with a scythe, which was laborious work but resulted in a smooth lawn for the wedding. Every chair in town had been collected and hauled to the barn, stacked to ensure they were ready for the special day. Long, flat, wood planks lay across stacks of firewood, which would serve as tables for the reception.

Two days ago, Rich and Jess constructed a barbecue pit big enough for a side of beef. Emma, along with Dennis and Jose, had slaughtered a cow, hung meat to jerk in the new smokehouse, packed beef in water-softener salt, canned beef all day long in the pressure canner, and still saved enough for the wedding.

Yesterday, sunup to sundown, everyone baked and prepped food for the reception, finished their sewing, and prettied up the house and yard. Except for Lynn and Emma, no one knew that the women of Sunflower were doing their own baking and decorating of a wedding cake.

That morning, before dawn, the men put the beef on the barbecue. Lynn decorated the arbor with the pods and wildflowers that she and Emma had collected, then spread petals along the aisle between the two rows of chairs.

The only thing left was a few minutes of nervous waiting.

\*\*\*\*

Guests had started to arrive about a half hour before noon, the time set for the ceremony. The townspeople came on foot, horseback and wagon. Everyone wore their finest: the women in nice dresses if they had one, and the gents in suits, or at least their best western shirt and bolo tie. Many carried presents they had scavenged or made for the young couple.

"Run in and help Kelly get into her gown, would you, Lynn?" asked Emma.

"Me?" asked Lynn. It was nearly a gasp.

"Of course you. You are her bridesmaid aren't you? There are a few things I just *have* to get done, then I'll be in."

Lynn took off like a shot.

"I could smell the beef cookin' from my house, and that's a long way," said Bill.

"Glad to have you," said Rich. "Come take a seat, we can talk."

"I brought a peach cobbler, Emma, where would you like me to put it?" asked Janet Nichols, sticking her head through the open door.

"And I brought potato salad," called out Patty Johnson, Bill's wife.

"How about in the kitchen for now, ladies, and thank you. Let's keep it away from the bugs 'til we eat," said Emma, hurrying into the house herself. Janet and Patty followed. "I'll get the bride, I mean Kelly," she said, flustered. Janet patted her on the shoulder.

"You've got some time," said Janet. "I think it's taking Bea a little longer to get here with the cake because she's afraid of tipping it over. I told her not to worry—there isn't a wedding on this planet that has ever started on time."

Emma made her way down the hall to Kelly's room. "Ready, dear?" she asked, knocking softly.

"Almost," came the muffled reply. "Okay, come in."

Lynn slipped from the room as Emma entered, giving Emma a wink as she passed her.

A gasp escaped Emma when she saw Kelly for the first time in the *dress*.

"Do you like it?" Kelly spun nervously. "It fits, doesn't it?"

"Of course, of course, turn around." Kelly turned slowly in the small bedroom, the train catching on the bed frame. "Stunning, stunning… it's just… amazing," she sighed.

"Mom, you're rambling."

"Am I?" She composed herself, then turned back to her daughter. "Well, I should be allowed. The whole town's shown up. It's about time to start but..."

"But what?"

Emma didn't want to give away the *cake* secret. She thought for a second, then said, "I don't think Jared's ready yet." Why had she chosen that?

Kelly's nose wrinkled and she looked at her mother incredulously. "I thought he was already ready."

"I'll check and be right back, when it's time, to bring you out."

"Okay, hope your stuttering is better," Kelly called after her.

"J-ju-just... never mind," Emma said and headed down the hall. "It won't be long."

\*\*\*\*

Emma closed the bedroom door behind her and leaned back, thinking of her little girl as she appeared twenty years ago, her long blonde hair in pigtails. Wiping a tear from her eye with the sleeve of her shirt, she noticed Bea standing near the solar oven. Bea gave her the thumbs-up and winked one eye. That must be the signal for *the cake's here*, Emma thought.

Jared stood near the arbor, anxiously shuffling from foot to foot. Dennis waited in the middle of the arbor, dressed in his finest blue jeans, borrowed white shirt, and prayer shawl. Neighbors milled about the yard. Normally they would be waiting for music to begin to signal the need to take their seats. Emma frowned, wishing she had arranged for their porch band to play, but then again, they were all busy.

"Everyone, everyone, can I have your attention," Emma called out. "Would you please take your seats, the ceremony is about to begin." Emma saw Lynn sitting in the chair that they had positioned facing the guests on the bride's side, violin in hand.

Jess moved to Jared's side, nervously taking his spot, his hands in his pockets. Dennis leaned toward Jess and whispered something, and Jess's hands came out of his pockets and rested at his sides. With a final glance of approval and confidence that things were all in order, Emma motioned Kelly to approach the door. She gave her daughter a kiss on the cheek, then placed Kelly's veil over her face, fighting back tears.

"Mom, I need to tell you something," Kelly whispered.

"Can we talk after? I'm afraid if you say one more thing, I'll burst into tears and bawl all the way through the ceremony, and I won't hear a thing."

Kelly laughed out loud. "I just wanted to say I love you."

"I love you too." Emma felt her eyes fill with tears, but quickly composed herself. Leaning out the door, she waved—the signal for Lynn to begin playing *The Wedding March*.

Emma stepped out onto the stoop and held out her hand so that Kelly could steady herself coming off the step. There was a small, audible gasp from the assembled guests, and Jared reached up to wipe his shirt sleeve across his eyes.

Mother and daughter walked arm in arm toward the guests to the music of the wind and a lone violin. When they arrived at the closest row of chairs, Emma stopped and lifted her daughter's veil. She kissed Kelly on the cheek once again, then motioned for her to continue on down the aisle without her. Kelly's eyes, questioning at first, looked in the direction her mother had suggested. Her eyes met Jared's, and she was drawn to him.

Kelly continued alone. Her dress flowed out behind her. It was a simple but spectacular gown, fitted from the collar to her tiny waist, a reminder of how painfully thin she had become in the last five months. There wasn't a wrinkle in its many yards of aged, cream-colored satin. The skirt was full, the sleeves long and fitted with ten satin-covered buttons climbing up each wrist. It was boat-necked in that elegant 1960s style with thousands of tiny iridescent seed beads making delicate patterns near the neckline and over the skirt. The gown shimmered in the sunlight. Yards and yards of tulle hung delicately from a comb in Kelly's hair.

She made her way up the aisle to the arbor, toward her waiting groom. Jared reached his hand out to her and she took it willingly.

"You are so beautiful," he whispered, taking her hand. It took everything he had to take his eyes away from his bride long enough to guide them both to their places in front of Dennis.

"Dearly beloved, we have come together in the presence of God and this company," Dennis began.

Kelly struggled to hold back tears as she repeated her vows, then listened intently as Jared repeated his. The ceremony was a blur, and before she knew it, she heard Dennis quoting from the King James Bible.

*So God created man in his own image, in the image of God created he him; male and female created he them. And God blessed them, and God said unto them, be fruitful, and multiply, and replenish the earth, and subdue it: and have dominion over the fish of the sea, and over the fowl of the air, and over every living thing that moveth upon the earth. And God saw every thing that he had made, and, behold, it was very good. And the evening and the morning were the sixth day.*

"By the power vested in me by you, our good neighbors, and God, I now pronounce Jared and Kelly man and wife. Jared, you may kiss your bride."

Jared took Kelly in his arms and bent her backward, supporting her under her waist, pressing his lips against hers as the crowd cheered him on. He kissed her long and thoroughly. He started to lift her, then dipped her one more time. Kelly looked a little taken aback as Jared brought her back to standing. She felt for the comb on her veil and adjusted it.

Lynn played an upbeat piece that Rich had taught her for the recessional. Jared and Kelly started back down the aisle, now husband and wife. The crowd stood and clapped, tossing agave seeds that Lynn had been collecting for weeks into the air. Whoops and hollers abounded as the bride and groom ducked and weaved, trying to escape the barrage of seeds.

Jess waited in front of Dennis for Lynn. Still playing, she met him in the middle and they made their way back down the aisle together.

Dennis lifted his arms joyously skyward, motioning for the crowd to follow. Some picked up their folding chairs, taking them to the makeshift tables, before joining the receiving line near the back stoop.

Emma and Lynn stood next to Kelly, Dennis and Jess next to Jared, until each neighbor was greeted and thanked for coming.

"Let's eat," Emma finally said.

A cheer rose from all assembled as Dennis and Rich made their way to the fire pit. Both donned heavy work gloves and stood at opposite ends of a heavy metal plate. Smoke rose in a massive plume as the cover cleared the pit. The men's muscles visibly strained against their shirtsleeves as they lifted, revealing a dark brown, crispy, glorious side of beef. Another cheer.

"Bride and groom first," Emma cried, handing Kelly and Jared their plates and hustling them to the pit. Lynn grabbed for the bride's train and lifted it just as Kelly started moving.

Rich took a long, two-pronged fork and held it in the air ceremoniously. "Bride's choice," he exclaimed. "My dear, what shall it be, rib or steak?"

Kelly pointed to a fatty piece near the shoulder and Rich dug the fork into the tender flesh, lifting her out a queen's portion amidst more cheers.

"Thank you, kind sir," Kelly said.

"Now for the king." Rich bowed to Jared.

"It all looks heavenly," Jared replied. "Give me what you will."

Kelly and Jared lifted their plates above their heads and shimmied through the crowd toward the "sides" table. She and Jared took small portions of everything offered. There were baked beans, spaghetti with spaghetti sauce, canned pineapple, green beans, peach cobbler and potato salad.

"Can you believe this?" asked Jared. "I think everyone turned out, except a guard or two. I heard that James and Kurt drew the short straws."

"I'm sure some of the men will relieve them so they can have a nice meal too." Kelly smiled. She bent sideways toward Jared's chair and said, "I love you."

He bent toward her and kissed her. "I love you too."

Bill brought Kelly and Jared another small plate of meat and set it between their two empty plates, saying, "Eat up, you'll need your strength." Everyone within earshot laughed, and the party continued.

When the meal was over, Jose and Rich came around the house with an end table. Rich held an index finger to his mouth, signaling the crowd to be quiet. They placed the small table behind the bride, between her and the house. Emma placed a large lace doily over it and went to Kelly's side, distracting her with small talk.

Bea appeared at the kitchen door. "Attention, attention!" she said. "The ladies of Sunflower would like to present a surprise." She opened the screen door widely and stepped off the stoop to give the other ladies room to emerge side by side holding the cake.

The cake was snow white, three tiers high and decorated with beautiful pink frosting flowers.

*A more beautiful cake has never come from a professional bakery*, Kelly thought. She stood and squeaked, "Oh my, how did you...?" She glanced at the ladies holding the cake, then at Lynn and her mother, then back at Jared, mouth agape. Lynn lifted her train as Kelly started for the cake table. Kelly turned and motioned to Jared to join her.

"It took every last ounce of shortening we had in the entire village to make the frosting," said Bea, proudly beaming from ear to ear. "The cake is from everyone in town. Six of us made it yesterday and we finished icing it here, today."

Kelly shook her head in disbelief, then raised her gaze before she spoke. "You all have been so wonderful..." She began crying, overwhelmed at their kindness.

Jared placed his hand on her shoulder and continued where she had left off. "Yes, we can't thank you enough for doing all of this for us. It's a truly beautiful wedding, the most memorable wedding ever," he exclaimed.

"Cut the cake," cried Janet.

"Yeah, cut the cake!" Eager voices echoed her sentiment.

Emma scurried about, getting the cake knife and a small plate from the closest guest table.

"What should I do?" Kelly whispered anxiously. "I've never cut a cake this size!"

"Just cut a small piece for you and Jared," Emma winked. "I'll handle the rest."

"Smear it in her face," called Rich, snickering.

"Make it messy," Jess yelled.

A small piece of cake rested comfortably in Kelly's fingers, poised for Jared's mouth. He opened up and tilted his head back, ever so slightly. Kelly dropped it in, following it with a quick kiss.

Next, it was Jared's turn. He took the small piece of cake that Kelly held for him and waited for her to open her mouth.

"Don't let me down," called Rich.

Kelly squinted at Jared, giving him the evil eye, cautioning him not to do it. At the same time, she let the hint of a smile lift the corners of her lips.

*Squish*, Jared ground the cake into Kelly's lips and face. Instinctively she pulled back, trying not to laugh the cake out of her mouth. *At least there won't be pictures.*

"Let me make it up to you," Jared said and proceeded to eat the cake from her face, ending in another kiss. Kelly let the smooth, sweet cake melt in her mouth. Roars of laughter erupted from those assembled.

"Good man," said Rich, slapping Jared on the shoulder.

Kelly and Jared made their way back to their seats with Lynn following dutifully behind, taking her duties as bridesmaid very seriously. Emma started to cut the cake as guests brought their plates up from their seats. The white, cloud-like layers were skillfully carved into generous pieces.

Everyone oohed and aahed over the cake, saying that they had never tasted any better.

"I don't know if it's better, or if it's just that I haven't had any for so long," Kelly sighed, closing her eyes and relishing every bite.

"Both," Jared agreed. "We have a truly amazing family."

"One more thing, everyone, please. We have a group gift," said Bea. Janet emerged from the back door this time, carrying the huge quilt. She reverently took it to the bride's table as the other ladies rushed to remove plates, clinking silver on ceramic. A small gasp escaped Kelly as the quilt was unfolded, revealing the swirls of colors that resembled fall leaves blown up against a picket fence. Emma stepped up and helped too. Soon every woman who had helped cut and piece it was holding the quilt from its edges, beaming as they displayed their work.

"What can I say?" said Kelly. "I'm overwhelmed." She ran her hand over the thickly quilted squares, feeling its fine texture under her palm. Tears stood in her eyes, but didn't overflow their banks.

The quilt was refolded and taken into the house. The party resumed. Kelly leaned into Jared, pushing him playfully to one side, and watched contentedly as her mom and friends reveled in her party.

****

Jared and Kelly, sidesaddle in her long gown, rode side by side on Hokey and Pokey toward the Branham's place. A winter breeze chilled them. Kelly's satin gown swished back and forth to the rhythm of her horse's gait as they moved through the long shadows that fell over the canyon. Dennis followed at a respectable distance behind as their armed guard. They were, after all, on their way to their honeymoon.

"Oh my gosh, Jared, wasn't it beautiful?" Kelly exclaimed, sighing deeply.

"Yes, and you're the most beautiful part." Jared blew Kelly a kiss from atop Hokey. "When I saw you coming down that aisle, I was sure I had died and gone to heaven. I wasn't expecting a long, white dress either. You practically floated."

"Thank you, kind sir." Kelly winked at him. "You didn't look bad yourself."

"Yeah. Tim Nichols, Janet's husband, loaned me this suit." He looked down at it. "Fits pretty good."

"I'd say. The whole day was wonderful: the arbor full of flowers, Lynn's 'Here Comes The Bride,' Dennis's beautiful ceremony, Rich's barbecued beef, all the wonderful food, the cake, the quilt—and then we had quite the hoedown at the end. It couldn't have been more wonderful. My mom slaved."

"A bit breezy, don't you think?" Jared shuddered like an autumn leaf in a stiff breeze.

"It's always that way up here in the fall. Besides, I refuse to say a single negative thing on this perfect day."

The sun made its final drop behind the cliff, leaving them in darkness. Kelly shivered too.

"Here, take my coat," Jared said, slipping it from his shoulders. He guided Hokey next to Pokey and attempted to hand it to her.

Kelly reached out, but reflexively reached back for her saddle horn when she tipped farther than she had envisioned. "Riding sidesaddle in satin on a western saddle is a bit tricky; I'm afraid I'll fall off. We're almost there. I can wait."

"I think I can see the turnoff up there. We'll get you inside." Jared spurred Hokey, then remembered what Kelly had said about falling off, so pulled back on the reins to slow him down. Hokey gave a whinny in protest.

Dennis yelled, "What's up?" in staccato.

Jared called back leisurely, "Oh nothing, we're good."

"Jared?" Kelly said, making sure she had his attention. "My mom told me there's everything we could ever need in that house: clothes, food, dishes, firewood, everything. Wasn't that sweet?"

"Wonderful. You and me, totally alone for three days. That's the best wedding present I could have imagined."

"Here we are," Kelly said, motioning with her head to the left.

Sure enough, it was the turn for the Branham's. Both riders eased into the driveway. When they got to the porch railing, they came to a stop. Pokey bobbed his head deeply at the prospect of jettisoning his rider.

"I'm coming," Jared told Kelly as he jumped from Hokey. "Stay where you're at, I'll help you down."

Kelly did not object. Jared stood with his arms outstretched, ready to receive his bride, and Kelly slid smoothly from the saddle into his waiting arms. A short kiss followed, then Jared swept her up into his arms, her dress billowing to one side. In one fluid motion, he climbed the steps.

"Hold up, you two!" Dennis called. Both looked up in surprise. He was tying Traveler to a tree not more than fifty yards from the house. The horse had a lawn chair, sleeping bag and Winchester tied behind the saddle. "We've got to clear the place."

Looking truly frustrated, Jared set Kelly down by the door. Instinctively he took her shoulders and moved her behind the door frame to wait for Dennis. "He's staying 'til his relief gets here at 2 a.m."

"You're kidding, out in this cold?"

"Yep, Rich told me all about it. We're to have a twenty-four hour guard for all three days we are here. Not in the house, of course." Jared screwed up his face into a funny expression that made Kelly giggle.

Dennis bounded up the stairs to Jared's side.

"I'll be right back," Jared told Kelly, puckering his lips softly. "You go in first, Dennis." Dennis looked at him questioningly, and a smile broke across Jared's face.

"Just kidding, man."

Dennis reached forward with the door key and turned it in the lock.

Jared lifted his eyebrows at the novel entry technique, then turned the door handle, cracked the door open and yelled, "Police!"

Dennis looked at him questioningly. Again.

"What?" Jared whispered loudly. "First thing that came to mind, habit," he said, shrugging his shoulders.

Kelly giggled. "Mom said there was an oil lamp and matches on the table next to the door."

"Got it." Jared called as both men disappeared inside.

Kelly waited patiently at first. Then she started to fidget. She didn't have a gun; there wasn't a place for one in her gown. *You've only been standing here two or three minutes,* she thought to herself. She slumped against the wall and continued her wait. Another two or three minutes passed before Dennis came through the front door, tipping his cowboy hat to Kelly as he passed.

"Good night, Mrs. Malloy," he said with a straight face and walked toward Traveler.

Jared appeared on the porch and lifted Kelly in his arms again. "There aren't any intruders in the house, Mrs. Malloy, but I can't say it's safe to go in, over the threshold with me, I mean."

"I'll take my chances, Mr. Malloy." She kissed him softly.

With that, Jared threw her into the air just a bit to reposition his grip, then strode forward. He slammed the door behind them by hooking the toe of his boot around the door and giving it a stern shove. The sound was lost to the wind.

Dennis returned to his horse and started untying the knots that held his equipment. He smiled to himself while removing his bedroll and preparing to start a fire.

\*\*\*\*

"Do you hear that?" Kelly said, sitting straight up in bed, clutching the covers to her neck and nudging Jared's shoulder.

"What?" Jared slurred, rousing from a sound sleep.

"That!" Kelly said with more alarm.

The sounds grew louder. It was a banging, but it had almost a musical quality. The volume increased by the minute.

"What the...?" Jared sat up to the side of the bed and gathered his suit off the floor. He hadn't bothered to look for anything else to wear before getting into bed. "Get dressed," he blurted.

"In what?" Kelly asked, looking down at the huge white dress in a heap on the floor.

"I'll find you something." Jared went to the dresser at the end of the bed and opened the top drawer. There was some kind of light-colored garment sitting in it, and he tossed it to Kelly. "Try this." With that, he sprinted for the front door and the din in the yard.

He peeked out the front window. There had to be twenty people with lanterns and torches. They were all banging rhythmically on pots, pans, or buckets. One of them even had a drum.

Kelly joined him at the front door, dressed in a long white nightgown. She put her hand on his shoulder and leaned forward to see too.

Jared sensed her standing beside him. "It's a mob, and I'm going to get to the bottom of it. You stay here." He went out onto the porch, dressed in the suit he had thrown back on. "What's the meaning of this?" he shouted.

"Bring out the bride, bring out the bride!" The chant grew louder each time it was repeated. The crowd danced around each other, raising their torches high.

"Dennis is with them," said Jared, leaning in through the front door. The moon cast a pale glow, illuminating the man at the back of the crowd. "He's shouting too. Emma, Rich, they're all here."

"Bring out the bride, bring out the bride!"

"I think they want you."

"But I'm not dressed," Kelly cried, taking a small step backward.

Jared took that same small step toward her. "You're dressed, you have fabric over you. Just come out for a second, maybe they'll leave." He put his hand out and motioned with his fingers for her to take it. She did, tentatively. "Come on," he said, pulling on it gently. "I'll be with you."

Kelly thought about the crowd and then Jared. *I'll trust him.*

They stepped together onto the porch to boisterous cheers and clapping.

The chant abruptly changed to, "Kiss, kiss, kiss, kiss..."

The young couple looked out at the crowd, then at each other. Jared raised his shoulders and his eyebrows. Kelly copied his movements exactly, then fell into his arms. The newlyweds kissed. Kelly tried to pull away, but Jared would have none of it and kissed her for a full minute.

The kiss was the finale of the evening.

The crowd turned and went as they had come, the banging fading little by little. Everyone left except Dennis, who sat back in his chair by the tree.

## Epilogue

Kelly Malloy fidgeted with the dials on the Clansman radio. The speaker emitted an unearthly, off-frequency voice. She slowly tuned in until Sam Wise's speech became normal.

"Hi, Dad. Our preparations are going well. Jose and Jess have finished the wagons. We have enough tack for two wagons and a spare set. The horses are mostly broken to the wagons already."

"How many total?" asked Sam.

We'll be six souls and seven horses. I'm hoping to keep the teams fresh. Over."

"Seven horses? That seems like a lot of stock to water in the desert. Over."

"We're going to need all of them to make the long, steep pulls. I'm afraid to cut down. If any wear out, go lame or get sick, we're stuck in the middle of nowhere. The water will work out," she said, more hopefully than declaratively. "We've gone over the topo maps in the Arizona Gazetteer a hundred times. There are wells and springs along the way. Jose has put water tanks on the wagons. Over."

"I'll have to trust you. Your friends sound pretty amazing and I never have been able to get you or your mother to change your minds about anything. Hey, Cowgirl, how's that new son-in-law of mine?

"Jared is *wonderful*," she said and looked at her husband, giving him a smile. "I can't wait for you to meet him in person. Over."

"I can't wait to meet him either. Are you set? Over."

"As set as we can be. Night, Daddy. Over."

Made in the USA
Coppell, TX
15 September 2020